When Babel Tower Is Falling Down

by
Alexander Raju

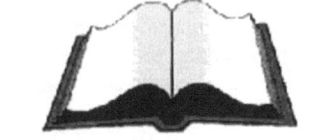

CCB Publishing
British Columbia, Canada

When Babel Tower Is Falling Down

Library and Archives Canada Cataloguing in Publication
Raju, Alexander, 1952-, author
When Babel Tower is falling down / by Alexander Raju. -- First edition.
Issued in print and electronic formats.
ISBN 978-1-77143-173-6 (pbk.).--ISBN 978-1-77143-174-3 (pdf)
Additional cataloguing data available from Library and Archives Canada

Cover image: *Tower of Babel*, by Pieter Brueghel the Elder is in the public domain.
People having a break from an argument © konradbak | CanStockPhoto.com

Publisher: CCB Publishing
              British Columbia, Canada
              www.ccbpublishing.com

To my family for all their support and for sharing their lives with me, especially to loving children, my daughter Xandy who made my life worth living and my son Xandeep who every previous night confidentially reminded me his birthday as well as the birthdays of his mother, of his grandparents and even of mine, which I always forget...

Other works by Alexander Raju

The Haunted Man (1997, Second Edition in 2009)

Upon This Bank and Shoal (2008)

Poles Apart on the Same Bed (2011)

And Still Plays the Abyssinian Damsel on Her Dulcimer (2013)

Where the Green Dream Shattered

Ripples and Pebbles (1989)

Sprouts of Indignation (2003)

Magic Chasm (2007)

The Psycho-Social Interface in British Fiction (crit. 2000)

The Voice of Ethiopia (ed. 2008)

Behold, the people is one, and they have all one language; and this they begin to do: and now nothing will be restrained from them, which they have imagined to do.

Genesis 11:6 in the Bible

The Martian and Venusian languages had the same words, but the way they were used gave different meanings; their expressions were similar, but they had different connotations or emotional emphasis. Misinterpreting each other was very easy.

- John Gray in *Men are from Mars, Women are from Venus*

CHAPTER ONE

Dark clouds were thickening in the sky. More and more masses of clouds were rushing towards the west and their contours were brightened when every time lightning flashed one after another on the distant eastern horizon. Heavy showers with thunder and lightning could be expected at any moment. The drizzling began and would last for half an hour, giving pedestrians sufficient time to reach their homes! And the heavy rain would continue for three hours, and that was the usual way of rain here in this closed, hidden and mysterious land of Ethiopia.

I was packing my luggage. I had only a single suitcase with a few pairs of dress, certain books I had brought from my home-library in India and two files, one containing my certificates and the other the photostats of my publications. What else should I take from Ethiopia to India?

Most of my clothes, I had already distributed among my needy neighbours. Some of my books and the copies of journals which I had brought from India were donated to the university library. Almost all the utensils in which I used to cook my food were given to the maid-servant who had cleaned my room and washed my clothes once a week throughout my two-year stay here. Now, only one more day was left for me in this country!

Tomorrow I have to collect my salary from the office, check my post box No. 89 and also No. 91 that belonged to my friend, for the last mail if any, and return the keys either to Anwar or to Kadir, the post office clerks, and say goodbye to my colleagues and friends in the university. That's all! My contract as

Associate Professor of English in this University ends then and there! Of course, the Department of English had forwarded to the authorities concerned the minutes of its decision to renew my contract for another two years!

Day after tomorrow, Ethiopian time one o'clock in the day, that is seven am, I must take my suitcase and go to the airport. At 8 am I must catch the domestic flight to Addis Ababa, the capital city of Ethiopia. Then, from there by 11.30 am, Ethiopian time 5.30 in the day, the next flight directly to India, saying goodbye to Ethiopia, the Land of Thirteen Months in a year! Of course, if my contract was renewed, it would be my two-month vacation trip to India!

A sudden flash of lightning and then an ear-breaking thunder! The frightening roar of the approaching rain and, then, the pit-patting of rain-drops on the tin roof of my rented house! No one would be out of this house at this time of the night, though it was only 8 pm, the usual time when I used to return after long evening walks with Rajesh, Salim and Worku.

Dr. Worku Singh was also coming with me to India, for he too had completed his two-year contract with the university. Of course, he had a plan to extend his contract for one more year, but there was no possibility, as the Ethiopian Ministry of Education did not consider contracts for less than two years.

And Rajesh! I really missed him a lot. He had left for India two weeks earlier. Otherwise he would be here to help me in packing my luggage, as he had been only halfway through his two-year contract. He used to tell me that he would go to India only after completing the tenure of two years. But suddenly, two weeks ago, he changed his mind and came to me with unusual enthusiasm and cheerfulness.

He said: "George sir, I am going home. I must bring my wife here. You know, without family, how dull and boring life here is! I asked Mr. Wondwosen of the Continent Travels to book a seat for me on tomorrow's flight. The fare is a bit high, but I must go!"

"You mean tomorrow itself?" I said with a shock. "What a surprise! Are you joking? What really happened to you? Why are you so excited? Can't you wait for a couple of weeks so that both of us can go together to India?"

"No! It's urgent! You see, George sir! I must bring her before she changes her mind. I am really sorry to offend you by changing my plan. I have to go, that's it."

I looked into his eyes! There was a peculiar brightness in them. In fact, under my compulsion, he had changed his plan of going to India by the end of the contract and had decided to come with me. We had planned everything; to go together to India and enjoy a few days of our vacation somewhere in a hill-resort, and this sudden change in the program would create some inconvenience to me.

What a change? I wondered. Perhaps, some accident might have occurred to some dear relatives, which he did not want to reveal to me! Nonsense! He could not hide anything from me. We were such thick friends, and how could he conceal things so important? It must be something connected with his wife!

Of course, some husbands are like that! There rises a sort of an urge of the spirit and, then, nothing on earth can prevent them from meeting their wives! I can understand such feelings. It's quite natural and even my friend can't ignore it or escape from its vortex!

Next morning, I saw him off at Sea Side City Airport. Later he rang me from Bole Airport of Addis Ababa, and said that the journey was nice and the next flight to India was on time and everything was okay with him.

"Well! George sir! I have something for you!" he said to me over the mobile phone. "I am sending you a special gift from here by post. Please do check your post box. As a writer, it'll be of much use for you. OK, Bye....!" The phone was cut!

In India, people used to add 'sir' with the names of teachers as a mark of respect, perhaps, a part of the colonial hangover! Of course, in Islamic countries, nobody bothered about such 'tails' to the names, even they addressed their father or grandfather with their usual names which was considered a taboo in India!

For the next two weeks I had been checking my post box but his so-called gift did not reach me. Well! The postal service in Ethiopia depended on the luck of the customers! Sometimes letters from Addis would reach Sea Side City within three days, then, you are lucky! But everybody may not be that fortunate, for them the post may take two to three weeks to cover the same distance! Rajesh might be joking! What gift could he send me from Addis? And that too was of much use for me as a writer! Perhaps, a couple of fancy pens! I thought.

Rajesh was my best friend. In fact, we became friends before he came to Ethiopia. He was with me in Muscat, the capital of the Sultanate of Oman, where we worked together; he as a teacher in one of the schools where I served as an Inspector of English, giving training to teachers in English Language, under the Ministry of Education. Even before that, we knew each other as college teachers in my hometown in Kerala, a southern State in India. Of course, we were working in two colleges run by two different managements.

In fact, we became real friends, I remembered, only on our way to Mumbai where we had to attend the interview, undergo our medical check-up and get our certificates attested by the Embassy of Oman, before leaving for Muscat. We traveled in the same compartment of the train, stayed in the same room of a mediocre lodge in Mumbai, went to the same hospital for our medical certificates and flew to Muscat on the same flight conducted by Oman Airways.

When Rajesh left us, I thought that at least we four would be there to go to India together. But Dr. Salim Mohammed also left a fortnight earlier. He told us that the wedding of his daughter was finalized and it would be better if he could reach home as early as possible. One day earlier, that much better, he pointed out. Of course, the wedding of a daughter was the greatest dream of every father, especially in India. A wedding cost the whole of one's earnings but the relief that gave was unexplainable. Naturally, to put down the burden of each responsibility, one by one, gave unusual pleasure in family life!

We promised to attend the wedding at any cost, though I knew that it was very expensive for Worku Singh to come from the northern part of India. Both of us gave Salim some amount as a gift for his daughter. We noticed the glow on Salim's face and he was quite jolly before he left for India. Dr. Ansari, one of our thick friends, said that he had asked his brother in India to send a Benares silk sari by parcel in Salim's home address, but it remained only as a promise and the parcel never reached Salim's house, as I later understood!

Dr. Ahmad Ansari also left us a day before, as his brother who was at Addis Ababa University had booked a seat for him. We requested him to stay an additional night with us so that we three could go together. Moreover, Dr. Worku Singh was also going to Delhi, unlike I who was going to Mumbai, so that they could keep company throughout the journey. But Ahmad was adamant, and no one could correct a teacher of psychology! And what was friendship for a man from a family background of textile business unless it brought some solid profit? We thought.

The three-hour rain was over! The sky was gathering the unused pieces of dark clouds, perhaps, for the next day's rain-festival! Well! Ethiopian rain was so benevolent towards the pedestrians that they would never get wet under heavy showers. There would always be a light drizzling for half an hour before every heavy rain, so that all pedestrians with or without umbrellas could reach their homes and save their heads! I used to thank the punctuality of Ethiopian rains, especially in Sea

Side City! Unlike here, the rain in Kerala was sudden and unexpected as if it had a deliberate plan to wet every pedestrian on the road!

A lightning flashed somewhere on the distant horizon as if to show the wandering clouds their way in the dark wilderness of the skies! I made a final check-up of the things in the suitcase, locked it and tied it around with a plastic rope for further safety. Then, I searched the air-bag for my passport, resident permit, air-ticket and money-purse, to feel doubly sure of their presence. Everything okay! And I felt relaxed for a sound sleep.

I climbed into my bed, pulled down the sky-blue mosquito net, the first thing I bought from Sea Side City immediately after my arrival. Thank you, my dear Net, for you protected me these two years from the much-feared malaria, believed to be common in Ethiopia! Mosquitoes flew around my net, singing their lullaby to which I was used to hearing. Just one more day and I would be at my home. No more songs from the agents of Malaria! Farewell! Dear singers of lullaby, I should give you two more nights, this night and the coming one, could you agree! Adieu!

The next morning after breakfast, I went to the university office, took my last salary, collected a few official papers, bid farewell to my colleagues and friends and had a last look at my office room, CUBA-248. For many years, those rows of rooms were used by teachers from Cuba, hence the building continued to be called Cuba, and mine was the second room in it. Moreover, I was the Fidel Castro there as all other rooms were allotted to the labor-supervisors and clerical staff!

The university campus had been changed into a wonderful garden! The main road was beautifully asphalted and the side-roads to each building were properly tiled or cobbled. On both sides of the road, jacarandas, gulmohurs, Flames of Forest and other shady trees stood with flowers to greet the visitors. Two years ago, when I first entered this campus, the roads were full of mud and slime, due to heavy rains. Then I had to walk carefully, hopping from one stone to another, paved on the road, avoiding pools of muddy water.

That was my last day on the campus. I walked by each and every small road that connected various departments, almost every part of the university, as I knew that it was, perhaps, my last walk along those newly paved paths. I watched those perforated rocks, thrown into the campus area in some volcanic eruption in the past. They had been the seats for calf-lovers of the university.

The trees in the campus gave cool shade. Even in summer, one would not feel the presence of the equatorial sun, just above the head. The old, rugged bamboa and daro trees, with a number of monkeys playing on them, the Flames of Forest with fire-red flowers, the leafless gulmohars full of violet and blue flowers and the humming xerophytes with thousands of multi-colored birds roosting on them – all were bidding farewell to me. Really I had lost a heart there in that campus, and that thought struck my mind like an epiphany, or a realization, or a revelation!

Suddenly, I remembered the post office, where I had to return the key of my post box and get back my deposit of 10 Birr. I entered the post office, opened my post box No. 89. I knew that I was going to use that key for the last time! A post box is a thing where you can test your luck! Yes! I was lucky, indeed! There, I found the parcel sent by Rajesh, at last! I was always lucky in Ethiopia, even at that last moment!

From the appearance, the parcel seemed to be containing a book or a diary; I put it in my air-bag. I also checked the post-box of Dr. Ahmad, as we used to do on alternative weeks, and found it empty. Then, I closed the account with the post office, of course, my deposit money was not returned, for rules changed as Kadir, the man-in-charge of the post office, said, and I returned to my rented house.

In the evening I had to attend a farewell party arranged by my friends and neighbors. It was a very interesting and warm party that I hurried home quite tired just for a sound sleep as I could not have my usual noontime siesta. I slept, hearing the mosquito-lullaby that strained through the sky-blue net.

Early morning I woke up, dressed, took my suitcase and air-bag, closed the front door of the house that welcomed me all these two years, and went out towards the taxi honking for me. Dr. Worku Singh was already in the taxi, and soon we moved towards the Airport. I bade farewell to Sea Side City, and to Lake Tana which always refreshed my everyday life there. Of course, Ethiopia has no sea coast but in the past days, it was natural that people considered the lake a sea and there was nothing wrong if a lake of more than 2,500 square kilometers was honored with the name Sea, and hence the name Sea Side City to that place flourished on the banks of Lake Tana!

Then, the airport, some twenty kilometers away from the city! Thank God! The flight had arrived from Addis Ababa which was supposed to take us on its return trip! And then, an hour's flight to the Bole International Airport! We got down from the domestic plane at Addis Ababa, and trolley-ed our luggage towards the queue for the next check-in for our flights; my friend Worku Singh for the Delhi flight and I for the Mumbai flight.

We sent our luggage, except our handbags, and they were on their way to the cargo section of the plane. It was time for us to separate because our destinations were different. Both flights were more or less at the same time, only half an hour's difference. We embraced each other and bade farewell. It was a heart-touching farewell! After all, we two were together for two years, facing all the hazards of living in an alien land!

For a minute we became sentimental; in between our native places in India there was a distance of about three thousand kilometers! Perhaps, we could never meet each other again!

Weren't there tears in our eyes? All these two years, we were like true brothers, walking together, eating together and living in the same house. 'North is North and South is South, and the two ends will never meet' was the slogan we heard in India! At least, both of us could prove it wrong!

The first flight was to Delhi and Dr. Singh moved to the waiting room. I had to wait half an hour more to move to the waiting room for Mumbai passengers. Then the announcement came that my flight would be thirty minutes late and, that means, one hour more for boarding the flight! My friend would have already been on the Delhi flight! And I had to idle away my time in the airport lounge, completely cut off from the outside world.

There wasn't sufficient time for me to take even a dog-sleep! At any moment, they might ask us to board the plane. Most of the passengers were a little anxious about the delay in boarding. Everybody wished to reach their homes, at least, a minute earlier!

Suddenly I remembered the parcel sent by Rajesh. I took it out from the air-bag in which I kept my passport and boarding pass. I tore open the packet and took out the content. It was a diary, fully written by Rajesh himself, for I was quite familiar with his exclusive style of handwriting. As I opened the diary, a folded paper fell down onto the floor. I took it and found that it was a note addressed to me. I went through it with casual curiosity.

My dear George Sir! Rajesh used to address me like that. Many a time, I told him to call me just George and not with the dangling colonial tail of a 'Sir'! Even the ten-year-old Ethiopian girl Kalkidan called me 'George', though it offended me a little at first, as it was against the practice in India, a little girl addressing an aged professor by his first name. Of course, in Ethiopia or in the Gulf countries, I heard children calling even their grandparents their names, which was a part of their

Islamic culture. But Rajesh and I were almost of the same age, he might be a few years younger than me, and I considered his calling me 'Sir' as mere formality. Of course, he honored me more than I deserved!

The letter began like this: For almost a year we have been living and working together and almost every day during evenings we walked miles and miles together, but I have been wearing a mask, hiding many facts from you, though you were my only intimate friend and guide, whom I respect more than anyone in this world.

Why Rajesh, all these formal beginnings? Cut it out straight! I was slightly embarrassed, rather annoyed, at the tone of his words, I felt as if reading somebody's will and testament or a sort of suicide note!

The letter continued: I was very happy and cheerful when, after a long break, we met each other at the university campus in Ethiopia. I remember how you were surprised and pleased at seeing me there quite accidentally. Well! Then, I was a happy man. I believed that I was the happiest man who ever lived on earth – with a beautiful, intelligent and assiduous wife, with a lovely and intelligent daughter, owning a few cents of land at least, in the town with a newly built, magnificent house on it – what else should one need for happiness?

I became quite impatient. Why all this nonsense! We knew all about each other's family. His wife Geetha, as far as I knew, was an excellent housewife. Even I myself envied her ability to manage the family, to host the guests in the most appropriate manner, to treat the relatives and to entertain the neighbors. Really she was a woman who always spread the light of love, affection and kindness in the family.

Tell me, Rajesh! What happened to her? Is your child alright? Is there a court case against your property and house? Well! I know that you built the house with a loan from the bank! Perhaps, you forgot to make the repayment! My heart was throbbing with anxiety!

I became so anxious that I continued to read the letter: Just two weeks after joining the university in Ethiopia, I got a long letter from my wife, Geetha, and it changed my entire life or even, shall I say, turned my life upside down! I hid everything from you and pretended as if everything was normal, in good faith, expecting another letter from my wife expressing her regrets and pleading forgiveness. All these months I have been waiting hopefully for her letter but in vain! Her letter was a shock to me that, at first, I was mad with anger, but gradually, I became silent, quite prepared to face my fate, whatsoever it was!

The letter continued: But how long could one remain a coward and escape from the realities of life? So I began to recollect my past days and decided to write them in a diary. Now the diary is with you, no longer have I needed it, you can read it and realize how much I suffered in Ethiopia and led a life of mental agony. I sent this diary to you as a penance for my sin of hiding certain real facts from you, my sincere friend. Moreover, no more I need this diary with me, because perhaps, it may fall into the hands of my wife and lead to another petty quarrel. Yes! At last, the expected letter came from my wife and I have been so excited that I was even ready to leave my job at the university to live with her.

Et tu Brute! You too were planning to leave this country without informing even your best friend and room-mate! I whispered. I knew many Indians were compelled to leave Ethiopia without informing the university authorities or the concerning ministry of education. It was natural as the university itself was taking an initiation for the breach of contract by not paying the house rent allowance agreed in the contract. Once the employer breached the contract, the contract itself was void!

Rajesh! You are very clever! If you don't want to continue

here, it is better to leave the country without telling anyone about it, even to your best friend! I thought with some bitterness in my mind.

A few more lines were there in the letter and I read them: I also have a plan to visit the ashram of my favorite Guruji who had been consoling me all these months. But it all depends on the situation. My wife had agreed to come to the airport to greet me. If we could come to a peaceful consensus, I will go with her to the ashram and then to our house and live together there forever; or if she agrees to come to Ethiopia, we will be here after the vacation.

May God bless your reunion, my mind mused. The union of the husband and the wife is God's will and so it is divine. Two individuals hailing from different backgrounds and having different mental formations are united into one single entity is really a miracle. As the scripture says: the husband and the wife will leave their parents and stick themselves to a single body! But, does it also mean the singleness of their minds? Is the unison of the body sufficient to keep the on-going of a married life? For the singleness of the mind, much sacrifice is needed, much patience and humility are essential. But who is going to make such relaxations in a world of self-assertiveness? Yet Geetha is wise; she can manage things in an effective manner. I tried to think that all's well that ends well!

Rajesh continued his writing: But if she sticks on to her foolish notions, we will go our own separate ways. Let her take all my property and belongings. For, I cannot live without her. I loved her so much that she has become a part of my body, life and soul. If the worse happens, my plan is to go for a pilgrimage to some holy places in India, spend a few weeks there in prayer and meditation, or meet that famous Guruji who is an expert in family-counseling, so that I may get peace and consolation. But remember, whatever happens, we will meet again in a perfectly happy situation, either in perfect happiness of conjugal life or in perfect happiness of the ascetic life. Thanks and goodbye!

The letter ended with an awkward signature of Rajesh, perhaps, he did it in his hurriedness to catch the flight. I folded the letter, kept in the diary and placed it back safely in the side pocket of the air-bag.

Of course, India has solutions to all human problems, whether physical or psychological, whether individual or social! India, the Land of Solutions! I was smiling as I boarded the plane to India, the flight that goes to Mumbai and, from there another flight to Kerala, my loving state.

Lunch was served by the flight staff and I took it half-heartedly, as I was thinking too much about my friend Rajesh. May the God who created man and woman, make them happy! I sincerely prayed for their happiness, for real conjugal happiness is rare these days! It is quite easy to break a life, and even if it is stitched together again, it'll remain a patchwork forever!

I looked through the window. Far below, the clouds floated like a soft cotton bed of some unknown fairies, and the plane was gliding over it. I could see the left wing of the plane, the joint of a piece of it seemed to be slightly separated and it vibrated terribly under the pressure of the wind! I could notice a cleft there, so that the piece might fly away at any moment, I thought. A shudder passed through me and I took the small Bible copy from my handbag and opened it with a prayer. Of course, we believed in such harmless superstitions, the opening page would guide you in such confusing situations, or we tried to find meanings suitable for our situations from the opening page!

My eyes fell on Chapter 11 of Genesis, and I began to read the passage wondering why this particular part was opened by chance! Of course, many a time I read that story and presented it as an ice-breaker to my students of linguistics. But in the flight, as I was scanning the passage, I felt a new meaning and timely relevance for it! And I read:

> Now the whole earth had one language and one speech.
> And it came to pass, as they journeyed from the east, that they found a plain in the land of Shinar, and they dwelt there.
> Then they said to one another, "Come, let us make bricks and bake them thoroughly." They had brick for stone, and they had asphalt for mortar.
> And they said, "Come, let us build ourselves a city, and a tower whose top is in the heavens; let us make a name for ourselves, lest we scattered abroad over the face of the whole earth."
> But the Lord came down to see the city and the tower which the sons of men had built.
> And the Lord said, "Indeed the people are one and they all have one language, and this is what they begin to do; now nothing that they propose to do will be withheld from them.
> "Come, let us go down and there confuse their language, that they may not understand one another's speech."
> So the Lord scattered them abroad from there over the face of all the earth, and ceased building the city.
> Therefore its name is called Babel, because the Lord confused the language of all the earth; and from there the Lord scattered them abroad over the face of all the earth.

Well! I read the passage two or three times and tried to find whether it had anything to do with Rajesh and Geetha! In the past whenever I read this part, I considered it a silly story to be told to small children in Sunday school! It's time for a deconstruction! I thought with a smile. My idea was to pass my time some way or the other!

The 'whole earth' signifies the unity of human life which has 'one language' and 'one speech' as its ingredients! Then, what is language? It is the human use of spoken or written words as a communication system! And what is speech? It is the ability for the act of effectively communicating by speaking! So, language and speech are two different things, and God decided to confuse not only their language but also their speech because a change in the language need not affect the speech, but at the same time, a change in the speech will definitely affect the language! Then why did God confuse both; confusing speech alone would have been sufficient! Well! It is said, God won't give problems without solutions! When God does something, it should be perfect; confusion means complete confusion but with a provision to rectify it with deliberate human efforts!

God created man in his own shape and image, says the Bible. He created man entirely in a different way; unlike the creation of animals, the creation of man was unique! Flora and fauna were created simply by his voice; man was created by his manual labor! No one could learn his mother tongue through the milk of his mother; in other words, no one could learn a language without manual labor and hard work!

If man is a rational animal, he must be a linguistic animal too! This means that man can degrade himself to the level of an animal, rationally as well as linguistically! Reason and language are only for human beings! Only human beings have reason and when reason does not work, they turn into irrational beings or animals! Similarly, only human beings have a language because only the vocal cord of human beings could articulate and produce meaningful sounds, as Noam Chomsky said. And when human beings fail to use language in an appropriate way, they turn into 'illingual' beings or animals!

During the long journey of life, human beings found a suitable place and decided to dwell there! A man and a woman meet each other by chance and decide to settle down permanently, without any intention to be 'scattered' abroad! They start building their new life; they preferred a hard-working life to a natural carefree life; they made bricks and baked them, instead of using the natural stones for construction! Stone and asphalt are natural while bricks and mortar are artificial! It would have been better if they had used either bricks and mortar or stones and asphalt! And it was the combination of one natural thing with an artificial thing that created problems in their process of building up an unbreakable settlement!

Instead of mining natural stones, they made bricks and baked them in fire. According to G. von Rad, fire is a universal symbol of civilization, art and craft; while bricks are the symbol of permanence and stability. Instead of the artificial mortar, they used the natural bitumen or asphalt which is easily melted in fire! Of course, the Tower of Babel is 'an attempt to meet human means by the peaceful means of invention, language, utopian planning, social cooperation, creativity, culture and technology'.

The man and the woman constructed their own private Babel Tower, their natural way of love making mixed with the artificial means of sexual voluptuousness, and in the fire of sex their dream of natural unity turned into a nightmare! The fire of modern civilization melted the natural bitumen and the baked bricks loosened and fell down, leaving no stone upon another stone!

There was always some privacy in married life and they tried to 'build ourselves a city and a tower', so that they would not be 'scattered' but would be of 'one flesh'. Of course, the phrase 'a city and a tower' had sexual connotations, as its purpose was 'heavens', the culmination of an act that leads to the heavenly bliss! And God saw that they were 'one' and 'nothing that they propose to do will be withheld from them'! In fact, it was the true conjugal bliss of perfect unison in which man and woman conquered 'heavens', forgetting everything else including God!

As human beings climbed up the 'heavens', God 'came down' and did two things; firstly, He confused their language so that their system of communication was completely disturbed and, secondly, He created a situation in which they could not 'understand one another's speech' so that they lost the ability to communicate effectively! This was the crucial point on which their mutually built city and tower fell down; even the natural asphalt could not hold the artificial bricks together! The unity was broken; the building of the city was 'ceased'; they felt separated, shattered and 'scattered'!

Learn the lesson from Babel! Man is a gregarious animal with individual and social responsibilities. Once married, man and woman become one in 'flesh' but as it is a small unit of society, their attempt to build a life for themselves is against the law of nature! They are allowed to enjoy all pleasures in life provided that blissful experiences should not make them forget God! The husband and the wife may face situations in which they could 'not understand one another's speech'; and they may feel one another's language pretty confusing, as every language is incomplete and insufficient to express the real feelings and ideas of one's heart! Then, only through deliberate and conscious attempts that they could bring back the bliss of unity and oneness! He or she who tries to love his or her life too much will lose it! See what the Scripture says: The man (or woman) who loves his (or her) life will lose it, while the man (or woman) who loses his (or her) life in this world will keep it for eternal life.

Of course, there is a force in nature that breaks the wall, as Robert Frost says, and brings together the two separate entities, but people build boundary walls thinking, 'good fences make good neighbors'! In the past the husband and the wife were 'no longer two but one flesh' but as time passed, due to the hardness of their hearts, they decided to live like 'two flesh', like two good neighbors!

There was a time when husbands went for work in faraway places, the wives waited with prayers for their safe return! Now the situation had changed completely; men and women lost their patience! The wife takes it as an opportunity for testing variety in sex! Other men follow her, for they have nothing to lose, tempting her with artificial sympathy and the poor woman falls into the trap of such womanizers! Alas! Gone are the days of Penelope who had waited patiently, avoiding the fortune-seekers cleverly, for twenty long years for her husband Ulysses, though there was little hope of his return after the Trojan War!

Dear Rajesh! I thought. We live in a hard world! All our concepts about family life have changed! We thought that premarital or extramarital sex was an unpardonable sin! But today, the so-called system of 'living together' has become a fashion and it is legal too! The husband and wife have become mere partners or mates, who can be changed like soiled clothes or worn out shoes! Divorces and remarriages have become very common even among Christians, though Christ gave strict warnings against them! We are quite comfortable with second-hand goods and public toilets!

I quickly turned the pages of the small Bible once again and scanned the Gospels to find what Jesus said about it. Soon I found it; the passage was from St. Matthews, Chapter 19, verses 3 to 12, and I read it word by word:

> The Pharisees also came to Him, testing Him, and saying to Him, 'Is it lawful for a man to divorce his wife for just any reason?'
> And He answered and said to them, 'Have you not read that He who made them at the beginning 'made them male and female,'
> And said, 'For this reason a man shall leave his father and

mother and be joined to his wife, and the two shall become one flesh?'

'So then, they are no longer two but one flesh. Therefore what God has joined together, let not man separate.'

They said to Him, 'Why then did Moses command to give a certificate of divorce, and to put her away?'

He said to them, 'Moses, because of the hardness of your hearts, permitted you to divorce your wives, but from the beginning it was not so.

'And I say to you, whoever divorces his wife, except for sexual immorality, and marries another, commits adultery.'

His disciples said to Him, 'If such is the case of the man with his wife, it is better not to marry.'

But He said to them, 'All cannot accept this saying, but only those to him it has been given:

'For there are eunuchs who were born thus from their mother's womb, and there are eunuchs who were made eunuchs by men, and there are eunuchs for the kingdom of heaven's sake, he who is able to accept it, let him accept it.'

I closed the Bible, kept it on my lap and relaxed for a while. What might be the significance of getting these passages for my reading? I thought. Perhaps it was because I was thinking too much about marriage and family life. Could Rajesh lead a happy life with Geetha? I thought.

Of course, the success of a family life depended mainly on the wife, though the husband could not escape from his responsibilities. I remembered the Latin saying: Mulier est hominis confusio which means 'Woman is man's whole bliss and joy'. There were ascetics who discovered bliss and joy without a woman but for an ordinary man life would be dull and boring without marrying a woman! There might be people who could find this bliss of life by marrying persons from their own sex but better from the opposite sex.

A gloomy thought passed through my mind while thinking about the sacrifice of my wife; she could not come with me to Ethiopia as she was seeking a daughter-in-law for my son! Xanthu should not feel that his parents had left him without caring for his personal needs, she said! Moreover, according to his horoscope, he was likely to marry a girl of low birth or a girl who was elder to him! Or if the marriage was not arranged within a year, it would be after a decade! Funny!

I remembered the agonized face of my friend and I murmured, "Dear Dr. Worku Singh! Here's a supporter for your pseudo-science!" I smiled myself, thinking about the mystery of human life in which a person was ignorant even about his immediate future!

Of course, usually husbands will not recognize the amount of sacrifice made by their wives! She might be waiting anxiously for my arrival after a long break. The humming of the plane disturbed my thoughts; I wished to fall into a deep slumber, in vain!

CHAPTER TWO

I adjusted my senses to the humming of the plane. No more enquiries from the hostess, no more restless movements of the passengers. Everyone looked calm and quiet, except for the persistent anxiety commonly found on the faces of those who were separated from the solid land to fly across the air currents, thousands of feet up above the sea! There was nothing to think about regarding the safety of our flight; if something unexpected happened, we would all go deep into the Arabian Sea, 'unsung and unheard'! Then, why should I think of such matters? I tried to relax in my seat. My thoughts were flying backward!

It was about two years before that we all came to this African country. No friends or relatives, except our willpower to face every adverse circumstance and our dreams to stir our enthusiasm. It was necessary for me to find a job somewhere on this planet since I had been officially retired from the college where I served for about twenty-six years! Of course, it was not the money that compelled me to accept this new assignment, but my active spirit that could not leave me idle. I could not be idle; the purpose of my life was not yet completed! My adventurous soul always whispered in my ears 'to seek, to find and not to yield'!

Then, I left my family, my neighborhood, my friends, my congregation, my society, my linguistic group, my State and my Country and crossed the Arabian Sea! First, I had to take a domestic flight from Cochin to Mumbai. At Mumbai, after the ordeal of hopelessly long hours of waiting outside the airport like a beggar, suffering the heat and the dry wind of the city, the security guards allowed me to enter into the air-conditioned atmosphere! Then, the boarding of the Ethiopian Airlines flight towards my destination!

Five and a half hours of flight over the dark waters; nothing except a few pieces of white clouds that hung outside my window! I heaved a long sigh of relief as the plane touched the Bole Airport of Addis Ababa, the capital of Ethiopia. Ethiopia, the land of the gods! Ethiopia, a country in the Horn of the Dark Continent! Ethiopia, the land of unknown diseases, wars, famines and natural calamities! Those were my strong notions about Ethiopia!

A strange feeling of familiarity overcame me! I felt I belonged to this country and, here, I must open a new page in my life! There onwards, Ethiopia belonged to me and I belonged to Ethiopia! Ethiopia, where legends turned into history! Ethiopia, the seat of one of the ancient civilizations of the world! Ethiopia, the country where one could see the stelae, one of the wonders of the ancient world! Ethiopia, where people could enjoy thirteen months of sunshine, as the Ethiopian Airlines advertised! Ethiopia, for me, a strange land of strange people! And I had to live here, at least, for the next two years, according to my contract with the Ministry of Education!

Taking my handbag, I exited the plane and walked into the lounge where I had to collect my luggage from the conveyor belt. Mr. Pull-ready was following me like a shadow as one of his suitcases was in my name. I met him while standing in the queue for the Ethiopian Airlines check-in at Mumbai Airport. The poor man was almost begging every passenger who had fewer bags in the queue to take one of his suitcases, as he had more than sixty-five kilograms, about twenty-five kilograms of extra weight, and for that he had no money with him to pay! It might be a trick of his, but he has taken the risk! And in this modern world, one should take the risk to become rich, and he dared it! Of course, most of the so-called members who came under the democratic majority, who took the risk, would end up in suicide; and that was inevitable in our system of capitalist democracy!

He moved from one person to another, saying, "Sir, I'm Pull-ready; Sir, I'm a teacher at an Ethiopian University. Please, see my Identity Card! If you have fewer bags, please take a small suitcase of mine with you. Sir, please do me a favor, Sir!"

No one was ready to help him. Of course, it was natural that they would not take baggage from an unknown person, for fear of prohibited things in it. Finally, he came towards me and made the same request. I had only about 18 kilograms with me, as I was allowed only 25 kilograms in my domestic flight from Cochin to Mumbai, and my old bath-scale at home betrayed me by showing 25 instead of the actual 18 kilograms!

I agreed to take his suitcase to Addis Ababa. There was a helpless man before you in need of genuine help and you got an opportunity to show a little charity without any expense! Oh, George! You're incorrigible! Never would you learn from lessons of the past! Many a time you faced problems in your life just because you did not know how to say 'no' in such situations! Your mother taught you, from your childhood onwards, that you should do at least one small piece of charity a day especially if it did not cost you anything! You tried to follow her advice and always landed in trouble, either in loss of money or loss of honor or both!

And those who benefited from my help did not even care about the value of my sacrifice; they ignored it like a useless piece of straw! Even that so-called Pull-ready did not thank me at least through an e-mail! I might be a fool to accept the baggage of a person who was unknown to me. Suppose his suitcase contained some explosives or narcotics? Then I would be arrested and put in the Ethiopian jail, perhaps, for years! Oh, no! Pull-ready wouldn't pull my legs, I tried to believe so!

Don't be a coward, you Professor George! 'Cowards die many times before their death, but the valiant tastes death but once'! At last, as it usually happened in such tug-of-wars, my heart won over my brain!

We received our luggage and walked out into the Ethiopian 'sunshine' or 'shoeshine' as my Ethiopian friend corrected it later! I was expecting the vehicle from the Ministry of Education to take me to the hotel as mentioned in my contract. But Pull-ready told me that it was foolishness to expect anything to happen in Ethiopia in accordance with the contract. Once you signed the contract, they would forget everything about it! He knew the Ethiopian Hotel where the Ministry had arranged facility for our stay and suggested that I share the taxi fare and go with him. Of course, it would be better to share the taxi rather than taking a separate taxi and pay an exorbitant amount.

He dropped me in front of my hotel and told me to go and check-in as he was going to his friend's house. Later I came to know that the vehicle sent by the Ministry to pick me returned without finding me and it was the clever idea of Pull-ready to take me with him so that his taxi fare would be shared! And no vehicle was supposed to be arranged for those persons, like Pull-ready, who came on a second contract!

I went to the receptionist and he asked me to share a room with another person who had come on the previous day with the same purpose as mine. Mr. Aweface was my roommate, a nice gentleman with thorough knowledge in his subject, provided that I used to keep awake the whole night, for he screamed and shrieked during his sleep. Naturally, every person who had to leave suddenly the warmth of his family life would scream and shriek in their sleep; I was not blessed even with that opportunity!

Next morning I went to the office of the Ministry of Education to find out the name of the university for which I was appointed. Before I could meet the officer concerned, Rama Rao, a person from Andhra Pradesh, greeted me and said, "Sir! Are you a new teacher to Ethiopia? I have been working here for the last one year. This year my wife also got an appointment but unfortunately in another university."

I saw his wife standing in another part of the corridor, carrying a boy-child in her hands. As we were talking, she joined us with an expression of utter despair on her face.

He continued, "Sir! I am working in Alemaya University and she got the job in Jimma University. Mr. Mepleased, the personnel officer, is not ready to change her university. Neither did he agree to give me a transfer to her university nor a transfer for her to my university! You know, she may suffer a lot with that small child in a place quite strange to her."

I guessed what was in his mind. There was a man and his family in sheer helplessness! I asked him, "What's your idea?"

"Sir, if you get the appointment in Alemaya, and if you are ready to go to Jimma, Mr. Mepleased will consider our case. Believe me, he promised us! You see, Sir, Jimma is one of the best universities in Ethiopia."

I stood there with a smile. Well! If Mr. Mepleased promised to do some favor for Rama Rao, it meant that Rama Rao promised something to him! And I knew that the Andhraites were manipulating things in the Ministry of Education in Ethiopia! Of course, that was great! A few years back, Andhra Pradesh was one of the most underdeveloped States in India and, now, if they could do what the Keralites had done during the time of Emperor Haile Selassi, I should not be jealous of them! In India, while all the backward States accelerated their progress, my State, Kerala, stood motionless, as if she were waiting for some orders from China or from America!

I understood his plan; in my place his wife could join Alemaya and, in her place, I would go to Jimma. As a newcomer to Ethiopia, all universities were one and the same for me. And I was there to face any kind of situation! Whether it was in Alemaya or in Jimma, it wouldn't make any difference for me. And their naughty child was smiling at me, as if he were making a strong recommendation to me for the case of his parents!

I readily agreed to their plan; who knew what would be drawn on my forehead by the goddess of Fate? Both of us entered the office and Mr. Mepleased opened the confidential file. I could see the tension and anxiety mounting on the face of Rama Rao! Mr. Mepleased went through the file, found my name and clicked his tongue and said, "I'm sorry! He is appointed in Sea Side City University."

Rama Rao went out of the room in utter disappointment. I got my appointment letter and came out. The child was crying loudly and his young mother was trying every trick to console him. Rama Rao was talking to another newcomer, in the same friendly and polite tone in which he had talked to me!

I returned to my hotel and checked-out, for I had to catch the afternoon domestic flight to Sea Side City. No Indian was there at the aerodrome; almost all of them might have joined their universities a week earlier! I was, perhaps, one of the late birds!

Of course, every big city in Ethiopia was linked with air-routes, as the road transport was very poor or impossible in the country! I rushed with other passengers and occupied the seat in a small plane. After an hour, I reached Sea Side City Airport and the university officer, Mr. Heavenlyfood, was waiting for me with his pick-up van. He was a fat man with striking personality and I wondered how he could work like a laborer! He helped me to put my luggage into the van and we went to the heart of the city. Instead of putting me in the Three-star Hotel, which had an agreement with the university, Heavenlyfood took me to a third rate lodge named Palace Hotel where I had to pay the rent from my pocket! And I had my first bitter experience of Ethiopia there in that brothel of a palace hotel! Later, when I demanded my hotel expense from the university, Ato Heavenlyfood reported that I had preferred that hotel for my personal convenience and that the university was not supposed to pay the rent!

He informed me that Palace Hotel was cheaper, but quite convenient. I argued that the university was supposed to arrange my accommodation, though, I knew, it was too late to search for a new hotel, at that time of the day, in such an unfamiliar place. But he pointed out that the teachers were supposed to pay the rent, and I could find an Indian family, trapped like me, staying at Palace Hotel so that I had to believe what he said! He forced me to pay the first day's rent in advance; perhaps, it would be his commission for supplying customers to that brothel of a hotel! He gave me the phone number of an Indian teacher, Dr. Tomsin Jose, and advised me to find a good rented house with her help.

The room-girl led me to a small room with a bed and a teapoy and, of course, a tiny bathroom attached to it, despite the hotel's royal name! Fortunately, the room was facing a beautiful part of the street, a junction of roads with a garden-like round-about full of flowered plants, a mango tree in the middle and sufficient neon bulbs spreading light everywhere and illuminating even my whole room.

I looked through the window and enjoyed the sight. Men and women, in small groups, were returning to their houses. After a tiresome day, I wished to relax and sleep. I remembered the bottle of scotch whiskey kept in my bag; of course, I must thank Mr. Pull-ready who had suggested to me to buy a bottle! That would be good medicine for all illnesses in Ethiopia, he told me.

In fact, Pull-ready, whom I had met at the Mumbai Airport, had enough money in his pocket, even to pay for his extra luggage if it were necessary! After sending his luggage and also the one in my name, to the cargo section, I noticed him moving towards the duty-free shop. I also followed him. He bought three bottles of scotch whiskey, that much Indian Rupees he had, and told me that such things were not available in Ethiopia. I was tempted to buy at least one bottle as I had only that much Indian rupees left with me. In my heart, I thanked the advice of Pull-ready, and I felt as if I had taken two or three pegs more, with three cheers to his health!

Moreover, I remembered the advice of my friend Dr. Rajuji who had six years of experience in Ethiopia. Before coming to Ethiopia, I went to his house to bid him farewell! We took a few pegs and talked about Ethiopia. His friend Dr. Nandu was also with us as he too had a plan to serve abroad!

Dr. Rajuji told us in the tone of an old priest, "It's very difficult to live there without your family! You can also live there without a family, but remember one thing! Every evening take a peg or two, drink it very slowly, sip by sip, until you feel sleep, take some food and go to your bed! Sleep till the sun peeps into your bedroom!"

I thanked Dr. Rajuji for his advice. But sleep was such a shy maiden that she wouldn't embrace you when you were badly in need of her! A few mosquitoes were singing around me as if they had pledged to chase away my dearest sleep! A madman was shouting and howling and performing strange calisthenics around the traffic-roundana in the street! I did not know how or when I fell into deep slumber!

Hearing loud noises from the street, I woke up. I looked at my watch and it showed 4.55 am. The noise was from the sweepers who were ready to clean the streets when the siren hooted at 5 am sharp! The mad man was innocently sleeping under the mango tree, covering his body with a torn rag and a sack of soiled clothes under his head, perhaps, too tired of his midnight exercises! I heard the siren, and the long palm leaves in the hands of the sweepers, which they used as brooms, began moving to and fro over the road.

I took my breakfast, of course, it was 'bread and banana' all these days, and rang Dr. Tomsin. The appointment was fixed for the afternoon, and she gave the details about how to reach her house. I talked to the other Indian about whom Heavenlyfood had told me, Dr. Maindoor, who stayed with his wife and two kids in the next room. In fact, he was packing his things to vacate the room and he told me that he was moving into a new place. I thought that he was shifting to a rented house! And, as there was much time left for me, I returned to my room and fell into another sound sleep.

When I woke up, I realized that I was a bit late for my afternoon appointment. I dressed up quickly, took a service-taxi and went to meet Dr. Tomsin. I got down from the taxi at a nearby stop and walked a hundred meters or so and found Tomsin and her husband, Jose, waiting for me at their gate. It was their pastime or hobby, as I understood later, to help those newly-arrived Indians in finding suitable rented-houses and honest maid-servants, and also in buying necessary furniture, cooking utensils and other household things like blankets and mosquito-nets. Of course, such things were inevitable for a healthy life in Ethiopia.

We went to see a house and, on the way, she said, "In the morning, we found a house for Dr. Worku Singh; and the house for you is very near to it. But I'm not sure whether the house is ready for use."

However, we met the house owner, Mohammed, who was living with his wife and three children in the same compound. It was his out-house that he planned to rent. Electrification and plumbing were going on in the out-house on wartime basis, and he demanded 800 Birr for the big house in which he was living, and 600 Birr for the out-house; but on condition that until he shifted his family from the present house to the new house which he was constructing at a nearby compound, I should stay in the out-house with three tiny rooms, including the kitchen!

I agreed to it, for I loved his compound that was full of mango trees, papaya plants and avocado trees. I also loved the presence of a family which would help me in not feeling loneliness. He took an advance of 800 Birr, but later, neither did he shift his family to the new house nor reduce the rent to 600 Birr! I had to stay there for a year, of course, enjoying the hospitality of Safia, he called her Sophia, his wife, and the nuisance of his three children, Mubarek, Salama and Babu.

We returned to Dr. Tomsin's house, took our tea and by evening I took a taxi and reached my room in the Palace Hotel. There was no sound of kids from the room of Dr. Maindoor, and I guessed that he had shifted to his rented-house. On the handle of my room's door, there was a folded paper and I thought that it might be a farewell note left by Dr. Maindoor, as he could not find me. I opened the paper and read it. It said, "I am Dr. Ahmad Ansari, staying in the room next to yours, and I will be back to meet you at 7.30 pm. See you then." And there was his illegible signature!

Another poor man dropped by Mr. Heavenlyfood, I thought. When Maindoor left, the room was given to Ahmad. At 7.30, Ahmad came to my room and we talked for more than an hour. He had the inborn talent of taking anyone into his side by his golden tongue! He told me that he had met some Ethiopian Muslims and they had promised to find a house for him, at a very low rate somewhere near to the Masjid.

Dr. Ahmad blindly believed that Muslims would not betray other Muslims and I could feel his prejudice towards people who belonged to other religions. Of course, nothing better could be expected from a product of Jamia Millia Islamia, I thought. One could not blame such people as their family background; the circumstances under which they were born and brought up, the educational institutions where they studied and the closed society in which they lived were so rigid, preventing every bright ray of secularism entering into them. Generally in India, people preferred to live with members of their own community and watched other communities with suspicion and fear, I remembered.

Ahmad was a short-statured young man who talked too much about himself, about his city in Bihar and about his studies in Delhi. But I liked him for his clever and calculative way of assessing persons and situations, perhaps, a talent he hereditarily acquired from the background of his business-family, and a friendship grew up between us, despite the differences in our religions.

Next morning, Ahmad knocked at my door and woke me up. He said that he could not sleep during the night as, every time, men and women came in pairs and occupied the nearby rooms just for an hour or so, they called it 'shorts', and left after paying half-day rent. He pointed out that the hotel rooms were mainly for the purpose of prostitution, and we should escape from there as early as possible. Of course, prostitution was not illegal in Ethiopia and most of the hotels and lodges minted money out of it. In India, even the legal husband and wife could not stay alone in a hotel room for fear of harassment from the police, I remembered. Later, I came to know that Sea Side City was one of the leading cities of Ethiopia in tourism and notorious for prostitution and, of course, it was also leading in the number of HIV/AIDS patients!

When Ahmad had gone out in search of his Muslim friends and their promised house, I too went out to fetch my usual breakfast of 'bread and banana' from the footpath. Quite unexpectedly, I noticed Dr. Maindoor sitting near a vendor-girl who sold guava fruits. He was bargaining in a loud voice and was trying to reduce the price, even though the poor girl sold the fruits at the lowest price! In Ethiopia, the footpath sellers neither increased the price of things they sold nor reduced the price on bargaining!

I ignored him and went to a shop which sold bread and to another shop for bananas. While returning after ten or fifteen minutes, I saw him still continuing his useless bargaining. He was selecting the best fruits from her pile of guavas, turning them this way and that way and pressing them and throwing them down as if he was not satisfied. In India, the footpath sellers would have beaten him for such uncivilized manners! He saw me approaching and, with a foolish smile, told me, "See, this girl demands 15 cents for one guava and she is not ready to give it for 10 cents! We must bargain, otherwise these people will cheat us!"

He was trying to get four guavas for fifty cents but the vendor-girl was adamant on sixty cents! Well! I used to get angry, of course, unnecessarily, on such occasions. Here's a shameless bourgeois who bargains with poor street vendors who sell their products at greatly reduced margins, who do their business not to build a shopping mall but for their daily living! I thought.

I said in a tone of deep indignation, "Do you get guava at this low price in India? What a shameful thing, Mr. Maindoor! Just for ten cents, you bargained for half an hour with this poor, illiterate girl in rugged clothes! If you have no money, I shall give you ten cents!"

He looked into my eyes, for a moment, in embarrassment, and mumbled with a hollow laugh, "No! No! I have money, but we must bargain for anything and everything!" Then, suddenly, I realized that he was not exactly bargaining with that girl but was secretly enjoying the guavas on her chest which could be seen through her torn clothes! Such sights gave the sexually starving Indians a sort of vicarious pleasure! It was my Sri Lankan colleague, Joken, who told me later, "Who said there is no poverty in India? You have poverty of sex!"

"Alright! You go on bargaining!" I said and walked away. I knew that he did not like my comments! There onwards, he never talked to me in a friendly manner! When drinking, dogs could only lick the water even from the great ocean! I thought. Ethiopians always loved and respected Indians more than Europeans and this petty and stingy Indian would spoil our name, I said in my mind. Moreover, among the expatriates, he was the teacher who drew the highest salary, as I came to know later. He would have befooled the members of the interview board with his unbeatable talent in bargaining!

As I turned towards my hotel, a flash of suspicion passed through me: Why is this man roaming near my hotel? He can buy fruit even from the neighborhood of his newly rented house! I waited for him, hiding myself from his view at the corner of the street.

I saw him coming with four guavas in his hands and entering into the Three-star hotel with which the university had some tie-up! I went to the hotel, enquired about him to the receptionist and came to know that he was staying in that hotel! He was clever enough to get a double room there at the cost of the university; and he cleverly hid that fact from us lest we would also get rooms there! In my heart, I appreciated his bargaining capacity!

Well! Why should I be jealous of him? Let him go his own way! Who knows about our fate here in this alien land? Any person can be terminated of his or her job at any time! Who knows who will continue here for more years?

I looked for Ahmad everywhere but I could not find him; he might be taking his food with some Ethiopian Muslims, I thought! In the afternoon, I shifted my luggage to my rented house, in the compound of Mohammed. I did not know when Ahmad vacated the hotel and went to his rented-house, perhaps, on the same day itself!

On the very next day, I went to the university by their bus. It was my first day in the university campus and I enjoyed it. As you got down from the bus into the university main square, a big hoarding with letters in blue welcomed you: GET YOUR DEGREE FREE...

For a moment, I was confused. There was a picture of a few girls and boys, pale and ghastly, skeleton-like youngsters in their ceremonial graduation costumes! Skeletons wearing the black gown and mortar board, holding the scroll of their degree certificates! I again read the full caption with the addendum in red letters: GET YOUR DEGREE FREE FROM HIV/AIDS. Am I here to work as a Professor... or as a social worker? I was confused for a moment.

Perhaps, both! Here, a teacher ought to be a social worker, if you love this land and its people. My eyes were fixed on another big hoarding in which a young boy and a girl, both blindfolded, running and playing in their ecstasy, quite unaware of the deep gorge ahead, were about to fall from a mountain cliff! Are these youngsters deliberately ignoring the danger into which they may fall at any time? I thought. As I came to know later, these boys and girls did not know self-control or the social laws of the outside-world's morality. And many of them got their degrees together with HIV/AIDS!

The bite of the same flea, as John Donne says, may unite these loving pairs of students by sucking blood from both, except that their unity shall not be in sharing HIV/AIDS! Thank God! They say that this epidemic won't infect through mosquitoes lest the whole world should teem with millions of HIV/AIDS patients!

I visited my department and met the Dean, the Head and other colleagues! I loved the place, the atmosphere, the climate and the people! What else was needed to work in a foreign country? I tried to become satisfied with whatever facilities I had! I realized that I was the first Indian who ever joined the Department of English!

The next day, Dr. Dinov, another Indian from Delhi, also joined the department. I talked to him and understood that unlike many other Indian teachers working here abroad, he had in-depth knowledge in his subject. We used to talk on various literary issues and consulted each other before delivering lectures to the students. However, later when he brought his family, I cut short my regular visits to him. Outside India, we used to think that there was a wide gap between those who led a bachelor life and those who lived with their family, and the gap was wider and deeper than the gap that existed in between Lazarus and the Richman!

I felt almost settled after a week's agony and anxiety! It was my habit to meet and acquaint with as many people as possible and, here too, I began my search. I enquired about people of my own Southernmost State in India first and then about those coming from other South Indian States and finally about those from North Indian States. Knowing about others was just like learning a new language! Whenever you tried to learn a language other than your mother tongue, the first words you come across would be either obscene words or vituperations! It was natural because people with some bad reputation would be more popular than those who were silent and selfish!

The second couple I met in Sea Side City, of course the first one was Dr. Tomsin and her husband Jose, was Mr. Priest and Ms. Pom. They greeted me and took me to their house for a cup of tea and I was quite impressed by their behavior, their unity, their friendliness, their caring for each other and a lot of good qualities necessary for an ideal couples. Made for each other, I said in my mind.

They went together to the University, returned home together, went to the market and bought things after consulting each other, they smiled to each other on silly matters and looked into each other's eyes with a sort of understanding and whispered to each other with confidence! They were in their middle ages but behaved like a pair of little sparrows, newly met for the season! Really I appreciated their care for each other!

I could not find their children with them and that might be the reason for their extraordinary intimacy, I thought. When children were born, the husband and wife would not get enough leisure time to care for each other, and both of them would be too assiduous, and a sort of unnecessary stress would dominate over their each and every activity! Perhaps their children were studying in India and, if so, they should relax and enjoy the days here!

The next day, I met Mr. President, of course I called him like that because his actual name was that of a famous American President, and his niece in the market. Both were teachers at the University, working for quite a long period and they knew each and every shop in the city. As we moved along the street, we noticed Mr. Priest and Ms. Pom alight from a shop and moving ahead of us. A cunning smile flashed on the faces of Dr. President and his niece, Ms. Sinja, and I noticed it.

Of course, it was the nature of Indians that they were always curious about others! And I was also not an exemption and I asked Mr. President whether they had any kids!

He laughed aloud and asked me, "Sir! Are you jealous of them? Don't you think they're very happy in their life?"

"Of course! I think of them as an ideal pair of husband and wife!" I replied.

Mr. President laughed again at my reply. He said, "Sir! Her husband is somewhere in India and as he works in a private company, he will not get leave to come over here. Moreover, they have one son and we heard that she had given a notice for divorce!"

His niece, Ms. Sinja giggled and said, "And Mr. Priest's wife is in India and they have no issues; the poor wife doesn't know anything about the amorous adventures of her husband in Africa!"

The image of the Babel Tower of an ideal married life fell

down in my mind and turned into mere rubble! Couldn't husbands and wives keep fidelity and faithfulness to their spouses, by sacrificing at least some of their pleasures? I felt a sort of moral indignation.

Later, when I met Dr. Elderking, a Professor and friend of mine, I expressed my indignation on such kind of relationships. But he had a different view and he said, "What's wrong in it? Even the Indian Supreme Court has accepted such 'living together' relationships as legal! Their spouses are in India and they found this life quite convenient and what is immoral about it? What about your friend Dr. President? He lives in the same flat with his niece and you don't find anything wrong in it?"

My God! Is it what they think about a person who lives with his sister's daughter? My Christian sense of morality was hurt in such cruel jokes! Of course, one could not blame Elderking as he was a Hindu and among certain Hindu communities in South India, a person was allowed to marry his sister's daughter! But here, Mr. President was a Christian, and how could such a relationship be possible in the Indo-Christian cultural background? Even among Europeans such a relationship was considered a taboo!

Some people get a sort of brutish satisfaction or sadistic pleasure when they cook up false stories about others! This might be common to all human beings all over the world, perhaps! I wanted to get the truth from the horse's mouth and talked to them face to face. My friends would say that it was none of my business and why should you get involved in it! But I could not leave things like that! And then came out the tragic story of Ms. Sinja, and I felt ashamed of myself for suspecting that poor woman and her uncle!

Her husband died when her eldest child was studying in the seventh standard! They were living in a rented-house with her meager income from a private institution; and she found it very difficult to make both ends meet. How could she give proper education to her two daughters? And as an Indian Christian, she could not appreciate the idea of remarriage. She felt as if her life was at a crossroads!

Then her uncle decided to help her by resigning from his job as the administrator of an educational institution, and deciding to join an Ethiopian University where both of them could work together. Though at first they were appointed in two different universities, Dr. President managed to get her a transfer to the university in Sea Side City, so that they could live together in the same flat.

My mind began to rebuild a new Tower of Babel from the rubble! True love has not completely disappeared from the face of this earth! There are people who help each other even in the midst of misfortune! There might be people who change their spouses just like tornout clothes! But still, there are many people who experience the heavenly bliss of conjugal life. As Anne Frank, the girl who wrote about her suffering during the holocaust of Hitler wrote, "In spite of everything, I still believe that people are really good at heart."

After all such positive thinking, the question remains: Why did they live together in the same flat? Of course, it was sufficient to arouse suspicion among other Indians! There is no smoke without a spark of fire! In the Indian way of life, even a brother was not supposed to sleep in the same room of his sister after a certain age! Only God knew the truth!

Most of us came here leaving our family, relatives and friends! A few were lucky to bring their family and for others, the circumstances at their homes would be different. There might be children who could not break their studies; there might be aged parents who needed daily care and protection. It would be a consolation to think that at least your wife was there at home and she could manage the affairs in your absence!

And you missed their presence! How much money could compensate the homeliness you had been losing every day, every hour and every minute! You needed the presence of your wife and children, your parents and dear relatives, your neighbors and friends! You might not feel their importance, once you were there, perhaps! Perhaps, you would be too busy that you might not get time to talk to them or engage in conversation with them! But you always felt their presence and that would suffice to quench your visceral fire!

Of course, when a child was born, you would feel happiness; you would feel the sense of responsibility! The child would be an encumbrance for you; but it would be a pleasurable encumbrance! Same might be the case with your aged parents; they were definitely an encumbrance for you but that too would be a pleasurable encumbrance! Your parents might be very old but they would make your life worthy of living! Only once they had left this earth, you would feel the grace of their presence!

I remembered a Yiddish proverb: "When a father gives to his son, both laugh; when a son gives to his father, both cry!" There were parents who could not adjust with their children and there were children who could not adjust with their parents! There were parents who preferred old age homes to the homes of their own children and there were children who sent their parents to old age homes! Relationships turned strenuous in these days!

When I said about my aged parents, who were in their eighties, to my Ethiopian students, I noticed the expression of wonder on their faces! The life expectancy in Ethiopia was 40 to 45 and many had lost their parents at an early age! Perhaps their parents would be lucky because, in this modern age, children were so busy that they would find it very difficult to look after them!

One day, my friend Dr. Dinov told me that he would not trouble his children, once he was old; he would prefer to go to an old age home. He said, "I know the problems of my children; of course, they won't have time or convenience in their busy schedule to look after their parents! We are educated people and we must understand their difficulty."

But wasn't there a note of sadness and helplessness in his words? In Kerala, the southernmost State in India, which claimed one hundred percent literacy, the most profitable business was to start an old age home! Almost every educated member from most of the families there had gone abroad and their palatial houses were left for their aged parents who lived in them like ghosts! Once a year, the children would come and try to send them to some old age homes for the sake of security, but most of the parents thought of it as a shameful deal, something against Indian culture!

I remembered the folktale quite popular in India. Once a benevolent king went out of his palace with his minister; both of them were disguised as common-men, to check the welfare of his subjects. On the way they met a very poor man and gave him a small bag of gold coins. The king asked him what he would do with the gold coins. The poor man replied, "One fourth of it will be used for paying my debt; one fourth of it will be given as a loan; one fourth will be thrown away and the last one fourth will be buried under the soil!"

The king and the minister were surprised at his answer and they demanded further explanation. Therefore, the poor man said, "The first one-fourth will be used to look after my parents and, thereby, I am paying back my debt; the second one-fourth will be spent to look after my sons and, thereby, I am giving them a loan which they have to repay when I'm old; the third one-fourth will be spent for my daughters and as they were going to their husbands, it'll be like throwing away the money and the last one-fourth will be utilized for cultivating my land which will help me to earn my daily bread!"

The king was surprised at the wisdom of the poor man and gave him another bag of gold coins; and thus, the story ended in such a way that we were enlightened by certain aspects of

Indian culture! But who was there to bother about such old sayings of practical wisdom, especially in this so-called modern age?

I remembered the words of Dr. Lexan, a cousin and a friend of mine. Of course, he was a Professor of Philosophy and he had answers to every problem, though often they were quite impractical! He said, "The problem with the modern generation is that they follow the wrong concept regarding discipline! Of course, it is very easy to control this world and its population if everything goes in a disciplined way! But that's quite unnatural and impossible, and we shouldn't expect everything will go on quite smoothly!"

He continued, "Our main complaint is that indiscipline is the order of the day! Parents say that children have no discipline; children say that parents have no discipline! Our brothers and sisters have no discipline; our friends and neighbors have no discipline! Teachers say that the students have no discipline; and students say that their teachers have no discipline! We foolishly believe that everything will be okay if we obey each other! 'Oh, wives! Obey your husbands!' That's what the scripture says. But the wives ask why not the other way? 'Oh, husbands! Obey your wives!' Our relationships are thus shattered on these rocks of discipline and obedience!"

After a minute's silence, Dr. Lexan said, "And what we want is freedom! But we don't know freedom from what! We aren't ready to accept what Rousseau said, 'Man is born free but everywhere he is in chains!' By chains, I mean not slavery but a sort of healthy relationship from which we have no emancipation! In fact, we're glued to life with these relationships; those who ignore human relationships find this life a heavy burden!"

Dr. Lexan was in a philosophical mood and he said, "And we forgot the significance of love! While we preach about love, in our hearts we know that we are cheating ourselves! We lost our basic sympathy; our genuine willingness for sacrifice! We are impatient and restless; we wish that everything must happen according to our desire! If something happens against our expectation, we will begin to hate ourselves and also blame others! We are not ready to accept our own frailty; we are not ready to assess the value of relationships! And that leads to the failure of our life!"

He continued, "Today we live in a world of misunderstanding, not only among nations but also among married couples! We think about the figurative meaning of words rather than their literal meanings and this leads to vulnerable misinterpretations. The result varies from petty quarrels to divorces among married couples to simple exchange of shots in the border areas to great World Wars! Nations sign peace treaties, but before the ink dries on the paper, they declare new wars! Today the bride and the bridegroom with a smile sign in the marriage register and, before the ink dries on the paper, they snarl at each other and sign on their divorce notice! It is always better if married couples can remember the words of John Gray: When misunderstanding arises, remember that we speak different languages, take the time necessary to translate what your partner really means or wants to say. This definitely takes practice, but it is well worth it".

I always wondered how the conjugal life could become so formal1 how could you say phrases like 'sorry' and 'thanks' in such a casual manner in real family life? See the American serials like the OC and the South Park! Such serials show the actual social life in the USA! Of course, a society which has nothing like a culture of its own, but only an amalgamation of a thousand cultures, might behave like that!

Of course, Dr. Lexan had his own family problems but he managed them with a magical snap of his fingers! One day he said, "Don't allow your family problems to pester your daily life! Try to nip them in the bud; try to kill them in your mind!

Problems are insects and your mind should be an insecticide! You spray it, 'Psheeew!' and the problem's gone! It's simply because there's no problem without a solution!"

"But don't forget that certain cockroaches survive pesticides!" I said with a smile, and he also joined with me to enjoy the joke.

Next day I was on my evening walk and I unexpectedly met Dr. Dinov. He used to walk with his wife and I was surprised to see him alone on that day! His wife, Lashie Dinov, was suffering from diabetes and the doctor had advised her to walk a few kilometers every day. She observed fasting at least twice a week and avoided all kinds of sweet dishes! She walked every morning and every evening but the level of her blood-sugar remained the same! The rest of her time she spent with her yoga and prayers! But they were all of no use!

Dinov told me that he wanted a new house. He was living on the ground floor of a three-storeyed building and the way for other residents to go upstairs was through his drawing cum dining room! The two families who stayed on the first and second floors of the house always passed through his launch and this irritated him. He told me, "You see, there's no privacy! Both of us are caged in our bedroom of a prayer-room! We can't talk freely; we can't eat freely; we can't sleep peacefully! How long could we go on like that? On weekends, I would like to have a drink or two! How can I take my drinks in the bedroom? It's even impossible to quarrel with my wife or shout at her, for fear of the neighbors! Are we dead bodies to live silently forever? How long could we pull on without having some petty quarrels with our wives?"

I agreed with his argument. There must be, at times, some petty quarrels between husbands and wives; this would add spice to their conjugal life, provided that such quarrels should be in a good spirit and they should not brew up hatred towards the spouse!

I smiled to myself thinking over the strange relationships among husbands and wives! Some husbands drink to quarrel with their wives and some others quarrel with their wives to drink in the pubs! The so-called Indian culture was so funny and rigid that men would rather go to brothels to see the naked body of a woman than to see that of his legally married wife! I remembered my friend Prof. Mozad, may God bless his soul, one day after a few drinks, confessed to me his pathetic fate! His wife belonged to a traditional orthodox Hindu family and she was too pious to show her nudity even to her husband, so that he had to seek other sources!

In India, once there was the 'devadasi' custom as well as the concubine system and, even prostitution was a socially accepted institution! Certain Hindu communities in South India still followed the system of 'little home', the system of keeping an extra wife! In the past, rich people used to spend their nights enjoying the music and dancing of girls belonging to a particular caste! Of course, as my Sri Lankan friend, Joken, said, "If Indian husbands went after prostitutes, one could blame only their wives!"

There are men who torture their wives and wives who torture their husbands; both groups enjoy a sort of devilish pleasure out of it! Some husbands serve their wives like slaves and some wives serve their husbands like maidservants; both groups get a sort of happiness out of it! Here, who wins and who loses, nobody knows!

Conjugal relationships were so strange and queer that outsiders could not interfere and take quick drastic decisions! Each couple is unique in this world and their ways of internal and external adjustments are unpredictable!

Some husbands, being fed up with their wives, go for long pilgrimages or enter into the life of an ascetic! Some wives, in order to eschew the sexual approaches of their husbands, show excessive religious faith and engage in prayers and rites! Of course, indifference and passive approaches to sex mars the sanctity of conjugal life!

But think in another direction! If Mrs. Leo Tolstoy had been tolerant and merciful to her husband, the world would not have had a great writer! If Fanny Browne and Maud Gonne had not rejected Keats and Yeats, respectively, would we have had such great poets in English literature?

I remembered the story of a great writer who always came home with injured feet or wounded fingers only to get the nursing care of his wife! She would come with hot water, lotion, antibiotic ointments, cotton and plasters; slowly wash the wounds and carefully bandage them, taking at least an hour! All this time, he had enjoyed the pleasure and thrill which he could not have felt even in the bedroom!

I remembered the popular Sanskrit saying about the qualities of an ideal wife:

Bhojeshu mata; karyeshu manthri;
Rogeshu daasi; shayaneshu Rambha!

The meaning can be put like this:
At the dining table, she must be like a mother;
In administration, she must be like a minister;
At the sick bed, she must be like a nurse;
And in the bedroom, she must be like a whore!

Of course, this might be from the male point of view, and similar lines could be composed from a female point of view about the qualities of an ideal husband! In the modern world, it would be difficult for a woman to be an ideal wife but if she wished to become one, the husband should also be an ideal one!

In married life, both the husband and the wife should feel victorious, only then, conjugal life would become worthy and meaningful. As the poet wrote: Man's excessive lust turns him a conqueror; he makes space in the void, feels himself victorious and annexes the place with his powerful phallus! Woman's deep lust too turns her a conqueror, fills the space made by man with his essence of life and, then, cruelly rejects his powerless phallus! Victory to man and woman and their irresistible desire for mutual annexation that they willingly conquer, sharing happiness with each other, and find human life wonderful!

CHAPTER THREE

A sudden jerking of the plane made many of the passengers wake up from their sleep. Of course, Ethiopian pilots were experts despite the poor maintenance of their planes, I thought. Our plane was piercing the thick darkness of the sky over the Arabian Sea. There was enough time to brood over and assess my two years in Ethiopia. I slipped into my memory, once again.

The Sea Side City University campus was in a natural botanical garden with hundreds of trees and singing birds that you might feel as if you were in Tagore's Shanti Niketan. It was situated on the southern coast of Lake Tana and on the western banks of the river Abay or the Blue Nile adding a pleasant atmosphere. There were a lot of volcanic boulders scattered all over the campus which served as natural seats for the students who waited for their next class. In short, as I wrote to my former colleague, it was a university situated in a botanical garden or rather it can be called a Jungle University.

My friend, Dr. Brahanu, in his study about the university campus, stated that there were sixty-three tree and shrub species belonging to thirty-four families, identified there by his students. About eighty-nine species of birds, including the rare endemic bird Wattled Ibis, were also identified. Moreover, the fauna of that university campus included amphibians, reptiles like snakes, lizards and chameleons, and mammals like bats, porcupines, rabbits, mongooses, rats, monkeys and wild cats, and they all had made that place their safe haven. A lot of domesticated mammals of different groups like cows, dogs and cats also lived leisurely in the campus.

The students freely moving here and there, boys and girls hand in hand, sitting in pairs on the beautiful boulders scattered all over the campus gave you the feeling of Plato's university in his Republic. The boys were lean but were strong and they moved carelessly around the campus with a desperate look in their eyes. The girls were bony and beautiful and they moved everywhere in their tempting fashionable dress, exposing too much of their body beauty. Owing to their uncontrollable life, the glittering of dream in their bright eyes used to change into dim, dull and despair-stricken as they reached the age of thirty, as they married some dullards who were at least twenty years older than them, who gave them a minimum of six children to look after or left them for new preys, usually after giving one or two brats for their care! I felt worried. But there in the campus, weren't these girls the real cause behind the tired looks and shaggy appearance of the boys?

I saw girls and boys freely moving in pairs, hugging, caressing and kissing which were strange for a person from India. Many of them were sitting under the shade of trees; boys resting their heads on the laps of their girls and girls sitting on the laps of boys, perhaps, enjoying the hardness of their groins!

Both the natural and manmade gardens enhanced the beauty of the campus, giving temptations for the students. The hog-paths in the woods were decorated with fallen petals of the Gulmohar flowers and used condoms. As I went into my department along a short-cut in the garden, I saw a boy sitting under a tree and his girlfriend was lying in his lap keeping her face in between his thighs! Of course, it was the vigorous movements and hissing noise that tempted me to look towards that part of the garden. The boy looked at me and I could never forget the helplessness in his eyes; they were like the eyes of the street dog that locked itself in the body of its bitch!

But these people were highly hospitable, I mused. I watched

them and realized that, at last, I was in 'the land of a thousand smiles'! The people respected Indians more than Europeans. The students were highly disciplined compared to Indian students. Adversity might have disciplined them; I could see in their eyes, hope and optimism about a great future. And Ethiopia was growing fast, galloping into progress and nobody could rein her growth. I began to feel proud of becoming a Professor in Ethiopia.

Could I bring a change for these people? It was just like missionary work for me. Of course, I would get my salary for my normal work but I should give them more of my talents, I decided. If I gave my service with a full heart, at least some youngsters would change their way of life and think seriously about life. Could I be successful in that mission?

My Ethiopian colleagues think of teaching just as a profession. The habit of chewing the narcotic leaves of the chat plants converted not only certain teachers but also many boys and girls into dullards. I was surprised seeing teachers who should be models for their students used to eat Qat or Chat and even they selected their mates from the students. They thought of whatever good or bad they did as part of their culture. One day, one of my colleagues, Mr. Spreadinglight, argued: "You cannot change the culture of our students. Never!"

"I can! I can do it easily!" I said with confidence. "Because what you call culture is only your tradition and practice which are stages of a civilization-fixation or stagnation. The word culture is strictly related to values of society which are the same to you as well as to me. According to our culture mother comes first, the father second, the teacher third and God comes only in fourth place! 'Mata, Pita, Guro, Daivom' is the accepted saying in our place. I can tell you how changes came even to the poor, illiterate laborers, let alone our students!"

"Interesting! Tell me your story!" Ato Spreadinglight said with a cynical smile.

I continued, ignoring his pessimistic tone: "You know my office is just near the labor office where the casual laborers on daily wages gathered and idled their time waiting for the call from the administrative office. It is natural that they used to make noise, greeting, talking, laughing, discussing, arguing and quarrelling in a very loud manner, at times, even forgetting themselves. They are simpletons and prone to slight provocations and the usual excitements! From early morning to evening, except for lunch break, their disturbance continued and I made a notice in Amaringa, with the help of Ms. Mebit, our office secretary, who made a neat computer print-out 'Ebekachew Dimtsachew Kensu', 'Please reduce your sound', and I fixed it in front of my office door. The laborers seemed a bit offended or rather annoyed at the notice, for it was the first time they'd seen a daring notice as such, especially on the door of a professor, curtailing their natural freedom which they had been enjoying for a long time. They loudly read the notice, and also my name, in a mocking tone, of course, but by the second day their sense of culture activated and they began to talk in a hushed manner. On the third day onwards I could notice a sea-change among them."

"If such a notice was fixed on similar situations in my place in Kerala, the laborers there would tear it down first and would amplify their noise! And that's their culture! But in Ethiopia, you can do miracles with youngsters. Just make them feel that you are concerned about them. I visualize the dawn of a bright day fast approaching this small and wonderful land in the north of the Dark Continent."

Mr. Spreadinglight seemed to be shocked at the enthusiasm and sincerity with which I talked. He left me silently, nodding his head to a new approach towards students, there onwards. Honestly, I had not seen students anywhere else as disciplined as Ethiopian students. Even the grown-ups were well-disciplined. Functions in the auditorium continued until late midnight without the supervision of a single teacher. Girls and boys behaved in the most disciplined manner, and such a situation could not be imagined anywhere in an Indian campus!

I went to the canteen. There were many canteens in the university campus, two of them for the students, one for the teachers and another for the employees, where one could see even the President of the university, or the Vice Chancellor as we call it in India, sitting at a lonely corner slowly sipping his hot tea to pass his idle hours. The teachers' café was usually shared by the students and we did not mind them with us as we too were like them; we didn't like to spend much money on refreshments.

We used to take only black tea, as they had no idea of milk tea, in fact, it was not tea but a kind of decoction prepared with dried leaves and cinnamon bark, and adding a lot of sugar into it. Sometimes, on tedious days, we took either bunna, the black coffee; the name etymologically came from Bunno, an area in Ethiopia notable for coffee plantations, or makiato, the milk coffee.

"You like coffee, aren't you?" I heard the voice of my colleague Ms. Jerusalem from a nearby chair. I was watching the students who in groups of three or four shared their food from the same plate, at times, putting folded pieces of injera, the flat bread made of fermented teff-powder into each other's mouths.

"Oh, sure!" I said. "We start our day in Kerala, with a glass of black coffee in one hand and a newspaper on the other! We have coffee plantations in Kerala and the coffee plants might have first come to our place from Ethiopia. An Arab, who noticed that some sheep which ate coffee leaves and seeds behaved in an excited manner, tested it and found the secret of its vitality, as the story goes in Ethiopia. He might have taken it to the outside world, and thus, we also got it, centuries ago."

"I know that Ethiopia had trade relations with India in the

past," she pointed out.

"This is what the Ethiopian history says! But with which part of India, they are not sure about it, and they think of the big subcontinent as something like Ethiopia! In fact, Ethiopia, in the ancient days, had trade connections mainly with Kerala, the southern-most State of India, as the sea winds and the water currents helped their marine vessels to reach exactly the Malabar shore of the Arabian Sea, a direct sea route from Africa. Owing to this natural convenience that Pêro da Covilhã in 1473 and Vasco da Gama in 1478 could reach this coast directly from Aden and Cape, respectively."

"Unfortunately we don't have that special coffee ceremony, as you have in Ethiopia," I commented in a low voice and then ordered for the bunna, the concentrated black coffee. I knew that the word coffee derived from Kaffa, a place in Ethiopia where the coffee plants were first found. "Even though Ethiopia produces and exports coffee, the price of coffee powder here is double compared to that in Kerala," I commented.

The honey bees flew around us and even settled on our cups. There was more sugar than needed for a beehive in my cup that I offered a spoonful of it to them. They might be satisfied with my kindness that they no longer tried to disturb me! Though the Ethiopians used much sugar in their tea and coffee, they didn't add much sugar to their food items. It seemed God deliberately benumbed certain taste-buds on their tongues. Otherwise how could they keep the per capita consumption of sugar in Ethiopia at less than three kilograms a year, the lowest rate in Africa, so that Wonji Sugar Factory near Addis Ababa could export much of their product! For Ethiopia, the bee or tazma is a special symbol of hard work and prosperity.

Girls and boys were really enjoying the lunch break, as if participating in a food festival! The rich girl-students liked their own company. They never cooperated with others even for sharing their lunch; they came to the canteen in small groups of two or three girls of the same feather!

Walking, like cranes, on their high-heeled shoes, they came to the counter and the leader, who had the purse, asked in an arrogant manner: "Dhoro wot?" Is there any chicken curry?

"Yellam." No, said the young man sitting at the counter, casually looking at her half naked breasts.

"Ebek thibs?" This time, it was a dish with small pieces of roasted boneless mutton.

"Yellam!" At this the girl showed a wry face of disgust.

"Oh...keyei!" she said in a different accent. "Misto?" This time, it was mutton curry with an egg in it!

The man at the counter smiled and nodded his head cheerfully, for he knew how to handle these fashionable girls from Addis Ababa. Some gravy with pieces of mutton picked up from the lot, spread on an injera!

The boys preferred the less priced kai wot, the mutton curry with bones, for they liked to suck the bones! They knew that asa dulets, the boneless fish curry, was only available at medium hotels like Sea Side City Hotel.

It was quite surprising that in a country where many people starved to death, how the people could waste much of their food! They used to leave a good part of their food on the plate as waste, of course, it was too difficult for one person to finish one full injera, and they did it as part of their culture! After the lunch break, I noticed some boys carrying this waste in large baskets towards a centre from where it was distributed among the poor. I remembered the Ethiopian saying: One cannot fill his belly and sleep with ease; while his brother's stomach is empty!

One day I talked to Dr. Worqu Singh about the hardworking nature of Ethiopians. The teachers were so enthusiastic in their work. They were so sincere, especially in their extra work related to Distance Education, Continuing Education, Extension Education and Kiremt or Summer Education for which they got some extra payment that their sincerity seemed to be quite exhausted when they came to attend the regular students. Except for the senior teachers, no one had the hypocrisy of the Indian teachers. Though their salary was reasonable, under the changing circumstances, the amount seemed to be too insufficient to manage their daily domestic and social life, I felt so.

"It's the fate of all salaried government employees all over the world," my friend Dr. Singh said. Every first week of the month, they're heroes; by the second week, they're zeroes, by the third week, they're beggars and by the fourth week, they're destitute!

Their condition turned worst since the banks had begun to offer them housing loans! Once the monthly installment was paid to the bank, they found it very difficult to make both ends meet; and for their unavoidable celebrations of holidays and festival days, for which Ethiopia had no scarcity, they had to borrow, making their future days gloomy and desperate. No wonder, most of them felt some grudge towards the expatriates, who received a better payment under the United Nation's scheme for developing countries. Many of the teachers misunderstood the contract of the expatriates and they thought that the expatriates' salary affected the economy of Ethiopia. Unfortunately they did not know the fact that we had been paid under the UNDP, of course, my colleagues were always ignorant about the political dealings of the government.

The teachers enjoyed all modern facilities in teaching. All of them were given computers with internet facilities, and, instead of giving simplified lecture notes which suit the standard of the students, they downloaded the American internet material and supplied them to the students, slightly editing the matter here and there. Many of them used the computer either for playing games or for watching pornographic pictures! Well, it's all common with people of the so-called third world!

Most of the teachers kept a certain distance from the students. My colleague, Mr. Spreadinglight, one day warned me in a most affectionate tone, during the first semester itself: "Be professional as a teacher when you deal with the students. Don't make too much personal contact with them. You may land in trouble. You are new to this place and you don't know Ethiopian culture. Don't show any sentiment to them. They are like wild animals, never to be tamed. They will nag you like anything and your job itself will be at stake. To study or not to study is their business."

It seemed that my Head of the Department, Mr. Zoom, was very particular that more students should be failed from my class! He insisted that I must fail at least ten percent of my students. Ten percent 'A' grade means ten percent 'F' grade, he said to me! His idea might be that I should not get any popularity among the students! While other Ethiopian teachers were taking 12 hours a week, he gave me up to 18 hours! Of course, other teachers were taking extra classes for which they got extra money. I did not complain; to whom had we to complain or was there any benefit by complaining? The bull that pulled a heavy cart, shouldn't complaint about the weight of its balls! I remembered our local saying.

Of course, after a week of submitting the grade report of the students, two of my students, one Mister Dametew and another Miss Zafu, came to me requesting to raise their grades or else they would be thrown out from the campus. Dametew fell at my feet and Zafu warned me that she would commit suicide! In fact, they scored good marks but some students should be failed to show the credibility of my valuation, according to the head of the department. I was quite helpless in helping them! According to the rules of the university, any change in grade should be reported within three days of the submission of the list, and all grade sheets should go through the head of the department!

I remembered the words of Mr. Spreadinglight. I must be

professional; I should not show any sort of sentiment towards students! In fact, I was surprised at the attitude of Mr. Spreadinglight. First I wished to ask him for what he meant by the word culture. Secondly I wished to ask him whether parents in Ethiopia were just as professional in the treatment of their own children. And thirdly I wished to ask him whether a teacher could be just professional.

I, as a teacher, always loved my students and my affection towards them was not merely professional. A student-teacher relationship can be compared to God-man relationship. Even the position of God is second only to a teacher as the latter is physically present to the student.

I remembered my Ethiopian students coming to me with confidence and saying: "Teacher!" They even used to call professors like that; and continued: "It's the first time we see a teacher who is ready to give personal advice in the class. They are the key-words of success in life rather than of formal success in the examination. Thank you for showing your personal interest in our career, unlike your Ethiopian counterparts!"

I was very happy to work in Ethiopia mainly because of the secular feeling among my students. I did not know how long it would be continued. In India, people thought more about their religion before they engaged in friendship. After coming to a foreign country, Indians used to forget their religious or regional differences. But at the heart, they were all aware of their religious, linguistic or regional differences!

I remembered, on a hot day, Worku, Ahmad and I went to the teachers' café and ordered tea. Soon, Professor Fluteplayer and Mr. Prestige Mussalman came there and sat with us. Though they were Indians, we always tried to avoid them due to their petty regionalism, narrow-mindedness and common cunningness. Unlike me, Dr. Worku was clever enough to stay away from discussing controversial issues in their presence and, if necessary, he knew how to give them tit for tat.

While taking the tea, Ahmad complained about the common toilet which was very near to his office-room. He pointed out that the Ethiopians were throwing used toilet paper here and there, and he could not even sit in his room because of the horrible stench coming from them.

"In many African countries, people do not even use toilet paper, and Ethiopians are far better than others," Professor Fluteplayer made a joke.

"Perhaps, the Italians and other Europeans had taught them to use toilet paper," Worku pointed out some historical reason.

"No! I don't think so!" I said. "According to Reidulf Molvaer, the khat eating Arab tourists who had been in the hotels of Addis Ababa, on their 'booze and sex safari', used to throw toilet paper in and around the commode instead of flushing them as Europeans did. The room-boys, therefore, kept a basket near the commode so that the tourists could put the paper in it, and the practice still goes on."

"Do you mean that the Arabs don't wash their bottoms?" Prestige Mussalman raised his voice.

I tried to cool him down and said, "My dear friend, Indians are generally very particular to use water for cleaning their bottoms, but Europeans in general and the civilized Arabs in particular, use toilet paper."

The face of Prestige darkened and he announced, "Remember, the Arabs are Muslims and they use water!"

"Of course, before they go to the mosque!" I retorted.

"Leave the topic! Let's move, I have a class," Worku intervened and the discussion came to an abrupt end.

I was quite embarrassed at the fanatic approach of some people; they closed their eyes and created darkness! There might be people in every religion who believed blindly that their religion was the greatest one in the whole world! Though Prestige Mussalman was such a fanatic, we could not blame all

Muslims. My friend Salim Mohammed was a Muslim but he was never a fanatic; he respected and loved all religions. Of course, the secular attitude of Dr. Salim attracted me and we became thick friends within a short time.

I remembered the words of Mark Twain, "Never argue with stupid people, they will drag you down to their level and then beat you with experience." I tried to calm down myself. Of course, there were many intelligent people who conveniently ignored their conscience and argued irrationally for the false practices of their religions!

Fluteplayer laughed aloud, enjoying the argument, cleverly without taking sides. Of course, we knew that he was a bat, when he was in our company, showed his wings and declared himself a bird, and in the company of Prestige, showed his teeth and declared himself an animal! Of course, this world is for such eels, I thought.

While returning to our office-rooms, I said to Worku, "Doctor, I always wonder why modern civilization fails to bring some sort of unanimity among various sects of peoples of this world! Everybody claims that he is highly civilized, and what do they mean by the word 'civilized'?"

"Well! Every civilization depends on the geography of the area concerned," spat out the geography professor in Dr. Worku Singh.

I laughed aloud and said, "Well! Let's come to this conclusion. A civilized man is a person who keeps his mucus in his pocket! A civilized Englishman is a person who cleans his shoes now and then with his handkerchief. And a civilized Indian is a person who always spits left and right and not in front of him."

"....especially, when the wind blows against his face!" Worku completed the sentence and we laughed at the joke.

On the following evening, I exited from the house for my usual evening walk, expecting Dr. Worku on the way. Dr.

Tomsin called my name aloud and I turned to see her and her husband together with another person, beckoning me to the place where they were standing. To my surprise, my friend Rajesh was with the couples. In fact, I never expected him there; he had told me that he would not come to Ethiopia!

He told me that he came to Sea Side City on the previous day and found a house with the help of Tomsin! I enquired about his wife Geetha and their daughter! He was in a jovial mood and we went to Tomsin's house for tea; and I had to cancel my evening walk for that day.

The next Saturday, I went to the market to buy some vegetables. I saw Dr. Tomsin and her husband Jose were making long bargains and buying things. In fact, it was Tomsin who bought things and Jose always stood a few meters away from her just holding the carry-bags. He seemed quite restless when his wife continued to bargain on the price of certain paltry items with the shopkeepers. He would be angry with her talkativeness and usually made certain foul comments at her, of course, in his dirty language. And she faced his substandard language with a sharp look or a blushed face.

She held a doctorate degree but her husband could not learn that much! I always felt a sort of inferiority complex reflecting on his face, and he compensated for it by using foul language while talking to his wife! However, they understood each other and adjusted their life accordingly. And they were in Ethiopia to make money for the education of their children in India!

The Jose family was the first one with which I had some close relationship in Ethiopia. They gave me much food for thought and, that night, I brooded over their conversational language. No language is perfect or complete in itself and, perhaps, the so-called obscene words in every language may be the most natural means to convey our genuine emotions, provided that the persons engaged in conversation must be generous enough to understand each other.

In certain Hindu temples in Kerala, the worshippers used obscene language to please their goddess! Of course, all impurities might be removed from the refined language, like the so-called refined oil, but it also became artificial at the same time! Look at the illiterate families swarmed in the slums, their crude and uncivilized language may hurt the ears of the educated. But those people also know the language of the heart which covers a multitude of sins! I thought.

The story of the Babel Tower in the Bible might be an apt example to prove how even the greatest ambition of man to reach heaven was left incomplete just because the builders could not understand each other's language! Married life is a humble effort on the part of the human beings to reach heaven; and the language used by the husband and wife plays a very crucial role for the successful completion of it. I mused for a while.

Every word we use has an explicit and implied meaning and we are all aware of the lexical significance of it. But how many of us can understand the language of the heart which can be expressed by absurd sounds and illogical or unsociable words? In intimate relationships like family life, the use of such a language is quite common. If the partners can understand each other, they attain heavenly bliss; if not the result is estrangement or divorce! My thoughts moved into the wilderness!

On Sunday afternoons, we friends used to sit in the house and discuss national and international affairs and, sometimes, even personal matters! On that day, we were talking about the difficulty in finding suitable spouses for our children! Of course, almost all of us were above the age of fifty and most of us had children nearing their age of marriage!

The issue was put forward by Mr. President who said that his middle-aged HOD Mr. Danny was not marrying as he could not find a virgin among Ethiopian girls! That was the first time I was hearing about an Ethiopian who bothered about such matters! Most of the Ethiopian boys and girls had pre-marital sex and the society thought of it as an inevitable experience in life! Some of them preferred to marry mothers of children!

"Here comes a Daniel!" I shouted like Shylock, and said, "No doubt, he will die a chronic bachelor!"

"Even in India, it's the same case," Dr. Worku said. "Once the horoscopes are matched, we enquire about the girl and sometimes find her pregnant or as mother of a child!"

Dr. Dinov, who wore more than three rings on his fingers, as recommended by certain astrologers, said, "I don't care for such foolish pseudo-sciences! I'm not even a conservative to insist that my children should marry from my own race, caste or religion; let them go and find their own spouses whom they like!"

"It's because you have only boy-children!" Dr. Ahmad retorted in an angry tone. "Men have the freedom, they can marry on experimental basis and if they don't fit his whims and fancy, just desert them, and search for fresh ones! Be one among us, you can marry legally up to four, and illegally more!"

"Whether the leaf falls on the thorn or the thorn falls on the leaf, the damage is only for the leaf!" With a long sigh, Dr. Worku quoted a local saying.

After a moment of silence, I said, "Well! In India, the women developed a sort of dependence culture which cannot be erased from their mind with our high-talks on feminism and women's empowerment! Otherwise they should be geniuses like Jhansi Rani, Sarojini Naidu, Kamala Surayya, Medha Patekar, Ajitha, Arundhathi Roy, Kiran Bedi, Meera Nair, Gauriamma, Phoolan Devi and so on!"

Dr. Ahmad supported me and said, "Yes, that's true! Our girls, for every silly problem in their married life, come to their parents for solutions! If their husbands desert them, they would return to their parents with full confidence that they would be received at their homes, even they resist the tortures of their husbands because they knew that their parents would support them!"

"And as Qathafi said: 'To ignore natural differences between man and woman and mix their roles is an absolutely uncivilized attitude, hostile to the laws of nature, destructive to human life, and a genuine cause for the wretchedness of human social life,'" I said, quoting from the Libyan Colonel's the Green Book.

Our Sunday evenings were not only entertaining to our hearts but also augmenting to our knowledge! On other days, we used to spend them in our own way, depending on the situation.

Worku and I enjoyed our evening walks. One day, we were on our usual evening walk. Suddenly, a cyclist stopped in front of us and asked whether we were the new-comers from India. He was a young man and we felt a bit embarrassed at the phrase 'new-comers'. He introduced himself as Sajeev, working in the Technical School in Sea Side City for the last four years. He was a man of about twenty-eight, from Madhya Pradesh in India. He used to go to the gymnasium and he was on his way back home, he said. After talking for a few minutes, he said, "Sorry, Sir! I'm a bit late today. My wife will be angry if I'm late! Sorry, gentlemen!"

Sanjeev hurriedly pedaled his bike home. When he moved away from us, we laughed at him saying, "A man from a gymnasium and is afraid of his wife!" Of course, we all laughed at others and called them 'hen-pecked' and boasted about ourselves in the absence of our wives!

I thought about the ridiculous nature of conjugal life! I had seen many skeleton-like, unhealthy persons easily control their fat, healthy wives! And the wives behaved as if they were afraid of their husbands! Here is a person with a well-built body who turns himself into a mouse before his wife! How funny this husband-wife relationship is, I thought.

I said: "Dear doctor, now I doubt the sanctity of what the philosopher Lao Tzu said. Do you know what he said, 'Being deeply loved by someone gives you strength; loving someone deeply gives you courage!' I must either find out new meanings for the words love, strength and courage or ignore their practicability in married life!"

Dr. Worku suggested that Sajeev's wife might be from a wealthy and powerful family and their marriage was conducted in a hurry-burry! They might have thought only about the smartness of the boy and not about their horoscopes!

I was a bit angry at that comment, and I said, "Dr. Worku and your bloody horoscopes! You see, if the husband and wife love each other, there's no question of your pseudo-science!"

Worku replied in a serious tone, "Don't mock at the mysterious sciences of India, Dr. George. First study them and, then, if you don't want, just ignore them. But I believe there's some truth in such sciences. I am not ready to take risk and I'll conduct my children's marriage if only their horoscopes are matching."

I kept quiet at his words but wondered whether there was anything believable in such supernatural sciences. Of course, a marriage in India is a social institution, a social necessity rather than an individual affair or mutual sexual attraction as it is in Europe. Cultured people control their sexual instincts for the benefit of the society. If human beings are rational creatures, they cannot go wayward, engaging in sex with many women, even if they are all his wives in polygamy! In the case of animals, Nature itself has regulated their sexual instincts, making it seasonal unlike human beings who are capable of sexual life throughout the year.

There are individuals who think that it would have been better if they had been born in a tribal culture as it is in Arabia,

Africa or in modern Europe, where they act freely with their sex, changing their mates or adding the number of their wives. Man is blessed with rationality with which we built up a civilization. But in the name of tradition or religious practice or culture, how can we ignore the discipline of our civilization? I thought.

I remembered a discussion on the topic with my friend, Dr. Dinov. I told him the Ethiopian way of love making, sex and marriage! Unlike in India, here the girls and boys moved freely and lived together without any fear of society! They married each other without least bothering about their pre-marital sex life! Husbands won't care whether their wives have children in their earlier love affairs!

Dr. Dinov said with a laugh, "This is called 'the rhythm of blood' as D.H. Lawrence puts it! In India we're twice removed from nature! For us sex is not a biological need; it's a social need! In India, everything in human life is a ritual! And as W.B. Yeats says, 'The index of human civilization is in its rituals!'"

He always talked like a researcher, quoting from different authors! I argued with him and said, "The strict discipline of India has created a sort of fear complex especially among our girls and they look at boys as if they are all rapists! And the boys do not know how to 'look' at the girls in a normal way, but 'stare' at them as if they are all whores! Of course, our culture has made us abnormal human beings!"

"But, remember, the rhythm of blood theory can be applied only to animals; their behavior is instinctive!" said Dr. Dinov. "Human beings are different, especially the civilized ones; our reflexes are conscious and regulated by learning. We are controlled by reason and we have social laws to punish those who behave irrationally! Of course, man is an animal but a gregarious animal!"

Perhaps, I was jealous of those who lived as tribal-people in a civilized world! It might be my sexual jealousies that force me to look down upon the system of polygamy and changing mates! See the Arabian Muslims and the Ethiopian Christians who lived according to their sexual instincts! How easily they changed their wives! Let's excuse Arabians and Africans, for they could not raise themselves to the level of what Allah or Igzabier or God expected Man to be! God created only one Eve for Adam, then, why do the Christians, Jews and Muslims think of another mate, if they are truly religious? Does it mean that their belief in God is only superficial, something like a mask? If Jesus clearly said that it was adultery to marry a divorced woman, then, why do the so-called European Christians practice divorce and remarriage?

I felt real indignation against the fake morality of religions. Worku went to his house and I reached my house only to hear my telephone ringing continuously. It was a new voice and the person at the other end said, "Hullo, Sir! I'm Blisso'life. I invite you for a lunch this Saturday at my house. Please also tell Dr. Worku Singh that I invited him too. See both of you by 11 am on Saturday."

Worqu had neither land-phone nor mobile phone and it was natural that he requested me to convey the invitation to him. Moreover every Indian in the university knew that we were thick friends. But I did not know much about this Blisso'life, except that Mr. Glory, a friend of mine, once requested me to buy from Addis Ababa certain vegetables that were not available in Sea Side City. They were for Blisso'life, he said, and the money would be paid when the things were brought. I bought vegetables worth about twelve dollars and my friend Mr. Glory took it from my room for Mr. Blisso'life.

Mr. Glory was a young teacher in computer science living with his wife and little daughter! He was in the Department of Computer Science and he was never involved in the personal affairs of others! However, every news in the university first reached Mr. Glory and I used to wonder how it happened!

At first I thought that it was only a joke of Blisso'life! I wondered why he was arranging such a party for the Indians, and one of his friends told me that it was his habit to honor the newcomers with a feast. Of course, it was magnanimous on the part of Blisso'life, I thought, as the main idea of every Indian abroad was to save as much money as possible. I had seen even certain Indians who thought twice before taking a cup of tea from the café!

On Friday, I came to know that my friend Dr. Ahmad and Dr. Salim were not invited to the party. Perhaps, Mr. Blisso'life might have missed them, I thought. So I rang him and told him their phone numbers, of course, indirectly requesting him to invite them too. I didn't insist the case of Mr. Prestige Mussalman, as he was not so intimate with me! Mr. Blisso'life invited my friends but, later, I came to know that Mr. Blisso'life had an inherent prejudice towards Muslims! He was a fanatic who foolishly believed that all religions, except the Hindu religion, should be wiped away from the face of this earth!

Later he told me that it was because of the Muslim invasion and forceful conversion that his forefathers, about five hundred years ago, had to leave Saurashtra in North India and come to South India, where the natives still considered them as outsiders. Well! I could understand his indignation; perhaps, it had sprouted from a sort of identity crisis!

By lunchtime, we were all at the house of Mr. Blisso'life. His wife, Ms. Holybook, was a kind of 'made-for-each-other' type and I found her quite happy in greeting every guest. The couples were really cooperative and, perhaps, as she was only a homemaker, it was for her entertainment that her husband invited all these guests to the house.

Mr. Blisso'life never allowed any of his guests to keep silent; instead he compelled them to talk on any subject under the sun. He loved discussions and arguments; and Ms. Holybook also participated in such heated dialogues!

Mr. Sanjeev was there and I enquired to him why he did not bring his wife. He told me that she was sick and she could not travel in auto-rickshaws. He invited a few among us for a similar lunch at his house on the very next Sunday. In fact, we were starving for such social gatherings, as we had left our families in India. We all readily accepted the invitation.

I noticed that my friend Rajesh was not among the guests. I asked Mr. Blisso'life about it and he said that he had invited him twice, as he pretended to be busy when he first invited him. Of course, recently there was an evident change in the nature of Rajesh; he became rather gloomy, lackadaisical and indifferent. I realized that he was no longer that Rajesh whom I had known for years! Might be some sort of misunderstanding between husband and wife, I thought. And it was inappropriate to become involved in such matters, then.

Mr. Blisso'life introduced Dr. Honey Rao and his wife, Victoria Rao, to me. He was pretty old and looked seventy to seventy-five with his silver hair but his wife seemed fifteen to twenty years younger than him. Seeing my embarrassing look, Rao told me that he had been working in a university in Hyderabad for about 40 years and, then after retirement joined some private institution until he got the chance to work in Ethiopia.

He said, looking at his wife from the corner of his eyes, "In fact, this is a 'vanavasa' or life in the wilderness for us, according to the Hindu practice! We have almost completed all our earthly duties and are quite free for the call of God! My elder daughter is married and she is with her husband in Hyderabad. My second daughter is studying in London and my only son is an engineer married and settled in Hyderabad itself. My wife and I wish to visit a few holy temples in India, for which we need some extra money, and that's why we came to this country."

I appreciated his enthusiasm and vitality even at this late

age, a time to take rest with his son and family, playing with his grandchildren! Later, Blisso'life told me confidentially that Dr. Rao and his wife had some misunderstanding with their daughter-in-law and, that was the reason for their so-called 'vanavasa' or 'forest-life' in Ethiopia! Even Lord Ram had to suffer fourteen years in the jungle, and it might be a part of fate!

Dr. Worku Singh further pointed out that 'vanavasa' was a stage in life! It was like a penance, a step before the blessed life, which everybody must undergo sometime in their life like Lord Ram and his wife Sita, the hero and heroine of Valmiki's epic poem, the Ramayana.

I realized that Dr. Rao was philosophic, and was not joking about his life; he was telling us about human destiny!

Even though Dr. Rao was quite jovial and always talked with a smile on his face, I noticed a shade of sadness behind that veil of pleasant appearance! It might be the Indian curiosity that compelled me to talk to him more and more so that I could extract some facts about him! He talked like a philosopher and I loved his matured way of conveying ideas.

"Dr. Jhoaj!" he said. He always pronounced my name like that! He continued, "We all brought up our children expecting a peaceful retired life, didn't we? We hope that our son and his wife will look after us, we will look after their kids, and days will pass quite smoothly until one day the old generation will give way to the new generation and vanish into brahma or eternity! Am I right?"

"Of course!" I said nodding my head. "But if our children think in a different way, what can we do? They may think that their old parents are a debt, or an additional burden on their head! That's the attitude of the modern generation!"

I remembered what my friend, Dr. Dinov, once said, "It's all immaterial to think about an old age with one's children! I would rather prefer a life in the old age home to a life as a burden to my children! Of course, my London-settled children may not get time to even make a phone call! If they could enquire about our well-being at least once a week, that itself would be more than sufficient!"

Dr. Rao said in a low voice, "In fact, my son loves the traditional way of family life but his wife is a bit possessive! Possessive means too possessive that she won't allow him even to talk to us! She thinks that he is complaining about her drawbacks to us! When their kids come to us, she forbids them or scolds them and asks them to go and study! I am worried not about us but about my son and his wife! How my grandchildren, who learned such lessons from their parents, would treat them once they got aged!" Dr. Rao laughed aloud as if he were telling a joke!

I remembered the case of my cousin Pepin and his wife Merlin who were working in the Gulf. Merlin was so possessive that she allowed him to talk to his mother, sister or relatives only in her presence! When he came on leave, he used to spend the evenings with his friends over a drink, and she made a hell on such days! She did not allow his friends to visit the house, pointing out that it was not good as she had two girl children! Of course, she pretended that she did all these things just because of her love for her husband and his family! One could only remember the Senegalese saying, "An inhospitable wife wraps her husband in a tissue of ridicule!"

Some wives are like that, I thought. They are in a way jealous of their husbands, about their social contacts and friendships! It is a kind of inferiority complex that compels them to behave like that! If the wife feels herself to be not good looking, the situation will be worse; she will never allow her husband to talk to more good looking girls, whether they are relatives, neighbors or students or even sisters or sisters-in-law! Life with such a wife is worse than the torture in hell!

Why should one blame women alone? There are many husbands who suffer from an inferiority complex, especially if their wives are beautiful. They will secretly watch the movements of their wives, and if they find them talking to some men, may be relatives or friends, the jealous husbands will create a hell of a night! Dr. Babuji, my colleague in India, locked every door and closed every window of his house before he went to college, keeping his good-looking wife alone in the house! But such cases happen only in India, a country that is trapped in hypocrisy and chained to the past, a country that hesitates to move forward fast!

I suddenly remembered the case of my colleague, one Mr. Thai whose wife was suffering from extreme nymphomania! She patiently waited for her husband Thai to go out for work and, then, beckoned to men who passed by to come to her bedroom! It took a few months for him to find out her problem and, then, he locked her in her room and went to college! But, through the open window, she continued to beckon others; however, by then, the regular pedestrians came to know about her illness and avoided that route! At last, Mr. Thai had to sell his house after his retirement and go away to a far off place, where nobody knew about his wife's mental disease, so that he could get suitable alliances for his children.

It was not the case of women alone, I thought! My colleague Mr. Eyepot was a person who suffered from a similar type of illness! His wife was very beautiful; she was a soft natured woman with wheat complexion, a color appreciated by every male in India! He had two girl children whose future depended on his reputation! But he ignored all these and went after certain black-complexioned women who sold their flesh at a cheap rate! At last, when he realized that it was a mental problem, he set out for a long journey, reached a metropolitan city, took a room in a posh hotel and committed suicide!

I was brooding over such family relationships, enjoying the sweet smell of the food items prepared in the kitchen, and Mr. Blisso'life shook me by the shoulder and said, "Come on, Sir!

Everything's ready! Come and have your lunch!" We all rushed to the table where, perhaps, a hundred varieties of food items were arranged for the buffet!

The lunch was so heavy and all of us ate heartily! It seemed as if the husband and wife were in a sort of competition in making us eat from every dish! A pure vegetarian lunch! There were north Indian and south Indian dishes; three or four types of rice preparations with different side dishes, sweet items, fruits and salads! A spoonful from each item would make our stomach burst! In fact, I was amazed at their hospitality. When we bade farewell, Ms. Holybook even requested that we take a parcel of food with us, as is the south Indian custom, which we thankfully refused.

Life was quite fascinating in Ethiopia. The climate was good; the people were very hospitable; the students were enthusiastic and the colleagues were cooperative. And I decided to move to the new house of Dr. Worku for convenience and to save some money!

By the end of my first academic year, many of my expatriate friends were terminated from service. Many Ethiopian teachers who had been undergoing higher education abroad came back successfully and the university had to terminate the service of expatriates in order to accommodate the returnees.

The first smite was on Dr. Tomsin. It was said that her Indian colleague, Mr. Handsome, played a safe game and got in the good book of the Head of the Department; he could retain his job and Dr. Tomsin turned out to be the victim. Hearing the news, Mr. Jose went back to India leaving his wife in Sea Side City as she wanted to try her chance in some other university, of course, to save her honor. I felt sorry for her since she was the person who helped me to find a house and to fetch my household things, when I was only a stranger in this country. Fortunately, she got an appointment in another university with a better salary, she claimed.

A colleague of mine, Dr. Reeba, the American lady, was also terminated from service and nobody knew the reason! One day I entered her office to bid farewell to her and she was packing her books and papers. She took out the map of the United States of America, which was affixed to the wall in front of her table. It was a unique map on which she had circled certain areas with her marker-pen and she always kept it as a treasure.

I asked her about the importance of those circled areas and she told me in a sad voice, "These are the areas where the Red Indians are concentrated. You know that they were the rulers of America but now they live at the mercy of others! The English people came and conquered our land. Millions of people were killed in the battles and we had to retire to certain pockets in the country. The invaders' aim was not merely to occupy our land but to wipe away our race and culture from the face of this earth! We became homeless in our own country; we starved to death! In the pretext of helping us, they gave us contaminated food and a lot of us met a slow death; they gave us blankets stained with the germs of various infectious diseases and many of us died of smallpox! Wherever I go, I keep this map with me; it reminds me about the sad plight of my ancestors and present condition of my blood-relatives!" There was utter helplessness in her wet eyes!

All those who were terminated from service either returned to their mother country or secured placements in some other universities in Ethiopia. Of course, some new expatriates came and joined certain departments where there was vacancy.

Dr. Worku and I rented a colleague's house near the university and decided to share it. Our new house was in between the houses of Mr. Handsome on the left and Dr. Elderking on the right, which reminded us of the position of Jesus Christ on the cross!

Dr. Worku was a Hindu and I was a Christian; he was from North India and I from South India! Our mother tongues were different! The subjects we taught in the university were different too! However, there were many things in common between us. Both of us loved research activities and continuously produced articles. Both of us loved long distance walking and seeing new places. Both of us loved and respected each other's religion, prayer and abode of God. He prayed in his room before a small idol of Lord Vighneshwara and I prayed in my room before my own painting of Jesus Christ. Both of us prepared food together and we ate whatever was prepared or available. I could never find a similar friend anywhere in this world, I always thought.

Lord Vighneshwara or Ganapathy was the god of impediments, who controlled all the expected or unexpected obstacles in the smooth running of our life. Dr. Worku prayed earnestly before the Lord as he knew that there were some impediments for the marriage of his son and daughter. As a traditional Hindu, he blindly believed in horoscopes and he found it very difficult to get matching horoscopes of a girl or a boy for his children. When the horoscopes matched, the persons might not have either education or property or smartness or family background! And years were passing one by one adding age to his children! At this situation, only Lord Vighneshwara could find a solution, and he fell flat before the Lord with total surrender.

In fact, his devotion influenced me so much that I too, after my prayer, went to his room and joined his prayer. Sometimes, while he was absent from the room, I secretly placed flowers before the Lord, for I too, like any other human being, had many impediments in life. Of course, the belief that some super-human power was there to help us in our utter helplessness would galvanize and strengthen our willpower!

Dr. Worku had given strict instruction to his wife and children that they should telephone him only once a week and also at 8 am on Sundays, unless there was an emergency. They never broke his order and that not only reduced the phone bill at home but also lessened his anxiety about them. Well, there was a clear understanding between he and his family and they knew his language! My family members in India did not care for such timings; they rang me at odd occasions and if they did not call me for two days consecutively, I felt much stress.

Mr. Handsome and Dr. Elderking soon became thick friends as they belonged to the same locality in India. A calf goes only to the cattle flock, as the saying goes! Both of them looked at others with suspicion and considered friendship as mere familiarity, something for the sake of convenience! They enjoyed criticizing other Indians and laughed at them either about their caste or about their creed!

They did not know that we were all from India, far away from dear relatives and friends and we needed help from friends some time or other, especially in emergency situations. For instance, if somebody suddenly fell ill and he or she needed timely help, the friends would be very helpful. Mr. Handsome's wife, Artqueen, was carrying and she developed an extraordinary appetite for certain strange dishes, and this change in taste was common among pregnant women. We believed that it was our moral duty to help her, and this brought us closer to their houses. We helped them in preparing certain special dishes, especially with the spices which I had brought from my home. Of course, Mr. Handsome was very particular in fulfilling all the desires of his wife and I loved their company. Even he could find a small job for Artqueen in the university so that the family could meet their extra expenses.

Gradually, Elderking became one of our best friends and we used to spend the evenings together with the accompaniment of beer or gin. Once he was drunk, he would begin to show his Dutch courage, bringing out all the nonsense of his mind! Mr. Handsome had no minor vices like smoking or drinking; but he had the spirit of an Iago in him, a sort of jealousy for nothing, 'a kind of motiveless malignity of a motive hunting villain', as I noticed later!

One evening, after two pegs of gin with a few drops of lemon juice, Elderking said, "In India, I was the King of my college; everybody respected me; everybody obeyed me! Here, I'm like a beggar; nobody cares for my qualifications; nobody cares for my professorship! I don't care for anyone; I have enough and more money at home; I have all facilities there, and why should I bother about my job here?"

The first part of his speech was understandable; I heard many people talk like that after a few pegs. It reminded me about the Rana, the title for the kings of Nepal, then living in a hundred-roomed palace in Sagar, Madhya Pradesh. He had rented a few rooms of his palace for us, the university students in order to meet his expense on drinks. His only daughter was in England and she used to send him some money and it was insufficient for an ex-king. During Saturday evenings, he used to drink too much and invited us for a mock Durbar. Then he would act as the king and we as his subjects, and this drama was really entertaining. With all the pomp and show of a king, he would say, "I was one of the kings of Nepal! When democracy came, they took away my kingdom promising me a huge amount as Privy Purse! But now they stopped paying it and I have to rent my palace-rooms just for my daily bread!"

Of course, what he said was true and I saw tears in his eyes. He would continue, "Therefore, you are my subjects and it's your duty to protect your Rana!" He looked at our faces in a helpless manner! Then one of us would say, "We are your subjects and you are our Rana! We will fight for you till our last breath! *Bolo Rana of Nepal ki jai!*" We all shouted, "Victory to the King of Nepal!" The Rana would laugh aloud in the typical royal manner and, as he began to snore, we would leave the room silently.

The last part of Elderking's speech was obscure for his

friends but I knew the hint. I had been appointed in the School of Graduate Studies as a Principal Advisor to the Dean and I saw a letter sent to our office by his Head of the Department in which he pointed out that Professor Elderking was not teaching the subject in which he had taken his degrees. In Sea Side City University, it was a serious drawback, a relevant reason for termination! Of course, it was not his mistake as the University appointed him after scrutinizing his qualifications! I kept quiet and did not like to make any comment on it.

Another evening, he told me, "Do you know why I have come here? I have to make money for the marriage of my secret daughter. She is studying in the secondary school. Her mother calls me regularly." He continued his story as if he were in a dream.

I was shocked at this news. I knew that in his part of the country, there was the system of the 'little house' or sub-family. Some people, along with their first or legal family, kept a secret family. But it was a tribal culture of the past and educated people avoided such extra marital affairs. But, after all people, Professor Elderking! I never expected that he had such a life. He told me that his second lady was a Christian and she remained unmarried, waiting for the day of his returning to her. In fact, I could not believe his story; I knew some people who cooked up such stories as a pastime, especially after a peg or two. He might have emphasized the word 'Christian' either to impress me or to degrade me, I thought.

Moreover, I noticed that Elderking had the habit of telling such bombastic stories of sex-adventure such as he had slept with the girl whom we met on the road or with a lady who swept the floor of his building.

There was a fifty-year-old poor woman, who served as a guard of our nearby house and, one day, seeing her he declared, "See, yesterday she came to my bedroom; I didn't like that hag but she insisted and I was helpless!"

After a week, the sixteen-year-old daughter of that woman happened to come there and he declared, "Last night, she was with me in the bedroom. She is really wonderful and she taught me many new techniques!" He used to tell me that he had slept with almost all his research students and many of them, even the married ones were still inviting him!

I was smiling at my heart, even Seetha, the heroine of the Ramayana, noticed the handsomeness of Ravana, the giant! Even God could not predict what would be in the heart of a woman! He continued to describe his amorous activities, and I considered them only as the reaction of a sexually failed person who suffered from some sort of inferiority complex!

How could his wife tolerate a husband who had illicit relationships with other women! It was said that the Hamar girls of Ethiopia loved men who had sex with many women; I read it in a book written by Desta. But I was not sure about the Indian wives!

One day, Dr. Worku and I went to see Mr. Rajesh. He was deliberately avoiding all kinds of companies! Much change had come over him after coming to this country and we wished to enquire about his problems. But he always kept quiet and, if he talked, the words were very limited. He went to the university, took his classes punctually and returned home as early as possible. It seemed that he was avoiding even me, his onetime intimate friend!

One day during our evening walk, we saw Dr. Honey Rao and Victoria Rao; they were also on their walking exercise! We greeted them and said in a joking manner, "My dear oldies! In this age, both of you must be with your grandchildren!"

"Oh, it's our fate!" Dr. Rao heaved a hot sigh. He continued, "Or perhaps, it's my mistake! I tried to preach some philosophy to my daughter-in-law and that caused all these problems!"

"Of course, it was! Because you forgot the saying: Don't chant the scripture to the fighting bull!" Mrs. Rao said, without looking at the face of her husband. I saw Rao's face turn red!

I tried to soften the situation and said in a pleading tone, "Well! Please tell us, Sir, that philosophy so that we can avoid similar problems!"

Dr. Rao said, "Well! One day we were all taking our dinner and my daughter-in-law came with a plate of food and, then, switched on the television. I told her first to enjoy our food and then the television serial because both of them were for the same purpose of entertainment, pleasure and satisfaction! Of course, it was only a simple statement but she, who might have had an exchange of hot words with her husband earlier, mistook my comment! She shouted that she had been working in the kitchen to feed all of us and when she wished to see something on the television, we were objecting to it! I tried to explain my stand and told her that every work whether it was cooking or gardening or teaching or typing, one should think of it as a means of entertainment and then it would give the person concerned perfect satisfaction; of course, many people worked only for the pleasure of getting their salary! She replied that she had been working in the kitchen, cooking and washing the plates, washing the clothes, cleaning the house and did all sorts of odd domestic jobs without any payment and everybody in the house had been down on her! She continued that we were insulting her because she had no salaried job and was living on the pension of others! As days passed, the atmosphere at home was so tense that it was necessary that either she or we should leave the house; and we decided to leave!"

Dr. Worku Singh who always took matured decisions said with a smile, "Such a simple matter and you couldn't ignore it still! We are too old to quarrel like kids! Why can't you develop the spirit of reconciliation at this age?"

Mrs. Rao nodded her head and said, "Of course, our daughter-in-law telephoned us and begged pardon and, once the contract with the university ends, we'll go back!"

The old couple went to their house and we walked in the direction of our house. We were very happy at their decision; at least one problem of one family was solved! We thought.

Many a time, we invited Rajesh to our house but he never came! One day quite unexpectedly he came to our house and it was a very auspicious day. We had another visitor, a priest from the Indian Orthodox Church, Very Reverend Father Thomas Ramban, who was teaching in a seminary in Ethiopia. His craze was travelling and on his visit to Sea Side City, some Indians told him about me, he said, and thus, he happened to be our guest.

Ramban is an ecclesiastical position in Orthodox churches, just below the position of a bishop, and they followed strict celibacy. I knew that they never ate meat but only fish, and we all went to River Abay which is the source of the Blue Nile that made Egypt a fertile land! Of course, Egyptians never taught their students that it was Lake Thana in Ethiopia that was the source of the Blue Nile; instead they taught them that the small river named White Nile that flowed from the eastern mountains of Sudan and joined the Blue Nile at Khartoum was the source of their river! The reason is quite simple; while Sudan is an Islamic country, Ethiopia is Christian! See, how far the fanatic spirit of religions can go!

Rajesh was all in praise for the priest! He told me that it was wonderful to have a life without family, leading an ascetic life, thinking the whole world as one's ancestral home, without any worries about wife and children, and without any botheration of one's own life even! We noticed a few boys angling fish and I bought a few very good fish! Rajesh told me in a hushing voice, "Wait! Let's see whether the Priest would pay the money! He has no family and unlike us he has no extra expense; what is he doing with all the money he gets every month?"

I ignored him and paid the money, keeping the propriety of a host, and I knew that celibates were more miserly than married people! We all went back to our house to prepare the fish before it was too late for dinner. I changed my dress and began to clean the fish. Soon Reverend Father Thomas Ramban also offered his help in cleaning the fish; he came wearing my lungi tucked up like an expert cook!

We fried the fish one by one and it was a delicious dinner! Of course, eating such hook-boned fish was a Himalayan task for north Indians like Worku Singh and Ahmad Ansari but Rambachan, Rajesh and I finished our fish quickly, as we were Keralites with experience in eating such fish!

Dr. Ahmad used to laugh at the fish eating habit of Keralites, and he commented, "You people have pouches in your cheeks, like that of monkeys, where you keep all the fish bones stocked while eating!"

Once Father Thomas bade farewell to us, Rajesh told me, "I always thought that human life would be meaningless without a family! But after meeting the Ramban, I feel that individual life has a special significance in this world and, the only question is whether one is happy or not while we are on this side of the grave!"

Dr. Ahmad Ansari used to come to our house at least twice a week and, on such days, I fried fish as a special dish. Once a month, he invited us to his house too and he gave us very tasty biriani and chicken curry. Of course, he was an expert in preparing non-vegetarian dishes. Sometimes, Dr. Salim also joined us and we enjoyed such evenings.

How long could we be together? How long could we enjoy this life? Who knew what would happen to us or to the members of our families in India? Anytime, anything might happen and that would, perhaps, turn all our calculations upside down!

One day, on our way to the market we saw Dr. Honey Rao, of course, it was Dr. Worku's idea to walk all the way to the market. Sometimes, many things in our life would happen without our intention, and we called it coincidence or 'nimitham' in Malayalam, which might lead us to greater events!

Seeing a small crowd, we rushed to the spot and found Dr. Rao lying on the ground, sweating all over! Vegetables from his bag lay scattered around him! The Ethiopian crowd gave way for us, realizing that we were Indians, and somebody offered a bottle of water which I sprinkled on his face and he opened his eyes! His eyes rolled as if looking for somebody and his lips whispered in Telungu language, "My wife! My wife!"

We consoled him and, later, carried him to a Bajaj Auto. I gathered the vegetables and put them in the bag. Our plan was to take him to a hospital but he refused and asked us to take him to his house immediately. He might have something to tell his wife, as a last wish, and how could we deny it, lest our conscience would not forgive us if something unexpected happened to him! Gradually, he recovered and became normal. He got out of the auto-rickshaw as if nothing had happened to him. He opened the door as usual and called aloud to his wife to prepare some cool drinks!

He told us not to say anything about what happened to him and we kept mum! After taking the cool drinks, we continued our walk to the market! We saw Dr. Muse and enquired about the present condition of his child. He was a newly joined professor and he came to Ethiopia only to make some money for the treatment of his only child. His ten-year-old boy was suffering from some peculiar kind of intestinal problem which was not diagnosed by the doctors! He left his wife with the child and the treatment was going on in Vellore. He always seemed absent-minded, perhaps, due to personal worries!

One day, Dr. President requested that I go with him to a Baptist Congregation and I went with him to see what they were doing! There I met the pastors Pr. Dallas and Pr. Jona, the former preached and sang, and the latter sang and played on his guitar! But both these Europeans were unanimous in one thing; both of them married young Ethiopian girls!

My friend Dr. Muse told me in a hushed voice: "There are people who legalize their sins! Muslims marry many women and do not consider polygamy as sexual immorality as it is legalized through Shariat Law! The Europeans who work in underdeveloped countries used to marry the natives and cleverly escaped from the sin of sexual immorality!"

I said: "My opinion is that Christians should not betray their conscience by marrying the native girls of the country where they work as missionaries, despite their availability! Of course, Dallas and Jona, as Europeans, might be following the Christian principle, unlike the Muslims, 'one wife at a time'! Or they might have found that marrying those girls was cheaper than appointing them as maidservants! Moreover, it was a kind of adoption, and if you adopted an Ethiopian, certain charitable organizations would provide your monthly expense!"

Pastor Dallas talked on that Sunday on the topic 'God is Love' and he tried to justify his marriage with an Ethiopian girl, quoting a myriad of verses from the New Testament! Of course, I loved his way of presentation and I went to his congregation on the next Sunday too! Then he talked about Anti-Christ and declared that every Christian denomination, perhaps other than the Baptists, and every other religion in this world, were followers of the so-called Anti-Christ! I felt as if he were talking on the subject, 'God is Hatred!' Of course, later in a confession he said that he was once a drunkard and drug addict and was relieved by Jesus, but I ignored his confession as I knew that he was still an addict, an addict to his own way of understanding Jesus Christ!

We continued our private conversation and Mr. President said with a smile: "But, if he were a true Christian, why did he not follow the advice of St. Paul who said to Corinthians, 'It is good for a man not to marry!' But here we must understand their problem! Well, as Paul said, '...since there is so much immorality, each man should have his wife!'"

I mused: "Perhaps, those pastors were too clever to legalize their sexual immorality!" Well, I stopped going to his congregation though he invited me many times for a lunch with him! He knew that salvation could be brought only through soup!

Of course, there are a few priests, pastors and leaders, irrespective of religions and their denominations, who are genuine, God-fearing and fully devoted to God and man. But there are some who think that the way to heaven is through their mouths and some others who think that it is through their genital organs! Both ways are true to a certain extent for laymen but not for those who directly or indirectly earn their daily bread in the name of God!

The question was whether one could marry any woman from any country or any other race just because you did not want to become immoral? And, of course, when later you could easily leave her, if she had no objection, and the Ethiopian girls were so magnanimous that one could leave them at any time! Was this the Christian principle that Christ preached? Funny! If God created Man in different colors or races, there should be a reason for it, and man should not try to change it through intermarriages lest they should face the punishment of impotency and barrenness among their progeny!!

My thoughts went on in this line: The European way of understanding Christ made them believe that it was okay if one should have only a sexual relationship with one's own wife, and it forced them to marry girls for a day, or a few more days, and then divorce them mercilessly! Well, Pastor Dallas! I could not predict the secret intentions of your heart, only God knew the thoughts of your heart or the culmination of your fate! Pr. Dallas, I loved your prayers, but your preaching and your interpretation of the Scripture were not only horrible but also simply foolish, especially for an Indian who chewed and digested even the great Hindu religious philosophy!

Dear Dallas! Dear Jona! Do remember the verse: The body is not meant for sexual immorality but for the Lord, and the Lord for the body! Of course, you could justify yourself because St. Paul also asked: Do you not know that he who unites himself with a prostitute is one with her in body? For it is said, 'The two will become one flesh!' If it was so, you should have been saving the soul of an Ethiopian girl, and I had no objection for that! The possibility of the contamination of your holy body by uniting with a prostitute's body is equal to the possibility of the deification of her body by uniting with a pastor's body! Or even there is the possibility that both bodies would be neutralized in sin as the two became one flesh!

Divorce and remarriage had become very common in Europe, especially in America. Many of them changed their spouses as they changed their dress. Most of the men and women had premarital or extramarital sexual relationships! Listen! What the scripture says: Flee from sexual immorality!

A simple signature on the Wedding Register would never cleanse your sins! Remember the words of St. Paul: All other sins a man commits are outside his body, but he who sins sexually sins against his own body. Therefore such sins were unpardonable as they were against both our body and soul! Could we not honor God with our body?

CHAPTER FOUR

I could not forget that Sunday; it was the thirteenth of May, 2007. As usual on Sundays, I woke up thirty minutes after my time-piece had sounded the alarm of the weekdays. On weekdays, I had to wake up at six in the morning and, then only, I could be ready after the morning routine to walk a furlong and catch the university bus. But Sundays were more than holy days for me because the Holy Mass was in the Amharic language; they were holy days on which I met my friends who lived far away from my residence, and also I could buy fresh fish from the nearby market.

On that Sunday, I took my breakfast of 'bread and banana' and dressed hurriedly, as the priest of the Catholic Church, Father Flower, had informed me that there would be an English Mass which I should not miss. I attended the Mass and, then, joined the priest for a second heavy breakfast. Of course, Father Flower was a priest who believed in developing relationships between man and man rather than man and God! He was a priest who realized the importance of 'Soap, Soup and Salvation' among his congregation. Later when he was transferred from our church to Rome with an ecclesiastical promotion, I stopped going to the church!

After saying 'goodbye' to Father Flower, I went to the nearby market and bought a bunch of fish, reached home and began to cook my lunch. I cleaned the fish, cut it into small pieces, put the masala and placed it on the stove. I also took some rice, washed it, poured sufficient water and placed the utensil on the second burner. As the cooking process began, I went to my dressing room and prepared the table for pressing my clothes. When lunch was ready, I kept it on the stove by itself, as I was not hungry after the two breakfasts. My partner, Dr. Worku had gone to Addis for the renewal of his Resident Permit and was expected to arrive home that evening.

After completing the ironing of my clothes, I took my lunch and decided to take my favorite noontime siesta. Suddenly, I heard continuous knocks at my gate. I thought that they would be made by the urchins from the neighboring houses who always disturbed me at odd times! As the knocking continued vigorously, with a curse I went to open the gate. To my surprise, it was Salim Mohammed, and he seemed worried to the core! Never had I seen Salim in such a disturbed manner. He closed the gate himself and rushed to my house and I followed him quite confused by his abnormal behavior.

Suddenly Salim turned and embraced me; then he burst out crying. I stood there in utter bewilderment, mumbling useless words of consolation. I thought that somebody at his home might have passed away; I knew that his aged mother had survived a brain-stroke. I brought a glass of water and he drank it in a single gulp. Gradually, he cooled down and told me what really had happened.

His eldest daughter was studying in an engineering college in another State in India. As he belonged to a traditional Muslim family, his relatives opposed the idea of sending a girl to a college far away from the house. But, unlike other Muslims, he took the firm decision to educate his daughter. She had completed her course and written all the examinations. They were all waiting for her return but, just at that time, a phone call came to his wife informing them that she had eloped with a boy who had been studying in the same college. The informer also told her that the boy was not only a non-Muslim but also a person who belonged to another language group. Hearing the news his wife fainted and fell, and it was his elder brother who informed him about the matter. His relatives complained to the police and went to the place in search of the girl.

"I'm waiting for a call," Salim said. "If they find the girl, they'll call me; if it is bad news, I won't live a minute more! You know, what happens to such foolish girls! Every day, newspapers come with horrible, heartbreaking news! How girls are raped and thrown on the railway tracks! How many girls are sold to the agents of the red-streets in Chennai or Mumbai! Ah! My child! How foolish she was!" He again burst into tears.

I patted him on his shoulder and said, "Look, Salim! Nothing will happen to her! She will be safe. It's not so easy for him to run away with a girl like that! The police will find them. Everything will be alright. What you need now is the courage to face the situation."

"How could she do such a thing to me?" Salim was sobbing. "How could she run away with a boy whom nobody knew? My dreams are shattered; the honor of my family is thrown to the pigs! What is the future of my other children? That silly girl didn't think about me or my 'khandhan'! I'll kill that 'kafir'; that pig who trapped my child! I'll cut his neck like I cut the neck of a goat!"

I kept silent for a while. Let him speak or cry and relieve his sorrow! It was the fate of all fathers! You always thought that your daughter was only a child and did not notice her physical growth! One day she suddenly came to you and rubbed her breasts against your body as if she were trying to remind you that she had grown up! It was just like the action of your pet cat rubbing her tail against your leg simply to remind you that she wanted her share of food! You were shocked to the core when she said looking straight at your face that she was in love with someone! And like George Banks, the protagonist in the movie *Father of the Bride*, you felt as if you were an old shoe!

Salim looked again and again at his mobile phone. He was so impatient that one time he tried to throw the apparatus against the wall! I shouted at him and asked him to be a normal person. I knew that such a situation would naturally make any Indian abnormal.

Salim said, as if he had taken some strong decision, "I'm leaving this job; I'm leaving this country! Why should I work here? I came to Ethiopia to make some more money for her marriage. Now, for whom should I make money? Lost, everything's lost, lost forever!"

I said in a quiet voice, "Listen, Salim! You can't leave this country so soon! Now, it's examination time and you are supposed to complete them and submit the grade reports of your students. You can't play with the future of your students! For every problem, there's a solution! Today's children don't know anything about the culture of our country or about the honor of our family! It's all mere calf love; it won't last!"

The mobile phone rang and Salim went out of the room with it to get a clearer signal. I followed him and noticed his facial expressions. A sigh of relief came from Salim; he seemed a bit relaxed. While listening to the phone, he turned to me and nodded his head as if he heard good tidings. I went to the kitchen and prepared some ginger tea. I poured it into three glasses, two for us and one for Dr. Worku who would soon arrive from the airport.

Salim came into the room, took the tea and sat on the sofa, inhaling a deep breath. An ordeal was over, I thought. He told me that his relatives could find the girl at the central police station, a few miles away from the Engineering College where she was studying, as they had informed every police station in the city. They brought the girl back home, requesting the inspector not to file a case as it would tarnish the name of the girl further, and to release the boy with a warning. Salim's brothers promised him that they would look after the girl until he returned from Ethiopia.

A heavy storm was over! I heard a knock at the gate and

opened it. Dr. Worku came in at the right time; he could drink the hot tea. Salim winked at me and we kept the matter as a secret between us. I changed the subject deliberately and said, "Welcome, doctor! We were waiting for your opinion on the marriages in Ethiopia. You know, here marriage is not necessary; man and woman can live together and have children without any legal or religious sanction! How strange it is!"

"Well! It's strange to you because you are born and brought up in a different culture," Dr. Worku began his harangue. He continued, "Marriage has developed into a strong social institution in India. Of course, it took centuries to constitute such a highly effective social system. Unlike in America, we give more importance for social freedom than for individual freedom, in this matter. When a matured man and woman decide to stay together, a family begins there and it becomes the smallest unit of the society. Whether they beget children or not is insignificant and Indians usually do not leave or divorce their spouses on the issue of infertility. Take the case of our friend, Blisso'life and his wife, Ms. Holybook, for instance. They have no issues but they live as happily as anybody else. They care for each other, they love each other, they bear each other and they lead quite a satisfied life.

I interrupted and sang the Malayalam saying in a solemn tune:

Grief to those who have no children,

More grief to those who have children!!

Dr. Salim looked meaningfully into my eyes; I averted his look and continued, "In Ethiopia, men leave their wives just for the reason of infertility! Who knows by whose fault it is so? Everybody blames the woman and not the man! Fortunately, Ethiopian women are clever enough to get children somehow before they are divorced! Of course, the husbands think only about the number of children in his house and not about their fatherhood!"

"Polygamy is common here," Dr. Worku said. He continued, "It seems both Christians and Muslims have a competition here in marrying as many girls as possible. Unlike in other countries, in Ethiopia, Muslims can marry up to five and Christians up to seven! In India, polygamy is allowed only for Muslims. Of course, Ethiopian society is changing so fast that their strong binding to tradition is loosening day by day!"

Salim, who was silent all the time, came forward at this point. He said, "Of course, according to our Shari-at law, under certain conditions we are allowed to marry up to four girls. Only those, who are rich enough to protect their wives equally, are allowed to do so. But, now-a-days, it is very rare in India; occasionally it is practiced by illiterate and uncivilized people. For instance in Kerala State, Muslim women are so conscious that they would not allow their husbands to marry one more woman!"

I agreed with him and said, "That's true! In Kerala, Muslim women are so educated that they won't allow their husbands to bring a second wife. If they do, I think, the Muslim women of Kerala are courageous enough to cut their throats! They prefer the civil laws of the country and don't care for the primitive laws of a religion. And that's why in many places, Muslim women are not given higher education by the male-dominating community."

"But I wonder why in Ethiopia, where the Orthodox Christian Church is the official religion, divorces are quite common!" Salim brought back the subject to Ethiopia.

Dr. Worqu came to my help and said, "Most of the marriages in Ethiopia are conducted without the permission of the church so that the church cannot get involved in the divorces of such couples! In the Orthodox churches, you can see two types of marriages, one of fresh man and woman and the other of experienced man and woman, the parents of two or three children!"

"But in our church, the priests won't allow the marriage of a pregnant woman, as there is a possibility of marrying two women at the same time if the child is a female!" I pointed out and everybody laughed at the idea.

We talked for about an hour. Salim seemed a little restless and I guessed his feelings. We stopped our discussion and we all went out for the evening walk. On the way, Salim got a taxi and he went to his house.

The next day, we, the teachers in the department had a hot discussion over the significance of sex in human life. In Ethiopia marriage was not fully recognized as an inevitable social institution and it was not illegal or irreligious if men and women lived together and produced children. I wondered why even the Orthodox Christian Church allowed such anti-social activities. When I asked my friend Mintesenot about it he said, "If you marry a girl at the church, it is very difficult to get a divorce!"

I laughed aloud thinking about these people who anticipate a divorce even before they fix their marriage! I pointed out that marriage is a highly developed social institution in a civilized society and if man and woman live together without the approval of the society, it is not only illegal but also immoral.

My Ethiopian friend, Mr. Clearsight, argued that there was nothing wrong in such a life as sex was a biological need and the whole responsibility was for the individuals concerned. He said that even in highly civilized societies like those in the United States, men and women used to live like that and nobody was bothered!

The sanctity of marriage might not be of that much importance, I thought. In India, there is not much individual freedom and that's why the society insists a sort of license for men and women to stay together. As Indians enjoy excessive political freedom, they forget the necessity of individual freedom in the intoxication of power and property. Only the richest, the poorest and the anti-social elements enjoy real individual freedom in India! Religious sanctity would be vaporized in the heat of money, or practical life! Recently, the Supreme Court of India has legalized the system of 'living together', perhaps due to the unnecessary involvement and harassment of the police!

"Of course, there was a time when people believed certain sexologists who argued that there was nothing wrong in 'living together'," I said. "At the same time we should not forget that there were lechers and whores in every society from ancient days onwards. The problem in America is that when they give more importance to the individual, they are compelled to ignore the society! No doubt, individuals form society, but for the proper growth of the individual, a proper society is needed."

I continued to point out that sex was a biological need for animals and birds and not for human beings. "For birds and animals, sex is for procreation while for human beings, it is a means for pleasure; and procreation, in most cases, is only an accident. Moreover, we live in an age of semen banks and test-tube babies, in which sex is not at all necessary for procreation!"

"You think only about the legal side of man-woman relationship," Mr. Wellspoke intervened. "Don't you care for love between a man and a woman?" he asked.

"Love is an abstract idea like truth and beauty," I replied. "Of course, true love is ideal and is inevitable in a happy married life. But under normal circumstances, the so-called love depends on the person concerned, and it is relative. The root of a society is in its smallest unit of a family, and when a man and woman live together, a new family is formed. Both individuals must get mutual protection and feel equal responsibility. By nature, man and woman are not physically or emotionally equal, especially because the burden of pregnancy is only with the woman. Therefore, their rights and obligations must be cemented with a legal sanction by some social authority."

Mr. Clearsight continued to argue that sex was a basic need and other responsibilities came only afterwards. "It is the responsibility of the individuals concerned to be cautious about further consequences like the birth of a child or the transmission of venereal diseases. And, of course, it is quite easy as we live in a world where preventive measures can be taken against them. In many countries even abortion is legal."

But I opposed his argument and said, "Man is a rational creature. Don't forget that human beings can also lead a celibate life, completely abstaining from sex. And if you are mentally perverted, you can also lead a private life of a gay or a lesbian provided that you must get a legal sanction for it. Prostitution, like marriage, is another social institution established from the ancient days onwards to satisfy individuals who do not like to marry for personal reasons. Moreover, the human body is formed in such a way that it is easy for an individual to get sexual satisfaction even without the help of a partner. In fact, it is a social crime to degrade the smallest social unit of a man and a woman to that level of mere prostitution, that is, a sex life without legal sanction! However, if an individual feels sexual desire for another individual, two individuals with equal rights are involved, thereby the smallest unit of the society is involved and, therefore, they cannot ignore the sanctity of a legal and social sanction."

I knew that my argument had no relevance in a country like Ethiopia where prostitution was a legalized profession! It was time for the lunch break and no Ethiopian can withstand the temptation, or continue to sit for a second more in his or her seat after 12 noon! "It's not only illegal but also immoral," said Mr. Wellspoke. We all laughed aloud and dispersed for lunch.

Mr. Spread-n-growth was my colleague with whom I had to do peer-teaching. He taught in his own way and I could not complain as he was the most senior among the staff. He was a 'chronicle bachelor' but always enjoyed the company of young girls. It was said that once he loved a student but she complained to the university about his sexual harassment that he was dismissed from service for a year. Fortunately, he got a scholarship from England and he went there to take his masters degree.

He rejoined the university and continued his amorous games very confidentially. Recently a few more complaints about him reached the department; this time not only from girls but also from boys! His taste might have changed; and the warning letter given by the university would, perhaps, help him to pursue his doctorate studies!

I wondered how people like Mr. Spread-n-growth became psychiatric cases! In communities in which circumcision was compulsory, sodomy might be quite common. I remembered the argument of a sexologist: If circumcised, the male will lose sensitivity at the tip of his genital organ and, so, such people seek unnatural methods to get sexual satisfaction. However, sodomy was not common in Ethiopia even though both the Christians and Muslims underwent the initiation ceremony of circumcision. The Orthodox Christians could still be frightened with the fire in Hell and with the stories of what happened in Sodom and Gomorrah!

In the United States of America, every child born is circumcised even without the permission of the parents! Islamic society there became successful in spreading the notion that circumcision would save men from cancer on the penis or in the uterus! A circumcised doctor will circumcise others as if he were taking revenge! These doctors do not know what an immoral thing they were doing or what a cold-blooded crime they were committing through compulsory circumcision, with which they were making men indifferent to a natural sex-life, making men fascinated with unnatural sexual pleasures! They were denying the heavenly bliss of conjugal life to an innocent generation crying helplessly on the tables of the labor wards in American hospitals! The so-called elite Americans who made much ado about cruelty shown against animals conveniently ignored this cruelty against human infants! What a contradiction!

The Christians in Ethiopia follow Jewish tradition rather than the Pauline way. In the apocryphal Gospel of St. Thomas (Logion 53), it is quoted as Jesus said, when his disciples asked him about circumcision: If it was really important, your heavenly Father would have seen to it that you came into the world already circumcised from your mother's womb.

When I told the story of Mr. Spread-n-growth to Dr. Elderking, he quoted a Tamil saying:

Mudinthavarku sadhikirarkal;

Mudiyathavarku bodhikirarkal!

Those who can do, do it; those who cannot, advise! Well! Why should I worry much about the morality of these people? The world would go on like this forever! I thought. And for Elderking, Ethiopia would be the right place to continue as far as he could drink draft beer, with two Ethiopian girls sitting either on each thigh or one on his lap, rubbing her breasts against his face and the other on his shoulder so that he could kiss the folds of her waist!

One day, I got a message in my mobile; it was 'Happy Easter' from the new teacher Mr. Ramesh! Of course, it was his habit to send such messages to everybody on every holiday, irrespective of its significance! We could understand when he sent messages like 'Happy Xmas!' or 'Happy Easter', but could not but laugh when he sent messages like 'Happy Republic Day', 'Happy Good Friday' or 'Happy Second Saturday'!

And in Ethiopia, Christmas and Easter came a week after the internationally accepted dates! Or, once you were away from your family, who bothered about such festivals? What festival for a wild fowl!

However, I thanked Mr. Ramesh and wished him the same! Of course, his message reminded me to send similar messages to all my colleagues. Mr. Joken's reply was strange; he sent the message: "Sorry! I don't believe in such formalities!"

Next day, when I met him, he opened the subject and said in a serious tone, "Doctor George! Don't misunderstand me! I don't believe in religions; I don't believe in God! Of course, you lived more than twice my life, but my limited experience taught me more bitter lessons than what you experienced! You can't understand what experiences I had undergone as a Sri Lankan during those days of the Tamil Revolution! If there was a God, he would not be so cruel towards us!"

"But my friend! We used to turn towards God, when we face problems and tragedies in our life! Whether God exists or not is immaterial; what we need is peace and confidence! Of course, our belief in God gives us greater willpower to face our predicaments!" I tried to console his bitter feelings!

He raised his voice and said in an angry tone, "Sorry, sir! I can't agree with your preaching! You can't understand the severity of what we suffered in Sri Lanka! We were helpless before the brutality of the soldiers! We had to see with our own eyes when our mothers, sisters and daughters were raped by the soldiers! We had to witness when our parents and siblings were tortured and killed right in front of our eyes! There was no God to save us; if there was a God, he was sleeping conveniently to help the brutes!"

His fervent words continued, "And for the last and final fight, about 700 Tamil Tigers had been gathered in the forest under their leader Velupillai Prabhakar, but the American and Indian satellites noticed them and informed the matter to the enemies and they dropped their fire bombs on them! Within seconds, all seven hundred warriors turned into charcoal and smoke! And with them our hopes, our confidence in ourselves and our belief in God, everything disappeared like a fume!"

I stood in silence at his recrimination; I tried to find proper words to anoint his wounded heart! I realized that there was a sort of limbo in between us! I saw his eyes wet and his cheeks stained with tears! His voice came out through the sore-throat, "Doctor! Do you remember the lines of Dante in the Divine Comedy?

'Through a round aperture I saw appear
Some of the beautiful things that heaven bears!'

Nobody can understand the real meaning of these lines except a Sri Lankan! In fact, we lived through Hell everyday with only glimpses of heaven in between! And I believe what Dante's master Brunetto Lattini said in Inferno XV: 'Man makes himself immortal!'"

I tried to understand his sentiments! He spent most of his money on courting Ethiopian girls and he had a lot of girlfriends among whom he found those 'glimpses of heaven', perhaps! Of course, one could take risk with religious morality related to sin and hell, but could one ignore those facts which were stranger than fiction? I wondered.

Our evenings were fully occupied by discussions on various topics. Blisso'life used to visit us at least twice in a week and he made the evenings lively. He talked and argued on various topics like religion, culture, literature, language and politics. Such intellectual discussions enhanced our knowledge and we loved it. We were free to talk on any subject and exchange our opinions.

At first I thought that he was an open-minded man. But later, I came to know that he was a staunch Hindu fanatic who, at heart, hated all other religions, especially Islam because of its extremist nature and fundamentalism. This made me sad because I never thought that an educated man could become fanatic in religious matters! He always lived in the past. He boasted about India's four or five thousand-year-old culture and he attributed it only to Hindus.

In fact, all Indians were proud of it, irrespective of their religions! But Blisso'life never accepted it. The funniest thing was that he wished to go back to that so-called Indian culture of the Mahabharata times! He conveniently forgot the tremendous changes that happened to Hindu religion in the passage of time due to its contact with other religions! He deliberately ignored the natural amalgamation of various cultures into Indian culture which made it unique. Today's Hinduism was almost monotheistic, and if it was pantheistic, almost all religions of the world which allowed their believers to go for pilgrimages and visit shrines of saints were pantheistic at least in practice!

I tried to understand his arguments as I had developed an open mind in religious matters. One day I gave him a book on Christ, a sort of research work to prove that Christ did not die on the cross, but on the very next day; he returned it, saying, "I don't care whether Christ was crucified or not! I am not interested in any other religion other than Hindu religion; I am not interested in any literature other than Hindu literature; I am not interested in any other cultures other than Hindu culture!"

I was shocked at his reaction! Was he really a frog in the well? But he was a vociferous reader and I could not believe that he could believe in mere parochialism! Though I was born in a Christian family, I could not believe blindly many of the basic creeds and dogmas of the Christian religion. I knew the members of all these religions, whether Hindu, Christian, Islam or Sikh, followed more or less similar types of practices, if not with slight differences.

Well! Education alone could not make a man wise! As the sages say:

Chaturvedika tharo vipra,
Sarvashastra nipuno Indra,
Gyana agyananth karthavya;
Garvi papa rasarasa, garbhi paka rasarasa!

Even if you are a brahmin who learned all the four vedas, or

Lord Indra who learned all the six sciences (shastras), and if you are arrogant, your knowledge will serve only the purpose of ignorance, for the arrogant person cannot enjoy his knowledge, he is like the spoon with which delicious food is stirred but cannot enjoy the taste of it! And that was the miserable plight of Prof. Blisso'life! I sympathized at his self-assertiveness!

I wished to tell him, "Dear friend! You have a philosophical as well as a technological mind. They are two extremes which make a human being too rigid or a creak! You have also a sensuous mind and I agree that it is better to not be too sentimental. Of course, there are situations in human life in which one cannot give a straightforward answer like 'yes' or 'no', as our Academic Vice President told me when I applied to re-designate me without any encumbrances of any sort. However, it is always good to be a little sensitive or sentimental!"

Many a time, Professor Elderking warned me against talking religious matters with a fanatic like Blisso'life. But I continued to talk on such controversial subjects and maintained our friendship. In fact, it was Elderking who was a nasty fanatic in his heart, as I came to know later! After drinking, he talked too much in his Dutch courage against all other religions and all other religious institutions, including the Muslim College where he was working in India!

Blisso'life believed in the theory of rebirth and I too believed it. But he also believed that the present miserable life is the result of his sins committed in the previous birth or births, which I could not admit. As a childless man, he might be compromising his life with that theory, perhaps! It was surprising that though he believed in rebirth, he could not adjust with the fact that people could also take birth in other religions due to sins in their previous births!

One of the bad habits of Blisso'life was that he could never read a book with an open heart! Of course, he read a lot but only those books related to Hindu religion and ancient Indian literature. He loved music but only Karnatic classic music and old film songs and never cared to hear the western classic music or modern pop songs! He was an ardent capitalist and justified all its drawbacks including the atrocities of the United States! He loved democracy because he hated the totalitarian communists! Of course, the lack of individual freedom under communism is abominable but he was not ready to accept even its good aspects like socialism in education and state control of essential commodities, public health and so on.

"Read a book with an open mind, without prejudice, my friend, whether you agree with its content or not," I used to tell him. He replied, "Why should I? It cannot bring any change in me or in my attitude or in my opinion or in my belief!" Well. That was Professor Blisso'life!

I did not know why I respected and loved a fanatic like Prof. Blisso'life! There was a charisma about him. Basically he was a humanist but ideologically an extremist; the latter was the most dangerous! I respected Prof. Blisso'life but I revered Dr. Worku more, a pacifist!

Despite all such drawbacks, Prof. Blisso'life was a philanthropist at heart. Excessive egoism was a sin as it shut the doors of knowledge, I remembered. Well! Patriotism made us fools! There were people who pretended as secularists but at their heart they might be religious fanatics! And religion made us cowards too! I remembered the words of Nietzsche's Zarathustra, 'Do not be jealous of those unyielding and impatient men, you lover of truth! Never yet did truth cling to the arms of the unyielding!'

Dr. Salim avoided joining our discussions on religious issues, for him, all mysteries were for God to decide and man should not bother about them. Of course, he had many worries in his domestic life and he was not in a mood to discuss philosophy! We used to talk about our family matters and I suggested that he arrange for his daughter's marriage as early as possible. He had already contacted his elder brothers and uncles and requested that they find a boy for his daughter so that the 'nikah' could be arranged as and when he arrived home. Of course, he had no plan to return to Ethiopia, he told me, as he had one more daughter growing up. 'The cat that fell in the hot water will be frightened of even cold water,' I remembered a saying in my mother tongue.

The academic year was coming to an end and we had to complete all our duties. We had to wait one more month, according to our contract, to get our last month's salary and our air-tickets as well. Our contract with the university was coming to an end. If our contracts were not renewed, we would go back to India for good!

Dr. Maindoor seemed to be well-settled here. His wife got a job in a good school and his children were also studying there. In fact, he was drawing more salary than all of us; he could save his whole salary and manage family expenses with his wife's salary. Of course, his stingy nature and bargaining capacity helped him a lot in retaining a good bank balance. He expected to continue in the university, at least, for another ten years so that he could relax and lead a comfortable life at home, a sort of retired life even before retirement age. But the university was not ready to renew his contract and all his hopes were shattered. Man proposes; University disposes!

Dr. Dambay took leave from the university to pursue his research. It was really a pleasure for me to work with him and, in his absence, it would be quite boring. I decided to leave the work of a Principal Advisor to the Dean of Graduate Programs. On the basis of the request made by the Department, the University might be renewing my contract for another two years.

Though the university requested Dr. Worku to continue, he could not do so as the maximum period of leave sanctioned by his college was over by then. He had earlier worked for two years in Eritrea. And what he had left was only a year; the university renewed contracts only for a minimum of two years!

Dr. Muse faced the greatest tragedy; his contract was terminated in the middle of it. He was on the verge of tears, for he needed money for the treatment of his son. I tried to console him, pointing out that once you jump out of India, it was quite easy to jump out again! Attend the next interview and get an appointment in some other university, that's all!

Dr. Ahmad Ansari did not like to continue in the university due to his family problems; he wanted to rejoin his college in India so that he could spend his days with his young wife and small children, and he made every arrangement to sell his household things before it was too late. Moreover, with his business background, he knew how to make money by arranging seminars, workshops and symposia with financial support from the University Grant Commission in India!

Rajesh was always in a gloomy mood and he had not decided whether to continue his service or not. It seemed that he was expecting some miracle, some sort of good news from somewhere. In fact, I thought that he had secretly applied for some job either in India or in some other foreign countries, with a better salary. Of course, for the last few months, our friendship was a little strained due to his silence. He never talked openly and I could not find any means to know what was going on in his heart. I asked him many times to tell me his problems so that I could help him. When grief was thickening in one's mind, a burst of crying might give, at least, a little consolation; it was not merely a saying but a fact! Perhaps, he was crying aloud during his lonely nights!

Ms. Sinja resigned her job on health grounds before the completion of her contract; she requested the HOD give her a month's medical leave but he asked her to resign, and in Ethiopian universities the word of the HOD was the final one!

Dr. President decided to continue, expecting that his niece would return, after taking a few months rest, attending another interview.

One day, a gang of people who belonged to Mr. President's State in India, came to his room and manhandled him! When asked the reason, he said, "It's all the fault of my tongue, sir, just my loose talk! You say certain facts and others misunderstand your sincerity! I don't want to continue here, sir, I withdrew my request for the renewal of my contract! It's always better to keep your mouth shut while you work in a foreign country!" he said in a desperate tone.

He made a rasping noise by grinding his teeth; it was his habit to make grating sounds with his teeth! Of course, he had certain health problems and the assistance of somebody was highly necessary. Or, perhaps, he could not continue in a place where he missed the service of his niece!

Dr. Salim was also confused, whether to continue or not in the university, due to his family problem. He wished to conduct the wedding of his daughter as early as possible. If he could do it during the vacation, he wished to return and, therefore, he agreed to renew his contract. And if he could not arrange the wedding, he decided to stay at home.

To some people who had no doctorate degree, the university had already served the three months' notice for their termination and they had left the place before the beginning of the previous semester. Mr. Sajeev knew that he would be terminated by the end of the year and, therefore, he had secretly applied to a neighboring university. He took his pregnant wife and daughter to India well in advance, though he told us that it was for the purpose of giving a good education to his daughter!

One day Sanjeev came to my room on his bicycle and told us the facts. Fortunately, he was selected by a neighboring university, and gave the three months' notice to the university but the university, instead of waiting for three months, immediately permitted him to leave. He said that he was going to the new place soon. He said goodbye to us and that was our last meeting!

Of course, a few others also gave the three months' notice to the university as they got better jobs in other countries. Ms. Kishari had gone to England and Mr. Godwin had gone to Ireland. Mr. Glory had no doctorate degree but he managed, as usual, to be in the good book of his HOD! The service of Mr. Glory was highly needed for the Department and his contract was renewed by the university.

Prof. Elderking had one more year to serve according to his contract. Though he boasted that he was 'the king' of his mother college, I knew that he would not go back soon! On a single 'anger' one could jump into the well but with seven 'angers' one couldn't come out of it, as the proverb warned! And the poor, jovial young man, Ramesh! His contract was terminated; he could serve only for a year!

What happened to Mr. Handsome was quite surprising. Though he was in the good book of the Head of the Department, the university issued him a termination notice. Mr. Handsome's wife was in India for her delivery and she was planning to come back by the beginning of the next academic year, and the termination order was like a thunder out of the clear blue! However, he told everybody that he did not like the job in Ethiopia and would not return! He had played a foul game in the case of Dr. Tomsin and now it was his turn! Nemesis might have played her role well, though a bit late!

Mr. Fluteplayer decided to continue here until the university terminated him, as he was an already retired man in his own country. Dr. Prestige Mussalman, as usual, gave the publicity that he had given the three months' notice to the university. Of course, every year he did so as a part of his pressure tactics, so that the university would reconsider his salary! But it seemed that the Department came to know about his trick and it accepted his resignation! And Blisso'life and his wife stayed happily in their house, as if nothing would change this world! They were saving money for their next pilgrimage to the temples in the Himalayas, as they had already visited almost all other temples in India!

The case of Mr. Jerry, my Canadian friend, was the most shocking one! He was serving the university as an architecture and art historian and he had the dream of launching a School of Art! Following the implementation of the new Business Process Engineering system, many devoted persons were thrown out of their chairs and many inexperienced persons occupied new chairs! One among the latter became the HOD and he had some grudge towards Mr. Jerry! The new Head decided not to renew his contract.

There was a rumor that Jerry had fallen into the trap of an Ethiopian girl and he had to pay a good amount to settle the matter. I asked him about it and he told me that it was the trick of that Head of the Department. He had arranged for a girl to tarnish Jerry's image and thereby he could easily terminate him! Jerry, caressing his silver-white beard, winked at me and said with a cunning smile, "Wait, my dear friend, for a surprise; for this insult against me, I will take a sweet revenge, do wait and see!"

An abusive termination letter was prepared and served to Jerry by the HOD and its copies were sent to the offices of each and every governmental and non-governmental organization! It was the first time that a university in Ethiopia did such a horrible thing against a Canadian! In fact, the phrases used in the letter were so cruel and uncivilized that the issuing of such a letter was unbecoming for a university which is supposed to be the center of culture and civilization! It was all because Mr. Jerry tried to prove that the architectural style which Ethiopians call 'Gondarine' was nothing but clear Portuguese style! In fact, Mr. Jerry's idea was to live and die in this Ethiopian soil, but it seemed that the Ethiopians did not need yet another Portuguese connection! Did BPR mean Blood Pressure Raising system?

Dr. Worku's leave, taken from his mother college, was over and, as they refused to extend the leave, he could not continue in Ethiopia, though the university desired his service for two more years. Dr. Ahmad did not like to continue here as his purpose of coming to Ethiopia was only to get two years foreign experience which would help him to become the principal of his college.

As a man retired from an affiliated college under a university in India, I had no other option but to continue in Ethiopia. Of course, I was getting my pension at home, but to sit idle and waste away one's talents was unbearable, it was rather a sin. Possibly, the university would renew my contract for another two years so that I could come back after spending the holidays with my family.

Dr. Honey Rao, the oldest professor in our university, had one more year of contract and we thought that he would continue here! As Dr. Worku Singh was going back to his mother college, he wished to meet Dr. Rao to say goodbye! On that Saturday, we went to his house, of course, as a part of our morning walk! It was the habit of Dr. Worku to walk on a new route on every Saturday and I followed him wherever he went as part of his so-called geographical exploration!

It was about 11 am when we reached Dr. Rao's house. We knocked at the door and it took at least five minutes or more to open the door. He would be reading or preparing some notes for the next year, I thought. Seeing him, we were surprised to the core! All his joviality and smiles had gone and he looked like a ghost! He wiped his head and face with a towel, of course, he was sweating all over! I could not hide my shock and I asked him, "What happened, Sir! Are you suffering from fever or some other illness?"

"Nothing, Dr. Jhoaj!" he said in his usual pronunciation of

my name, bringing a smile on his face with much effort. "See, after the late breakfast, I was reading a book and soon fell into a deep slumber on the chair, perhaps, last night, I had no proper sleep! Or I may be getting a bit too old! Come and have your seats!"

He invited us in and we sat on the sofa. Dr. Worku asked him, "Sleeping is always good for health at this age, but why are you sweating this much? Have you checked your blood pressure?"

"It's nothing like that! I saw a dream while napping! It may be a warning, a sort of red-light alarm from the heavens!" he said with a blush on his face.

"It's really interesting! If you don't mind tell us about it; we too are approaching your age, aren't we?" I said with curiosity.

As we were talking, Mrs. Victoria Rao came with soft drinks and joined our conversation! She said with a sigh, "Sir, we are winding up our work here and leaving this country forever! You are our only friends, and why should we hide the facts? My husband is not well and he needs rest! We came here not for making money but to get some peace of mind and if we won't get that peace here, why should we continue to stay here?"

We agreed with her argument. I said, "Doctor! What she says is correct! We appreciate your spirit of adventure even at this age but one should also think about one's health!"

"Yes! It's decided! Tomorrow I'm going to take my last salary from Ethiopia! We've enough money to embark upon a holy pilgrimage!" Dr. Rao said with a deep sigh.

"Pilgrimage?" I asked in surprise. "It's simply nonsense! Sir! Go to your home and take rest for a few weeks! Then you can decide whether to go for pilgrimage or not! To live with your children and grandchildren is more blissful than any great pilgrimage!"

"But he doesn't like to go to his son and daughter-in-law!"

Victoria Rao said suddenly and, looked at her husband's face as if she had disclosed some secret!

"No problem! You can say everything; they are our friends!" Dr. Rao said with a pale look on his face. Then he recited a few lines from a poem:
"When grief accumulates in the mind;
A burst of cry will give a bit relief!"

His wife Victoria Rao said with a sigh, "After all they are our son and his wife! I'm ready to live with them; I'll work there like a servant; I won't show the right of a mother-in-law! What we need is some rice gruel, the balance of what they had eaten! But, brothers, he is worried about his daughter who is in London, that's the most important matter for him!"

We looked anxiously at Dr. Rao's face! He nodded his head and said in a low voice, "Look here, friends! I'm a Brahmin!" He took out his holy-thread from beneath his shirt and showed it to us. Then, with a deep sigh, continued, "I sent my second daughter for higher studies in London. I worked hard in the university and sent her fees regularly. She completed her studies very successfully and joined a firm for practice. But then, for a moment, she forgot her father, her family, her community, her language, her religion, her culture and everything that made her what she is, and married a European! They live in London; it's for the penance that we wish to go for pilgrimage!"

We sat there without even breathing for a minute! He continued, "I told you about a dream I saw a few minutes back! Do you want to know what it was! I was on my death bed, waiting for the last breath! My son came to my side and whispered in my ears, 'My sister has come from London; she asks your permission to see you!' I shook my head sideways and said in the loudest voice I could make, 'No! Never! I don't want to see her face!' I breathed heavily as if I were taking my last breath! And then, you came and knocked at the door!"

We sat there like statues! How could we console him? He

continued, "I know what is going on in your mind! You think, such incidents are quite common these days, and it is better to forgive and forget and come to some sort of reconciliation! But I cannot; I'm not a willow plant to move up and down in the wind or storm and stand erect when they pass! I'm an oak tree and my branches will not move in the wind but when the heavy storm blows, it'll break all the branches! There's no room for reconciliation in my heart! I'm a professor who gave moral messages to my students throughout my life, and my daughter betrayed and disgraced me! I'm ashamed of myself; I can't raise my head due to shame; I'm disgraced to the core and my life became worthless!"

He was breathing heavily and we were in an embarrassing situation! I touched on his shoulder and said, "Sir! Please relax! Please forget such things! The modern generation is like that; they don't know the sentiments of their parents!"

He looked sharply into my eyes and said, "It's easy to advise others! I can forgive her but I can't forget! She shouldn't have done such a thing; because she was born out of my blood and marrow! For her sin, I must undergo the penance!"

We sat there silently for a while. Soon Dr. Worku changed the subject and we began to talk about the convocation of the students and also about our travel to India. We said goodbye to the old couple and walked our way towards home. I tried to wipe my tears secretly without being seen by Dr. Worku.

Dr. Worku became philosophical as he used to do on similar situations! He said, "As we grow older and older, our involvement with this world and its ways, with people and their habits, even with our dear and near ones, should be reduced. Then, we will feel a sort of placidity as we approach our last breath. Dr. Rao seems too much involved and death may be too horrible for such people!"

I replied, quoting from Prophet Jeremiah, "The heart is deceitful above all things and beyond cure, and who can understand it?"

After a few moments of silence, Dr. Worku said, "The dream is perhaps a warning for Dr. Rao! Once a man happened to see God and he fell before him in obeisance. God was pleased and He demanded the man to ask for a boon. The man said, 'Please inform me before my death, that's the only boon I want.' Years passed and, one day, the man died! He met God and complained, 'You promised me to inform me before my death but you didn't keep your word!' God replied, 'How can you say that I didn't inform you! Many times I sent you warnings but you always ignored them! First I made your hair grey but you dyed it black; then I made your eyesight dim but you bought spectacles; I loosened your teeth but you replaced them with false-teeth; I reduced your hearing ability but you bought earphones! You ignored all my warnings and now you're complaining to me!"

Dr. Worku Singh was always like that; for everything, he had readymade stories, sayings and quotes with him! We walked silently but felt a sort of heaviness in our hearts!

At last the convocation day arrived together with the heavy rain. Students in their black gowns and the mortar boards on their heads queued up in the rain for their entrance into the hall. Most of my colleagues were in black and red gowns as they had no doctorate degree. I was in the black and blue gown with a blue velvet hood over the shoulders and the mortar board with a bunch of blue threads hanging from it. In most of the Indian universities convocations had been stopped years ago so I did not get the opportunity to wear the ceremonial dress there. I really enjoyed the colorful graduation ceremony!

Usually expatriates never attended the convocation program as the program was in Amharic. But I loved the pomp and show of all such festivals and carnivals, irrespective of its nature. They might be arranged to celebrate a particular occasion, religious, cultural or social! Why should we oppose them in the name of nationality or creed? Enjoy every such opportunity and that was my attitude, as well as of Dr. Worku.

After the function, many of my students came to my office to take their photographs together with me. My student-friend Mr. Mengistu invited me for lunch at his house and I went with him. The family had arranged a great reception for their young graduate. Mengistu told me that all the expense of his graduation was met by his brother who came from the United States for a short visit. He continued, "In fact, he is not my direct brother; he is the son of my mother's first husband with another woman. His parents died years ago and we are the only relatives for him." Many neighbors and relatives came to the house with flowers and other gifts. Tella, the local beer, was served to all, and it was followed by a heavy lunch.

My Ethiopian friend Mr. Sam invited me to spend the evening in a traditional house. The Ethiostar Lane in the city was full of traditional houses where one could enjoy traditional music and dancing. Boys and girls in their traditional dress danced and sang; a young man played on the traditional drum and another young man played the single-stringed musical instrument named masinqo. I knew the masinqo player; his name was Awabech which means joker! While the dancers took a rest, he told stories or made fun of the spectators.

There were Americans, Indians, the Chinese, the Dutch and Canadians among the spectators and Awabech made humorous comments about them. The Chinese people monopolized the construction works in Ethiopia as they could quote the lowest rate in their tenders. It was not necessary for them to spend money on labor, for most of the laborers were brought from Chinese prisons, it was said. China had a good business with Ethiopia; even very small items like pens and pencils to electronic things were imported from China. Seeing a Chinese engineer among the audience, Awabech sang, of course, with the accompaniment of his masinqo:

The Chinese have very small noses;
How can they smell with such tiny noses?
But Ethiopians also learned to smell
Now with imported Chinese noses!

We laughed aloud understanding the sharp sarcasm in his words. Some of the traditional songs were to attract married men. In one song, the singer said:

Why do you waste your youth
With that old wife of yours?
We will sing and dance for you,
Why not come and enjoy life!

No hot drinks were served in the traditional houses! Small bottles of St. George beer were served among the customers! People came there mostly to enjoy the oral literature of Ethiopia, in which the writers and singers enjoyed maximum freedom!

On the other side of the street, there were so many nightclubs, illuminated with flicker lamps and colorful automatic bulbs. Girls in scanty dresses welcomed guests and entertained them. Ethiopian and European cultures go side by side in this city!

Mr. Sam and I were talking about the changed attitude of the people. We walked along the lane hearing the music from the traditional houses. Suddenly a beautiful young girl in fashionable dress and hairstyle came to me and said, "Sir! I know Hindi; I am Tsahay which means Suraj in Hindi! Shall I come to your room?"

Mr. Sam walked forward a few steps and I was embarrassed. In India, if you refuse such an offer, they would call you bad names! Mr. Sam saved me from that awkward situation by calling me to his side. I said, "Next time!" to the girl and scurried away! Later, Mr. Sam said that she was a sex worker! Suraj means the sun; but this Suraj could bring only darkness in the lives of her customers! I thought.

Many a time I saw her coming out of the hotels in the city. One day, I saw her coming from the church with a child walking with her. She was in her traditional Ethiopian dress and she walked with a bowed head! Perhaps, she was betrayed by her man; he might have left her after getting her pregnant! And she might be forced to become a sex worker, just to find food for her and her child!

One of my Ethiopian colleagues, Dr. Fullgate, once said to me, "See! Ethiopians have their own culture; no one can change it. We won't allow it!" But I knew that even the smallest ethnic group in Ethiopia would say the same thing!

I wished to ask him, "Is prostitution a part of Ethiopian culture? It is the legacy of the Italians who ruled Ethiopia for at least five years. Is circumcision of Christians a part of Ethiopian culture? It is the culture of the Middle East. Of course circumcision of female may be a part of African culture and so Ethiopian too! But how long could we continue such tribal initiation ceremonies in the name of God? Is the nightclub culture Ethiopian? It is American; in Ethiopian cities poor girls display their flesh for the customers of the clubs! Well! Come to the graduation ceremony; is it Ethiopian culture? It is European or, specifically, the English culture and the poor people of Ethiopia spend a huge amount to see their children wear the black gown and the mortar board! Dear Dr. Fullgate, Ethiopia has changed a lot by amalgamating various cultures!"

Almost a month of free time; we had already submitted the grade reports of our students. So I requested my wife to send me a few canvas boards; I used to paint during vacations. I had a plan to solidify an idea that was lingering in my mind for the last thirty-five years. It was a scene from John Keats' poem *Eve of St. Agnes* which I learned for my BA course. Porphyro comes to the bedroom of Maidelyn with a plan to elope with her, but finding her in a dreamy sleep, hesitates to wake her up, and plays a soft tune on his flute! And all these years, I could not paint that scene.

My wife sent me the parcel and I opened it. While unwrapping the inside cover, I noticed that the canvas board was wrapped with a local newspaper, the Malayala Manorama, in my mother tongue! I scanned the paper quickly and a snippet caught my attention. It said, "Children refused to accept their mother who had eloped with the servant." The paper was dated August 30, 2008. The news said that the father of the children was a central government employee working in another State; at the time of his transfer, he asked a servant to look after the household affairs in the latter's absence and the servant really 'looked after' the family! Within a few weeks, the government employee's wife eloped with the servant, leaving her two children in the house. After a few months, the servant-lover deserted her, as it usually happened in similar cases, and she returned to her children. Her son and daughter, both of them were college students by then, refused to accept her as their mother!

I felt really proud of those children's courage. Among human beings, just littering a child should not be the criteria for motherhood! I also felt proud of the street boys of Ethiopia who never thought about their mothers who had left them in the streets but managed to find their means for survival!

"What's happening to our men and women?" I asked my friend Dr. Worku Singh. After our usual evening walk, we were sitting on that pleasant evening in the Millennium Café for tea. I continued, "It seems that our belief that marriage takes place in heaven is completely wrong! There was a time when husbands left their wives and went abroad or faraway places for jobs for the well-being of the family and the wives patiently waited in prayer for their safe arrival after a year or two! And the husbands spent their days working hard and nights dreaming of the good old days he spent with his wife and children! But now the wives wait for an opportunity to get a different sexual experience and there are many gigolos around us to give them free service as it is quite safe for them! They may be either servants or drivers or an intimate friend of their husbands! These bastards were waiting for their chance to get the profit for respecting and obeying all these years their husbands, and the wives foolishly think that it was an honor from their side!"

Dr. Singh replied that it might not be the need for sex but the eminent need for care which provokes these women to fall into the traps of these womanizers! He continued, "Of course, there are many nymphomaniacs among our women but many of them are not so. But these lechers, who have nothing to lose, if the sex is with another man's wife, tempt them with slavish obedience and cunningness that the poor women used to fall victim!"

We sat there talking and, then, an Indian engineer came towards us, greeted us and introduced himself as a trainer in a private company. His name was Sreeni and we were impressed by his manners; he never smoked nor took intoxicants, unlike us! But later, I came to know that he was living with an Ethiopian lady. He had his wife and children in India and, with the spontaneous sense of moral indignation; I told him frankly that he was a criminal in India.

Sreeni explained in an apologetic tone, "It's not my fault, Sir! She doesn't believe in marriage! Of course, she had married an Ethiopian first but, after the birth of a boy-child, he deserted her and married another woman. It was a shock for her and she decided not to marry again in life. Meanwhile, a Dutchman came there as her neighbor and she served him until she had a girl-child. Later, she met a Chinese engineer, who had been there for the construction of roads, and had her second girl-child from him. Now she wished to get another child from an Indian and that's why I stay with her!"

How cosmopolitan she was! Shouldn't we encourage such women who sacrifice their body for the unity of human races?

But how could a woman degrade herself to the level of a public latrine? I wondered.

On a drizzling day, my young Ethiopian colleague, Mr. Zalem, told me with sheer indignation, "I wonder, how the youngsters in India could tolerate you, the conservative elders! If a man and a woman fall in love, let them marry! Why should you think about their differences in race, caste, creed, language and culture as far as they love each other? What the hell others bother about their private life? Well! If they cease to love, let them divorce! Do you mean that, in India, individuals have no freedom even to love each other?"

I listened to his argument and said, "Mr. Zalem! Let's begin by asking: What is Love? It's just like the question: What is Truth? Silence would be a better answer! But generally what I have seen in Ethiopia is not love at all! You meet a girl; you are attracted by her and you declare: I love you! The poor girl believes your words and falls flat! After a few months, you repeat the same procedure with another girl; she too falls flat; you forgot your earlier love; divorces or leaves the first one; marries or keeps the second one because you feel better love with the latter! If you call it love, I will keep my silence!"

I continued, "In India, I have seen quite a lot of women and men who live as widows or widowers just because of their true love towards their dead spouses. Of course, it's a kind of platonic love, and true love has an element of divinity in it. You may call it foolishness, if so, lovers are fools!"

"But it's all against the freedom of the individual," Zalem insisted.

I patiently said, "In India, men and women have the freedom to love and marry. But in most cases, the women have to lead a miserable life and society cannot do anything against it. The social restrictions reduce the misery of women, at least, to a certain extent. Of course, if women are economically self-reliant, the case may be different. Marriage, divorce and remarriage are not a problem among the richest and the poorest people; they have nothing to lose! But think about the middle class women who are well-educated but unemployed! They know only to dream and, usually, their innocence and credulousness are exploited by clever males only to throw them later into gutters!"

I continued, "What you call love is not 'real love' but 'tentative love' or a sort of erotic love in which the element of conjugal love is less; one day you feel it towards one girl and on another day to another girl; the so-called love becomes a mask for the sexually perverted individuals to engage in promiscuity or adultery! Have you ever tried to take the list of those women who have been deserted by their so-called lovers, at least in this small town? Those poor women live in the foot-paths, selling corn and sugar-cane, or even their flesh, to feed their children! In true freedom, there is right as well as obligation; obligation without right is slavery but right without obligation is hooliganism!"

It seemed that Mr. Zalem was not convinced and, as a male, he would never be! Here, in Ethiopia, they played with their life and the result was the increase in the rate of HIV/AIDS patients! And the elders had no voice as they themselves were sinners!

The same issue came up when I was talking with Mr. Compensation about the slow progress of Ethiopia, in particular, and Africa, in general. He was a very sensible and courageous person who talked with witty and humorous anecdotes. "There's something wrong with the African psyche," he said.

I said, "See, Mr. Compensation! I'm not a male chauvinist or a supporter of patriarchal domination. One fact I must point out as a reason for this slow development; and many times Prof. Blisso'life and I talked about its sanctity. All over the world, except in Africa, the children are brought up under the supervision of the father, the so-called head of the family. In Africa, traditionally children are brought up by their mothers, and fathers play little or no important role in shaping the mindset of their children at an early stage. Of course, in Ethiopia, the system is gradually changing and, I'm sure, within a few decades, one can witness a drastic change in the tempo of progress here."

"I wished to see that change but an expatriate could not stay here for a long time. 'Something is rotten in the streets' of Sea Side City! I could feel the stench of fear emitting from every quarter! Even officials of high rank were afraid of taking decisions of their own and, when problems were faced, instead of solving them immediately, they kicked them into another's court! How long could they play this game of irresponsibility?" I wondered.

Once Dr. Worku said, "The problem with Ethiopia was that they had no administrative continuity. The Dictator Hailemariam Mengistu had an effective secretarial administration but when the democratic government came, they wiped away every trace of the former system and reshuffled everything, except, thank God, his land reforms! This example they followed in every office, even after fifteen years of democracy!"

I interrupted him and said, "By the way, sometimes fate is too cruel to interfere even into administrative matters of a ruler! See! What happened during Mengistu's dictatorship; there was a severe famine that shattered all his great ideas! Of course, he made every effort to solve the problem but the people turned against him as if he were the cause of famine! And the Americans made use of that opportunity! The same thing happened in India too during the time of Chandrababu Naidu who launched an IT Revolution in Andhra Pradesh! Unfortunately there was no rain for about five years there and people complained that he concentrated only on the cities and not for the farmers or the field of agriculture!"

Worku, a bit irritated by my incongruous comments, continued his argument, "What I mean is, even today, experienced people were transferred to new offices and in their places the unfamiliar and inexperienced people were appointed as heads of administration! The newly appointed people completely ignored what their predecessors did. By the time the new heads learned the system, they would be transferred to other offices!"

Business Process Engineering was imported from America to speed up the matters. But could one cross the river in an anchored boat? You rove harder and harder with all your might, the boat appears to be moving but never reaches the other shore! BPR or no BPR, life will continue just like in the old days, in its worst condition! I remembered the words of Benjamin the Donkey in George Orwell's *Animal Farm*.

Power leads to arrogance, arrogance to cowardice and cowardice makes people blind and deaf! Once, Prof. Compensation asked me, "What is wrong with Ethiopia?" I said, "The Ethiopians are not ready to think differently! They don't like even different tastes in food. Shall I make it clear through a parable? Milk is very good and nutritious and you can use it as such or with tea or coffee. You can also make curd with it and, then, it gives another taste. The curd has an upper layer of cream or butter with yet another taste. And cream is the best part of milk! If milk is information, curd is knowledge and the cream is wisdom. A people who are reluctant to change the information gathered through their experience into knowledge or wisdom cannot progress in life."

I continued, "Perhaps, adversity has its own blessings! The Ethiopians generally do not like to make profit. They cultivate land only to produce whatever is needed for their daily bread! There are merchants but they sell things and make profit only for managing their daily needs! They are satisfied with what they get and they pray, in its literal meaning: Abba dho chin hoy….yehlat enjirachne siten sarei……Our Father who art in Heaven….give us this day our daily injera!"

I said, "A few Ethiopians, including high officials, think that expatriates work here only for money! They do not know the spirit of service or adventure! Can they calculate the price of social life they lost in their own countries? Can they evaluate the price of family life they lost by coming over here? The difficulties of traveling: waiting at the airport for hours, carrying luggage, the insult of customs officers, the opening of the tightly packed suitcases for silly reasons, the security check-up in front of those who look at travelers as criminals and the queuing for immigration clearance – my God! How much is the price for all these ordeals? Then the domestic flight with the same procedure and, then, the train or bus or taxi journey to the house…!"

I continued, "The funerals of dear relatives, the wedding ceremonies of blood-relatives, the small enjoyments of domestic life – all are lost just for a few dollars! Most of the money we get here is spent either in this country or on the way while going for vacation. Can they understand the cost of living in India or in Europe?"

Yes! One could not wait that much time! It was high-time for me to leave this country. It's too unbearable for me to continue my service here! I remembered the saying: Stop singing while the voice is good!

That evening, I got an unexpected telephone call! The voice asked, "Is it Dr. George? I am Rajeev Gupta, the brother-in-law of your friend Sajeev! I am working in Mumbai and your phone number was given to me by Sajeev!"

I said, "Well, Mr. Rajeev! I haven't seen Sajeev for the last couple of months! Is there any problem with him? I only know that he had left our place and joined another university!"

"Well! The problem is not with him; it is about us, for my

only sister!" He continued over the phone, "Are you sure that he joined some university? Currently he is here and he wants to take his wife and children with him to Ethiopia! But we have strong doubt about his sincerity! In fact my sister wants to file a case of divorce against him! Dear doctor, please tell me the truth; we can't risk our sister's life, you know!"

What should I say to him? In fact, I did not know whether he had actually joined the university, though he told me that! There should be some serious problem in their family life! I asked him to tell me the details.

Rajeev Gupta told me that his sister was in the house of Sajeev for her second delivery and her in-laws looked after her in the absence of her husband. After leaving his wife and daughter under the care of his parents, he might have returned to Ethiopia to join the new job, I thought.

Rajeev talked to me over phone for more than forty-five minutes and that showed the seriousness of the situation. He said, "When she delivered the second daughter, her mother-in-law could not tolerate it and she tried to kill her! Fortunately on that night she managed to escape with her children and took refuge in a neighbor's house! In such a situation, how could we believe her husband and send her and the children with him to Ethiopia?"

I thought for a while; here's a life and death question! I know Sajeev, his wife and his first daughter. In India, there were still some conservative parents who believed that the gender of a child was decided by its mother! How could we convince them that it was the 'Y' chromosome in the father that helped the birth of a male child! And Sajeev was an obedient husband who even worshipped his wife; perhaps due to some inferiority complex in him!

Whatever was the situation, I decided to save and protect their married life. I told Rajesh in a harsh voice: "Dear Mr. Rajeev! Listen to me with an open heart! Here's the question of a family on the verge of a break! Please don't take any foolish steps based on a quick decision! About Sajeev, I give you a hundred percent guarantee; once they are in Ethiopia, he will properly look after his wife and children! Don't be afraid of any wrong action from Sajeev's side! If anything worse happens, I will be responsible; you can take my word for it!"

Rajeev said over the phone, "I believe you, doctor! I hope my sister's life will be safe there! Thank you very much, sir!" He cut off the call.

Our land phone was in the bedroom of Dr. Worku Singh. I placed the receiver on the cradle and turned to exit the room. Casually my eyes fell on Lord Vigneswara's idol, worshipped by Dr. Singh. I felt a sort of smile on the face of Lord Vigneswara, perhaps, the Lord was appreciating my courage in saving a family life!

Dr. Worku and I walked many more miles during our evening walks! We were spending our days quite idly, waiting for our last month's salary. One evening we met Mr. Joji, who had married an Ethiopian girl, walking along the street with his girl-child! The child was fair complexioned like him but her hair was curly like her Ethiopian mother! Every year, he wished to go to India to see his first family but the university never gave him air-tickets since he had married an Ethiopian girl!

Every two weeks, Mr. Joji used to visit Addis Ababa and brought us hot news. This time, he announced that the Government of Ethiopia had decided to separate universities from the grip of the Higher Education Authority and, so the universities could directly recruit expatriates for teaching. No longer could the Higher Education officers in Addis be involved in the appointments of staff in the universities. He also said that the education officer in Addis Mr. Mepleased was arrested under charges of corruption and was undergoing imprisonment!

He also disclosed to us that Dr. Priest and Ms. Pom were likely to be terminated from service! The Ethiopian teachers who had been on their doctoral studies were returning to their mother department and there were no more vacancies for expatriates! Of course, they could not lead a free life in India, as the prejudiced, hypocritical society in India could not tolerate such dubious relationships; they would definitely find placements in some other university in Ethiopia!

Many times I tried to meet Mr. Heavenlyfood but I could not find him in his office. I had an obligation towards him, not because he was the first Ethiopian who called my name, hugged me to his shoulder in the Ethiopian style and brought me from the airport to the city but he had requested that I give him an Indian shirt! One day I met his friend Mr. Weldearegay and asked him for the whereabouts of Mr. Heavenlyfood.

He laughed aloud and said in his unusually loud voice: "He is in Addis; in fact, he is in prison for a month or so! Don't you know? He was arrested a month ago on corruption charges! Of course, he will be here within one or two days!"

It was shocking news for me. Mr. Welde explained that it was an old case; it was alleged that as the finance officer he had helped the former President of the university to escape to the United States with a huge amount! Welde said, "Of course, Mr. Heavenlyfood was innocent; he simply did what the President asked him to do. For that crime, the university punished him by demoting him to the post of an ordinary clerk and now he is undergoing the second punishment! And what happened to the former President who took away the money, do you know? How long could one live in America without a job even if one had good savings? There is a rumor that currently he has been working there at a gas station!"

After two days, I met Mr. Heavenlyfood; he hugged me shoulder to shoulder. He behaved as if nothing special had happened to him! I thought that prisoners would be starving in Ethiopian jails, but Mr. Heavenlyfood had put on much weight within a month! As I was leaving for India, I invited him for lunch with a few bottles of St. George beer; and then to a textile shop for a shirt of his size, perhaps XXXXL, which would be rarely available in India!

As the days of our departure fast approached, one day, Rajesh came all of a sudden, announcing that he was going early, without waiting even for the clearance from the university. He did not mention the reason clearly but just said that he wished to bring his wife to Ethiopia. After all, that was a good decision, and he went to Addis by the next morning!

Of course, he was friendly enough to ring me from Addis Ababa, before entering the plane, just to inform me that he had sent a parcel for me. After two weeks, Salim also followed him, as the wedding of his daughter was fixed. Finally Dr. Worku and I were left; we decided to go together to Addis Ababa and from there, he would enter the flight to Delhi and I to Mumbai.

There was a heavy jerking, perhaps, the plane fell into some air-currents, and the string of my memory broke! I looked through the glass window. The sky was grey and I could see the flashes of the golden rays of the morning sun. The plane pierced through the flakes of clouds and I saw the city of Mumbai below me like a collage work. Soon the announcement of the pilot came that our flight was going to land at Chatrapati Shivaji International Airport. Had Shivaji known that his name was given to the airport or to the railway station constructed by the British, he would have been turning in his grave! I smiled at the pettiness of the Indian politicians!

How fast time is running! I wondered. Everything happened as if it happened yesterday! Two years seemed just like two days or two weeks! How many people I met! How many places I visited! How many events I faced! All passed through my mind as if in a film running in 'fast forward' mode!

The plane landed and I heaved a long sigh. At last I was back in my homeland! I came out after collecting my luggage, clearing my immigration and buying two bottles of Scotch whisky from the so-called duty-free shop; of course, we would get it at a cheaper rate outside! I took a pre-paid taxi to the domestic airport from where I had to go to my hometown.

There were two terminals and the taxi driver dropped me at the wrong place. An airport officer told me that it would be better to take an auto-rickshaw, as I had a suitcase with me, and go to the other terminal. He introduced an auto-driver who agreed to take me there for ten rupees, though it was actually a walk-able distance as I came to know later. I did not know the place and the auto-rickshaw moved through many streets; the driver from time-to-time told me that there were traffic blocks on many roads that he had to take some shortcuts! Instead of five minutes of travel assured by the airport officer, he took about twenty minutes and I was shocked to see again certain buildings which I saw a few minutes earlier! I remembered the stories of many travelers who were cheated by auto-rickshaw drivers and I felt a fireball in my abdomen!

I told him in a friendly manner that I wished to take my breakfast and, therefore, to stop the auto-rickshaw. He replied, "What do you say, Sir? You told me the airport and how can I leave you on the way? That's not fair, Sir?"

"How much is the auto-charge?" I asked him.

"If I ask you one thousand rupees, do you give me?" he said. "We are not rich people like you, sir, but that doesn't mean that we take more money for traveling in our rickshaws."

Fortunately I saw the terminal entrance, about a hundred meters ahead, and asked him in a loud voice to stop the auto-rickshaw. I pushed my suitcase half out of the rickshaw and was ready to jump out of it whenever it slowed down its speed.

"Okay, give me three hundred rupees," he said in a cool voice.

"Before the airport officer, you agreed for ten rupees and now you demand three hundred? I shall give you fifty!" I said. I wanted to avoid a quarrel with him.

Three auto-rickshaws were following us and he slowed down his vehicle. He called them aloud and said, "Brothers! My auto ran for three hundred rupees and he is not giving the money! He says fifty only!"

He stopped the auto and the three other auto-rickshaws also stopped in front of us. One of the drivers laughed aloud and said, "Only fifty rupees for seeing the whole city of Mumbai?"

I jumped out of the auto, took my heavy suitcase and ran towards the entrance of the terminal. I did not turn my head to look at them; I heard them shouting, "Hey! Hey!"

I saw an airport officer standing at the entrance. Somehow, I managed to reach him and asked him the way to the 'check in' area. The auto-rickshaw drivers thought that I was complaining about them to the officer. They cleared from the place as quickly as possible; and I saved fifty rupees. I still wonder whether that airport officer who had recommended that particular auto-rickshaw would be getting a share in the whole business!

You might be cheated by any one at any time, if you are lucky, you could escape with a sigh! That's India, and at last, I reached India! I remembered the words of Gail Tredwell, the author of the Holy Hell, "When you think about India, there are two ways. Either you can think about the extreme poverty, beggars, lepers, disease and theft or you can think about the simple life-style, richness of color, density of delightful aromas wafting through the air and the down-to-earth joy of the people despite their poverty". The former way of thinking might be spontaneous but I would prefer to be optimistic by thinking in the latter way!

I could relax the one hour flight to Cochin Airport, the nearest one to my hometown. At the airport, my wife would be waiting for me. From there, about two hours ride in the taxi-car and we would reach our home. My home, my sweet home, at last!

CHAPTER FIVE

At last I was in my own house constructed under my own supervision! I knew every nook and corner of it, and I proudly moved everywhere in it, touching the doors, windows and walls, caressing the furniture and feeling the warmth of homeliness. My son, Xanthu, had already arrived there from the capital city where he was working. Somehow he had come to know about the date of my arrival and he was there at the house a few hours before my arrival!

I opened my baggage and took out some packets of chocolate-items which I had bought from Mumbai Airport; I was not sure whether I bought them from the duty-free or duty-paid shop, for they charged a cut-throat price, and I handed them over to my wife to be distributed among relatives and neighbors. I took out my books and journals from the suitcase and placed them on the shelf of my home library. I emptied my handbag; the dirty clothes that should be washed, and the two bottles of scotch whiskey, bought from Mumbai, should be kept secretly behind the books! Then I saw the diary of Rajesh and took it out and placed it on the table, so that I could remember to read it.

By evening, my wife and son went shopping, of course, to buy certain special things to celebrate my arrival. I hurriedly took my bath, went to my room and prepared a cocktail. I saw the diary of Rajesh and began to read it; of course, sipping my drink, for it would take at least two hours for my wife and son to come back.

On the first page of the diary, it was written as a title or something like that, 'The Autobiography of a Failed Husband' and below it, 'Chapter Last but One', and then at the bottom of the page, like a dedication: 'To Geetha, the first and last woman in my life.'

I laughed aloud reading the title and thought how funny these fiction writers are! Rajesh had sent me only one diary and, then, what about the previous chapters? He would have forgotten to send the first diary in which he wrote the other chapters, I thought. Or he would have deliberately kept those chapters as a secret! Perhaps, he was in the process of writing his autobiography by attempting the chapter last but one! And could anybody write only the last but one chapter of an autobiography?

Once again I read the dedication and thought for a while. Could a man love his wife better than Rajesh? Of course, Geetha deserved him and he deserved her, a sort of 'made for each other' and, by now, they might be so happy in their house. Rajesh was a good writer, quite fluent in language, and I enjoyed reading his diary as if I were reading a novel! I began to read.

"Heavy dark clouds rise up in thick masses from the eastern horizon. Layer after layer, they roll up above my head in the form of huge spirals. I can see Lake Tana spreading like a shroud over the lifeless body of the earth. Dark clouds are gathering over it every moment thickening its massive size. I am quite frightened like a child. Can they hang on in the sky like that for a long time? Can they lose their grip in the sky and fall down upon my head, crushing me flat to the earth? Can they turn into hailstones and fall down to break the heads of the pedestrians? Can they split into drops of water and fall scattered over the ground? Can the wind drive them away to another part of the sky and save my head?

"For the first time I see like this the pure turquoise blue color in the sky. I have seen almost all the colors in the sky; all the seven colors not in the form of a rainbow but quite separately spreading one third of the sky. I have seen the whole sky, the pure blue sky, without a single speck of cloud. I have seen even pure white sky, gray sky, yellow sky, red sky and violet sky. I have seen hundreds of colors changing in the sky within half an hour, at an early morning, while standing on Tiger Hill in Darjeeling. But this turquoise blue sky, which I used in one of my paintings in a unique way, is seen for the first time in my life.

"Poets say that every cloud has a silver lining! I look for a silver lining at every curly edge of the massive cloud rolling up in the sky. Not even a spot of shining! Not even the hope for a glittering! The whole sky is now turned dark and blue! If it rains, the dark clouds will be thinned into grey ones, I am sure. But this turquoise blue color, what will happen to it? Is it a sign of death, the end and the vacuity?

"The cold wind is getting stronger and stronger! I see lightning flashes in the sky. I hear the rumbling and grumbling of the clouds, turning into thunder! I feel one or two cold drops of water fall on my forehead. It's quite sure that the rain will fall! It's always better for the dark clouds shower away rather than hanging above the head without any grip, arousing tension and anxiety to those who stand under it! It is like a tug of war; you try your best to keep the victory on your side, and pull the rope with all your might, until you feel exhausted and then let the rope slip from your hand, so that the opposite side will fall flat to the ground!

"I desperately look for a tiny ray of light; but it's all dark, thick darkness to the core! Let there be rain! Let there be heavy storm! Let there be lightning and thunder! Let there be heavy flood! And together with the flood, let me be flowed away into nothingness!

"Now it's time for the lightning to strike on my head with a loud thunder and split me into pieces! Now it's time for the showers to wash away my body and soul into eternity! All your hopes and dreams about future must come to an end within a split second! Then, you will be no more, dust returned unto dust! And mere dust only!

"After living with a wife for a period of twenty-five years, she fails to understand your love! After living with your child for more than a score of years, the child fails to understand and love you! Or is it vice-versa? It may be better to say that I failed to understand or love them!"

Then, there were a few asterisks, denoting the break in the narrative. I was anxious to know what happened to Rajesh. I continued to read his diary.

"Darkness was crawling into my heart; it got stuck and thickened there, resisting the entrance of every ray of light! I felt all my hopes and fears about the Dark Continent turn to be quite irrelevant and immaterial before the cruel letter of my wife. Only a few days ago I arrived at this African country and it was the first time that I could step on this mysterious land of the charcoal-skinned people. I had landed here with the great dream of paying back all the debts there at my native place in India. Also I wished to save some money for the wedding expenses of my daughter. And also a small account reserved for my old age! But all my hopes and dreams turned upside down within a week, as I received the first letter sent by my wife.

"Geetha's letter was shivering in my hand, no, it was my hand that was trembling! I sat like a statue on the sofa, being unable to believe that the letter was really written by my wife, by the mother of my only daughter. It was only a few days ago that my wife and I, together with our daughter, had celebrated the twenty-fifth anniversary of our wedding, and how could she change all of a sudden into a person of just the opposite nature, within a few days after my leaving for this African country? Can a wife or any human being for that matter, change so suddenly, that such a chemical change occurred in her, turning white into black or black into white? Are we human beings a mere rebirth of chameleons? Can a person pretend a natural conjugal life for such a long period, about a quarter of a century?

"Of course, this letter was not written by my wife Geetha! I tried to convince myself. Someone is trying to make a fool of me! Such things are quite common now-a-days! Telephoning wives in the voice of their husbands, sending telegrams or e-mails to husbands in the name of their wives, writing letters by the so-called well-wishers to the parents about the immoral life of their sons or daughters, dropping notes on the faithlessness of the lover or the beloved by detective Iagos and similar incidents are quite common these days! Perhaps, this letter too is of some such gimmicks of some jealous neighbors! Of course, my Geetha could not write such a letter!

"Perhaps it's all fun for her. She used to quarrel with me on silly issues and after a few hours or, in certain issues, one or two days, we patched up our misunderstanding and joined with a sort of doubled love. Then, we felt as if we were a newly married couple! And this letter must be another prank of that silly girl, I thought. A successful marriage requires that you fall in love many times, always with the same person, as Mignon McLaughlin says. But how could I be sure about this time?

"I felt darkness piling up in my eyes. The letter was gaining more and more weight in my hand and I tried to hold it tightly in my hands. I tried to believe that it was a fake letter! But this handwriting, it is unmistakably Geetha's; I could recognize it even in the dim light. Anywhere and everywhere I could recognize her beautiful handwriting, each and every letter with its peculiarities, and my mind tried to cop up with the fact that it was Geetha's letter. But within a few days, how she could transform herself into a strange creature, I wondered. Even a chameleon would take a few seconds to camouflage!

"Yes! Somebody, perhaps, is blackmailing her! 'Write like

this or I'll shoot you!' or something like that! In that case, she is in danger. Then, the life of my daughter is also in danger! All of them are under some kind of threat! Oh, God! All these days I was there and no one dared do such a thing! And, now, just as I was away for a few days, and thousands of miles away in another continent, these blackmailers snatched the opportunity and entered my house! I must ring the police! Or it's better, to first try the house, and sense the danger!

"I tried the mobile. No sound for a few seconds, and then a sort of grumbling and, then the voice 'Hello!' Sure it's the voice of my Geetha!

"I could recognize her voice, even in its most inaudible manner! I heaved a sigh of relief! For a moment, I could not say a word. Again the voice came, now it was very clear and free from disturbances.

"Er....! Well! What's it? What happened there? Geetha, are you there? It's me...Rajesh!

"'Oh! It's you! Well! It means you got my letter! Nothing more to say! Goodbye!'

"She hung up the phone, for the click sound of the handset sent a bomb-blast into my ears! I felt the darkness rush into my brain, and I tried to clutch on the wall, but slipped down. Someway I sat akimbo on the floor. I did not know what was happening to me!

"Does it mean that the world's coming to an end? Does it mean that the sky has rolled off like a sheet of paper and the stars lost their grip in the sky, and are falling one by one on my head? I felt my head reeling!

"I breathed heavily, I felt as if I was not getting sufficient oxygen. My shivering fingers groped for the letter that had fallen down somewhere on the floor. I sat there completely blank, no feelings of senses, in a sort of vacuity!

"I heard the rumbling of thunder, up above my head, somewhere in the African sky! It's not the rainy season here, I thought. A few drops began pit-patting on the tin-roof of my house with a frightening sound! It must be hailstones, I thought. Let the hail crush this house, so that it can fall on me and shatter my head into pieces!

"It's all going to end. All the sweet dreams of a retired life are shattered and disappeared into thin air. No more hopes of a peaceful old age under the protection and care of a patient wife! No more loving and constant enquiries about health and illness from the daughter, or the lisping voice of the grandchildren! All vanished like the flash of a rainbow!

"Never could I patch up the broken strings of life! Why did it all end up like this? The long, restless life for the last twenty-five years! All the helter-skelter running to make both ends meet! And the fond hopes of a retired life! The lovely wife, the loving grandchildren, a few cents of land and the shelter of a beautiful house – all disappeared within the wink of an eye! A peaceful life, managing the needs of everyday life, a little luxury of a puff of a cigarette or a few pegs of brandy once in a while, and the little savings to give as pocket-money to grandchildren – all finished within a snap of the fingers! And it's too late to begin again! Too tired even to think of a new beginning! How true it was when the great writer Leo Tolstoy said: 'The only absolute knowledge attainable by man is that life is meaningless!'

"It was really a race and never did I try to look back! Only going forward! Why should I turn back if everything was intact at home? I had complete confidence in myself, complete confidence in my wife and child, and then, why should I look back? Run forward and grab success in life! I had gone far ahead that I could not realize that my home was on fire! The flames were gutting down my sweet home, together with my faithful wife and innocent child!

"Where did this all start? Where did I tumble on the stone, slipped and fell down flat on the ground, never to be returned to the starting point? Was I a total failure as a husband and as a father? It's all clear like daylight! Mine is a life failed to the core! Or is it a life defeated, if so, by whom? I was immersed in deep thought.

"I managed to climb into the bed. The wrinkled letter was in the fist of my right hand. I wished to read the letter once again to see whether it was really written by Geetha. But I hadn't the courage or equanimity to open it again! Slowly I fell into a heavy-some sleep, keeping my wife's letter, resting on my heaving hairy chest, where once she had rested her face, close to my heart! I slipped down and down into a sound sleep, hearing the lullaby, hummed by the malaria-carriers of Africa....!

"I woke up from my sleep as if I had seen some nightmare! I switched on the light. I was sweating all over even though cold wind was blowing outside. My heart was palpitating and I heard the beating of my heart drumming in my ears! For a second, I felt darkness creeping into my eyes and a sort of dizziness engrossing me. I tried to rest my head on the pillow but it was all wet and cold with my sweat. I wondered what was happening to me. Was it some kind of a blood-clot in the arteries or a mild stroke in the brain?

"Geetha's letter was lying on the bed; perhaps, her letter would have raised the level of my blood pressure! Her letter was more than a shock I could suffer. Of course, shocks were not new to me; I had survived at least three other fatal shocks in my life! But through your letter, my dear Geetha, you gave me a real fatal shock, an unexpected blow that shattered even the very foundation of my existence! I wished to cry aloud or shout so that my wife Geetha could hear my voice.

"Next morning I went to the university, as usual, but I could not engage any classes. My mind was going out of my control. By evening, I went for my usual walk but my legs led me to the banks of Lake Tana, and I sat there watching the waves. The dark clouds which I saw on the previous evening might have melted down into showers. The waves were beating against the volcanic rocks scattered by the force of nature on the shores of the lake. I watched the rocks carefully. They were perforated rocks, created in the normal course of some volcanic eruption, and the waves were trying to strain through them. Can these hard rocks absorb the coolness and freshness of the blue lake? Or can these cold waves strain through the hard rocks? I thought.

"These waves are the waves that blow against my heart. And my heart is hardened, like these volcanic stones, in the passage of time, experiencing all the stresses and tensions of a life! If only my heart were perforated so that the coolness of these waves could pass through it! I looked vacantly into the lake. How rigid and opaque is my heart, it could not allow even any poetic fancies and fantasies to pass through it.

"Every heart, like these rocks, may not be so opaque; some must be transparent and porous, allowing the rays of light, the coolness of the water and the notes of natural music to pass through them! Otherwise, life will be so hard that one cannot survive the test of years! Yes! I must learn to survive the beatings of all the strong waves against my life. I tried to relax myself, sitting on a volcanic rock, watching the evening sun setting in the western horizon, beyond the vast Lake Tana.

"I felt difficulty in forgetting everything about my wife's letter and relax there on the banks of Lake Tana. I wished to write to my wife, all about my life. Or I must write everything in a diary and, later, send it to her! Or, at least, she could read it after my death, if it happened earlier! Yet, my dear Geetha, I couldn't ignore or forget the shock your letter had given me!

"I remember the first shock I received in my life, in December 1977, years before I met you and received you into my life. Then, I was a journalist in the north-eastern States of India. After seeing the unique 'sunrise' from Tiger Hill in

Darjeeling, I went to the Deer Park, with my friend Rajendra Bhandari, a Nepali young man, to interview the great Sherpa Tenzing Norgay who, together with Edmond Hillary, conquered Mount Everest for the first time.

"We met Tenzing, wearing an ivory-colored suit and a scarecrow hat of the same color, sitting on a chair in front of the Mountaineering Club. During the interview, I asked him, 'Who reached the summit of Everest first, you or Hillary?'

"He laughed aloud and said, 'Of course, it was Hillary!'

"In those days, many people believed that it would be Tenzing who reached the summit first, because he was a resident of the mountainous areas, more accustomed to high altitudes, than Hillary. I asked him again with the cunningness of a journalist, we studied in our schools that both of you reached the summit at the same time. But how could two persons step together on the summit of a mountain?

"'That also is possible!' He laughed aloud with the simplicity of a child and continued, 'I told you, it was Hillary who reached the summit first!'

"In fact, Tenzing was only a 'sherpa', a person who carried things of the mountaineer, employed by Hillary. And Hillary had every legal right to claim his success. I wished to touch the feet of that great man, in our Indian fashion, who was still sincere and humble in allowing his former employer to take all the credit of that great adventure!

"From the Mountaineering Club building, I moved towards the Deer Park, together with Rajendra. I was actually in the thrill of meeting Tenzing Norgay, my childhood hero! We saw a few deer standing in flocks due to the severe cold. Then we walked towards another part of the park named Rose Garden, a wonderful world of roses blooming with flowers of a hundred different hues!

"It was early morning and no one else was there except Rajendra and me. Suddenly, Rajendra turned towards me and asked, 'Why do these Indian dogs come to this part of our country? This is our Gorkha Land, and you bloody Indian dogs snatch away all our employment opportunities! Every Indian dog here should be killed, only then, we could live peacefully!'

"I was shocked to the core; I looked into his eyes; I found the cruelty of a wild animal stagnant in those eyes! I realized that he was mad and he was planning to kill me! If he had killed me in that deserted place, nobody would be found guilty! Perhaps, the news-dailies would bring a snippet captioned 'Journalist killed: Gorkha Land extremists suspected.'

"Supporting his point with a smile, I walked fast towards the Club where I could find some people. Rajendra was following me and I started running towards the Club. I reached there and saw many young mountaineers basking under the hot sun. With a long sigh of relief, I looked back and saw him standing silhouetted against the blue sky, about fifty meters away from the Club building, like a lion disappointed at the unexpected escape of its prey! I managed to reach the house of my colleagues, Jeeth Raika and Arun Thapa, and took the evening bus to my newspaper office, saying 'goodbye' to Darjeeling.

"Of course, later Jeeth Raika and Arun Thapa begged my pardon and said, 'Dear George! We're really sorry! We forgot to tell you that he had been suffering from such fits on certain occasions! Please do forgive us!' I forgave them, but I could never forget that incident, because it gave me such a shock that would last throughout my life!

"The second fatal shock was from you, my dear, and you might have forgotten about it. How could I forget it as it was for the first time you behaved in such a hysterical manner? It was in November 1987 when we were living in a rented house in the city, as my brother evicted us from his house. Of course, you were angry towards my parents, brothers and sister, and every other person who put our life in such a dilemma. My income was very small and the expense of the family including the rent was too high. As usual, I never irritated you with financial problems; I managed it somehow in my own way.

"It was noon-time and you were in the fits of some sort of hysteria. After a few exchanges of hot words, you started abusing my mother who had suffered a lot in bringing up her children and you even addressed her as 'that littered-woman of yours.' It was intolerable for me that I gave a slap on your face, of course, not with all my strength! Though it was a light warning, I felt guilty about it afterwards, for it was quite unbecoming of an educated person like me. But you reacted in the most horrible manner; you became fiendish; you took the scissors from the sewing machine and struck me at the back of my head! I felt blood oozing out of the wound and I went out of the house silently!

"I soaked my handkerchief in cold water and pressed it to the wound so that the flow of blood stopped after a while. I walked along the street towards the center of the city, silently crying all the way and cursing my fate to live with a hysteric! That was the first day in which I came home over-drunk!

"Well! After that incident, I never raised my hand to punish you in a similar manner. It was not because you did not repeat the same insulting words against my mother; I knew that you were incorrigible! It was not because I was afraid of the sharpness of your scissors, I would rather prefer death by your hands! I realized that no one could correct a self-assertive person, especially a mentally perverted person! Even if you put a fool in the mortar and pound, that person would never leave the foolishness! In fact, my religion and community had made me a coward; I wanted to live as a man who married only once in his life.

"I remembered the words of Goity, the Hamar girl, in Fikeremarkos's novel *The Land of the Yellow Bull,* when her husband finds it 'difficult to beat a lover,' she retorts, 'That bastard coward! He let me pass by it peace as I foresaw instead of whipping me; I am rather the husband and he is the wife!' It is said that the Hamar women in Ethiopia respect only those husbands who flog them regularly. A husband who ignores beating his wife is considered a coward or a female! And see how a European woman in the novel, Charlotte Alfred, reacts, 'Only a proud and tough man could lash to tame her and ride with her love.' Such punishments increased their love and desire for sex, they believe! Even they think that a man without premarital sex with many women is not a man but merely a woman. If a man continues his extramarital sex, the women are ready to become his third or fourth wife!

"You might have heard the story of that poor woman, Maria, who suffered every day her husband's blows on her back when he returned from the toddy shop! Every day by 10 pm you could hear her shrieking 'Ooyiow' following her husband's fist falling on her back 'bhum…bhum,' and this continued for years! One day her husband died and the neighbors heaved sighs of relief thinking that the poor woman had overcome the torture of her husband! But on the same evening by 10 pm the neighbors heard the same sounds 'Bhum…bhum' and 'Ooyiow' and they came out to see what was going on! The widow was throwing a coconut up into the air and was catching it on her back! She said that she could not sleep without a few blows on her back! See! How strange is the relationship between a husband and a wife!

"Perhaps, my dear, my love and tolerance might have effeminated me in your eyes! Of course, you violently reacted because of the first shock but, later, might have recognized that I was 'a proud and tough man!' The so-called great Indian culture has made our men and women mere cowards! Here, in this land of the hermits, only the anti-social elements could survive!

"Despite all our civilized learning, there are always certain tribal elements lurking in our psyche. It is a fact that there are women who love to be punished by their husbands! Such punitive measures are like mild shock treatments given to mental patients. Of course, wives also would resort to similar measures against their husbands and, thus, great writers like Tolstoy are created! But, unfortunately, my dear, the shock you gave me on that day was so unexpected that, thereafter, I could not take you to the innermost part of my heart!

"Again after a decade, it was in September 1997, that I received my third fatal shock. I was walking along the riverside with your uncle, Junkuson, whom I loved and respected like my own father. In a very low tone he talked to me and, at first, I could not understand what that old man was driving at! He told me in a pleading voice, 'My wife is like your own mother! She is too old for you! Why do you run after her? Please leave her alone! God will not forgive such sins!'

"I looked into his eyes, for I could not believe my own ears! His eyes seemed begging to me with an expression of utter helplessness! Tears began to flow from my eyes and I ran away from his presence. For many months, I could not forget that innocent, pleading expression on his face! If my wife or somebody else had warned me about his fits of paranoia, I would not have felt such a deep shock! People generally try to keep the psychiatric problems faced by themselves or by their relatives a secret! And they don't know that such hiding of facts will only complicate the situation!

"Sometimes, I am forced to believe that paranoia is hereditary, and your uncle's illness may not be a coincidence! Otherwise, how could it affect you too! Your behavior at times reflects the symptoms of paranoia! Perhaps the unexpected changes in your attitudes and your depressed moods are surely the outcome of such an illness! In fact, I am a bit late to realize such strange abnormalities in you; I thought of them as normal dispositions of women in general!

"Yes! Psychiatric problems, from hysteria to madness, are the greatest tragedy in human life! When a person loses his or her senses and becomes mentally abnormal, no one can predict to what extent he or she will go! Such persons deserve immediate medical treatment rather than sympathy. Of course, people become mentally abnormal due to hereditary, physical or ideological reasons! In the case of hereditary reasons, one can't help it, it's merely part of fate! Physical reasons include a tumor in the brain or some other blood-clotting in certain veins. Mental abnormality resulting from addiction to drugs, narcotics and alcohol can also be added to physical reasons.

"But the most dangerous mental abnormality is caused by ideological reasons! I must say from my experience that blind belief in a particular creed or theory, whether it is racial, religious, political or cultural, will lead to the abnormality of the mind. Theories like the superiority of the Aryan race are capable of creating many Hitlers! Religions give birth to fanatics and fundamentalists; the believers turn extremists, especially, when they cannot rationally or scientifically prove their beliefs! Many people are tempted to accept mere superstitions as philosophy as they have been propagated in the name of God!

"Blind belief in certain political systems and cultural practices will also lead us to mental perversions. Theories of male domination and feminism can tempt individuals to behave abnormally. It is always safe to keep a distance from all these so-called principles, dogmas and theories; for we must realize that all of them are different tactics cleverly employed for the domination of a group or of an individual over another.

"It is generally believed that it is the mind that controls the body, but the mind varies according to the individual concerned. Doesn't it mean that the body is controlling the mind? In fact, the mind-set is formed by the body-set. For example, a person who suffers from lung diseases will be a hot tempered one. Or a person who suffers from stomach or intestine diseases will be restless to the core. Such people will show symptoms of stress, tension and depression. Of course, you suffered from some chronicle illness of the intestine and, my dear Geetha, which might be the cause of this sudden change in you. I really feel sympathy towards you and consider your illness as part of your fate and of mine!

"My thoughts are going wayward, my dear Geetha! I don't know to which category you belong! Does your problem relate to hereditary reasons or to physical reasons or to ideological reasons? Perhaps, all of them work together in your personality! Yet your innocent face appears in the mirror of my mind. Are you really abnormal? You might be influenced by the whims and fancies of some feminists! Even Adrian Rich, after a period of feminist-hangama, lived happily with her husband and children! If so, why can't you?

"Each sentence in your letter is engraved in my brain; they were so deeply carved into my heart that I failed to erase them. In your letter you blamed me and said, 'You made me a mental patient! I had to take medicine for depression secretly just because of you!'

"Does this mean that you knew your problem and you cleverly hid it from me? I never expected that you have been suffering from such real problems! I thought that you might have written that letter in the fit of anger or disappointment, for such hysterical reactions were quite common among women, and men never took them seriously! And now I understand your problem, you cook up stories only to defeat me!

"All these years, I thought that I was a good husband! What a fool I was! What do you know about what was going on in the mind of your wife? Soil and woman will smile, as our proverb says. When the farmer works hard on the soil, expecting good harvest, the soil smiles, mocking at the foolish farmer who does not know that drought or flood will destroy his dreams! And

142

woman smiles when you take her child in your arms and say, 'Oh, my child' for she only knows whose child it is! If I failed as a husband, there is no meaning for my life. Death is the only solution!

"Every unexpected death is an accident or a coincidence and every expected death is a welcomed one or a suicide. About accidental deaths, one cannot do anything and let it be left to fate. And fate always is very cruel! Fate was too cruel to me that only through my death, I can take revenge!

"Welcomed deaths are suicides. And suicides are related to cowardice! Yet suicides are either due to a physical or mental attempt of the person concerned. And they are the blessings of fate! For example, an aged person who suffers from all kinds of illnesses wishes to die and his death is what he desired. Some others who feel themselves at the end of their tether wish to die and they do physical attempts to die. Both are one and the same!

"Hence, if a person who lived a major part of his family life quite unsuccessfully or his success was not at all recognized by his wife and children wished to meet a normal death, it would be a desired death!

"Why should I live? Why shouldn't I die? I was brooding over the mysteries of life and death. One thinks that one has gained a lot in life and attained everything a human life could bring! One fine morning, he gets the information that he has been living in a make-believe world and his life was actually a total failure. In such cases, there is no excuse for him to prolong his life. He desires death and fate sanctions his wish. Well, all's well that ends well!

"I wished to write to Geetha, 'You won't see me alive again. You will be happy when you see me when I reach home in a coffin unexpectedly.' I thought first that it would be a shock for her. But after deliberation, I decided not to give her such hopes! She would be happy of getting relieved off my grip of a married life! She would also cry like Mrs. Mallard, the protagonist in Kate Chopin's short story, *The Story of an Hour*, when she heard the news of her husband's death in a train accident, 'Free! Body and soul free!' But can Geetha be so cruel to be so? Only God knows her inner heart. Even God couldn't predict what was happening in a perverted mind! All these twenty-five years, I couldn't understand what was going on in her mind! And how true is when the poet wondered, 'Is there a person in the whole world who saw the real heart of a woman?'

"A life without a real life is equivalent to death! And your life, which you nurtured and brought up all through these years of your youth has shattered to pieces and there is no life left for you, I thought. And there is no time left for you to re-start everything, perhaps, rectifying your mistakes and refilling the gaps you made, not deliberately but in good faith that everything you did was good for the family. And who knew that everything would be turned upside down, just by a letter reaching you from your wife! It's all your unchangeable fate! A life wasted and only fit to be thrown into the dustbin, I thought.

"I glanced at her letter once again. She wrote the letter in an uncontrollable manner, like a fiction writer crazy with the fits of imagination! Of course, Geetha, you were always in a world of unproductive imagination! You always lived in a world of useless fantasy and of non-creative dreams! I recall the words of Daniel, the protagonist in Monica Dickens's *Flowers on the Grass*, 'You're living in a dream world and calling it reality; God, if this is what life is really like, give me death.'

"You loved fondling with your illusions! You got a sort of sadistic pleasure while cooking up false stories about me! Of course, illusion is the first of all pleasures, as Oscar Wilde once said. You imagined untrue things about me to vitiate and humiliate me in your mind and enjoyed it as a pastime by deceiving yourself! Of course, everything you can imagine is real, as Pablo Picasso said, and you consciously tried to turn your illusions real!

"Oh, Geetha! Will you please stop this nonsense! My mind cried in silence. It is not good to abuse me like this, as you used to do throughout our married life! Then, I was staying with you and I forgave and ignored your abuse because I knew your mind, and I loved you so much! But now, as I live far away from you, in this lonely place, without any sort of access to your real presence, you should not have written like this! There's a limit for a person's patience! Please, Geetha! I beg you, not to test my patience! My mind pleaded in silence. You see, dear! One can't go on like this forever!

"Your letter, my dear Geetha, was a flood of complaints and accusations leveled against me and my personality, and I would be drowned in that quicksand! Storing all these murky and nefarious thoughts in your heart, how could you live with me sharing my body and mind? Were you a disguised monster or a vampire with whom I had to spend my nights innocently? How could you smile at me keeping all these sinister ideas hidden at the depth of your conscience?

"But, remember, all these years you never told me about any one of them! I was neither aware of them nor they passed my notice! In fact, I was quite innocent about them. If you had brought them into my notice earlier, I would have rectified them or found a solution for them. You never gave me a warning; you never gave me a chance to see to them! Perhaps, you were keeping all of them in your mind to get a better opportunity to shatter my whole life! Even God would not pardon you because it was a sin against your own soul!

"Perhaps, this was the right time to punish one's husband! I was retired before I came to Ethiopia and I had authorized you to all my bank accounts and pension benefits! As a homemaker you never got any monthly salary, you had to ask me even for your petty expenses, and I thought it would be an exciting experience for you to draw money every month! Of course, even if I died, you would get half of my pension every month without any fault!

"I always believed that I had been safe with the members of my family, especially with my wife, until your letter, through which you opened your real self, reached me. To be frank, your letter shattered all my beliefs and confidence in everything and everybody! There are sadists in the world; of course, they include sadist husbands and sadist wives. I never expected that my wife would be one among that group! And that miserable fate of a husband would be on my head!

"Geetha! Your reaction towards my sincerity was so negative that there is no room left for me for further explanations! You humiliated me to the core of my life! Your accusations were not mere complaints! You actually struck at the root of my moral existence, my very entity! As far as my conscience is concerned, I have been perfect in my moral beliefs and practices. I always respected the voice of my conscience and never acted against it. And I have no regrets about my ways of life.

"Are you living all these years with me like a slave? How did this idea enter into your mind? Of course, you were a homemaker or a housewife as we used to say in India. But you were the mistress of the house and I never interfered with your reasonable rights!

"If you had felt your life slavish, why you did not tell me frankly your problems? Did I ever curtail your freedom? Even if so, why you did not disclose the secrets of your heart to me? As Martin Luther King Junior said, 'Freedom is never voluntarily given by the oppressor; it must be demanded by the oppressed.' I foolishly believed that you had been enjoying your family life! And that was my mistake!

"But the ideology of slavery is entirely different, my dear! If women were suppressed by men, the reason was that women conveniently preferred to that way of life! In our tradition, the head of the family was the husband and he took decisions in consultation with his wife, though mostly the decision was that of the wife and the husband pretended that it was his!

"There was a time, in Ancient Egypt, when the slaves fought each other in order to get the chance of to be buried alive with the dead body of the Pharaoh! The landlords under the Zamindari system never killed their tenants directly but sent other tenants to kill those tenants who opposed him! During the British Raj, the English people controlled Indians with the help of those Indians who too were slaves like others! But there was not even a single occasion in which I dishonored your individuality as a woman!

"Whatever I did during all these years were true to my conscience and, I believe, they were not against the will of God. And I tolerated your humiliations, as I believed in the mercy of God. But now, sitting in this far-off place, I feel your perverted thinking so unbearable that I fail to tolerate it. Of course, I tried hard to ignore it for the sake of my deep love towards you and to my only daughter. But how could you, taking up the rights of a wife, continue to harass me like this!

"Of course, we live in a world of women's empowerment and there are new laws to protect the rights of women and prevent torture against them! And men live in a world of hypocrisy and vanity, in their own make-believe world of male domination in which to disclose his suffering and torture is considered a shame! But that does not mean you can allege any kind of nonsense against me, my dear!

"In your letter, Geetha, you mentioned with utter disgust about our last night, the night before my flight to this African country! How could you call it our last night, my dear? Does it mean that you have taken the final decision? Was it really our last night? God forbid!

"Like the first night in the married life of a person, the last night also remains ever green in his or her mind, isn't it? About my first night, I could only remember that it was the first time in my life that a strange girl was sleeping with me on the same bed! That was enough for me to remember it throughout my life!

"But how can I forget the so-called last night, the night of bidding farewell to you, Geetha, just before coming over to this alien land! In fact, it was not a full night but the small hours of the day, it might be 2 am, as you had mentioned in your letter.

"I felt rejuvenated, as those moments recycled in my mind. I was in the study room upstairs, waiting restlessly for her movements in the bedroom. Every moment seemed longer and longer, and as I could not waste time, for early morning we had to go to the airport, I was engaged in the last minute packing of my inevitable books and papers which were highly essential for preparing my lessons in the university where I got the appointment.

"Of course, a week ago, I started packing my travel bag by placing books and other necessary items in it to avoid the last minute hurry-burry, but on that evening my brother Anish, who was more experienced in foreign travel came 'to tie up the bag,' carelessly removed most of the things out of the bag formally declaring that the bag, according to our old bath-scale, weighed more than to be carried in a plane; the maximum weight allowed in a King Fisher domestic flight was only twenty-five kilograms, as Malvi the travel agent who arranged my air-ticket warned.

"From the thrown out things, I had to select a few books and, of course, medicines which I could not leave at home, and to replace them in the bag. I also had to write one or two letters which should be mailed in India itself, for I did not know whether I could send them fast from that African country.

"But, all the time, my ears were sharp towards the bedroom where I expected you, my dear Geetha, at any moment. It was only after midnight that Anish and his family left the house. I heard the sound of utensils in the sink you were washing. Of course, a lot of plates and glasses, aluminum vessels and their lids, pressure cooker and rice-pot – all had to be washed. And it was your habit that you never went to bed without cleaning the daily used vessels, and then sweeping the kitchen or scrubbing the floor, and you did not care how much time it took! And I knew that you could be a model for any housewife in the matter of cleanliness of the kitchen and neatness of the house in general.

"Having finished my packing, I came down the stairs and cast a look at you. I knew that it would take at least half an hour more for you to complete your dish washing! I went up once again to my study and quickly looked into some unfinished work. I had to send an urgent letter to a friend and, so, I started writing it.

"'It was 2 am when you completed the letter and came to the bedroom,' you wrote in your letter. But I started writing the letter because you had not come into the bedroom! Otherwise I would have avoided the letter writing. No! Now I remember! It must be the letter for Prof. B. Gupta to whom I had to send a Demand Draft as subscription to his journal, and if I had not sent it, who would send it? And the DD would be outdated by the time I returned from Africa! As I had started the writing, shouldn't I finish it? Of course, I completed it but it took some more time to find the stamps kept in the useless jewel-box, and then the tube of gum to fix the stamps and the flap of the cover, and then to write the address on the cover!

"Soon I heard your steps in the bedroom. You were shaking the dust off the bed-sheet and were spreading it on the bed, as you used to do before going to sleep. With all the hurriedness I completed my work because I knew your habit, once you were in the bedroom; you went to the bed, pulled the blanket over your head, extended your hand out to put off the light and started sleeping or pretended to be sleeping! I was sweating with my work so fast completed; because I knew that I should hurry down to spend the last night with my wife, the last one before my flight to Africa.

"In fact, I came down to the bedroom, without writing the address on the letter, to see whether you were ready to sleep. But then you had entered the bathroom and I heard you brushing your teeth. I thought of saving two or three minutes, by that I could run upstairs and complete the address. I went up and completed the writing within seconds and ran downstairs.

"Well! I was not sure about the time for I did not care in that situation to check the time, the whole night was ours, I thought. I was never punctual in my life, and I did not consider punctuality as a great principle in human life! There are certain people who think of punctuality as something great! But if they want to keep punctuality, undoubtedly, they must have set aside or avoided certain other very important programs. How can I keep things aside as I have to attend a lot of urgent work which I cannot postpone to another day?

"I believe that punctuality is only for those selfish and heartless fools who are systematic in avoiding most of the work that come their way, just for the sake of punctuality! They claim it as a great credit. But for them too, things may not go as they imagine, and sometimes even Mr. Deesikay, the great publisher in our native town, a synonym for punctuality, himself was late for meetings at Darsana Auditorium due to a flat tire or a procession of some political party that blocked all the traffic into a standstill!

"Perhaps I had taken about five minutes! Within those few minutes, you had gone to the bed and covered your head with the blanket, as usual, as if you were trying to avoid me! And I had to use some force to take the blanket off your face. From your face, I realized that the night was spoiled, for you never knew how to utilize properly the free time of your busy husband!

"Well! There was some mistakes on my part too, it would have been better if I stood near you in the kitchen while you cleaned the plates and glasses; instead I was engaged in writing letters! 'I am sorry, my dear! I am very sorry!' I said in a polite manner. If it was on some other day, I would not have begged to you that much! But that being a day before my trip to Africa, I must stoop to any level! I thought.

"Of course, I had some selfish motive to bring you to lovemaking! Whatever be the previous nights in our life, this night must be remembered for at least a year! Mainly because I could feel your real warmth only after about ten months and I should keep that night's experience in my memory throughout that period! Of course, after the tedious work of the day, both of us were too tired for an amorous act and, yet we managed to have it, with a half heart! Instead of an enjoyable night, we felt it a boring and tiresome night, and we started sleeping; though even without lovemaking, we could have slept peacefully!

"It is natural that after an amorous act, one might feel that it was not necessary, but by the next morning some faint memory of it might remain in the mind of the concerned as a refreshing event! But in your memory it was a black night which you could think in its worst form! But now my confusion is what happened to you later in my absence!

"Just after a week of my travel, how could you think of that wonderful night in a negative way? How could a wife complain about the failure of a sexual act in which both the persons were equally responsible? Was it not an act of giving, taking and sharing? Perhaps, our minds were travelling in two different directions!

"Well! I remember it as the submission of a heartless woman; there was a sort of vacuity in your mind! In similar situations, those who did not know about the proper utilization of the available time and place would feel like that! Throughout the night, you were thinking of my late coming to the bedroom and, then, how could you enjoy the real presence of your husband! You thought only about the time '2 am' and nothing more about the night! What a silly woman you are!

"The waves in the lake have subsided except for the glittering of the ripples. I stood up and went to my room. I wanted to take a deep sleep forgetting everything about Geetha's letter. But goddess sleep seemed to be angry with me or she was waiting hesitating outside my bedroom like a new bride! I wished to remind Geetha about our first meeting, for no woman could forget such delicate moments in one's life! And writing is the only way to pass my sleepless night!

"My dear Geetha! You don't know how much I was sentimentally attached to you from the very moment of our first meeting. It might be a part of my eccentricity of a future writer that I had a peculiar notion in mind about my wife. I believed that I could easily recognize my rib-bone, at any moment! Of course, I saw many girls, as our custom and tradition demanded, but I could not find my future wife in them.

"At first, I used to go to see girls with my relatives in a rented car with all the pomposity of a ceremony of 'seeing the girl!' In certain cases, my father and brother even insisted that I marry the one we had seen but I could not marry a girl who was not tallying with that image of the dream-girl in my mind. They were all fed up with me, as my young brother himself was in a hurry to marry, and I began to think that the girl of my dreams was not yet born!

"Then, the proposal of your case came, and half-heartedly, I came to see you. Without any showing-off, without the accompaniment of relatives, without any taxi car, I came to your house all alone by a line-bus and walked all the way to your house, breaking the usual formalities of 'seeing a girl!' I might have thought that if I had not liked the girl, I could keep it a secret from my relatives!

"I was restless in your house, for it was evening and I

wanted to return home as early as possible. I wanted only a glimpse of the girl to make sure whether she would be mine or not! Your grandmother came and talked to me, your mother came and talked to me and I cursed myself for not bringing any other relatives with me! At last, you came with a cup of tea!

"I saw you and a flash passed through my mind; I recognized my lost rib-bone, my only wife and partner in my future life! In fact, I did not see your face properly, I saw only your fingers on your hands that carried the cup of tea, but I could recognize my own body by seeing any part of it! I knew that you were mine, the only person to complete my life, the partner for whom I had waited all these years. I knew that I should not lose you by chance and I decided to make you mine at any cost. Could one allow some others to cut off a part of one's body and go away like that! I found you and my heart recognized you, for you were my dream-girl, the image of a strange girl who had been haunting me all these years in my dreams, without showing your face clearly, from the day of my maturity onwards!

"A few days before our engagement, I asked you to come with your mother to a famous temple a few kilometers away from your house. In fact, I wished to speak to you openly and freely whether you agreed to marry me with a full conscience or not. I knew that, as an educated girl, you would have your own ideas, concepts or preferences concerning marriage. I wanted to know whether you gave consent for this marriage under the compulsion of your mother and relatives or not.

"I came with my sister to the temple and, about two hundred meters away from the temple, I saw you standing at the entrance of the temple compound. Seeing a flash of smile on my face, my sister looked towards you. She had not seen you or even your photograph, but from a far distance, she could recognize my choice and she said, 'Brother, at last you got the girl of your dreams; no doubt, your selection is excellent!'

"I talked to you and I understood that your consent to the marriage was not under any pressure from the members of your family, but it was at your own will. As a person with a 'clean-heart', I did not like to marry a girl who had once given her heart to someone else. Of course, it was very difficult to get such girls in these modern days, but I wished to try my luck. And you conquered my heart; I never thought about another girl, before or after, to come into my life. I remembered the Tamil saying, 'Kidachongele kattikirtavide; pudichavale kattikirth,' marry the girl whom you like and not the girl whom you get!

"Then, your uncles and brother came to my house and were satisfied with my family. It was our custom that when a bride came to the husband's house, she should bring her father's share which gave her equal rights in the family. Usually the Christians in the southern part of Central Kerala hesitated to give girls their proper share and tried to keep it for the boys. My father declared that we should not be cheated by your uncles! But my mother said, 'Don't bargain for her share; here's a girl liked by our son; let him marry her whether they give her share or not!' I only wished that my wife should not come to my house like a beggar-maid so that my brothers would laugh at her. As Shakespeare said, '…worthless peasants bargain for their wives as market men for oxen, sheep, or horse,' and I could not stoop to that level! Of course, your uncles tried to reduce the amount to the lowest level and my father agreed to the amount they suggested.

"Of course, my house was in a village and it created certain problems for you. It was natural that you felt much inconvenience in a house to which you were new. As it was part of our tradition, nobody bothered about the sentiments of the brides. Gradually, they used to adjust with the new surroundings in their husband's house. Even for many weeks after our wedding, you could not adjust neither with the members of my family nor with the environment there.

"I realized your difficulties and allowed you to spend more days with your mother. You felt that my mother was dominating over me and your sense of possessiveness could not tolerate it. As a woman who had been managing my family even in the absence of my father who had to work thousands of miles away from the house, she had the right to supervise everything, or she expected so. Of course, as her eldest son, she might have showed a bit more affection towards me, and you hated even that!

"Did you expect that once a man was married, he should 'leave his father and mother and cleave to his wife,' as it was said in the Bible? Of course, what happens in our tradition is that 'she leaves her father and mother and cleaves to her husband!' What is said in the Scripture is only a general truth! And I could not think of it as a directive principle! So, when you insisted to continue your studies, though it was expensive for me as I had to spend much money on travel, I allowed you to do so. I also thought that it would be a good outing for you, to be away from the loneliness of my remote country house.

"Moreover, adding fuel to the fire, I got an appointment as lecturer in a college in the city, with a one hour journey from our house. I had to go early and come back late. But I was happy to note that you had somehow adjusted with the household works. When you began to continue your studies in the same city, I thought that you would be very happy as we could go together! But I was in a fool's paradise, as it is clear from your letter.

"You wrote in your letter, 'Even in those early days of our marriage, you did not like to walk with me or sit together on the same seat of the bus. It was because you were at least eight years older than me.' Strange are your complaints, my dear Geetha, and you made them after living together for about twenty-five years! I appreciate your memory power, but you remember all the bitter experiences and not even a single sweet experience in our life! Funny, indeed!

"Your words take me back to those early days of our marriage, my dear. You were only twenty-one and I was twenty-eight and that much age difference between the bride and the bridegroom was quite natural in our community. Rather the difference was comparatively lesser in our case. Of course, you might be thinking of those classmates of yours who were engaged in calf love, and who, by chance, married and ended up in divorce! In our country, marriages among the matured people were only arranged with an age difference of five to ten years, and the male was always older, as you know.

"Well! You continued your studies in a college in the city where I was working as a teacher in another college. As a teacher, I always tried to be a model for others, especially for my students, who used to travel together with us in the bus. Of course, it might be my maturity of mind attributed by education and culture that prevented me from becoming an exhibitionist.

"In fact, ours is a sexually jealous society, and the people never tolerated such exhibitionists. When a man and a woman sat together in a public transport bus, even if they were husband and wife, other passengers felt jealous of them, and made vicious comments about them. Indians always suffered from the poverty of sex! In European countries, even lovemaking in public places was ignored by others. But our society was not that much civilized or rather uncivilized. Perhaps, it was not a matter of civilization, because in African countries like Ethiopia, men and women walked in pairs hand in hand or kissed each other on the public road. But in our reserved society, even husbands and wives were not permitted by the so-called protectors of morality to walk holding each other's hand. The spectators used to make dirty comments about them, 'It seems they're going to fuck on the road itself,' or something like that!

"In the bus you were getting a student's concession ticket, and the bus conductors generally would not like such ticket holders to sit even with their husbands or wives. And as you know in our place, seats in the bus were reserved for women, and men sat on general seats. Despite many general seats vacant in the bus, on rare days, you always sat on the reserved seat so that I could not sit with you, and if by chance I sat near you, some ladies would enter the bus and ask me to vacate the seat. And you never sat on the general seat, giving me an opportunity to sit near you without any fear or tension that I should have to leave my seat at any moment.

"Of course, I always loved to walk with you. Don't you remember how we went to our family temple, walking the three kilometers from our house, along the muddy paths of our village? But I know that you think only about those weekdays on which we walked about a kilometer to the bus-stop, from where we took the bus to the city. The morning bus took forty-five to fifty minutes to reach the stop near my college and I had to sign my attendance ten minutes before 10 am. If only we got the 9 o'clock bus, I could reach the college somewhat on time. As a student, even if you were late, it would not make much difference or create any official problems for you, but my case was different.

"Don't you remember, my dear, that never could we complete our household works or take our breakfast sufficiently early so that we could walk to the bus-stop in a relaxed manner. Most often we were running to the bus-stop to get our 9 o'clock bus. Then, how could I walk with you, freely engaging in amorous talks? And in those days, you neither made any complaint nor reminded me of my impropriety, at least once, on my part. After all these years of our married life, now, you find fault with our age difference! As you could not complain about my physical fitness, you blamed my mental maturity! Even Boccaccio could not imagine such a trick from women!

"Years later, when a proposal came for our daughter, of course, she was only a final year student in the engineering college; you made an ugly remark in her presence, about the boy's age. You were giving me an indirect clever dig! You forgot that every word and every action of parents will create some inerasable marks in the heart of children.

"Every father will feel proud when a marriage proposal comes to his only daughter and, naturally, I too felt so! All of a sudden, I became too conscious of my duties as a responsible father and began to make plans for the marriage. I imagined my daughter standing with a bowed head, magnificently dressed as a bride, on the specially decorated stage in front of the shrine and its deity. And as I was standing behind her, all in a solemn mood, all my invitees impatiently waited in the temple premises for the early completion of the ceremonies! And the bridegroom in his elegant formal dress stood by the right side of my daughter waiting for the sign from the priest to tie the holy thread around her neck, and garlanded each other! And I heaved a long sigh of relief as every formality was done in an auspicious manner, and then, rushed to the hall for the reception and other formal procedures! But it was all merely a dream of a too excited father!

"Our daughter was twenty-two years of age and the proposed boy's age was twenty-nine, a difference of only seven years between them! And was not that difference of age quite a normal thing all over the world? But then my daughter's words came out, 'A man of twenty-nine can be a good father but not a good husband!' How silly she was! Generally it is said that we are all under parental influence and each of us falls in love with a mate who has qualities of our parents! Dr. Carl A. Whitaker once said, 'From early childhood on, each of us carried models for marriage - femininity, masculinity, motherhood, fatherhood, and the other family roles.' But here the case is just the opposite; here is a daughter who prefers a model just opposite of that of her parents!

"The society generally followed the system that the husband must be older or taller than the wife, though personally I believe that there is no problem if a woman marries a boy who is younger or shorter than her, as it happens in the United States where rich widows keep gigolos! Anybody can have sex with any person of any age but sex alone is not the basis of a marriage! However, to retain physiological happiness throughout life, it is always better to have a wife a few years younger to the husband!

"Marriage is a social institution and, therefore, the couples have to follow the rules of the society! In Ethiopia, the usual age difference among married couples is twenty years. They follow the age difference of Joseph and Mary, the parents of Jesus Christ! Men consider thirty-six as the right age for marriage and for the girls it is sixteen. It may be because of their tradition followed right from the days of Queen of Sheba. And of course they lead quite a happy married life. For a normal marriage, the boy should be older than the girl, and a difference of eight to ten years won't make any difference. But, of course, one cannot accept the system in the Islamic countries where aged men marry sixteen-year-old girls! Then what's wrong with my daughter?

"I understand it! It comes very clear to my mind! She expressed only the thought in the mind of her mother! She was hitting me below the belt! Were I not twenty-eight or twenty-nine when I married her mother who was twenty-one or twenty-two then! I remember, from that day of marriage onwards, wasn't she so unhappy about the age difference? Like mother, like daughter! Just incarnations of utter foolishness! But how could I tell my daughter that I am physically and mentally fit even now to have another marriage, a marriage with a young girl, if not possible in our country, in another country where such marriages are acceptable?

"Society gives us certain foolish notions and we become slaves to them! What else should I say? And the funniest thing is that you do not know that there are young men who are too old in their mind and body, and old men who are pretty young in their body and mind; and as a woman you could never understand such things! As the Red Indian jury, in Jack London's short story, says, 'Behold! Age is never as old as youth would measure it.'

"You complained in your letter, 'You never took the family for an outing, never for a picnic or an excursion.' What a shameful lie! You forgot that we never had sufficient money for such extravaganza! Though I never disclosed my financial problems to you, you could have very well realized the fact that during those days we had been running on thin ice! Every month we had to visit your house or my house, and such journeys cost a lot of money. Of course, such travels were not in a taxi-car which would cost my whole month's salary! But we enjoyed our small trips though they were in public transport buses, didn't we?

"In fact, you could never enjoy travels in a bus. Whenever you were in the bus, you looked anxiously through the window of the bus and sat on the seat as if you were expecting an accident at any moment! I noticed you sitting with the eyes of a timid rabbit or of a frightened deer! Always you kept silent in the bus, as if the driver would be careless! It might be the accident which had occurred to a bus in which you used to go to school; fortunately you were not in it on that fateful day, which led to the death of your teacher and a few other passengers including your friend's mother. There onwards, perhaps, you always traveled in a tense mood! Whatever the reason, you not only appreciated such travels but also made my journey miserable!

"Of course, in this modern world, everybody lives in an environment of stress and tension. There might not be a single person in this age who did not experience some sort of stress, at least, once in life. But most of the people knew resilience or adaptation and they managed to make their life happy. Of course, a small amount of stress is useful for a better life as it adds enthusiasm and courage to our personality. It also makes life spicy and vivacious giving real motivation in our pursuits. It keeps us always on our toes so that our life becomes adventurous. But I wonder, why after all these years of married life, you failed to adjust with me or adapt to a healthy life!

"I remember how we went for our honeymoon trip to a neighboring State, of course, in a public transport bus. At an odd bus-stand, the bus stopped and you wanted to go to the restroom. I showed you the place, you went there and returned but you did not tell me the fact that you could not use the toilet as it was dirty, lest I should have advised you to use it somehow as the bus would stop only after many hours. As you were controlling the 'hydraulic pressure' of urine for long hours, it led to urinary infection, causing severe pain for many weeks both in the house as well as in the hospital. This experience also might have made you frightened of bus journeys. And you never knew how to adjust with the situation!

"Fortunately, there was no sign of urinary infection while we moved here and there, visiting palaces and gardens, and staying at your uncle's house. It was our bad luck that we could not return together, as there was no train service due to the damage of rails caused by the sudden floods! And you were not ready to take the risk of traveling the whole distance back in a bus! I could not take more leave from my college, as it was my probation period, and so I returned alone in a bus and joined duty on time. You stayed in the house of your uncle for a week more, until the rails were repaired and the train service resumed. You came back by train and I was there to receive you, and I thought that everything was perfect.

"On the same evening you developed severe pain in your

stomach, both of us thought that it was due to some food poison, for which some local native medicine was given to you. It was impossible for us from our village to go to the hospital during the night and you agreed to go to hospital the next morning. After my strenuous work in the college and a long bus journey to the house, I was so tired that I fell into a deep sleep. You could not sleep due to severe stomach pain; it was not because of food poison as we thought but urinary infection, as later the doctor said. You told me later that you were rolling on the ground due to pain while I was peacefully enjoying my sleep! You did not try to wake me up; you decided to suffer alone! Our dog Tiger came to our room and licked your feet and expressed its concern and sympathy, you said later; and I had not had even that much love expressed by a mere dog!

"Next morning we went to the hospital and the doctor admitted you there for a week. Unfortunately, you developed allergy towards the tablets given to you, and they affected your beautiful teeth. Of course, you had such beautiful, pearl-like teeth, of which you were always proud, and when they were affected by the medicine, you began to hate me! Well! I must admit that I was responsible for your illness, and I could not blame it on any other person, as urinary infection is common, as doctors said, during the honeymoon period! I accepted my mistake though it was not a crime on my part as your spouse.

"You suffered a lot due to tooth decay, and every time suffered tooth pain, you cursed me! You were very sad about the loss of the power of your teeth, though I tried to console you in many ways. Later, you were very happy when I began to lose my hair, and as I became bald-headed, you cheerfully said, 'We're equal in our disappointments; I lost my teeth and you your hair!' In fact, these were situations in which we should make a joke of it and enjoy the funny acts of fate. Instead, you took it very seriously and without any sense of humor, used such matters only to belittle my personality!

"Again, you wrote in your letter, 'You never took me to a big hotel for some delicious food!' But did you ever ask me to go to a big hotel or to a particular hotel? Many a time I suggested such ideas and requested you to prepare a plan for outing but you always postponed it. You had problems with your stomach and you could not eat many of the food items served by the big hotels. Even ice-creams you did not take due to the infection in your throat! Though you liked spicy foods, after taking it you suffered for a week or more. Doctors advised you not to take spicy food.

"Of course, I could not justify myself the faults I committed. I loved all kinds of food items, spicy or non-spicy, vegetarian or non-vegetarian, cooked or uncooked, seafood or bush-meat, native or exotic, Indian, Chinese, Continental, American, Italian, Arabian or even African. I practiced like that, for I did not know where I would get a job, and if it were in China, I would have eaten the middle part of the snake! And you were always jealous of my eating habits!

"At the same time, you always told me, with pride and honor, about your exciting experience in certain big hotels where your uncle Ryan or your cousin Bobby took you. Of course, once in a lifetime, they could take you, as they lived far away from you! And you never remembered those days in which I took you to big hotels; you thought of it as the normal duty of a husband! When I took you there, either you complained that you were not hungry or ordered some simple dishes pointing out your stomach problems! Others can force you to eat anything and everything, for they do not bother about the consequences. But as a husband, I must care for your ailments as well, for you are not for a day for me but forever. And the funniest thing was that you had never complained about such matters all these years, just heaped it up in your mind for a vulnerable moment in my life!

"You think that I came to Ethiopia to enjoy life! What kind

of enjoyment is here for a person like me? Could I enjoy delicious food here! I was a non-vegetarian throughout my life and I always loved non-vegetarian food. Of course, when you prepared it and gave me in a beautiful plate together with your loving words, it surpassed the taste of every other cuisine! And you are also a non-vegetarian. You might be thinking that I have been enjoying delicious food here in this African country!

"What I prepare here is something strange which one can call either vegetarian or non-vegetarian! Those vegetarian fanatics in India may be confused when I say so! But I say the truth and truth only! Do you think that onion is a vegetable? Do you think that tomato is a vegetable? Do you think that green chilly is a vegetable? Do you think that a few drops of lemon juice or a pinch of salt are vegetarian? You are wrong, my dear vegetarian friends? I mixed all these things and ate it as if it were a non-vegetarian dish! This was my food for months! And truly, you must see how deliciously I devoured it! Of course, I prepared fish one day and it tasted like a vegetable dish to me! It is the mind, not Botany or Zoology, which makes a vegetable dish non-vegetarian and a non-vegetarian dish vegetarian! And I passed my days in Ethiopia like this!

"Of course, I was a busy man. Though I was not a workaholic, I worked more to make some extra income. You knew that we were not persons born with golden spoons in our mouths! There is an adage in the Spanish language: The poor man is a lean ant that runs here and there, working day in and day out while the rich man is a fat frog that sits quietly somewhere with his tummy and big mouth! Most of my running was not exactly worth remunerative. You get some fifty rupees with which you wish to buy some sweets for your children; you enter a bakery and buy biscuits or sweets and pay sixty or seventy rupees; and the net result is that you are a debtor of ten or twenty rupees! And that was my life in those days!

"I wished to make our home a real heaven! I knew money

alone could not make a heaven of one's life; but without money, life could not be a heaven at all. I remembered the Amharic saying: The salary of America, the food of China, the house in England and the wife from Japan will give you a heaven on earth; the salary of China, the food of England, the house in Japan and the wife from America will give you a hell on earth! And I was never a dreamer!

"In those days of youthful adventure, I had full confidence in myself and in my fate! I knew that everything would go according to my plan. I had a hundred percent faith in my fate, for I knew that my fate wouldn't cheat me, of if my fate betrayed me, I would be consoled as it was my own fate! I used to recite the lines of Henry David Thoreau:

'Whate'er we leave to God, God does,

And blesses us;

The work we choose be our own,

God leaves alone!'

I tried to do myself the lion's share of my works and left very little for God to do, for at least somebody must be there to support Him in his too busy schedule! But that made all the difference; I had to work hard, breaking every bone in my body, beyond my physical and mental capacity! Nobody knew my real agony, except God, not even my wife whom fate gave me as a partner in my joys and sorrows!

"Of course, I ran helter-skelter not only to make a little money but also to get some honor. Besides my usual work in the college, I was engaged in various social, political, religious and cultural activities! You might not have liked such a person as your husband! You liked an average clerk who does his usual work in the office and returns to the house as quickly as possible! You never cared about the honor given to you by the members of the society just because you were my wife!

"I always loved to be free from all these hectic activities, either imposed on me or accepted by me. On those free days, I really wished to enjoy my time with you. For your sake, I was ready to go with you to the cinema, to the hotel or for shopping. But then, you procrastinated such cheerful moments either pretending illness or some other lame excuses! Of course, I believe that such excuses were not deliberate! You did not know how to utilize the free time or the mood of a busy husband, and to make married life a wonderful experience. If I could not give you memorable moments in your life, the mistake is totally yours. You suspected my honest enquiries about your health, and deliberately prevaricated only to make complaints later!

"'Why did you marry, after all, you don't care for a domesticated life?' you asked in the letter. What answer should I give you? I remembered the Tamil saying, 'Kalyanam anavankaluku oru kavalei; kalyanam aavate unkaluku aayiram kavalei;' for those who married have one problem, those who didn't marry have a thousand problems! Well, to say it frankly, I did not want to have a thousand problems!

"'Why did you ruin my life if your interest was in social life?' you wrote in the letter. Can we have a life bereft of social life, do you think, my dear? When your life and my life join together, there does begin a social life, don't you think so? Can we separate our life from our social life? As George Lamming said, 'The proximity of our lives to the major issues of our time has demanded of us all some kind of involvement.' Of course, there are many who remain neutral but for me to remain neutral is equivalent to exile! To feel exile in the midst of your own society is worse than death! This sense of exile will make you feel about your inadequacy or irrelevance in the society! Your existence in the contemporary society itself will become insignificant! One should have been born somewhere in a jungle in the Paleolithic or Neolithic age!

"Of course, I extended my small service to the communist party, not because it was above corruption but it better cared for the poor and the helpless at least in words! After Christ, it was

Marx who thought about the poorest of the poor. But Christian religion became a toy in the hands of the capitalists whose watchword was charity! Let us keep communism with us, only it could give us a wonderful dream! Of course, it may not have a future, just like any other dreams! Even China replaced Karl Marx with Milton Friedman!

"My dear, I can understand your feelings; you wished for a reserved life! But your desire to always have a private life of your own is so deep rooted in your psyche that, I'm afraid, it may even pass into our daughter, making her too un-adjustable with a conjugal life!

"How could a person become so selfish? Especially a woman, the most venerated Mother Image of our culture! Geetha had written in the letter, 'You were all for helping others but they always ignored your service!' Well! It's true that I rendered my help to others, of course, whatever was possible in my limited capacity. But I did them without expecting any returns from the beneficiaries. I did just my duty as any other human being would do to his fellow beings. Of course, the beneficiaries of my help, most of them, were my own relatives or friends and how can I expect anything from them! They did not enquire about our well-being, at the time of need, and that was not important. No need to feel offended at their reaction as what I did was mere free-service.

"It is not a simple thing to do possible service to others! And the benefit we will get, surely, not from them but from God, sometimes as luck or chance! Even Albert Einstein, the great scientist, believed in luck! But the fact was that I could not do service to them even sincerely. I could have done it in a better way, I always thought with a guilty conscience. Most part of my so-called service was only to help some students to get admission in some colleges where I had friends! And remember the words of Alan Loy McGinnis: 'There is no more noble occupation in the world than to assist another human being, to help someone to succeed!'

"But what social life is there for me if there is no place for my wife and children in it? Well, those employed persons, of course, have a social life in their specific areas of employment. What about a housewife like you who have been perfectly managing the household duties? You too have your own social life, among our neighbors! Even though, I haven't had that much contact with them, you managed to keep healthy relationships with them all and I was so proud of your ability in such matters! Even I recognized only one-fourth of the persons whom you knew in our neighborhood! Now, I understand why this unfortunate idea came into your mind! Perhaps, you are jealous of that huge crowd that assembled in the auditorium on my last day at the college, to give me the send-off! Of course, I agree that it was due to my social contacts!

"Despite all my social activities, I know that my social or political contacts were very poor that I could not even help you in securing a job. I gave you every moral support for your studies. I took you to many places for your written tests. All those written tests were mere farce as we all knew. I met the Board Members of many cooperative banks; I was ready to give them whatever amount they demanded! But nobody was there to take the money!

"'Money is implied in it but recommendation is the main criteria,' they said. The banks governed by the Congress Party appointed people who got recommendation letters from Governors and Prime Minister's personal secretaries; the banks governed by the Communist Party appointed people who had strong influence inside the party circle. What was I for them, after all! You always thought I had some connection with party leaders but you did not know that I was nothing for them!

"Many a time I reminded you that a regular salary was not at all important for happiness. Of course, it might help to reduce the burden of financial problems. I read somewhere: Happiness is not a destination, it's a journey / Happiness is not tomorrow, it's now / Happiness is not a dependency, it is a decision / Happiness is what you are, not what you have. Did you ever try to be happy with what we had? You were always in stress and you failed to adapt physically, mentally and emotionally to a change. You ignored the fact that a small amount of stress is useful as it adds flavor to our life.

"There are a lot of husbands who watch their wives with jealousy, I have heard so! But do you think that a person like me can degrade myself to such a husband? I was rather proud of you! But for the first time in my life, I see in you, a wife who is jealous of her own husband! When a wife begins to watch her husband with jealousy, envy and malice and, at times, even with disgust and hatred, his manner of going to the office, talking to the people whom he meets on the road, smiling to those whom he encounters, sharing the grief of his friends, extending his helping hands to needy relatives, attending public functions as their honorable chief guest, giving speeches at literary or religious meetings, and what-not, even when writing poems or stories – the reason for such a behavior is as clear as daylight, and it can be diagnosed even by an ordinary person! Yes, I must console myself believing it all due to the wrong curves of lines on my head or palms!

"You used to complain that never did I cut jokes or make comments that aroused laughter in your presence! If ever I did so, somewhere else, it was just situational and most of them were about my own foolishness! I always loved to make fun of my own actions, thoughts and experiences! But you always considered them as degrading or shameful to you as a wife. Well, my dear, comedy represents life worse than what it is, as I used to say in my classrooms!

"Now, I realize why you wrote, 'What are your smiles and laughs in the college, with your students and colleagues?' If I say that I won't smile or laugh in the college, it will be untrue!

But you misunderstood the smiles and laughs which you heard over the telephone. Many a time I tried to convince you about the situation and still all your complaints are the repetitions of such clarified incidents! For all your suspicions, I explained my position and told you several times that I was really innocent, and they all happened as in the normal course of life! Of course, every time you had an axe to grind!

"As you could not forget or forgive such incidents, I recollect one of such incidents. When the phone rang, I who usually never attended such untimely calls had to take the receiver, as other teachers were busy in a discussion on departmental affairs. From my facial expressions and tone of talk, Joyce, the lady teacher with a big mouth, realized that the call was from you and she made some funny comments ridiculing my intuition, and everybody laughed aloud. I gave a tit for tat and that too aroused a much louder laugh. And that was the end of it! But were I a comedian to make irrelevant funny scenes to make others laugh? Think for a moment! Or don't think about such incidents, for you lost forever the God-given talent to think aright!

"I have a few friends here and I know how their wives write or talk over the telephone to them. They are not speaking in my language but I can feel their warmth and love, for to recognize love, knowledge of a language is not needed! Their wives may be illiterate housewives but they know how to love their husbands! Many of them will go back home only after two years; until then their wives are ready to suffer their absence for the sake of the well-being of the whole family. You are an educated person and that may be the reason for your perverted approach to life!

"As the days of my retirement approached, I became a bit more sentimental, perhaps! I have my social life and that is different from family life. If I show sentiments to my friends and students, it's because I am leaving them forever, yet my sentiments to my family are reserved, for they are mine forever. The sentiments I have shown to my students and colleagues may be just a show of the moment but the love and affection for the family is genuine, and there cannot be any comparison!

"Your mental perversion makes you think wrongly of every such relationship, and you observe them with a sinful eye! But I can't stoop to such a level to confess before a too clever wife like you! Stop your nonsense and think like a true partner in my life or at least like a normal person! Your attitude is the other side of the coin played by my daughter! Please, don't make me a madman! There's a limit for everything!

"Geetha wrote, 'You used to turn away your face, and you didn't like me to come near you or talk to you.' With a guilty conscience, I do accept your complaint. I should not have done so, and it was quite unbecoming of a true husband. But unfortunately you came to me only when I was smoking or just after completing my smoking. And you knew that I had the habit of smoking three or four cigarettes a day, or on drinking day, one or two more. Of course, the smell of nicotine is intolerable even to me, and how could I embrace you with my bad smelling hands, and kiss you or talk to you with a stinking mouth?

"It was my guilty conscience that deliberately avoided your presence on such situations. Moreover, neither you liked the smell of cigarettes nor I liked to smoke in front of my dear ones. That was the reason, when I returned from the college, I used to go upstairs without caring your presence, and came back to you after washing my nicotine-stained mouth and hands and my foul smelling feet that were kept in the socks throughout the hot day! You didn't realize the dignity and prestige I enjoyed when I returned to you thus! But, by then, you had turned away from me and disappeared from my sight! And that was my fate!

"And about smoking, I know it is injurious to health as the statutory warning on the cigarette packet reminds us. I am sure that you were aware of my habit of smoking, on the very first day of our first meeting at your house. Your worker in the house followed me secretly and saw me smoking at the bus-stop and informed you about it within an hour! Of course, I am not justifying my bad habit! I know that passive smoking is also harmful, if I believe the words of the anti-smoking experts! At least, after that teacher of our nearby women's college, Ms. Mamona, got a verdict from the court declaring 'passive smoking is also injurious to health!'

"As a former advocate, I know that everybody can file such a case for the benefit of the public and so long as there is no defendant, an *ex-parte* decision will be taken by the court. She or anyone else could file a case against chewing betel leaves and areca nuts as it caused cancer, driving vehicles as their smoke gives lung disease or engaging in intercourse without condoms as it leads to AIDS!

"We hypocrites used to ignore such cases and verdicts and continued to do such minor evils for relaxation. And, of course, a court is not supposed to make such verdicts, especially on matters related to the cultural or traditional habits of the people. Neither the judge who made a verdict in his passiveness or ignorance nor the teacher who filed the case in her enthusiasm or arrogance is benefited from similar situations! And the idea that passive smoking is more dangerous than active smoking is equal to the idea that coconut oil contains more cholesterol than the American palm oil!

"How funny are the decisions of our courts, based on certain make-believe research and its deliberately twisted results? Can the smoke of the cigarette be more toxic than the carbon monoxide emitted by thousands of vehicles in our cities? Of course, I will never be an advocate for smokers. But if I smoke just to refresh my mind or to stimulate my imagination, a rare gift of nature, how could a government or a court of justice issue orders against it? And as a part of my formal manners, I refused to smoke before you and my children. But I never imagined that such decency on my part would lead to the breaking up of a conjugal life!

"There was not even a speck of honesty, when you wrote, 'All these years, you did nothing in my presence that could be remembered in my life!' Did I ignore anything deliberately which you asked me to do? Oh, Geetha, you think too much in the wrong way and even forget the truth! Your accusations are nothing but raw lies! I fumed for a moment with anger. I could not tolerate such an insult on my individuality from my wife!

"After a few minutes, I smiled to myself and argued, I hope that, at least, one thing I did in your presence, which you could remember forever! That's our daughter! Don't you agree? You might say even that too was not of my deed! Any woman can say so, unless the husband should go for some DNA test! However, to a person who remembered only the evils of married life, that lasted for a quarter of a century, what should I say, especially, as I am living now in a distant land?

"I remember that you always wished to ride on a motorcycle or in a car. Even before our wedding, I had my driving license but I could not buy a car or even a bike due to financial problems. Moreover, a minor car accident that occurred before our marriage had given me such a mental shock that I was afraid to drive a car. Yet, I would have freed myself from that phobia if you had insisted to buy a car but you never did so. Had your brother Kapildev encouraged and helped, I would have bought a car!

"Of course, you quarreled over every silly and unnecessary matter and never tried to convince me through pleasing words. You did not know to advise but only to order or complain, and that would never enter into my heart! You used my own words against me! Words are angels that can be converted into devils! They can be made sweet as well as poisonous! As Sri Sri Ravi Shankar says, 'If you manipulate words, it is a lie; if you play on words, it is a joke; if you rely on words, it is ignorance; if you transcend words, it is wisdom!'

"I looked at her letter, particularly at a question she asked! She had written, 'Can you give back my past life?' My God! Was our married life for the last twenty-five years such a hell for her? But she never gave even a hint about it all these years except for a few heated words during petty quarrels which were quite common among loving couples! And what about those hundreds of happiest days which we spent together when we felt our life so heavenly? How could you forget or ignore those wonderful years which we spent together? And she wrote whether I could give back her past, as if her past with me was so miserable! Well! If I ask you the same question, how would you answer me! Like you, I too, or in that case all human beings, wished to get back their past life! Like T.S. Eliot, we used to ask the question silently, 'Where is the life we have lost in living?'

"Suppose I say I can give back your past, of course, I am sure I can do it in an emotional way, if you are willing, you will immediately ask, 'Can you take me back to the days before our marriage?' That's pretty impossible for me! 'Can you take me in a motor bike; you and I as a young and newly married couple, and ride through the streets of the city, while all others enviously watching us? Can you lift me up, like my favorite film actor does with his heroine, and run around the trees?' Such will be your desires and how can I satisfy such silly ambitions of your erstwhile life? My Geetha, you were in a world of foolish dreams before your marriage and this question that arose in your mind after a long married life of twenty-five years was the reflection of those immature calf-love days! And the remedy for it is only in the safe stock of the Almighty!

"Well! My dear! We began our family life in a very humble way. I was a self-made man and our family was a self-made family. Nobody was there to help us! Like birds, restlessly flying here and there and collecting twigs, fibers, cotton and fallen feathers to make and beautify their nests, we worked hard to change our house into a home. When we bought each utensil in the kitchen or each piece of furniture in the drawing room, how proud and happy we were! Later, one after another, we could fetch cooking range, music system, television, refrigerator, washing machine and so on. But you never enquired how I got the money to buy all such things! All of them were bought under hire-purchase systems and I was always in debt! I did not like to trouble you with such financial constraints. I preferred to be tension-free at my home; I did not like to discuss financial problems in the bedroom! Do you think of it as part of my male chauvinism? But we are not Chinese Communists to discuss the nation's Five Year Plans in our bedroom, are we?

"In the letter, Geetha had complained that 'her husband,' that was I, came home, especially after the construction of the new house, 'only for sleeping!' Well! There was some truth in it, I must admit it. I tried to locate the situation. What was my salary then, after all the deductions of the Provident Fund, tax, union subscriptions, chitty-installments and repayment of the housing loans, both at the college and at the nationalized bank? Only Rs. 2000/- per month! In the second year of the completion of the construction of the house, one more increment in salary, and made the net income Rs. 2750/- On the third year, with yet another increment, it went to Rs. 3600/- Only after getting the UGC scale that I could stand on my legs! How could a person manage all the household expenses, the education of the children especially, with that meager amount?

"I did a lot of odd jobs, of course, not telling about them to you, dear Geetha, and ran the family somewhat smoothly. As the Ethiopian adage says:
Love without money
Is a hive without honey!

So, whenever there was a chance of getting a hundred rupee note, I rushed for that work. I believed that it was unfair to tell such things to my wife and put her in anxiety, or perhaps, I thought that it was degrading myself to tell my wife about such humiliating things, especially when her nature was full of unnecessary vanity or snobbishness. Even if I had told you that I worked three hours for just a paltry amount, you would have turned your nose up at my helplessness! You and your dear relatives, even those of mine, would have laughed at me with sneer and disparagement, I knew!"

I heard the noise of opening the front door! My wife and son had returned from shopping. It was her habit to buy from the bakery something ready-made to eat on such occasions and I rushed down, placing a marker in the diary of Rajesh. My guess was right, there were samosas and cream-buns, and a lot of other things, and I felt Xanthu a bit extravagant whenever he came on leave! Now-a-days, boys were getting jobs and a regular income, as and when they came out from their studies, and they turned spendthrifts soon, I used to think.

CHAPTER SIX

The climate in Kerala was so humid that I hated to go out during daytime! Owing to heavy sweating, whenever I went out, I appeared as if walking under the rain! Of course, I loved Ethiopia mainly because of her wonderful and lovely climate!

Next morning, as we were taking our breakfast, Ms. Joyce, my former colleague came to the house. She had to attend the wedding of our colleagues' children! The bride and the bridegroom were the daughter and the son of our colleagues!

"Didn't they invite you to the wedding?" she asked with regrets on her face.

I said in a tone of indifference, "Once a person is retired, who bothers about the old friendship? Nearness breeds friendship! Of course, I'm a conservative and I don't like to attend weddings in which colleagues' children marry each other or a teacher marries his student! We used to teach our children that our colleagues' sons and daughters are their own brothers and sisters!"

She laughed aloud and said, "Of course, we teach our students, 'India is our country and all Indians are our brothers and sisters!' That doesn't mean that we should not marry each other!"

I ignored her joke and said, "In Ethiopia, I have seen teachers dating with their students! In these days, it is common that teachers wed their students, and you may think of me as old-fashioned if I say that we, the old generation, neither ogled at our students nor thought of them in sexual terms!"

"Oh, yes! The whole world came to an end when your

colleague Corin married his student!" She teased me, giving a clever dig at my contention.

"Of course, their case was different; they knew each other as neighbors even before she became his student! Well! It's time that proves the sanctity of our traditional beliefs and practices!" I replied in a tone of surrender.

But Joyce insisted on her opinion and said, "Sir! In these days, it is always better to take spouses for your children from the families of people whom you know! For instance, suppose I make a proposal for your son, and if the girl is one of your former colleague's daughters, you must think about it!"

"I'm sorry, Joyce! I can't entertain such proposals! I had my foolish principles, you may think of them as anachronistic statements of a conformist but I stick to them!"

"George sir! It goes without saying what you are!" She taunted me and continued, "You don't know the latest trend among our students! When a good looking girl comes to the college, boys are after her! First they enquire about the financial background of the girl, if her parents are Gulf-returned or if she belongs to a family with good financial background, immediately they stick to her like flies on a piece of candy! The cleverest and luckiest one traps her! Now-a-days, the boys come to the college not for their study because they knew that even if they study hard and get a job, it is very difficult to get a girl of their choice as life-partner!"

I foolishly tried to dig in my heels and she left the house without telling who the girl was of her choice for my son! Of course, I didn't want to know! My wife and son also went with her as they wanted to give some clothes for dry-cleaning. I went to my study, poured a peg of whisky, diluted it with some water and began sipping it! Of course, I never wasted such moments of freedom!

I was anxious to know what Rajesh had written in his diary! I wished if he had told me his problems, I would have tried to mediate! Of course, he did not know what Mark Victor Hansen said, "Don't wait until everything is just right. It will never be perfect. There will always be challenges, obstacles and less than perfect conditions. So what? Get started just now. With each step you take, you will grow stronger and stronger, more and more skilled, more and more self-confident and more and more successful."

His words suited every venture in life whether in sports or in cultivation, whether in education or in family life! But there were situations in which no advice would work; then, everyone had to suffer whatever was destined for the person concerned! I opened his diary with a long sigh and began to read.

"'You spent a lot of money on drinks,' you accused me in your letter. Do you want to call me a drunkard? Or do you think that I have been an irresponsible head of the family who spoiled the happiness of the family by drinking too much? Well, that was the language of garrulous women of our neighborhood who happened to be your conscience keepers! Perhaps, there is some fact in your complaint, as I took a drink or two once in a while, or even drank too much on a few occasions, during the latest five years of our married life.

"Of course, you knew that, as a part of my social life, I used to have 'company' with my friends on rare occasions or on unexpected holidays declared in the college following some students' strike! And I accept that it became regular in a week or two, and that too was in a limited way, following the construction of our new house. But that was not to make a fool of me before you or in the eye of the public! Can a professor in a reputed college stoop to that level? If ever I stooped, it was before you and I am not ashamed of that. Where should I have to unmask myself and come to my real self, if it is not in front of you, my wife?

"Well, as you know, for the last two years, my friends Corin and Balzac were not on good terms, we even couldn't use their rooms for the get-together, as we used to do. And to enter the bar was unthinkable due to the heavy bill they charged, for me and my friend Mr. Odds with whom I used to take a couple of pegs. Then, the only chance was an unexpected invitation from our friend Binu, who used to celebrate when he got a bottle as a gift from someone. Most of the time, it was not on my expense but only sharing the drinks at the expense of some generous friend, and there was no chance of drinking too much. Of course, sometimes there may be a grand get-together and on such occasions I might have drunk too much, and that too was during my last year in the college. In fact, you did not like my social contacts and your complaint against my drinking was only an indirect means to express it! And you did not know the saying that an ex-alcoholic is worse than a teetotaler!

"Perhaps, you thought that we could save some more money if I stopped drinking! Of course, you did not think about its adverse effect on my health, or believe 'smoking or drinking alcohol is injurious to health' and such funny statutory warnings! A recent study by Neer Bersilai of Albert Einstein College of Medicine, published in the Journal of American Geriatrics Society, says: It is not dieting, exercise or good habits that decide the longevity of a person but genes. I was never suicidal in smoking or drinking and I used to leave my life completely at the mercy of my fate!

"Though it's not an excuse, I must admit that I had a bit more tension as the countdown started for my retirement. My tension was mounting as I was worried too much about the marriage of our daughter, usual and unexpected expenses at home and the debt at the college and in the nationalized bank which could not be managed with my pension alone. And the extra money which I could get from taking contact classes at the Seminary or at the Open University or at the Distance Education Center was only a pauper's bowl. And the workload there was too much compared to the paltry amount I received.

"I was running, like a dog that caught fire on its tail, with the 'one aim, one purpose, one business' to grab maximum income while continuing in service. Even I couldn't spare Sundays on which they conducted the bank tests! And you thought that it was because I did not want to come with you to the church or to spend the hours of the holiday at home with you and our child!

"Of course, we had to face more financial constraints after the construction of our house. Wasn't it our dream to have a beautiful house of our own? But the financial commitment was above our expectation! Well! I don't regret my decision to build a house; it is the dream of every homeless citizen in our country; and I take the full responsibility of all the financial problems thereby occurred to us. I came to Ethiopia, particularly because I had to pay back the bank loan on our house. As Mervin Kitman said, 'A coward is a hero with a wife, kids and a mortgage!' and I don't know whether I am a coward or a hero!

"But the construction of the house was not on my decision alone! You also were longing for a house of your own! Of course, you approved my decisions when I took them, praised me if they resulted in success, and blamed me if they failed! I ignored your assassinating criticisms, as I respected the great stoic philosopher, Epictetus, who said, 'Man is basically free and has to choose, but within what is in our power; to choose from what is not in our power is none of our business; and we are responsible for what we choose.'

"As a teacher, could there be any possibility of getting a bribe or such illegal means of income for me? So the only way I could find was to value as much as possible answer scripts from the University. Though the payment was not immediate, I could at least hope to get it sooner or later. And of course, I could manage to get the maximum number of answer scripts, which any other professor under our university ever received for valuation! Sometimes I had to treat my friends in the university office to reissue the declined paper bundles in my name.

"Only half or less than half of the scripts thus got were brought for home valuation and the rest were kept in the college, and I valued them either at the library of the Centre for Research or at the General Library, which would be of less distraction. You can't imagine the number of answer scripts I valued at the college, perhaps, three times more than what I brought to the house! I accept the fact that you helped me a lot to prepare the mark lists. But what about those hundreds of mark sheets which I myself prepared, sitting in the library of my college?

"Now, Geetha, in your wicked mind the question would arise, 'Where has gone the whole lot of money thus you amassed?' and, once you even asked me so! Yes, the money which I spent including it in my salary, for the education of our child, for the maintenance of the house and for the general expenses at home was nothing but the extra amount which I earned!

"Of course, I couldn't spend anything for your personal needs! I thought that you were a part of my body and soul and I always expected a peaceful retired life with you without any financial worries. But now I realize that a woman can never become an inevitable part of the body and soul of a man! A woman is a woman, for frailty thy name is woman! But remember, whenever you asked, or whatever you asked, I never denied!

"Well, when I returned home so tired and fed up after the valuation of answer scripts, on certain days, I used to take before food, one and a half peg, and never more than that, from the bottle which I bought and kept in my study room, or from the bottle sometimes offered by my brother-in-law or cousins. But that too was not in such a manner to destroy the peace of our family life or to mar our relationship as husband and wife.

But within your mind you blew up such normal occasions into something like historical events! Just for that reason, you insulted me in such a way that no other wife had done so far! And you may ask, 'Did I insult you?' and your mind will remain incapable of realizing the insult you directed against me! As the poet says, 'Even though the cow's udder is full of milk, the mosquito sits on it drinks only the blood!' And you were such a type!

"Only God could give you replies to your dirty suspicions! I wonder how you could write, 'Just before you left this country, you took me to a hill resort with the families of your friends just to make me a witness to your buffoonish manners and foul-plays after drinking.' Well! Was it necessary for me to take you to that faraway place, to that wonderful land of scenery, just for making you a witness to my Dutch courage! What an utter nonsense! I could do it, if I wished, anywhere in our house itself! But I thought it would be a change for you, spending some time with other like-minded people, especially with the wives of my colleagues! All other members in the company heartily enjoyed the trip except you! You also appeared, as far as I could remember, to be happy with the picnic. But now, I see that it was all sheer pretence and hypocrisy on your side! You imagined strange things which others could not even dream of! You were full of conceit and your whimsical conclusions spoiled the mirth! It's all my bad fate, nothing but my cursed fate!

"My dear! I know the reason for your disgruntled and discontented family life; you wished to become an employee in the government service, that was your greatest dream, and you did not get one! No doubt, if the husband and wife together contribute to the family, life would be quite easy! I remember how happy you were when you worked temporarily for a few months in a government institution. You could prove your mettle, especially with your enviable handwriting! You had every talent needed for managing an office single-handedly. On the day of salary, you made a hearty shopping and brought home a lot of necessary things, including costly and delicious sweets and cakes from the best bakery in our city. I was also proud to see you coming home with a happy face and in a jubilant mood!

"After a year, to your utter disappointment, you lost that temporary job and you did not get another one despite all our efforts. You began to blame me for not getting a job for you in some government or private institution. Of course, I could have found certain menial jobs for you but that was unbecoming for the status of a college lecturer's wife! As you know, in ordinary private firms, the proprietors offered jobs and gave salary for beautiful ladies not merely for doing the office work but also for satisfying their personal needs! Only a male could understand such Indian situations! And you found it very difficult to adjust with a boring life at home, especially after spending a few months of active and assiduous days!

"I always tried to justify your unemployment and tried to make you happy at home. All my efforts turned futile before your assertive nature. On principle, I was against the system of both the husband and wife working and drawing salary from the government services. Of course, many couples in our country were government employees but I considered it unpatriotic and immoral! I believed that it was sheer injustice if both the husband and wife drew salary from the government of a country where unemployment was so 'acute and unwieldy' a problem that many well-qualified youngsters turned desperate and even committed suicide. Our governments were adamant in limiting the retirement age of the employees to fifty-five, thinking that it would reduce the number of the unemployed, but were they ready to make a law that both the husband and wife should not draw salary from the government treasury? Then, you could see the real sanctity of our so-called holy marriages!

"It was Adolf Hitler who tried to solve the unemployment problem in Germany by ordering one of the married couples to resign the job. Though he did it in good faith, the consequence was terrible! All those Christians who considered marriage as a holy sacrament, preferred to continue in their job by getting legal divorce and staying together illegally! Young men and women lived together as bed-mates without any legal or spiritual sanction! Of course, money covereth a multitude of sins! Our beliefs in religion and culture are merely superfluous, and we ignore them as and when we face a real trial or ordeal in our life! By my soul, I was always against the system in which both the husband and wife drew salary from the government service; one should resign and join some private institution. Well, you would laugh and say, 'You're the fox in the adage; when difficult to get, the grapes taste too sour!'

"The main problem with you, I believe, was that you did not like to be criticized! In fact, what is criticism? It really opens a way for us to correct ourselves. If husband and wife criticize each other, it is creative criticism and not assassinating criticism. Don't you want to be corrected? No person in this world is perfect, and the tragedy is that many of them won't get a chance to be corrected. Whenever I complained, you misunderstood it as an accusation leveled against you! Accusation is entirely different from complaint. Husband and wife are living human beings and not mere dead bodies. Dead bodies won't make complaints, and do you prefer the silence of the cemetery in our conjugal life?

"If husbands and wives have no complaints, it simply means that they live 'like dead bodies!' And a person who is not ready to listen to the advice of another person, whether he or she corrects himself or herself, that person surely is a psychiatric case to be treated by alienists! Sometimes, I felt sympathy towards you, as you developed a mind equal to that of a mental patient at times!

"Of course, a wife has the right to advise her husband, sometimes he may correct himself or he may not be in a mental condition to correct. Whether he corrects himself or not is immaterial. But if you keep quiet and suffer your husband, it is a sin. Rethinking about one's actions or correcting oneself is a miracle or something divine and it happens unexpectedly. It is like conversion into another religion or political party; it happens spontaneously and without much rational thinking.

"Therefore, if there is something wrong with the husband and wife relationship, it must be frankly expressed and, thereby an opportunity must be given. The idea must be kept in the air so that one could correct oneself as and when the time comes. For ideas are alternatives waiting on a crisis to serve as the catalyst of change, and it is a crime, or rather a sin, if corrigendum is not suggested by a sincere spouse. Of course, neither such corrections are mandatory on either side nor the negligence of them is an excuse for divorce!

"In the United States, divorces are common because the couples usually have different cultural backgrounds. When I say cultural difference, it also includes very meticulous aspects related to sexual behavior of a person. They generally believe that a married life is something personal, related only to two individuals. They don't think that it is a small unit of the society and their divorce affects not merely the individuals concerned but the whole society.

"There divorces are granted by the courts as quickly as possible because the judges think about it as an individual affair. A matter concerning the society should not be decided so fast! The double-bed system of our modern times may arouse petty quarrels that lead to filing a case for divorce, and, in western countries, the court gives a verdict before giving the couples sufficient time for rethinking. But our case is quite different. We are born and brought up in the same culture if there is a problem that must be purely personal, related to the psychology of either of us.

"My dear Geetha! You misunderstood my ideals; of course, some of them were not practical like any other ideal! But how could you suspect my faithfulness to you, after a life of many years with you! In fact, you were jealous and self-centered! You never loved me! If you ever loved me, you loved me as you had no other choice in a society like that of ours! You loved me as if it was the duty of a wife; you loved me as it was a custom in married life! Neither you were sincere to yourself nor to me!

"My dearest! It is natural that the realities of life erode the vision of marital bliss! Anybody can say, 'I love you or we love each other!' But love is an ideal stage or an abstract idea or an imagined acme, like God, that anybody can misuse the word for justifying one's selfishness! To survive in marriage, more than love what we require are adaptability, flexibility, sympathy and kindness. A deep sense of humor and an imagination strong enough to feel what the other is feeling will give additional fragrance to conjugal life. Of course, genuine love is an added spice like fragrance to gold!

"We live in a society in which only Philanderers, Romeos, flirts, sycophants, womanizers and shameless and garrulous chatterers could survive as good husbands! Persons who are serious by nature, who are reticent and taciturn, are kicked out by oily-artists who have neither obligation nor responsibility towards the weaker sex!

"And what is this genuine love? As members of a Hindu family, we did not get the opportunity to read the Bible of our Christian neighbors. If good things are there in the Holy Books of other religions, we must read and try to follow them. In the New Testament of the Bible, there is a unique passage about love. It says, 'Love is patient, love is kind. It does not envy, it does not boast, it is not proud. It is not rude, it is not self-seeking, it is not easily angered, it keeps no record of wrongs. Love does not delight in evil but rejoices with the truth. It always protects, always trusts, always hopes, always perseveres.'

"My dear, we are mere mortals and it may be very difficult to follow such rules of love literally. But this passage can be used as a touchstone to measure the quality of our love, the sincerity of our hearts. At least, it will help us to test our love, to see for ourselves, how far we are true to ourselves!

"Well! You might have expected a perfect person as your husband or rather a husband who behaved perfectly like the person of your dreams! But you forgot that the most committed person in the world will still fail you sometimes because he is not perfect in every way. Perfection is an abstract word which gives a concept of the highest point which nobody can attain. It is a word like truth, beauty, love, freedom, equality and so on; the meaning and the depth depend on the conviction of the individual concerned. One cannot reach the acme; the nearer you get, the farther it moves away like a mirage in the desert.

"Dearest Geetha, you know that my background was different from that of yours. The society in which I lived and the village circumstances in which I grew might have an impact on my mindset. And you never tried to correct me through your loving kindness, if you had something like that with you! I would have fallen at your feet and obeyed you like any other domestic animal if you had not used words that hurt me like strikes of flogs and whips!

"If our married life is a failure, as you believed it so, I'll not be the only culprit; you are also a partner in it. And we must have to undergo the penance for it. Perhaps, your relatives forced you to agree to our marriage, as your father had died by your childhood. If that's the case, how truly Shakespeare's character Lord Suffolk asked, 'For what is wedlock forced but a hell, an age of discord and continual strife?'

"Of course, in a male-dominating society, it is the duty of the husband to manage the financial affairs of the family, and every wife secretly enjoys that tradition. If there is no money, the wife has the right to order her husband to bring it somehow! The husband runs even haphazard to make both ends meet! If he is late, then the wife asks, 'Where were you spending the whole time? You must be with your other wife or some girlfriends whom you met in the street!' It was useless to argue with such a wife. 'Seveit kha ketber; hadow kabo hasot, hadow kabo krshi,' says a proverb in Tigringa language of Ethiopia. There are only two ways to please a wife; you give her either a lot of money or a lot of lies! And that's why I always kept quiet before your wrath. But my silence irritated you much more than my late coming! Many a time I told you, 'My dear, please forgive and forget it! Let's make best the most of the time we do have, Geetha, please?'

"But my pleadings were mere cries in the wilderness! I knew that forgiving and forgetting are like oil and water though people always lump them together! One may forgive but never forget; one may not forgive but forget only to remember as and when the opportunity comes!

"My dear Geetha, are you not a believer in God? Are you not a member of a theistic religion? Well, I know that all these religions that were so busy being about everything except God! If there is anything divine in us, they are tolerance, forbearance, sacrifice, humility and patience which are purely humane! Well! We are not too late, my dear, time and tide wait for none, though love is beyond the sickle-reach of time and space. Neither could the wane of beauty nor the decline of health nor the symptoms of aging come as impediments before true love!

"What you wrote in the letter is true, I admit it! You wrote, 'Your going to the African country is different; it's not like your earlier going to the Gulf country.' You're right, my dear, for when I went to the Gulf, I desired to return alive to you! But, now, after receiving your letter, if I return from this African country, it would be different! It would be my dead body coming to you in a coffin! And you know it better! But as my last wish, will you please take the money which I sent to the bank? Of course, you have the ten blank bank-cheques with you which I gave you before leaving for this place! Well, get the money in fresh hundred rupee notes, stuff it into your wallet, and go shopping, as you always desired, and learned it from your cousin Bobby's wife, Valina!

"'There you can fully engage in writing literature,' you casually wrote in the letter. I understand the inner meaning of your words! As writing literature is a heavenly talent, your inner conscience cannot hate it but at the same time you are jealous of my talents in writing! My dear Geetha, I know quite clearly that with my literature there is no benefit either for you or for others or for the world! But it has been giving my mind peace and solace. It purifies my mind and my soul is purgated! That is the only reason why I write. But even in my remote dreams, I did not know that my wife would turn to be a person without common sense or sense of humor or aesthetic sense, who always failed to understand my stories as 'stories'! That too is the curse of my fate!

"You asked in the letter, 'Why do you work in a foreign country?' And you also give the answer, 'I know the reason! You want to escape from me! You want to lead a wayward life! And Ethiopia is, perhaps, the best place for you! My cousin who had visited that country gave me a detailed description. Girls come to the house and knock for spending nights with foreigners; and I know that you are not so clean in such matters!'

"How could I explain to her all the practical sides of Ethiopian social life? Here, there are many people like me who sacrifice their life for the sake of their family. Their wives may also say the same things! I tried to console myself. Winnow the grain when there is wind! I wished to work as far as I have health. It's for my family; it's for conducting the wedding of our daughter in the best manner and, of course, to feel myself the satisfaction that I am doing something for me or for the country.

"I left you there, repudiating all the family pleasures, mainly because I could send money to you and you could utilize it as if it was your own salary. I gave you the cheque-book signed so that you could take my monthly pension! I knew that you were a person who thought of your life meaningless without a job and an income of your own! My lips struggle with a smile of scorn or sneer! Here's a wife who suspects your honesty and integrity, Rajesh!

"I love the philosophy of my friend Dr. Worku Singh who serves as a Professor of Geography. He is also of my age, perhaps a few days younger than me though he looks a few years older than me due to his grey hair. He is very practical to adjust with any situation in life. 'Everything is fine; no problem!' or 'Everything happens for good!' He used to say to me. Yes! I appreciate his attitude and confidence!

"It is your attitude towards life that should be changed! As my friend Mr. President, a professor in the Department of Management said, 'Attitude is the way of thinking about or of behaving towards somebody or something.' Of course, there are common aims for all married lives, but it is the special aims of each married life that make conjugal life wonderful! The husband and the wife submit themselves before each other and forget their selfish motives, giving chances doubling their talents, to make their life successful.

"Look at a glass half filled with water, one can say that it is half full but the other can say that it is half empty! Looking at a zebra, one can say that it has white stripes on a black body but another can say it has black strips on a white body! My dear Geetha, try to understand facts through observation and experience!

"There was a time when neighbors helped each other in solving family problems. Now they are all waiting to see how their neighbors solve their problems themselves! If we fail, my dear, we will turn a mere laughingstock for them! Learn a moral message from this story, my darling! A young mosquito came to a room with her mother, and as they were flying to find a suitable person to drink blood, the little one noticed the people in the room clapping and encouraging them! She told her mother about it and the mother replied, 'My dear child, they are not clapping to encourage us but to kill us with their palms!'

"Don't believe what your neighbors say, my dear! Our skills, knowledge, hard work, aptitude and attitude can make an ocean of difference in our life! Always remember that environment, experience and education together make our life a success. The environment at your home, during your childhood, gave you a myriad of unforgettable experiences that etched into your character! Have you ever tried to create humorous situations in which we could laugh heartily? Instead, you made silly things more serious and serious things highly vulnerable!

"I know that our society will not allow women to live alone; they try every way to harass such women whose husbands have to leave them alone and go away for work. Moreover, in the present age, nobody likes loneliness; everybody craves for 'society, friendship and love!' In our society, women are neither self-sufficient nor capable of managing the family single-handedly. Society made them believe that they are invalid, and they conveniently accepted it as their weakness only to escape from their responsibility!

"A few decades ago, the men of Kerala left their wives at home and went for jobs either in North India as army-men or in the Gulf countries. Their wives suffered a lot under the jealous and cruel eyes of their in-laws, looking after the household works and nurturing their children! Every moment, they prayed to God for the well-being of their husbands and spent their nights soaking their pillows with tears! But in those days, money was quite insufficient for them even to manage with their daily needs; they had to wait for the monthly meager salary sent by their husbands!

"Now, things changed; husbands began to send pretty large amounts; if insufficient, the wives could take money from their accounts as their husbands had given them signed blank cheques! The more money came, the more needs for their wives! Delicious food, costly dress, posh house, comfortable travel facility and luxurious living conditions! What they lacked was only the warmth of a male who could share their beds! And that too was readily available as men were waiting to offer their sex-service if there was no obligation! And thus, every day, newspapers brought the hot news of housewives eloping with their servants, rubber-tappers, laborers or drivers!

"My dear Geetha! Loneliness is horrible, whether it is for you or for me! I also suffer here like you but I am always thinking about your suffering: Poor girl! How could she manage alone all the responsibility of a family; nobody is there to help or advise her! Relatives and neighbors look at her with envy and jealousy; they grin at her grinding their teeth, 'Let her suffer; her husband sends every month truckloads of money!' Or cunningly they come to you expressing their sympathy, 'This much money is enough, my dear! Ask your husband to come back!' Could you understand the irony in their words!

"You believe their words in your innocence and think, 'Yes! Why should I suffer alone here? After all he is enjoying his life in a foreign country; whatever he needs is readily available there! I am his wife and I have my rights over him; I can't allow him to go on like that!' I imagine how you are burning with anger, angst and despair!

"I am not criticizing you! I can understand your situation! You think about your present and I think about our future; that's the difference! Old age needs much savings and we cannot depend always on charity! Of course, I don't want to live long to suffer the attacks of senility and geriatric illness! But I believe in Divine Mercy which 'Gives even affliction a grace/ And reconciles man to his lot,' as William Cowper's Alexander Selkirk consoles himself while living in the uninhabited island of Juan Fernandez!

"Of course, our experiences and events we witnessed turn reference points in our lives and we draw conclusions from them which serve as guidelines for our future. You always tried to assess your husband on the basis of your experience of people in and around your childhood home! Coming to education, you thought of it as a means to make a living! But it also teaches you how to live which you conveniently ignored!

"You are a person made up by your environment! As far as you are not ready to change, you are illiterate! As Alvin Toffler says, 'The illiterate of the twentieth century will not be those who cannot read and write, but those who cannot learn, unlearn and relearn.' You tried to learn but never tried to unlearn and relearn! Of course, you are a person created by the so-called discourse! You cannot go, think or see beyond that discourse, as Miguel Foucault suggested.

"For instance, every individual who belongs to a social group like tribe, clan, caste or religious denomination has his own prejudices against those groups to which he has no affiliation. He learned only to hate other groups and not to love! But as Nelson Mandela said, 'People learn to hate, and if they can learn to hate, they can be taught to love.' Of course, unlike hatred, it is not necessary to learn love. Love is instinctive and spontaneous; it is one of the primordial emotions. Hatred, at the same time, is not an inborn instinct; we learn it from our environment! And our instinctive talents may be, at times, drowned in our acquired knowledge!

"It is said that the greatest discovery of the modern generation is that man can change the way he lives by changing the way he thinks! The problem with you is that you always think negatively! Some sort of inferiority complex is haunting you, I am sure! But remember that no one can make you feel inferior without your permission! Only by controlling your thinking, you can create an attitude; and see, attitude is a choice! As Professor Doumbledore in J.K. Rowling's *Harry Potter and the Chamber of Secrets* says, 'It is our choices that show what we truly are, far more than our abilities.'

"What matters most is how you see yourself! Remember the story of a coward cat who was afraid of rats! One day he looked into a mirror and saw his reflection; he felt that he was no more a cat but a lion! And that changed his whole life! What you must do is to reconstitute your attitude towards others and towards yourself! A healthy attitude towards life will kindle hope in us and, if hope is dominating in us, peace, faith and love will follow automatically! And keep the flame of hope always live and it should never be extinguished!

"I remember my master in Tae-kwon-do telling me, 'If you want to break a couple of bricks with your palm, don't look at the bricks but aim down at the floor below the bricks and, then, strike so that your palm breaks the bricks and touches the floor! Usually our aims are superfluous that we cannot reach our deeper aims or achieve our greater goals! Try to believe that whatever happens is good for you, and that's our Indian culture!

"Mr. President's advice was remarkable, isn't it my dear! We are in this alien land not to live a life but to give a life to our family. We wish to give a good future for the members of our family. Good food, good clothing, good ornaments and a good living for them. We burn and melt away giving light and heat to our next generation!

"You just think about this situation as a husband! As you struggle hard to make both ends meet, your wife and children think of it as your fate alone! Even your wife sometimes feels that it would be a better life with someone else and she even curses her fate of being legally attached to you! What she desires is a better living and a better future for her children. All the love and respect she showed to you during your early days of marriage was only for the realization of her dreams of a carefree future which you failed to give her. And what's left for you is this life! No other options to prove your sincerity as a loving husband. So here you have to face life as it comes to you!

"One day, my friend, Dr. Singh, was in a philosophic mood and he said, 'I remember the lines of Kabir Das that gave me always a sort of justification:

Rahim nij man ki vyadha, man hi rakho goy /
Suni atilenhei log sab, banti na leinhe koy //
Let your grievances be kept in your heart,
Those who hear them won't share your agony,
But only they make you their laughingstock!'

"Yes! That's why all the people who work in foreign countries, pretend happiness and say that their life is better there than anywhere else. They add exaggerations in every aspect! When I asked one of my friends why he told others about an exaggerated salary, though he was getting only one fourth of the amount he told them, he replied in a casual manner: Why shouldn't I say an exaggerated amount? If I starve, they won't give me their salary and if I have, I won't either give them a penny! Yes! That's the fact! They ask, 'What's your salary?' just to satisfy their sadistic instinct. So it is always better to exaggerate things to the maximum so that they grind and gnaw their teeth and melt themselves!

"'You were never a 'neat' or 'clean' person,' you wrote in your letter! If I were not neat or clean who else would be neat and clean? Didn't I wash my face, hands and feet to keep me neat and clean? Didn't I take a bath every evening before I came to sleep with you? In what other way should I become neat? I understand your evil thoughts and pun lurking behind such words!

"Though you quarreled with me for my occasional smoking

and drinking, never did I say a dark word against you; and then, it was your last strategy in your declared fight against your clean husband, to throw slime at my face, by accusing me of lechery and adultery! You began to criticize each and every movement of mine, just like the saying, 'when you don't like your spouse, whatever he or she touches turns a crime!'

"Did I ever suspect the chastity of my wife? For God's sake, never did I have such mental disorders! But you always defamed my purity! Of course, husbands would never say that their wives were wayward. But there are women who proudly announce their husbands go after other women, perhaps, to declare indirectly that their husbands are still virile and sexually potent, as your friends in our neighborhood used to say about their husbands! My dear Geetha, I always believed that I got a chaste wife just because I have been pure and chaste. If you haven't committed adultery, you can also believe me so! And if you don't think of me as chaste and pure, it means that some bitter memory of an unbecoming incident lay hidden in your subconscious mind, and I am helpless!

"It is the environment that creates a perfect person; a perfect husband or a perfect wife! You might be born and brought up in such a surrounding in which your relatives led a wayward life so that you were forced to think all human beings were like that! You could have become a perfect wife if your environment was appropriate. As John B. Watson, one of the founders of Behaviorism said, 'Give me a dozen healthy infants, well-formed, and my own special world to bring them up in and I'll guarantee to take any one at random and train him to become any type of specialist I might select – doctor, engineer, artist, merchant-chief, and yes, beggar-man and thief.' And your world made you an impatient, suspicious and timorous wife; and I could not blame you but my unjustifiable fate!

"'You are a person who led a wayward life in the past. You had connections with many women in yesteryears. You even contacted prostitutes and about such matters you wrote in your stories. There are many secrets in your life which I do not know. I have been living with you all these years, and I know that you are a person whom I cannot understand.' Geetha's letter continued like this....!

"How should I react to these baseless allegations from my wife who lived with me all these twenty-five years? I have to pick up them, one by one, and analyze them. Here's a woman who doesn't know the mind of a writer! His world is a world of fantasy when he writes. He can experience anything and everything as if they have really happened. How could I explain my weird dreams which I presented through my stories in the most realistic manner? If she believed them as genuine experiences, it simply means I am successful as a writer!

"Now I realize why you were so indifferent while we were in the bedroom. Perhaps, you were irritated by my lovemaking! You imagined that whatever I said or did there was a mere repetition of what I had said or done to some other women in the past! Of course, I wrote some stories imagining that the protagonist of my story had such experiences! Unfortunately, you had no sense of humor to understand a writer's mind!

"I remember, your mind was wandering through some jungles while we were together on the bed! Perhaps, you were in half-sleep or were feigning sleep! Of course, every woman is physically lucky in that way. She could easily point out the failure of a man, but a man cannot prove it against her! It's God's curse on man that the whole burden of proof in this case is only upon him!

"What really was your problem? Was it physical or mental? In a situation in which man and woman forget the whole world and concentrate only on the heavenly bliss granted to them in this mortal life, you try to become too rational, don't you? I could well imagine what the dirty thoughts were passing through your mind during those amorous moments! Perhaps, you were thinking how I would have dealt with those fictitious whores of my stories! Or you would be worried about your chronicle sickness, or about the tiredness you felt the next morning! But remember, I always respected your sentiments, for I could not become a brute before my wife! Were I trying to fuck the wooden *Niobe* like Gunther Grass's *Truzinski*; if so my fate too would be on a double headed axe! Don't forget, my dear, that I loved you not only with your talents but also with your weaknesses.

"When you speak about my past life, you may be referring to my life as a student in North India. But that was not a wayward life, as you think, my dear Geetha! I was a disciplinarian in my life and I knew my goals to achieve in my life. No deviation could I make there; no compromise at all! I was a studious person and my aim was to acquire knowledge more than even getting a degree. I knew my limitations and I tried to overcome them. As a student, I strictly followed the 'brahmacharya' or celibacy prescribed for students by Indian sages. I had no time to flirt with girls, talking to them on silly subjects, as some other students used to do. I did not allow any person or situation to deviate me from my purpose in life.

"I always valued human life; I knew the real worth of it and no frivolous thought could change my resolution on life. I wanted to always be different from others. You were a woman who compared me with persons or friends or students whom you knew. You also compared yourself with similar persons whom you acquainted. You forgot the saying, 'If you compare, you are insulting yourself.'

"For years I have been teaching boys and girls and I know the difference between each individual! Rarely could I find a girl student with high ideals or souring motives in life. They study just to get a job and then a husband and a settled life. I cannot blame them as they are mere products of our social milieu. And you too are one such woman. As you said you could not understand me, for I have been different or wanted to be different. I feel quite helpless before your foolish notions about me!

"You say that I had relationships with many women and, especially with whores! Here, you not only insulted my moral outlooks but also my integrity and honesty. All these years I lived with self-respect. I never allowed any person to contaminate my body and soul. I believed that my body must be kept clean and pure for my life's partner. I could not be a victim of temptations.

"Many people keep their morality and character due to the lack of opportunities in their life. But in my case, it was a sort of blind belief in the so-called 'conscience' that prevented me from immoral actions of any sort. Perhaps conscience might have made me a coward, as Shakespeare's Hamlet says. Yet, for this, I am indebted to my religion and its belief in God. All crimes are justifiable according to civil and criminal laws if there are no evidence. But in religion, a crime is a crime, or a sin is a sin, whether there is ample evidence or not, as the omnipresent God is the judge. I loved that philosophy and strictly followed it in my life. I respect a religion only for that part of its belief. As Christians think, if every sinner is pardoned quite easily, without any punishment, and is given the highest post in heaven, there is no hope for virtuous people!

"Of course, as a journalist, I had to visit many places including red-light streets. On my way to the north-eastern states of India, I visited the famous Naxalbari village where once the so-called 'thunder of revolution' resounded. A teeming village had been transformed into a deserted graveyard by the police force and soldiers! Young men were beaten into pulp and young women were raped mercilessly! When you had absolute power in your hand, the so-called Indian culture in your blood would shy away, and you could go to any extremes! Many of those youngsters took asylum in the streets of Siliguri, men as coolies and women as whores! The red-light street in Siliguri was known as Theen Number or Number Three! And I had to see the place to make a report.

"At Mumbai, I saw two red-light streets in those days, currently the number might have increased, and they helped me to contribute to my fiction. It was said that when Morarji Desai was the Prime Minister of Bombay, he felt much indignation against prostitution and issued orders against it! Then all the prostitutes of Bombay marched towards his residence and, in order to avoid their nuisance, he had to allow them to do their business at certain restricted areas like Kennedy Bridge and Kamatipura. It would not be incorrect if I nominated him as the godfather of red-streets!

"All these visits to such obnoxious places couldn't make me a lecher or womanizer, could they? I was honest in my work and to my honor as well. And as a man, how could I prove my virginity through clinical analysis? In the case of a maiden, a man could take her for an anatomical test and see whether she was a virgin or not, or that's what the science says! It is unfortunate that an unmarried man cannot prove his chastity! If you want, I am ready even for a lie-detector test? But you are a woman who shuts her eyes and creates darkness! In fact, you deliberately fabricate things in accordance with your imagination! And I am helpless before you, my dear, I am in utter vacillation!

"Why I should say all these things to a woman like you, I thought many times. I know that you are incapable of understanding such grave matters. But you are my wife and my married life is now at stake! In this human life, a major part is conjugal life, and your partner in life is no small thing. Her desires and complaints should be heard with patience, though they were frivolous and negligible. It was because many a woman failed to rise above her basic, instinctive way of life and thinking!

"Well, I had the habit of writing short stories and, of course, you read them. I never kept my writings away from you or hidden somewhere. If I had kept them away, it was because you haven't that sense of humor to read and enjoy them. I allowed you to read them because I thought that every educated person had some sense of humor left at the bottom of his or her heart. I believed that once you write a story in true inspiration, it becomes public property. I don't find any fault with you in reading my stories or even my diaries. I wrote hundreds of stories about lovers, drunkards and prostitutes, to quote a few themes.

"Of course, as you said, writers were not supposed to have a family life! From the Greek period onwards, they suffered a lot from their spouses! I remember the words of my friend Dr. George, who came to my room one day and said, 'Rajesh! We should not expect that the members of our family are proud of our writings! Even my son Xanthu criticized me saying, 'Papa, nobody is going to become 'something' by simply writing a few books!' See, he loves only the money which I sent from here, but hates the simple pleasure I get from writing! And Rajesh, what do you think of the future of those books which I have been keeping in my private room as a treasure? Perhaps, after my funeral, he will return to my room, collect all the so-called 'waste', sell those 'bloodless substitutes' to secondhand booksellers, or even make a pyre of them!' I remember, Dr. George was on the verge of tears when he said these words to me!

"I heard people say that philosophers and writers failed in their married life, but I believe that it must be their failed married life that made them philosophers and writers! Perhaps, it was my philosophical outlook on life that helped me to prolong my life! I used to think that human life is like the peeling of an onion! The peeling itself is the exciting part of it! You are actively engaged; you get the pleasure of doing an action; all your senses are activated; you are involved physically, intellectually and emotionally; tears fall from your eyes; your facial muscles are tightened to a sort of wry smile and, finally, an overwhelming relaxed mood of 'post-purgation' encompasses you! You feel quite satisfied of completing a job though the outcome of your work is nil or nothing!

"Many of my stories were lost in my carelessness and some of them are still kept as manuscripts and a few of them are published. A few among my readers appreciated the realistic presentation of situations in my stories. I was blessed with such an imagination that I could present life in a purely realistic manner. But you read my stories not as a 'sahridaya', a quality of appreciating aesthetic beauty, but as a mere wife reading the autobiography of her husband! I repeat, you lacked the sense of humor as well as common sense! You failed to realize or appreciate the outsider in me!

"I remember the words of the Great Russian writer, Anton Chekov, who wrote more than 4000 letters and more than 1000 short stories: One has only to sit beside a haystack in order to imagine oneself in the embraces of a naked woman. Well! I used to play with my imagination. I used to solidify those vaporous dreams and reveries that came to me unexpectedly. Of course, I felt quite restless if I could not write down my fancies. And I realize, I was mad or crazy, as you used to say, at least on certain occasions. I am sorry, my dear, I was quite helpless!

"I admit there was something wrong with me or you made me believe so. At times, I imagined situations in which I myself was really involved or persons to whom I have real acquaintance were involved. When I wrote stories, I was really present in that world; like the great John Milton who wrote about heaven and God and became blind at the glaring light that flashed from God sitting on his throne in Heaven, as some critics said. My reading, learning and thinking helped me to create reality out of vacuity. And as an ordinary woman you could not distinguish and see the difference between the reality in imagination and the reality in actual life. I am helpless, my dear, I am helpless before you and I accept my complete failure before your arguments!

"Of course, writers are different from other ordinary people; they are blessed with certain supernatural gifts! They can create things from nothingness; therefore, they are very near to the Great Creator! When certain subjects enter into our hearts without our knowledge and disturb our equanimity, we think about them deeply and write down the results of that thinking in the best possible manner! That's what we writers do! But anybody can earn this gift through meditation and hard work! Unfortunately you hated both the talents!

"Can you love me, or are you foolish enough to believe them, if I admit that all those things I presented in my stories really happened in my life? But how can I be so dishonest to my life and insincere to those principles which I have been cherishing all through my life? Even if I make a fake confession, you won't accept me, I am sure of it!

"According to Christian tradition, to say that you aren't a sinner itself is a sin and you are doomed forever. There are Christians who used to make false confessions before their parish priests, where yearly confession is compulsory if you wanted to attend its general body meeting. Even those who haven't committed sins cooked up stories to please the priests and concluded their confession saying, 'I also used to tell lies!' And if one says to the priest, 'Sorry, Father, I couldn't do any sin to confess before you,' he would be angry and ask him to go to the altar and sit on it!

"But tell me, my dear, what really was my sin that you cursed me to the tortures of Hell, as Christians do according to their belief? You wrote, 'Let that part of the body with which you have sinned be rotten.' It's a general curse that any part of my body may be decayed! What a cruel heart you have! How can you think of such a curse over me? And after all these years living with me, snatching the whole utilities of my body, saying such a nasty thing about my chaste body! Is there any wife in this world who wrote her husband such abusive words? I'm sure no part of my body is going to be rotten until I am dead and buried. But we live in an age of cancer where anybody can be affected by it irrespective of his sins! So if some cancer affects my body, you can easily establish that I have committed sin with that part of my body! What a clever idea! You've thrown the stone ahead of the running dog!

"Do you want me to become a psychiatric case like St. Augustine who considered usual and common actions, even simple ordinary doings, as sins and confessed them? Am I supposed to cry like him, 'Make me chaste and continent but not yet,' and repent sin which I haven't committed? But I know that Augustine's *Confessions* is only a literary masterpiece of the writer. In 354 AD, in a Roman Town called Tigashe, Augustine wrote his *Confessions* which is wrongly accepted by many as an autobiography! I consider it only as one of the best melancholic novels I have ever read. If the genre of novel could be traced back to that period, Augustine's *Confessions* would be the most realistic one! The protagonist in *Confessions*, repents his so-called sins of plucking a few pears from a nearby orchard, not to eat but throw at the swine merely for the fun of it; and of looking at girls and 'boiling over' or living for fifteen years with a woman unwed and having a son named Adeodatus, meaning 'by God given.' The protagonist undergoes a sudden change at the age of 33, and he rushed into the garden, flung himself under a fig tree and in a passion of weeping, poured out his guilty heart to God, like King David who cried, 'But thou, O Lord, how long? How long, Lord! Wilt thou be angry forever?'

"Shall I cry like that, 'But thou, O Geetha, how long? How long, dear? Wilt thou be angry forever?' Will you be happy if I strike on my chest and cry, 'mea culpa; mea culpa; mea maximus culpa,' as it is written in the Latin Liturgy of the Roman Catholic Church? What a pity! To confess before the wife those sins which were not committed by the husband? If it were to please a priest, it's okay, but to please a wife!

"Of course, the story of Augustine, I heard first from my mother's mouth! When she narrated the story in a sad tone, I remember, tears appeared in my eyes! She appeared to me just like his mother, Monica! It may be the impressiveness of her storytelling that prevented me from sins and sinful situations! But who is here to understand the sincerity of my words? How long should I 'chant Vedas to this angry wild-bison?' Though I am not a sinner, your letter surely will make me one! But remember, Geetha, every curse has a curse on itself! If it doesn't work on the cursed person, it will boomerang towards the person who gave the curse! It's about you, I'm worried, my dear!

"I pondered over the Chinese proverb which I had read in a student magazine: Govern a family as you would cook a small fish – very gently.' Perhaps, I have been governing my family with an iron-hand, I thought. I was trying to analyze my mistakes as a husband. But I could not recollect even a single instance of harsh behavior which couldn't be easily ignored by Geetha! 'If it is the case of clay utensils, they may usually touch or knock at each other,' as the saying goes.

"In a family life, the husband and the wife feel themselves one, and if one of them makes a complaint or critical comment, it is only for the common benefit. Such petty quarrels are not supposed to arouse hatred or vengeance against the partner. In fact, they serve to enhance the sweetness of their relationship. He or she takes up a particular issue just because of his or her confidence in the other! But if one's heart is not pure or if it is filled with selfishness, then, such petty quarrels will brew up hatred and disgust in the mind of the accused spouse. If things go on like this, there will never be true conjugality in the world!

"Is modesty a pretension? Are manners mere affectations? Sometimes they happen so! But once applied in personal life, it is self-destructive, and in social life deceitful! And you have been practicing them throughout your life, my dear Geetha! By deceiving yourself, you marred the heavenly purity of our conjugal life! You shattered the confidence which exists naturally among married couples just like what we call souls in individuals! An acquired skill may lose its effectiveness in the passage of time; but if it is instinctive, it glitters more and more as the days pass, illuminating the individual and radiating brightness to others.

"Perhaps, I could not give you a life in accordance with your dreams! You wanted to live just like your uncles who were working outside our State or abroad. Whenever they came home, they spent money lavishly like water! Of course, you were trapped in the unhappy design: The unmet needs of childhood, the angry feelings left over from frustrations of long ago, the limits of trust and the recurrence of old fears; it was exactly like what Sigmund Freud, the great psychologist, described! I could not blame a person who would yearn to escape from that sort of a trap and the result could be a broken splintered marriage; thank God, it has not yet happened in our life!

"I confess, I could not cope with your financial expectations! With the limited income I got from my work, how could we spend like your cousins who depended on the Gulf-income? If I had been a rich man, you would have loved and respected me! I remember the Yiddish saying, 'If you have money, you are not only clever, but also handsome too, and can sing like a nightingale.'

"Unfortunately, you do not know about the real life of the rich! Do you think they are all happy in their family life? There are many skeletons in their closets, my dear! Their love is a mere showing-off, their actual life is full of secrets and they wear masks before others! I was always faithful to you and you knew it! And that's why, through this letter, you smote at the very root of my fidelity!

"There were many people in and around us who led a life of luxury. They never cared about their future; of course, too much thinking about one's future might be foolishness. In tribal cultures, people spent whatever they earned, and when they had nothing, they starved! Could we live like lilies of the field or sparrows in the sky, as Jesus Christ said? In our case, we had to construct a house; we had to give the best education to our daughter and also had to conduct her wedding. Who was there to help us at the time of such needs?

"Could we lead a life as Charvakan suggested? He said: Yavet jeevet sukham jeevet; Ranam kritwa ghritam pivet! Make your body stronger even by borrowing costly food, and live happily as far as you live! But going to luxury hotels or buying costly food were beyond our financial limits! Don't you remember that, at least once in a while, I managed to fetch certain costly exotic dishes? Of course, you were not very particular about such things or you pretended so, perhaps, to please me! At the same time, you always praised the treats given by your uncles or cousins, once or twice, in some five-star hotels, only to belittle my efforts!

"Never did I wish to become rich. I knew the Navaho saying that a man could not get rich if he took proper care of his family! If both of us were employed, we could have enjoyed some luxury. But with the limited income of mine, wasn't it impossible? I know that your desires were quite simple, and it's natural that you loved to be above your relatives!

"Nevertheless, you have been an expert angler! You hooked me using my own words as bait! I remembered! I wanted to be an ordinary man in my wife's presence. All the hypocrisy and the masks of formality should be thrown away once you are with your wife. Man is fundamentally a man only! All the norms of civilization, culture and manners are acquired things and they will disappear when the real man comes out of it! And at times it happens so! Especially when you are quite private, spending your time with your wife. You say a lot of things and do many things when you are with your wife! Whether a man of social commitment can say or do such things is another matter! Society might have made us reserved persons! But the private life of a husband and wife is entirely different. There they must be like original human beings, perhaps, like the cave dwellers in their pristine glory and innocence!

"I know that you are very possessive and always wish for a husband who plays to the tune of the wife! Most of the Indian couples think of their spouses as their exclusive possession! Perhaps, the basis of fidelity between the husband and the wife in India may be this sense possession! But this sense also makes most of them paranoid! The words of Acharya Rajaneesh or Osho are applicable here, 'Love is not about possession; love is about appreciation!'

"I know a number of persons who, though reluctant to be free with their wives, go for the warmth of prostitutes. But near your wife, you are free; and the reservations of your mind vanish just like ice before the fire. But if the wife manipulates your words and deeds, the privacy of your life, no, even the very existence of your human life disappears! Every man and every woman gets relieved of his or her masks only in the presence of his or her spouse. In our case, my dear wife, I feel cornered by you at every word I uttered and at every action I performed! Really, now I feel quite afraid of you! I wonder how I have sustained or survived the very private moments of our conjugal life!

"Every moment I am thinking about the behavior and uncommon attitude of my wife, I feel horrified to the core. No husband could think of such a situation! It is natural that every husband and wife should be mere ordinary homo-sapiens in their bedroom. All the reservations and delicacies should be shredded down by them. Then only they could enjoy the mysterious pleasures of human life and feel the worth of this meaningless earthly life!

"You wrote in your letter, 'Now you can do whatever you like! No more there will be any trouble from my side. I am becoming more or less old! I am of no more use for you! I have crossed my forty-fifth year and my period is almost stopped!' Oh, Geetha! What a fool you are! Isn't it natural that the menstruation, in some cases, will be stopped by the age of forty-five? It is quite a common phenomenon and why do you worry about such things? Do you think that it will bring any difference in our family life? At times you are so childish and I fail to make you understand even certain simple things!

"Well! I think it may be a punishment for you! You always hated to be a woman. I remember how you cursed those days of menstruation. Of course, it was painful for you and it created much inconvenience. You know that it is a natural thing with every woman! But you used to cry, 'Oh God! What a punishment is this to be born as a woman! These bloody days of discomfort, and when it stops, the agony of pregnancy and, then, the travail of delivery....!'

"Every month, you cursed the natural blessings given by God! And you never cared about its value in human life! You forgot the suffering of women who could not deliver a child. A woman is anatomically different from a man and you know it. Suppose, every woman begins to worry about the growth of their breasts, what will be the condition of this world! You read the arguments of some feminists who preferred lesbian life and, that may be the reason, why you think in these abnormal lines!

"Perhaps, India is the only country where people mock at the body of another person, whether man or woman, old or young! They observed others indecently and checked whether they are tall or short, fat or lean, their hair, whether curly, scanty-haired or bald-headed, their breasts, whether large, small or dry, their tummy and buttocks, their demeanor and appearance, their way of talking and walking and what not! Indians are culturally uncivilized that they laughed even at physically handicapped people! The greatest merit of African culture is that they respect the human body, alive or dead!

"The voice of education, perhaps, contaminated the minds of our women! To become pregnant has become something shameful for them! To deliver a child or sometimes more than one child is a burden for them! To feed their children from their breasts is inconvenient for them! Just look at these educated Ethiopian women who think of their breasts as mere mammary glands and giving birth to children as something natural!

"Of course, our society is prejudiced with foolish notions! We laugh at those things offered by nature! We are very particular about another person's color, shape and appearance! Whether they are fat or lean, if so, to what extent they are fat or lean, whether they are tall or dwarf, or which part of their body is larger or smaller, are our main concern! Never did Ethiopians think badly of such natural gifts, and that is the greatness of their culture and civilization!

"My dear Geetha, be normal in your arguments! Can a leopard change its spots? Can a tiger change its stripes? The menstruation for a woman is like that, and you must accept it as it is, when it starts or when it stops! Of course, your family background and the social environment in our part of the country created confusion in your life. Your mother, who became a widow at an early age, might have cursed her useless menstruations! That might be her humble reaction towards a society that denied a re-marriage for her. The people who considered menstruation as something unholy and unclean might have created a stigma in your young heart. The superstition that if a girl-child is menstruating on an inauspicious day, it will create problems throughout her life also

211

might have influenced your mind, for your first menstruation, as you revealed to me later, was on a Saturday!

"Whether this superstition was good or bad, you suffered a lot during those days. You begin to feel tension even one week before it started, and continue to be in tension even one week after the period! All these three weeks you turned our family life into a hell! Then, you became normal and we enjoyed a peaceful life for a week, only to begin the next three weeks of horrors! But didn't I manage all these troubles silently and without any complaint? Now, you feel greater tension as you approach the days of your menopause! Well! My dear, if I could love you and bear with you during those painful days of your period, why couldn't I love you and bear with you the future painless days of your menopause? Be happy, my dear, and don't try to challenge the course of nature!

"I loved you as a woman, as my wife, and your problems, illnesses and difficulties are mine too. You cannot separate yourself from me as God united us as one body and one soul! I am not an animal to run after another female just for the sake of reproduction! Man is a not only a rational animal but also a gregarious animal, but, at the same time, man is the only animal on this earth that can feel love! The word 'love' is, perhaps, abstract like beauty and truth, they depend on the person concerned. But love can be noticed through its reflections of sympathy and sacrifice. If I could love you when nature blessed you with menstruation, couldn't I continue to love you when nature ceases the blessing? Menopause is quite natural with every female as she reaches middle age, but the love between the husband and wife will solve all its adverse consequences. For true love cannot grow old and age cannot exhaust it!

"Let me think of your problem in a different way! Perhaps, menopause might have caused a sort of paranoia and that was quite natural! You may remember the case of Kuroosa and his wife Omini, our neighbors. He was a teacher and he worked in a school far away from our village. His first wife had died following her second delivery and he married Omini, a beautiful woman from our neighborhood. She was very kind to his two elder daughters, even after the birth of her two boys. When Kurrosa retired, he got a good amount as gratuity and with that amount he could arrange the marriage of his daughters. However, as years passed, there came a sudden change in the character of Omini! She began to suspect her husband and she made his life miserable complaining that he had extra marital affairs! She did not allow him to go out of the house; there would be hell if she saw him talking to some ladies in the neighborhood! Some of us had to believe her allegations when she described her 'old man's amorous activities' in a believable manner! It was too late to realize that she had been suffering from some mental illness; the poor woman committed suicide believing the imagined story of her husband's illegal sexual relationship with some other women!

"Of course, you heard about certain wives in the Islamic countries who arranged young wives for their husbands. But we are Indians and ours is not a tribal culture and we cannot follow their uncivilized tradition! In such countries, there is no equality between men and women, no concept of love and respect for women and no idea about conjugal life; for them, women are just for sex and reproduction! Generally, they don't give proper education to their girls because education may create an awareness of equality in their minds, and that was what the fruits of the Tree of Knowledge did in the Eden Garden!

"Now, what really is your problem? I am sure that it is not merely psychological, though psychiatrists warn that such mental problems are common among women who face menopause, and you have learned about such things! Then, what troubles your heart? Perhaps, you never loved me! I remember, you always kept a distance in between us, and you never opened your heart for me! It's my fate, and I must suffer it!

"To whom should I explain my miserable condition? When you asked me how my life in a foreign county was, what answer did you expect from me? If I answered 'Life is enjoyable here,' then, you would reply, 'Yes! I know, you went there to enjoy life!' If I said, 'Life is miserable here,' then, you would ask, "Why did you go there? Did I tell you to go there?' If I replied, 'Oh, life is tolerable here,' then, you would say, 'I know it, everything is tolerable for you except me!' Was it the way of expressing one's love? Perhaps, it might be your way!

"Today, it is Christmas here! I can imagine how you celebrated Christmas there! You might be imagining how your husband reacted after reading the letter. You might be laughing aloud with sadistic pleasure, for inflicting pain on me with a letter. Wasn't your letter a bomb? Oh, God! How could my wife degrade into such a low level!

"And together with your letter, you sent a Christmas card too! The printed words on the card were so touching but, of course, it was written only by a commercial writer for whom the card-company might have paid a handsome amount! See the words: *Christmas Joys For You, Dear Husband. You are truly special, Dear Husband, and the Christmas season just seems like a good time to let you know how much you mean, and how warmly you're wished every happiness – now and throughout the year.* How lovely was the scribbling on the card! But from folds of the card fell down your letter that I took from the floor and read only to feel the shock for the rest of my life!

"You wrote in it: 'It's only a 'talk' that we are 'wife and husband!' For I haven't got neither a sincere letter nor an honest word from you! Of course, from the very beginning of our married life, you never talked much. And suppose you talked, it would end up in a fight! In Ethiopia, what else is the news about you? Life would be very pleasurable for you there as I am not with you! You can live a life as you like it! Even in those days of daring youth, you enjoyed the life of pleasures in North India! Now, the wife and the child might be an excess debt for you! The only thing is that the life of 'others' whom fate chained with you is ruined! My life is totally ruined. I only hope that at least my child should get a happy married life. I specially pray only for that!'

"Her writing ends with a piece of advice: 'Mutual love and faith is sufficient; and nothing else is needed! The life on this earth is worthy if there is peace and happiness in the mind!' What a wonderful idea, my dear Geetha! I never thought that you had such a powerful imagination! Or such a philosophical outlook on life! Well! Let me ask you one thing, my dear, as I have been totally confused by your letter; tell me frankly, are you getting some sort of sadistic pleasure by writing like this to me?

"I breathed a hot sigh and looked at the sentences on my diary. Can I end a twenty-five-year-old conjugal life like that! Can I find a trace of optimism in her last words? All these twenty-five years of married life, neatly sliced into two pieces with a single smite! I scanned the letter for some rare words of sympathy from my wife. No! Not a single word, instead of Xmas blessings she had sent only Xmas curses! In fact, her letter had transformed my Christmas into a Sad Friday, the day which Europeans call Good Friday!

"After living many years with a husband, enjoying or simply consuming each and every drop of his blood and sweat, there are wives who speak without any hesitation, like Ibsen's character Mrs. Elvsted, about their husbands, 'Everything about him is repellant to me! We have not a thought in common. We have no single point of sympathy – he and I.' Perhaps, I was also a specialist, as Hedda Gabbler thought about her husband: And specialists are not at all amusing to travel with; not in the long run at any rate.

"There were a few lousy lice in and around your

neighborhood, always busy in making fun of those husbands who were scientists, professors or priests. Such lecherous prigs would say, 'Oh! Look at those husbands, the scientists who smell chemicals deal with test tubes, the professors who smell cobwebs deal with books and the priests who smell frankincense engage in prayers! And their poor wives yearn for some free moments of sex-talks which their husbands cannot find. We must make use of such opportunities and we are always free at their service!'

"These anti-social elements were readily available anywhere and they were experts in trapping innocent wives with their 'tete-a-tetes'! In the presence of women, they forget themselves the dignity and honor and go on talking with them, flirting, courting, making a fool of themselves and enjoying a sort of vicarious pleasure, equivalent to intercourse! Of course, at times, some women love to hear such substandard gibberish prattles of womanizers, who are too cunning enough to behave like fools!

"Perhaps your mind still rebels at the thought of a life with a teacher, a man who doles out advice and impossible morals to people who patiently hear them and regularly violate them! Perhaps, one can't blame you, because you have been living with a teacher-husband for quite a long period! Of course, similar attitude will be developed among women when their faithfulness is only the result of conventionality of mind or tradition under which they had been brought up, and not of real virtue or discipline of the heart!

"Whenever others praised me for something or other, you burned with jealousy; I felt it in my heart! I think I know the reason. As Maugham's character Champion Cheney says, 'Women dislike intelligence, and when they find it in their husbands they revenge themselves on them in the only way they can, by making them – sore and angry and miserable and above all – fools.' And you did not know the warning given by

Shakespeare against 'ill office or fell jealousy which troubles oft the bed of blessed marriage!'

"Women are experts in making their beds; their husbands would appreciate their action expecting an unusual experience from them; but they make their beds for nagging and acquiring some extra materialistic benefit from them; and for the unusual experience, they won't lie on the beds they made but prefer the floor! And suppose they lie on the bed, they behave too formally that their indifference arouses disgust in the hearts of their husbands. As Somerset Maugham says through Lady Kitty, one sacrifices one's life for love and then finds that love doesn't last; the tragedy of love isn't death or separation, one gets over them, the tragedy of love is indifference!

"I always loved you. I have been in love with you since the first time I saw you! But my love has turned meaningless as you are not in love with me! Nobody is given a perfect marriage, as no one is perfect! But nobody can ignore the oath or promise made at the time of marriage. When two imperfect people got married, it was the promise that made the marriage and not the contract paper they signed! It is a promise made by two persons in the presence of an invisible God. A promise is a promise! A contract is only a contract, and it can turn voidable at any moment. Of course, it is good and it cements a promise as far as the partners take the words in its spirit and not in the letters.

"Of course, there are people who think of a contract as a mere piece of a contract-paper! Before the ink dries on the paper, they apply for divorce or go to bed with someone else. John Dryden, in one of his poems, asks:

'Why should a foolish marriage vow,
Which long ago was made,
Oblige us to each other now
When passion is decayed?'

"What do you expect from a marriage, love or happiness? Anybody can give love but happiness is something different, it includes responsibility, obligation, rights and sacrifice! Anybody can say, 'I love you!' because love is an abstract idea! And nobody feels the prick of conscience when they break their love, the phrase is turned, 'I hate you!' How funny it is!

"How funny are our writers! They shamelessly compare concrete things with abstract ideas! See, what Terry Lennox, a character in Raymond Chandler's novel *The Long Goodbye*, says: 'Alcohol is like love! The first kiss is magic, the second is intimate, the third is routine. After that you take the girl's clothes off!' Yet more funny is an explanation to love! 'Love is simply three kisses before intercourse!' See, how the great key-word for human existence is reduced to a momentary act of pleasure!

"It is said that lust makes a man old, but keeps a woman young! But I think that it keeps both man and woman young! Perhaps, lust makes both old but love keeps them always young. Of course, we were bound by lust and not by love; and one's love can be proved only through sacrifice and sympathy which we never tried in our life. Well, you always claimed that you loved me and tried to prove through certain examples. But all those examples seem to me frivolous and silly. They remind me about the line from Sir Walter Raleigh's poem, 'Tell love it is but lust; Tell flesh it is but dust.' Of course, in a fundamentalist or totalitarian country, the line can be changed like this: Tell love it is but law; Tell flesh it is but flaw!

"Love leads to mutual respect and honoring reciprocally. You tried to prove that you always honored me but the examples you pointed out were quite funny and awkward. My dear, Geetha! El honor ne se mueve de lado como les congrejos! It is a Spanish saying and it means honor does not move sideways like a crab.

"Your main problem may be that you have had no work-culture. And as a housewife you can't have it! A teacher's work-culture is supposed to be the best as it consists of discipline and hard-work. Take the cases of a businessman, a clerk or a priest; their work-culture will definitely reflect in their houses; the atmosphere in their homes will be typical of their occupations. Just take the example of time-management in their homes; it would definitely echo the system followed by the heads of the family.

"A clever housewife can easily become an expert in time-management, if she desires so! It is taken for granted that a writer is a failure in time-management because his work depends on his mood or what we call inspiration. Therefore, I believe that it is the duty of a writer's wife to adjust her time accordingly, if she is really interested in it! In your case, you are not at all interested in any kind of adjustments with time except in finding sufficient time to disturb your husband's heaven-sent moments.

"Now you may argue, asking questions like: Do you mean that I never encouraged your writing? Didn't I leave you alone whenever I found you in the travail of writing? Didn't I ask you several times to complete the stories which you left unfinished? Didn't I remind you the date and time for attending the meetings you agreed with the organizers? All these questions and a hundred other questions you put forward are perfectly right and I can't deny them. But I always felt the sardonic tone in your voice and that would be enough to put out the fire of enthusiasm in my heart. Your encouragements were not genuine or spontaneous; they came out of your propriety and formality. You tried to make such sacrifices with bitterness and hatred in your heart. Were you ready to leave me alone at least a few hours while I was in the mood of writing? Instead, you interpreted my mood for writing as my selfishness or lack of love! Well, it's all funny to argue with you on these issues!

"Of course, writing gave me a sort of relief; the free individual expression contributed much to physical and mental health! Aristotle said about catharsis, the purification of the emotions of pity and fear, and my writing helped me for the writer's catharsis! It purified me, refreshed me and rejuvenated me!

"Yes! I remember now! You did not like me talking to my students and friends; you alleged me of getting sexual pleasure from such talks! Gosh! How could a woman degrade to such a brutish level! One cannot imagine the ways of a crazy mind!

"I tried to find the reasons for her sudden downfall from that height of an assiduous wife to that of a jealous woman! Usually a wife falls into such abhorred state of mind due to three reasons, firstly, the persons with whom she has been living, secondly, the atmosphere in which she lives and thirdly, the things she imagines. In Geetha's case, perhaps, all three reasons might have brought her to such a depressed stage.

"Among the persons, who lived with her, I was one and so, perhaps, I also was responsible for her present mental condition, I tried to justify her. The situation of an unemployed woman who has always to depend on her husband also is another reason. And the third one is to pollute one's mind by sitting alone and imagining unnecessary matters which are quite impossible to happen. Perhaps, when Einstein said, 'Imagination is more important than knowledge', he didn't imagine its negative impact! And life will be happy only for those who control themselves by realizing the inevitability of these reasons. But unfortunately you think that I have been the only reason for your present depressed life, and that's my misfortune! I sighed in helplessness.

"And according to a study on Major Depressive Episode (MDE) made by the World Health Organization, India is first in the number of patients suffering from depression; the symptoms of the disease can be seen among 36% of Indians! The study was conducted on 89000 persons from 18 countries and revealed that about 120 million all over the world suffer from depression. With 33.6% the second place goes to Netherlands, the third place to France with 32.3% and the US stands fourth with 30.9%! It is also said that the age of starting depression in India is 31 years and 9 months!

"We live in the so-called modern age, my dear. We all suffer from a sort of disillusionment; our dreams have gone beyond our control! Here, on one side, young men and women try to evade responsibility and obligations at the cost of their progeny. On the other side, by leading a bohemian way of life in sex, a number of women are actually vitiating the honor of their vagina into that of a public latrine! Never a public toilet can be kept as a glamour room! Lechers use and leave it recklessly and the women struggle to clean the stains in vain!

"We are desert travelers, my dear, and we think that there will be a better oasis on the other side of the desert; we leave the little comforts of the present and seek the ideal only to realize that it was merely a mirage that betrayed our rationality. And once you leave a place, a return is impossible; at least, one cannot return with the same body and mind!

"Of course, in married life, the partners undergo a lot of traumatic experiences, if they try to probe into their own selves. If you think that your self is lost forever in the conjugal process of the amalgamation of the two selves in marriage and, thereby, try to go back to your past to recover that 'believed to be lost self,' the family breaks! And by the time you realize that your self was not really lost but was only diluted into one with that of your spouse, years would have passed and you would have lost much of the vigor and enthusiasm of life. In that process, you might have learned lessons and decided to make any kind of compromise, but that's natural with every aged person! Unfortunately, during our youth, we fail to differentiate between reality and disillusionment. Haven't you heard the famous words: And in the end, it's not the years in your life that count; it's the life in your years!

"We lost many heavenly moments; had we tried, by

reducing the heat of our arguments a bit lower, we could have turned our married life worthy in every sense! Contention, thy name is woman! If you had feigned a bit timorous, our life would have been more amorous! If you, pretending loving kindness, had demanded me to bring 'kalayana-saugandhika flower,' I, like Bhimasena, would have gone to the giant's garden to bring it for you! But your ego never allowed you to speak in a loving tone; you deemed bashfulness as a degradation of your feminine status! And now there's no use to cry over the spilt milk!

"But, my dearest one! Forgive me and forget all my mistakes! I might have committed many errors unknowingly in our conjugal life! I might not be a good husband to you or I could not grow up to your expectations! But there is sufficient time left for us, and I am ready to leave even my job in this African country. Why should I keep a job here if it is of no benefit for my wife and child? I know that I can love you more than ever! Just say that you are ready to compromise and love me. Just say 'yes' over the telephone and I shall be near your side! Won't you give me a chance, just one more chance, my dearest?"

There, ends his diary notes and, then, a number of blank pages. My eyes were wet and I wished to pour some cold water on my face. I prayed silently for the happiness of Rajesh and his wife. Oh Geetha! Won't you give Rajesh one more chance to love you! My mind whispered and I heard the chiming of the clock, which was considered a good omen!

I continued to ponder over his diary-notes. How could one believe what he had written, unless the so-called letter from his wife should be kept as evidence? Perhaps, the whole story was the outcome of his hot brain! Some fiction writers made their stories realistic by presenting them as if they had happened in their real life! They were like silk-worms that produced silk-threads from their own body with much effort, in order to be used by human beings to make their wonderful garments! Or they were like oysters that kept sand-particles in their body and suffered pain throughout their life covering them with their life-fluid, until people took them out as precious pearls to be used in their necklaces and other ornaments! Of course, Rajesh was a good fiction writer, and could not completely reject such a possibility as simple as that!

I casually turned the blank pages of his diary until, to my surprise, I found the last page with some more scribbling. I read it with much curiosity:

"I am very, very happy today, my dearest! At last my agony and suffering has come to a fruitful end. All these months, since your last letter had reached me months ago, I have been living like a 'live dead body!' Your telephone call has revitalized me! I am sure that your misunderstanding is over forever. The trauma and the ordeal are over and the next few days will be of recuperation and convalescence!

"My dear! What a fool I was to imagine a myriad of possibilities about your attitude towards me! I forgot what Boccaccio's character in Da Cameron, Filomena, says about women, 'We are sensitive, perverse, suspicious, pusillanimous and timid.' How true those words were in your case!

"It might be the good deeds in my previous births that helped me to regain my lost happiness! I know that you are regretting much over that cruel letter. I can see with my mind's eye how much you feel about it, my dear! Your wet eyes, your cheeks stained with tears and your lips trembling with sorrow – all I see as if in a vision. Don't worry, darling! The letter you sent to me will never see daylight again and it will never become an impediment to our happy reunion! I am burning it together with all other waste-papers. Let that fire purify our hearts and brighten our conjugal life."

That was the last page of his diary, and I understood why he had sent me that diary; he did not want to keep any evidence of those dark cloudy days. I closed the diary and kept it in my handbag. I must keep it as a confession-secret. I heard the gate of my house open, and the noise of my wife and son. I went down the steps to greet them.

CHAPTER SEVEN

It was a happy evening; my wife had enjoyed her shopping as her son was with her; she could pick up any item without a second thought of its utility! If she were with me, before taking every item, she used to look at my face to see whether I agreed to take it or not, and I looked elsewhere as if I did not care what she put in the trolley! Of course, such were the only occasions for the husbands to prove that they loved their wives and they had full confidence in them!

Of course, as the head of the house, I used to show a grave face in such matters as I must be a bit 'economic', traditionally husbands were supposed to be like that, but for my bachelor son, it was a golden opportunity to please his mother, for he did not know what would be his condition after his marriage!

Of course, the most important thing in human life are relationships; perhaps, what we call love is merely an abstract idea but relationships are real; and the success of life depends on how strong our relationships are and how many relationships we can maintain successfully without losing their sanctity. As Swami Vivekananda said, "Relationships are more important than life, but it is important for those relationships to have life in them."

I told my wife to prepare some fruit-drinks, perhaps to compensate her absence for a few hours but my son immediately went to the kitchen, opened the fridge and prepared some lime juice for all three of us. As we sipped the drinks, the doorbell rang and my son opened the door!

My friend Mr. Sanders was standing by the door and I was

surprised how he came to know of my arrival from Ethiopia! He was my classmate in high school and after graduation, he joined the B.Ed. course and got the job of a teacher, while I went for my higher studies, first a masters degree and then a doctorate degree, and roamed here and there to find a job!

I greeted Sanders and we went together to my study and talked a lot about things that happened in the locality during my absence. Though he answered all my friendly questions, from the expression on his face, I noticed that there was some problem troubling his mind! It might be some sort of financial problem, I thought! Could anyone manage their family in Kerala with just the salary, though the amount was not bad? Soon I remembered that his wife was working in a nationalized bank from where the employees would get loans at a very low interest rate!

Sanders was silent for a few minutes, and then I noticed blood rushing into his face; a sort of wild look appeared in his eyes! He said in a calculative manner, "Well! George, I am going to kill that bastard who spoiled my daughter's life!" He covered his face with both his hands and began to cry silently.

I was surprised at his sudden change! I knew that his only daughter was married to an educated boy from a reputed family! Both of them were employed in a leading IT company in a big south Indian city! As far as I knew the only problem with them was that they had postponed the birth of a child! Of course, almost five years passed after their marriage and it was a risk to postpone the birth of a child! Moreover, it was not a minor issue, as many Keralite-couples now-a-days happened to be childless!

He took out a letter from his pocket and gave it to me to reading. The letter was stained here and there with tears, perhaps! I glanced at a paragraph; she had written: "Why did God punish me like this? I studied for ten years at the Sunday School; I prayed every morning and evening; our wedding was conducted in the most graceful manner with the hands of a bishop in the presence of many priests and laymen! Why God did give me this miserable life? Even I lost my faith in God! But who could wipe away the lines of fate from one's forehead!"

She continued her writing, "When we face problems in life, we used to turn towards spiritual consolation! But where should we go when we face real spiritual helplessness? Whenever I look into the mirror, I see my face quite distorted; I feel as if the despair of the whole city is reflected on my face! I feel as if I were an ugly insect crawling in the shit of a modern city!"

"Nobody bothers about others in this busy city; by living among these huge skyscrapers of cement, steel and glass, my heart too is turned into stone or concrete! Sometimes, I dive into the depth of my past, into those days we spent together at home! In one way, I am happy here; my husband is quite caring, takes me to the hotel and offers me the most delicious food! We get regular promotions and salary hikes at the office; we have sufficient money to lead a luxurious life! But in the midst of victories and luxuries, the awareness of dissatisfaction in life beats its wings and shatters my hopes for a nest! My future is in utter darkness; all my enthusiastic efforts to achieve something in life turn in vain!"

I looked up at Sanders' face; he was looking somewhere on the horizon! I could understand the ocean of tsunami forming in his mind! I continued my reading: "Of course, we love each other and we cannot imagine a separated life! But he does not like to have a child! He thinks that a child is a burden in life! He wants to enjoy life, to drink life to the lees! He likes all the fun in life like eating, drinking, talking, playing, working, cooking, travelling, sightseeing and what not! But he does not like to have a child! We met a number of counselors, psychologists and psychiatrists, but of no use! And my life as a woman has turned into a big zero!"

I folded the letter without reading further and gave it back to Sanders. I was in utter confusion. How could I console this man? What remedy should I suggest for such a strange situation except the usual words of hypocrisy: Don't worry! Let us pray for them!

I asked him to relax but he made some lame excuse and hurriedly went out! I knew that he was really in a helpless situation. He was a man who believed that the immortality of the soul meant the immortality of the gene, and that immortality could be achieved only if you had a continuity of generations! And a person without progeny would not get salvation or 'moksha', according to Indian tradition!

In such a situation, the old generation would strike on their head and cry, "The Doom's Day has come! Women begging to men for sex and reproduction! It's simply unnatural!"

Once, together with Dr. Ahmad Ansari and Dr. Worku Singh, I visited Gondar in Ethiopia, where we saw a large, spreading tree with a mythological background. It was an aged tree, not much tall, but branches spreading all around about ten feet above the ground level. It was a kind of huge fig-tree and the name given to it was 'Jentekal'. People believed that when any branch of the tree touched the ground that would be the Doom's Day because then women would demand men to share their beds!

Such was the predicament of Mr. Sander's daughter, I thought. The problem was that they loved each other and no one could separate them! Of course, love is an abstract term; only a few people could fully experience it and, therefore, no one could ignore it! Usually, people like to give a sort of divine halo to it, as they used to do with all such unachievable things, and keep it away as something sacred or beyond the access of ordinary people! Naturally, many of us consider love as something abstract or immaterial or tentative like truth, beauty, freedom and equality, instead of making it simple and empirical.

In fact, love can be experienced, or even explained, only through its various ingredients like sympathy, kindness and sacrifice which are easily understandable. It is true that love gives one a sort of supernatural experience or a spiritual pleasure. That does not mean that love is something supernatural, something not attainable for ordinary people. A vast majority of people are not patient enough to wait till they get that rare experience.

There are people who think that the opposite of love is hate, and hate is just love gone bad! As Amish Tripathy's character, Veerbhadra, says, "the actual opposite of love is apathy;" a mindset in which "you don't care a damn as to what happens to the other person."

Then, what is love? "If you ask, I know not; if you ask not, I know," would be a better answer! Who could define true love? Of course, there were people who tried to explain what it is or what it is not! I remembered what my friend Rajesh had scribbled about love in his diary. He quoted the most wonderful explanation given by St. Paul.

I took a modern edition of the Bible and checked those verses; of course, holy books might offer at least some vague answers to our puzzles in life! I read that passage: Love suffers long and is kind; Love does not envy; love does not parade itself, is not puffed up; Does not behave rudely, does not seek its own, is not provoked, thinks no evil; Does not rejoice in inequity but rejoices in the truth; Bears all things, believes all things, hopes all things, endures all things; and Love never fails!

What a wonderful, ideal explanation! But how could ordinary human beings achieve such an exalted experience! Though those attributes were incomparable, were they sufficient for the modern age? A modern Paul would have added: Love advises, criticizes and scolds; seeks and gives justice; Love does not forget all things but forgives all things; Love is an obsession that acquires perfection through sacrifice and consensus; Love is a unique talent, a rare gift and a blessing for the selected! And so on...!

However, there is no use in shedding tears before a person who does not know the value of tears! It is true that family life is meant only for those people who are ready for some sort of sacrifice on his personal beliefs and convictions, for the sake of the members of his family, of his wife and children! Once Bertrand Russell told Dr. Abdus Salem, the Noble Laureate, that Gandhi was a cruel man, for forty years, he deprived his wife enjoyments of a married life!

It would be mere foolishness on the part of a person to ruin life just for the sake of certain principles. I remembered the case of my neighbor old John Papa's eldest daughter who after her marriage settled in the United States. They had no children but both of them loved each other and led a carefree life, eating, drinking and visiting friends. Once John Papa told me that they had no children because of physical disability of his son-in-law! They led a happy married life for about a quarter of a century and, then, he died in an accident! In the USA, one could keep for years a dead body in the morgue provided that the rent should be paid on time! She kept her husband's body in the morgue and every week she went there and saw her husband's body and returned home peacefully! This continued for about ten years and, later, under the compulsion of her friends and relatives the body was buried! I always believed that she kept the body of her husband in the morgue for ten years as a punishment for ruining her life!

Of course, sexual problems were quite common among our people and many of the married people from the middle class society kept such matters a secret! For the upper class and the lower class marriage and divorce are mere fun and they considered sex as mere biological need! They considered sexual intercourse as something insignificant like pissing or defecating! The case of the middle class is quite disheartening.

Every day the newspapers brought what a number of incredible news! The more the society considered sex as a taboo, the more rape cases occurred! On one side, we felt proud of our culture, but on the other side, we bent our heads in shame!

A sixty-five-year-old mother was staying with her son and, one day, the son brought home his fifty-one year old friend and helped him to rape his own mother! It would have been better if the son himself had raped his mother! Another news came in the paper was that of a grandmother who was staying with her grandson! The boy brought home his friend; both of them raped the poor old woman! What happened in this Southern State of India was indescribable! Did it mean that the Keralites were changing themselves into mother-fuckers and sister-fuckers?

After an hour, Sanders came back and I wondered what his idea was! When problems came in life, many of us would turn nervous so that some might seek refuge in drinks or drugs, some others harm themselves or commit suicide and the rest would become hermits. Of course, talking with friends would reduce the gravity of the problem, though it could not solve the same!

I thought that it was a new problem for him but he resumed our earlier topic as if he had forgotten the gap of an hour! Perhaps, he had gone out to take a beer to relax himself! A few minutes later, once again the doorbell rang, and this time it was my friend Dr. Lexan, our old Professor of Philosophy! In fact, Sanders had telephoned him to come to my house!

Sanders broke the ice and said, "See, Dr. Lexan! Here's a boy who bargains over the price of his sperm! It's the ugliest thing I have ever heard! See the helplessness of my daughter; here is a husband who doesn't want a child and a wife who badly wants to give birth to a child! She thinks that her life is worthless without a child and she yearns for the fulfillment of her mission as a woman on this earth!"

I realized that Sanders had already informed Lexan about his daughter's problem. Dr. Lexan placed on the table a few back-issues of Malayala Manorama daily, a local newspaper in Malayalam. He said in a casual manner, "You see, according to Islamic practice, every man is supposed to satisfy the desire of a woman, and he has the responsibility to make a woman the mother of her children!"

"I can't agree with your suggestion, Dr. Lexan!" I said in an angry tone. I continued, "The Islamic people misuse this opportunity and consider women as a sexual commodity! They use them only for their sexual pleasures and they engage in lechery as if it was their natural, divine duty! And we know that in this modern age of sperm-banks, a man's direct involvement is not at all necessary for a woman to get pregnant!"

Sanders shook his head and said, "Dr. George! That's true with unmarried women! But here the case is different; here's a husband and wife, married legally and spiritually, and the couples have their own rights and obligations; they also have a responsibility to the society! And their wedding was an arranged one, and not a love marriage, so that the parents also have a word on it!"

Lexan said without any sentiments, "You see, today such misunderstandings are common, and look at the number of divorces and remarriages! Man and woman are not ready to sacrifice their individual freedom. It needs some sacrifice in sharing a family life; no one could explain the divine excitement of a conjugal life; it must be experienced!"

Sanders seemed a bit irritated at the generalizing of his problem. He said, "But mine is a different issue; it's a case of life or death for me! You know that I don't believe in heaven and hell or even in life after death! But I believe in the immortality of the soul, and the so-called soul is just the gene for me! The soul of my forefathers became immortal through me, and mine will gain immortality through my children and their children! If my son-in-law doesn't give my daughter a child, he denies my immortality and, in turn, he becomes my murderer!"

Dr. Lexan shook his head and said, "That's quite strange! Why can't you think in a different way? I think, human life in itself is worth living and I don't care for a life after life! Life is the final realization and not the inevitability of death, as Albert Camus suggests. If your birth is not for the immortality of your father's gene, why should you bother about yours?"

I wished to reduce the heat of the situation and said in a jovial manner, "See, Sanders! It doesn't matter if you believe in heaven or hell, and don't bother whether they exist or not! But as John Lennon noted, we have to imagine them as existing; we might all be less judgmental of each other and be able to live in the moment! At least, I could feel happy thinking that my enemies would be in hell!"

Dr. Lexan was silent for a while, as if he were trying to remember the words of some other philosopher! Then he said, "Of course, there's an element of truth in what Mr. Sanders says! Let's keep theology aside and think practically! The idea of the immortality of the soul becomes scientific when you consider it as the gene or chromosome of man!"

I said with a sarcastic smile, "As Amitav Ghosh pointed out in his novel, *The Calcutta Chromosome*, if malaria germs can gain chromosomal immortality, why not human gene or soul?"

Dr. Lexan said with a gloomy face, "Yes! Those good old days when we thought that the marriage is performed in heaven are gone forever! Now, no one is ready to sacrifice his or her life just for the belief that they are united by God or in the presence of God! Well! We can't blame them as God is so busy that He waits too long to involve in conjugal matters! We want immediate solutions to our problems; we're too impatient to realize our own drawbacks! Of course, our life is too short that we cannot wait for a long time to come to an amicable solution!"

Sanders interrupted him and said in an assertive tone, "And that's why I argue for an immediate divorce in such cases! It is foolishness to continue to suffer an unsatisfied married life expecting that everything will be alright sooner or later! In the modern age, every individual has some mental perversion; if tolerable, prolong your married life; if unbearable, just break it as early as possible! That's my opinion!"

I said in a low voice, "But can we break an alliance or a holy betrothal simply like that? Do you remember the words of Dave Meurer who said, 'A great marriage is not when the 'perfect couple' comes together; it is when an imperfect couple learns to enjoy their differences!'"

"Stop your justifications, please, Dr. George! You can't understand the real situation. My daughter is a poor, innocent girl and she is incapable of taking a decision for herself! If I fail to advise her on time, her life will be 'a life licked by dog' as we used to say in our local tongue!" Sanders said in a loud voice.

Lexan said suddenly, "Of course, the decision is so crucial! If your daughter hasn't that willpower to manage her divorced life, she may blame her parents for her sad plight! Maybe Lord Buddha's advice seems reasonable: No matter how hard the past, you can always begin again!"

My wife brought us tea and our male-only talk was broken for a while. She greeted my friends and asked about the well-being of their families! She noticed the back-issues of the newspaper and asked whether somebody was going to start the business of used newspapers!

Dr. Lexan said, "We want to look at the matrimonial columns! You see divorces and remarriages are increasing day by day in Kerala, and anything may happen to anybody at any time!"

We all laughed at the joke. My wife pretended to be busy

and said, "I have some work in the kitchen; you're all nothing-to-do people, trying to find new topics for discussion!"

When she left the room with a smile, we began to scan the old issues of the newspaper brought by Dr. Lexan. There was a study on the alarming situation of divorces in Kerala State, especially in our major cities. In fact, we were all surprised at the information presented in that factual study made by certain young reporters!

Our small State Kerala had been on the world map for its beauty and for its spices, from ancient days onwards! It came into international notice when it gained credit as a place where the communist party came into power for the first time in the world through ballot paper! Now, it achieved another feather on its crown when it became the place where the rate of suicide was the highest in the world! The report also gave some statistics on the number of divorces in each city in Kerala. The pages of newspapers were filled with stories of mass rapes and murders of spouses! They were quite alarming!

I said with an air of concern, "See! It's quite interesting! Our Kerala State is far more advanced than certain European countries, at least in the number of suicides and divorces! Our men and women sign their marriage contract, and before the ink dries on the paper they divorce to make another contract! Funny! Don't you think that we're following the ways of the animals except in signing the papers?" I was burning with indignation!

Sanders interrupted me spontaneously and said, "Forget the rate of suicides! They are lucky; no longer did they suffer from angst or agony! Even in the so-called socialist China, every year about two million try to commit suicide and 287,000 become successful in their attempts; and it is 3.6% of the total deaths in the country! There is a 60% increase in suicide attempts every year and mostly the perpetrators belong to the age-group from 15 to 34!"

I showed them a snippet from the newspaper and said, "Look here! According to National Crime Records Bureau, Kerala State which has the highest literacy rate stands third in the ráte of suicides among the States in India; and among the Indian cities, our Quilon comes second! Last year 8490 persons committed suicide, 6409 males and 2081 females, of course, unlike in China, they belong to the age-group of 45 to 59! And the State of Bihar which has comparatively the lowest literacy rate in India also has the lowest rate in suicides! Does it mean that suicide has some connection with literacy and education? Perhaps, the more one is educated, the more one thinks about one's own future and the more selfish one becomes! And selfishness leads to suicide!"

Dr. Lexan said in his usual philosophical tone, "It's all the problem of communication; it's a common phenomenon of the modern age! The age of Damon and Damocles has gone forever; no more intimacy among friends or relatives! To whom could we reveal our unique personal problems? We live in an age in which even the priest to whom you confess your illegitimate relationship will eagerly ask for her address! Each individual lives in his own world as experience has taught him to look at others with suspicion! There's the communication gap between the husband and wife, between parents and children, among siblings, among friends and among neighbors! Of course, we try to communicate but we miserably fail in our attempts; and we have no patience to try again!"

I asked him in a sarcastic tone, "Do you mean that our language is insufficient to communicate our pestering issues? Nonsense! Don't forget that we live in a world where communication skills have developed into a science!"

"Of course, our communication methods have undergone a sea-change and we have improved them a lot! But haven't we developed ourselves accordingly?" Lexan asked in a polite way.

Sanders was in a disinterested mood. He said in a casual

tone, "After all what is there to communicate? From the days of Adam and Eve, we communicate simply our ideas, thoughts, emotions and experiences! We try to communicate even abstract ideas like love, truth, beauty, freedom and so on! Of course, when the heart is full, words are few! But then we try to communicate through meaningless sounds, gestures, facial expressions, tears and so on!"

Lexan interrupted him and said, "Yes! The problem comes when we try to explain the so-called abstract ideas! We try to insist ideas which are supposed to be quite simple, concrete and practical but our counterpart finds them complex, intangible and theoretical! Impatience breeds among the clients to such an extent that consensus becomes simply impossible!"

"Well! I understand why our award films and experimental films are very difficult to understand!" I said with a laugh. "Perhaps, they need a higher kind of oral communication!"

Lexan was becoming highly enthusiastic and he said, "Of course! Day by day, ideas are becoming stranger and stranger! There was a time when we thought that Michelangelo's Creation of Man was simply a realistic painting of perfect human anatomy but, now, we compare it with the human brain where man becomes equal to rationality! Can't you find new ideas coming up in the fields of science and arts? If five artists are asked to paint the picture of the same old tree, the result is five different paintings! Today, we wonder whether light travels in a stream or in molecules! Don't you feel that communication became more difficult due to the developments in economics, commerce and marketing? Many of our students get their higher degrees in Business Administration and Business Management but can they administrate the office or manage the people perfectly?"

Sanders joined his argument and said, "Yes! The more we study, the more complex things will be! We moved from autocracy to democracy and from Home Science to Family

Management, but life goes on without much change! Perhaps, it is high-time that we should return to our old systems, which is more or less impossible! Even our religions have lost their sanctity and how can we return to such corrupted institutions!"

I nodded desperately and wondered, "What's going on in this God's own country? Is it because our religions failed miserably? Does it mean that we became a pugnacious race? Have we lost all those cultural traits of dharma?" I asked with an air of indignation.

Dr. Lexan smiled and said, "These are the signs of an upstart society! Once we worried about our daily bread and pondered only about it! The more we became rich, the more we became selfish! We began to keep our eyes only on profit. We became more religious only to become more fanatic! Our moral manners and behaviors became mere formal showing off!"

Sanders interrupted and said, "I have a different opinion. You know, it is the energy that provokes us to engage in various activities. Normally, we use this energy in a fruitful way and make profit out of it. But some people are born with extra energy and they try to utilize it in better ways but fail in their efforts! Some of them could control it by engaging in spiritual activities, politics or social work; some others could use it for artistic and creative activities like writing, painting, sculpturing, singing and dancing! A few could suppress it by becoming alcoholic or workaholic! But a few others utilize their energy by engaging in criminal activities! And such people definitely deserve mercy killing!"

I agreed to the argument of Sanders and said, "In fact, a person with a passionate streak can develop his talents to destructive activities; he can become a thief, a rapist or a murderer! Or he can develop his talents to some creative activities like acting, writing, preaching, teaching and so on. Of course, one's natural talents should be channeled towards improving one's character, expanding one's horizon with continuous learning and establishing himself in creative arts or sciences! Instead of death sentences, the culprits must be given life imprisonment, allowing them proper facilities to develop their creative talents in a profitable way."

Dr. Lexan said in a philosophical tone, "Yes! That's cool! And I don't agree to that point of mercy killing! Of course, when we hear about the atrocities, tortures and cruelties on women, we feel too much indignation, and due to our excessive enthusiasm, we used to suggest death penalty or chemical castration to such criminals! But India cannot implement such uncivilized and primitive punishments for rape cases. Of course, in Islamic countries, the more-than-thousand-year-old tribal law is still practiced! Even HIV/AIDS is considered a taboo and such patients secretly brought to mercy killing! Uncivilized methods of punishments like public hanging, stoning to death and cutting off the head or limbs can be done only in a country ruled by fundamentalism or dictatorship. Even though such primitive punishments are given, theft, prostitution, rapes and murders are still there! It's because crimes are a part of human nature!"

"No law can prevent such things, I think. You know that I worked in an Islamic country for a few years and in one of its cities, there was a notorious woman named Ms. Abala, whose house was a brothel. Muslim girls, even from good families, served there, and most of the customers were the policemen! Of course, no one could recognize these girls as they came out after their work fully covered in black burkha and veil!" I pointed out.

Mr. Sanders was restless and he said, "At least, the Indian Criminal Procedure Code must be changed so that longer terms of imprisonment without 'parole' should be given to these sex-criminals! You see, every year rape cases and sexual abuse of children are increasing considerably in India, and punishments were given only in one or two cases! According to the Thomson

Foundation Reuter Survey, India is one among four countries in the world where women are not safe! Today, no court can punish a rapist because the evidence available may not be sufficient to prove the crime beyond doubt, and the concession of doubt will always be beneficial for the accused! The questions asked to the victim by the advocate of the accused are so mean and malicious that such questions could be answered only by street-harlots!"

"We cannot sail in two boats at the same time, my dear friends!" Dr. Lexan said. He continued, "On one side we talk about Indian morality and on the other side we practice all sorts of immorality! We say that prostitution is illegal, but it is here from the ancient times onwards! In every Indian city, we can see red-light streets with licensed 'sex workers'! Yet we frown upon it when somebody speaks about them and later stealthily crawl into such places covering our heads with a shawl! When will we Indians tear away this mask of hypocrisy? We close our eyes and create darkness! We make our laws only to help the policemen to make their extra income! We say that India is a free country but can we walk freely with a woman or stay together in a lodge? Even if she is your wife, the police come and harass! It is high-time that India should make a law allowing free movement of men and women without any hindrance from the police! Let them walk together, sit together or stay together wherever they like; it should be their right! And severe punishments should be given to those who try to harass them. Today, anti-social elements as well as the criminals in police uniform make use of the loopholes in law just to satisfy their sadistic instincts!"

I supported him and said, "Longer terms of imprisonment is the only solution! Today, suppose a cold blooded murderer is given life imprisonment, many times he could come out on 'parole' and continue his criminal activities and, as life imprisonment simply means twelve years of imprisonment, the convict could complete his term of imprisonment within less than eight years, deducting the holidays and other concession days! We all praise the American democracy and freedom but are we ready to accept their system of judiciary and punishments given to the criminals?"

I remembered what Rajesh told me when I asked him mockingly why he had left India and come to Ethiopia! He was very serious in his tone when he replied to me. He said, "I want to live in a country like Ethiopia where the culture is primeval, genuine and natural! In India, the culture is based on simple hypocrisy! The people behave as if somebody has imposed a culture on them; they live under constant fear, thinking what others would think about them! From harlots to ministers, everybody wears the mask of hypocrisy! They do all things which are illegal and immoral but before doing them they would put a shawl over their head! They are ostriches that duck their heads in the sand when the storm comes! How could a sensible person live there? Of course, we all love India as our mother country, but if you want to keep that love, don't live there permanently, just visit her once a year and return with sweet memories! That's all!"

Dr. Lexan supported the American system of punishment and said, "I think we can conclude in this way! Let the men and women go wherever they like and do whatever they like! If they get venereal disease or even HIV/AIDS, let them suffer the consequences! In certain Islamic countries, such patients are given injections of poison, even without any sort of enquiry! As medical castration of sex-criminals is not a legal matter but a medical matter, it need not be discussed among the members of the public. If a mental patient is given tranquilizing medicines or electric shock, it is decided by the concerning doctors. Likewise, let us leave the question of medical castration of the sex-criminals to the concerning medical doctors. Some of the criminals need it, some others not, and the concerning doctors of the jail will take the final decision. However, long imprisonment with a period of not less than thirty years without parole and concessions of holidays should be given to rapists and other sex criminals."

Sanders was still in his heated mood and said as if talking to himself, "I wonder, what the hell all our religions are for! They speak about morality, God and salvation but all the criminals are members of either of religions! No doubt, the days of the religions have gone forever!"

Dr. Lexan replied in a cool voice, "That's what Malthus said years ago that the poorer the people, the stronger would be their religious culture! The crime rate is increasing in India and that's a clear proof that India is progressing! When we were poor, we really believed in religious morality and our actions were controlled by our conscience; but now we are rich, I mean, at least we don't have any tension over our daily bread, religion is simply a luxury for us! Religion has become a fashion for the bourgeois and an entertainment for the petty bourgeois or the present lower class in India!"

I intervened and said, "Religion was always a part of power politics! It is an indirect way of keeping people under control in the name of God! The members of religions are helpless as their membership itself is a symbol of their identity and social status! Moreover, today, religion has become an unaffordable luxury! It is just like getting membership in a posh club! Once I questioned a bishop about the corruption of the church and the anti-Christian ways under which they operate, and he replied to me in a simple manner, 'If you don't like such things, better do clear off; we have more than sufficient numbers of obedient sheep in the flock!' Such is the arrogance of these religious leaders!"

I heard my wife talking loudly to Xanthu; it was time to wind up our discussion! I said in a concluding tone, "Let's hope for the best! And that's the only option left for the poor and the helpless! Hope is a delicious repast for the poor, according to an Ethiopian saying. Let's pray, my dear friends! That's the only reasonable thing we can do!"

I stood up, showing in a polite way my helplessness to continue the discussion! We all laughed aloud with a sort of mutual understanding and dispersed, promising to meet on the following day, if possible.

CHAPTER EIGHT

Next morning, I ironed my best dress and hung them on brackets, for ready use. The following day, I had to attend the wedding of Salim's daughter, Zeenath. Over the telephone, he had invited me and told me that he was so busy that he could not come to my house for a formal invitation. Of course, anybody could understand his situation!

Hearing the doorbell, I came out to see who was there at that odd time of day! To my surprise, it was Dr. Salim Mohammed!

"Oh, Salim! What a surprise! Come in; come in! I thought you have been busy with the wedding arrangements! Any new problem?" I asked him, while leading him to the drawing room.

"Everything's fine and okay," he said with a smile. "I thought I must come and personally invite you to the wedding."

"What nonsense are you talking? My dear Salim! You rang me and invited me, and that's enough and more! You know, I don't believe in these formalities! Do you think of me as an outsider in your family?" I said in a tone of indignation.

"Well! It's alright! But I wished to spend some time with you, doctor! Is that a crime? I want to relax for a while in your presence. Is that okay with you?"

"Chigre yellam!" I said in Amharic, as we used to say in Ethiopia. "No problem; you can stay here as much time as you wish. But I thought you were quite busy with the wedding arrangements!"

"Everything goes perfectly well until now! But, doctor, I'm in hypertension, till the wedding is over," Salim said. "I'm afraid whether that bastard or his friends would come and create some problems. He has nothing to lose, but I have everything to lose, my relationships, my honor, my family and even my life! If any such things happen, no more I'll be on this earth! Well! It's all happened due to the foolishness of my daughter!"

"Don't worry, my dear Salim!" I placed my hands on his shoulders and tried to console him. "Control yourself! What is to happen, will happen; for who can question the pranks of fate! You know what Clarence Darrow said, 'the first half of life is ruined by our parents and the second half by our children.' It's all part of the game!"

Salim heaved a long sigh! He was in a completely relaxed mood. I reminded him, "You know the nature of today's children; they grow fast as they eat the hormone-injected broiler chicken; they talk like their matinee-idols! Don't be embarrassed if I ask you something; of course, think of it as the foolishness of a friend! Can you believe your daughter? I mean, how far can you depend on her after all that happened to her?"

"Of course! I can believe her a hundred percent! You see Dr. George, this marriage alliance is her own choice! What happened on that day was not her fault; she told me the whole story! That boy was her friend just like other friends and they used to go to some restaurants to eat pizza or some Chinese food! There was a girl named Bency who was my daughter's classmate and she had some grudge or jealousy towards my child! When that boy came in a car together with other friends, my daughter also joined them! Using that opportunity, Bency called her boyfriend and both of them informed the matter to my wife, of course, simply to create a panic in the family. But their joke was too cruel! My wife, who was a bit credulous in such matters, immediately called my brother and told the matter. Soon my brother called his friend, Asharaf, who is an Inspector of Police working in the city where my daughter was studying. Within no time, they found the friends in a cafeteria and they told the facts to the Inspector. But, since there was a complaint against them, the Inspector told them that he could send them only in the custody of their parents! That was what really happened!"

"Then it's alright! Then, why do you feel tension?" I asked with a smile, though who could believe the words of children!

"But as the police involved, the boy took it an insult and he challenged my daughter. He threatened her of spoiling her married life even! See, how crazy these foolish boys are!" Salim said. There was clear anxiety on his face.

I tried to give him more confidence. We took our tea and talked for about half an hour. I asked him whether he had invited Rajesh and his family. He told me that it was his wife, Geetha, who took the phone. She said that Rajesh was in hospital following some minor ailment, and she would definitely come for the marriage.

It was news to me; I thought he was well-settled after that ordeal! I cursed myself for not going to meet Rajesh immediately after my arrival from Ethiopia.

Salim also said that he had rung some of our friends in North India, like Dr. Worku and Dr. Dinov, but they might not turn up for the wedding from such a faraway place. I found Salim quite relieved of his tension when he said farewell to me. I promised him that I would be at the wedding sufficiently early to control any unforeseen situations.

He held my hands and said, "Khudha Hafiz." I replied the same words. I watched him get into his car, with the pride of the father of a bride!

The next day, I was at the wedding hall, especially to give confidence to Salim. I knew that nothing ill would happen, as the boy or his friends would not dare enter the beehive of Salim's friends and relatives. However, Salim took me into confidence and told me that he had arranged for a few of his young cousins to intervene if an emergency situation arose. I looked here and there to see Geetha so that I could enquire about the illness of Rajesh. But I could not find her anywhere in that area. Perhaps, the condition of Rajesh might not allow her to come for the wedding, I thought.

The pandal was beautifully decorated with fresh flowers, and canopied with colorful canvas. On the platform, there were a few special chairs on which sat half a dozen old men with long white beard and turbans on their heads. Three chairs were placed at the middle of the stage, two of them facing each other and the other one facing the audience.

Soon an old Mullah, with a grave face, proudly came to the stage, sat on the middle chair and asked Salim Mohammed and his future son-in-law to sit face to face. The Mullah made a prayer in Arabic and asked certain questions to both of them. Then, he took the hands of Salim and the boy and placed them together, continuing his prayers. The wedding was over! Salim's daughter Zeenath was nowhere on the stage! And the guests turned towards the hot *biriyani!*

I saw Salim move into a side-room. I wished to congratulate him as well as the couple. After a few minutes, Salim came to the stage, holding the hand of the bride. Zeenath, in her glittering wedding dress, really looked like a houri! Massah Allah! How beautiful was his daughter! She came like a queen and conquered all our hearts! She walked elegantly and was lovely in her demeanor! Any young man, irrespective of his race, caste, creed or language, would desire to make her his own possession! Allah Karim! Let my words not cause any harm to her! Let them not turn an evil omen to her life! May God bless her with a long and happy married life, I prayed silently.

I wondered how Zeenath could overcome the difficult dilemma: to follow the tradition of her family as an obedient daughter, or to follow her emotional surge to marry a person whom she loved. Suddenly I remembered James Joyce's character Eveline Hill, the dutiful daughter who took the courageous decision at the last moment to return to her father, resisting the temptation of a free life in Buenos Aires with her sailor-friend, Frank. It might be her mother's uneventful, sad life which prompted her decision to escape the same fate by leaving Frank. But most of our girls are credulous and learn lessons very late! One provocation makes you jump into the well but even seven provocations cannot help you to get out of it! I thought.

I moved towards the couple and congratulated them. I looked into her eyes; they were quite innocent, shining with hope! Her face beamed with happiness and cheerfulness. Did it mean that women could adjust their lives under any circumstance? I felt that it was inappropriate to ask her about those black days! There was a sure sign of relief on her face. Did she really love that boy of her college days? Or was she trapped or blackmailed by that classmate of hers? Could she really love her legal bridegroom? Perhaps, the other boy would continue to blackmail her! She would have considered him as a friend and he might have misunderstood her friendship!

Every man and woman secretly kept a sense of possession. And in the case of man, he was tempted to use his muscle-power to possess the woman! Then, why did she run away with him? Was it really an elopement or a story cooked up by certain jealous friends, as Salim told me? Perhaps, she had no other option but to go away a few miles with him, away from her friends and relatives, and talk to him in a calm and quite atmosphere! She might know that he was a mentally abnormal person whom reason could not work anymore! He might have threatened her that he would kill her or even her father! Well! It was useless to analyze our past actions and to come to meaningless conclusions! I bade farewell to Salim and returned home.

I was quite worried about the hospitalization of Rajesh. He appeared to me even in my dream, with his tired face and dull eyes! So, next morning, I dressed up quickly and went to the house of Rajesh. I felt that the bus to his house was the most slow-moving one in the world!

Geetha had informed Salim over the phone that Rajesh had a stroke! Perhaps, Geetha would have requested Rajesh to forgive her and to forget everything about that letter which she had written in her fits of fury! Perhaps, both of them could not come to a proper understanding and settle their family issue. And Rajesh, as far as I know, was a sensitive man, quite incapable of bearing such shocks!

In Ethiopia, after getting Geetha's last letter, I had seen him becoming thin and gloomy. He had lost his cheerfulness, and become careless even in day-to-day activities. He did not care to shave daily or even comb his disheveled hair! He looked like a person suffering from some chronic disease. But what was the cause of his present illness? It might be the sudden change in climate. In Sea Side City, it was always an air-conditioned climate and once you come to the heat and humidity of Kerala, naturally you would feel some problem of acclimatization. Surely, it had nothing to do with Geetha's letter; I tried to believe so!

As the bus reached the stop near to his house, I got down and walked a few meters to his house. The gate was not closed and I entered the courtyard. The whole house and its surroundings appeared as if no one was living there. The garden plants were growing wild as if no one was tending them for months. The courtyard was full of dried fallen leaves and the front verandah itself was untidy with scattered newspapers and magazines thrown, perhaps, carelessly by the newspaper boy!

Soon I heard the sound of movements inside the house. I pressed the calling bell. After a minute, the front door was opened and Geetha came out. I was surprised to see her with disheveled hair and in untidy clothes! Her face was pale and eyes were swollen as if she had been spending many a sleepless night! She appeared so 'haggard and woebegone,' as poets might say.

"Oh! George Sir! What a surprise! Come in, please!" She greeted me with a hearty smile. She quickly smoothed the sofa with her hands and arranged the roll-pillows and cushions on it. She continued with a tone of apology, "I'm sorry, Sir! For a week I was in the hospital, and only ten minutes back I came to the house. Rajesh is in the hospital and, you know, how difficult it is to manage things both at the hospital and here at home!"

"Never mind!" I said in an easy way. "But what happened to Rajesh? What's his illness? How's he?" I was so anxious that I asked a lot of questions at a stretch!

"The doctor says that it was a stroke! A sort of mild hemorrhage! A few tiny blood-clots in the brain! But, of course, there's nothing to worry about! The doctor says he'll be normal within a few weeks. Well! Shall I prepare some tea for you?"

Even in distress, Geetha could not forget her hospitality, I thought. I stopped her and said, "No, no! You seem quite tired; please take rest. Moreover, I'm in a hurry. And I want to see Rajesh now, if possible."

"I'm sorry, George Sir!" she said sadly. "He's in the Intensive Care Unit, and they won't allow anyone to see him, at least, for a week! Only five minutes a day, they allow for me even, just for a glimpse of him! But the doctors and nurses are excellent; there's nothing to worry about such things. Well! When are you returning to Ethiopia?"

"By next week," I replied. "But I'm really sorry about Rajesh. What a sad thing! He came to India with great hopes and landed in unexpected troubles! I hope, both of you have settled your family problems, am I right?"

She looked at me with a kind of bewilderment or suspicion in her eyes and said, "Oh, that's all over! I'm really happy now, as he is here with me, at last! Did he say something about our misunderstanding?"

"Oh, yes! But it's okay! You know the depth of grief will be lessened when it's disclosed to an intimate friend! In fact, I read one of his stories in which he had mentioned some of your family issues." I lied to her in order to see her reaction.

Her face darkened for a second, or I felt so! Soon she brought back her smile and said, "Well! I know, he always writes about such silly things in his stories! But you heard only one part of the story! Do you think, he alone could write stories? When he left for Africa, I also began to write. Do you want to see it?"

There was some harshness in her tone. Before I could say anything, she went into the next room and came back with a notebook. She gave it to me and said, "George Sir! As Rajesh is back, I am happy in my life. I don't want my writing to create further problems in our life. I believe, you know everything about our life! Rajesh is so innocent that he cannot keep any secret in his mind! If I won't give this to you, you'll keep on hating me! In fact, I have been planning to burn this notebook before Rajesh returns from the hospital. As you're his best friend, and as you know our family secrets, I give it to you. You may read it and destroy it, okay?"

"Okay! Thank you!" I said with a smile; and I took the notebook. I might have felt a sort of sadistic pleasure at that time! I wanted to see if what Rajesh described was true or not. A simple and humble woman like Geetha could not be that cruel as he had presented her in his diary! Sure, it was all the whims and fancy of Rajesh!

I wished to change the subject. I said in a casual manner, "Well, leave it aside! What about your daughter, Radha? Did she complete her studies?"

I remembered their daughter's name; once Rajesh told me it was made of the first part of his name and the last part of Geetha's name!

"She's waiting for the result of her exam! In the meantime,

she practices in a private firm," Geetha said. She seemed in a hurry to return to the hospital. I promised her to return after a few days and bade farewell to her.

On my way back to my house, I was thinking how silly and frivolous matters destroyed the peace and happiness of a family life! But one could not blame Geetha's simple desire to lead a decent, normal life with her husband. And Rajesh undoubtedly was a jewel of a man; a man desired by any woman. He was handsome and healthy; educated and talented. Of course he was in his fifties but his appearance was that of a man in his forties!

Of course, he was a talented writer. It might be an abnormality for human beings to become writers! Generally most of them were slightly eccentric, but if so, there was some sort of eccentricity with every individual, man or woman! But to become a writer was possible only with heavenly blessings, and Rajesh had that blessing.

Leave aside his mental abilities and think of his material achievements! He earned more money than any person his age could earn through fair means. He was enthusiastic, adventurous and hardworking. He was a man disciplined by ethics and ideals. He was respected by all his colleagues and neighbors. Then, why Geetha alone could not appreciate him? Was he a jewel of gold on a swine's snout?

Well! All's well that ends well! Geetha could not hate such a great personality. "Hatred stirreth up strides; but love covereth all sins," as King Solomon the Wise pointed out. The absence of a husband might create such temporary mental problems and anxieties to a wife. But if both of them had love in their hearts, it would cover even a multitude of sins! Geetha, as far as I knew, was a virtuous woman. Of course, she could not be but the crown of her husband.

That night, I checked my e-mails and found a mail sent by Dr. Worku Singh. Worku conveyed the happy news of his son's engagement with a girl working in another office of his own company. I heaved a sigh of relief. At last, he could find a girl whose horoscope matched with his son's horoscope. Worku's prayers were heard by Lord Vigneshwara!

I wished to ask him about his daughter's wedding. But it would be inappropriate to enquire about it; he would have informed me otherwise. I could understand the tension of an Indian father whose daughter crossed the age of twenty-eight! Moreover, in her horoscope there was the evil eye of Mars and it was very difficult to find a boy with a matching horoscope! Worku had to pray more and take more fasting before the Lord of Impediments, I thought.

What nonsense was his blind belief in horoscopes? I thought with contempt. It delayed weddings of his children and created family problems. Was there anything true with this pseudo-science? Salim, as a Muslim, never cared about such things. The married life of many Muslims and Christians who did not think about horoscopes went on very smoothly. At the same time, the married life of many people, who were strict in observing the meticulous clauses of horoscopes, broke up in divorce! The only fact was that many people were not ready to take the risk!

I remembered the case of my former student Prabha and her husband Anil! Their wedding was arranged only after the strict word-by-word scrutinizing of their horoscopes by the brother of their grandfather, Warrior, who was a retired professor of Mathematics! Their horoscopes had matched 'ten out of ten clauses of matching,' he declared.

Anil was a postgraduate in commerce and he wished to get a government job, instead of joining his family's textile business! He wrote a number of examinations to get into the government service but all in vain! However Prabha managed to get a small job in a private company and that made his condition more shameful! He bought an auto-rickshaw and began to earn some money at least for his own daily expenses. But Prabha and her family thought of it as shameful to their honor and prestige!

I remember that fateful day; I went to my college in his auto-rickshaw. I noticed his carelessness in driving unlike on other days! I asked him, "Anil! Something is wrong with you! What happened to you? Any sort of family problems?"

"Oh, nothing, Sir?" he said in a dull voice. Again, after a few minutes, I found his vehicle went out of control and I asked him to stop it.

"Sorry, Sir! I will be very careful!" he said apologetically and continued his driving. After a few seconds, he asked me, "But shall I ask you something, if you don't mind, Sir?"

"Of course, Anil! Tell me your problem, please!" I said. As a professor I always enjoyed doling out advice to others! Of course, ideals are easier said than done!

"Sir! Is it wrong or shameful to ply an auto-rickshaw and earn some money so that you can avoid begging to your wife every morning for a few coins?" He looked at me through the mirror.

I remembered the sentences which I read somewhere in a diary, and told him, "Dear Anil! It is easier to protect your feet with the slippers than to cover the earth with carpet. I highly appreciate your decision, it's well and good for the time being but don't stick on to it! You are a qualified person and you will get a better chance! You see, every successful person has a painful story; every painful story has a successful ending. Accept the pain and get ready for success. Once you realize your mistake correct them soon."

The auto-rickshaw stopped in front of my college. As I got out, he said with a smile, "I realize my mistake and I know how to correct it!" A few hours later, we found him dead in his bedroom; he had injected some poison into his veins! To hell with the position of planets on which they were born; to hell with their horoscopes! I could not forget his innocent face, oh, God!

And what about the life of Rajesh and Geetha? Their horoscopes matched perfectly, as far as I knew. They belonged to the high caste Hindu families which gave much importance to horoscopes. Could horoscopes solve all the problems among married couples? No! Only tolerance, patience and humility could save a married life. One may not be a sage or a baba or a saint or a sufi, but a bit of sacrifice solves many a problem. As Joseph Addison says, "If you wish success in life, make Perseverance your bosom friend, Experience your wise counselor, Caution your elder brother, and Hope your guardian genius!"

No perfect couple ever lived in this world! Perfection in married life is created through love and willingness on the part of both partners. "We come to love not by finding a perfect person but by learning to see an imperfect person perfectly," says the American Philosopher, Sam Keen. In an age, when people changed husbands and wives as if they changed their dress, in which divorce was accepted as the only solution against misunderstanding, there's no hope for a sustainable conjugal life!

That might be the reason why the procedure of divorce was made very long and hard in India. But this delay also created a lot of misery among unhappy couples. I remembered the desperate situation of my friend, Professor Aby. He had two sons and he arranged their marriages in the traditional way. His eldest son, Deepu, an engineer whom any girl would desire, married a girl proposed by Aby's sister. During the early days of their marriage, she wished to spend more days with her mother and not in the house of the husband. Of course, it was normal that a bride would feel grief in leaving her dear relatives on a fine morning, which was the worst side of marriages in India!

By marriage, the man leaves his parents and joins with his wife, says the Bible. But in Kerala, the woman leaves her parents and joins with her husband! In fact, it was my friend

Joyce who reminded me of this contradiction among Kerala Christians! Perhaps, Deepu's wife was so emotionally attached to her mother that she ignored even her husband. Christians in India generally did not care for horoscopes and, if Worku Singh were here, he would have blamed their horoscopes! In fact, it was a psychiatric case and Deepu thought that it was curable, if a child was born to them!

Days, weeks and months passed, and there was no change in her character. In such cases, it was the mother who should compel her daughter to go to the husband but, in this case, the mother always wanted to keep the company of her daughter. Friends advised Deepu that his wife's decision might be changed if they had a child. He went to her house and stayed with his wife for a few weeks and managed to make her conceive. Some changes came to her mind and she returned to her husband's house. She delivered a girl-child and stayed with her husband for a few more weeks. One day, she packed her luggage and, leaving the child in her husband's house, went back to her mother.

Deepu was forced to file a divorce case. In similar cases, divorce was not an evil act; it provided salvation for the concerned! Of course, every divorce had its initial devastation like the first cut of the surgeon's knife, an inevitable, courageous step towards a healthy life!

But the story did not end there! Deepu's younger brother married a professionally qualified girl from a reputed family and the poor girl came to her husband's house with all the dreams of an innocent maiden. But Deepu's brother developed some sort of a phobia for having children; he foolishly believed that if he had a child, his wife too would leave the child, like his brother's wife, and go away! Dr. Aby feared that years would pass away, the poor girl would develop repulsive tendencies towards conception and their life would turn futile! It would be too late for them before they recognized their foolishness!

I remembered the situation of a cousin of my friend Professor Prepositions. On the first night of her wedding, she realized that her husband was impotent and she returned to her house! She had to wait for many months in order to get a divorce from an Indian court! And what about the church? The conservative priests, who shut their eyes and created darkness, believing the old saying that marriages were conducted in heaven, refused to conduct the remarriage of the divorced, especially the women!

And think, what happened to my friend and colleague, Professor Geevarghese! I cannot forget the tears in his eyes when he described his only daughter's story! He married her to a person settled in England who already had a European wife there and a child in that marriage! Keeping it a secret, that bastard came to Kerala and married an innocent girl only to destroy her future! And in the cases of both Prepositions and Geevarghese, the hypocrites of the church raised more objections to divorce and remarriage than even the court!

Deepu's wife was ready for divorce provided that she should be given the right to keep the child, a huge amount as monthly allowance and half the share of her husband's property! And the case went on for months and years. The poor boy who wanted a legal decision before a second marriage was trapped in the vortex of an Indian legal procedure! Law-abiding citizens were always punished like this! If he had married another girl secretly and had had a child, it would have been better; the Indian law would have ignored him! That was what happened in the case of Mr. Joji, one of my colleagues in Ethiopia.

Of course, Mr. Joji's case was slightly different. He had his wife and children in India and they were leading a happy married life. Then he went to Ethiopia for work. He had a beautiful maid-servant and circumstances compelled him to have sex with her. She became pregnant and he knew that abortion was quite a simple and common thing in Ethiopia. But that girl was clever enough to avoid it and, one day, brought some of her relatives and demanded him to marry her. There was no other way for him and he married her. They had a girl-child and they were leading a happy conjugal life.

Of course, what he did was a crime in India, at that time, and he would be punished if somebody complained. But who bothered about such things! Currently the Supreme Court in India legalized the system of 'living together', it is heard. But how could his legal wife file a divorce case against him as she would lose the father of her children? Let him live anywhere, with any woman, with any number of children, save she must have a husband and her children a father, at least, for name's sake! "Thanks to the Indian women's chastity, ceremony and decorum!" I murmured, remembering the lines from a poem.

Perhaps, if courts of justice could delay divorce cases, the couples might rethink and come to an understanding! Once, my Canadian friend Mr. Jerry supported my argument and said, "Divorces should not be granted so fast; it must be delayed as long as possible, giving sufficient time for rethinking among the couples. In Canada, unlike in India, divorces are allowed by the court as fast as possible. See my own example! If the court had given me at least two more months, the issue between my wife and I would be amicably settled. But the Canadian court allowed the divorce within one month of filing the case. We did not get time to think twice! And the result was that, after our divorce, I couldn't meet even my daughter whom the court ordered to be with her mother!"

Tears flowed down the eyes of Jerry; memories of the past days might have been rushing into his mind. Mr. Jerry, even in his seventies, had a striking personality and anybody can imagine how handsome he would have been in his youth. He began his career as an architect and used to declare proudly that he was a mason! Later, he acted in a few films; I expected it, for no film director would reject such a photogenic face! But as he took up the direction of a film, everything turned upside down; he lost all his money; he lost his wife and daughter.

"Didn't you try to find them? Could you meet them again?" I asked him with curiosity one day. "Nope!" he replied and sat silently for a while. Then he said, "I heard that my wife married someone else and my daughter was spoiled to the core! Of course, the Canadian court was kind enough to leave my son with me. He married a Mexican girl and they have a child who teaches his father the Mexican language and his mother the English language! Ha! Ha!"

Jerry laughed aloud until tears flowed from his eyes. He was an architectural historian who had spent most of his time among the ruins of the past. His future he could spend searching among the ruins of his own life, I thought. And only God knows how long the inter-caste marriage of his son could survive! May God bless and give them a long married life, I silently prayed.

I was not so pessimistic about inter-caste or inter-racial marriage and I knew a number of couples who lived happily with their spouses hailing from another caste or race. My Ethiopian friend Dr. Dambay married an American lady and they lived happily with their girl-child. I came to know more about them only when I began to serve the University as the Principal Advisor to the Dean of Graduate Programs. According to the American usage 'Graduate Programs' meant Postgraduate and Doctorate Programs and it was Dr. Dambay who recommended my name for the post. I felt really proud working with him as he was a hard-working and humble scientist. I knew his American wife Ms. Tamarind, and they appeared as a 'made-for-each-other' couple. It was not the race, caste or creed difference that led to divorce; it was the lack of sacrifice, patience and humility! I thought. I don't know whether there's a woman behind the success of every man; but if Dr. Dambay had become the President of the university, Ms. Tamarind would have been a life-force behind him!

Once he asked me, "How could the Indian scientists and thinkers marry ordinary women of their community and continue with their ideal research activities? I appreciate their courage to stick to their culture even though it's an impediment to their personal growth!"

He used to criticize those Indians who, instead of serving their own country, went abroad to make money! Though many offers came to Dr. Dambay from different European countries, he decided to stay in Ethiopia and serve her in his own humble way, together with his American wife!

But could we make it hundred percent sure that racial differences would not create problems in married life? In conjugal life, sex played an important role and the sexual habits of an individual depended on his racial culture, even though they had the same social or religious background. In a situation in which sex was only for procreation, there were not many problems. But among human beings, sex was beyond such limitations and, then, came the problem of proper understanding of each other's cultural habits. Soon despair or disgust on the part of either of the partners led to divorce! And it was always better not to take such risks.

Of course, in European countries where divorce or remarriage is easy, any person can marry as an experiment; if not palatable just get a divorce and try with another! But in countries like India where remarriage is a taboo, the system creates a lot of problems, especially for women. In Ethiopia too, nobody bothers before marriage whether the girl is a divorcee or a widow or a pregnant woman or a mother of many children! In India, the life of a divorced woman, or even of a widow, is so miserable that many of them prefer to commit suicide.

In the modern sensitive world of a mentally weak generation, even silly misunderstandings might lead to divorce! Perhaps our educated youngsters thought too much about their future! Or education might have taught them to plan their own personal life and not a reciprocal or social life! How could we blame our system of modern education alone? The problem was with our outlook on life. As Anatole France said: "An education isn't how much you have committed to memory, or even how much you know; it's being able to differentiate between what you know and what you don't!" Yes! It is true about human life too; many of us fail to differentiate between what we know and what we don't know about our life!

It need not be a misunderstanding that leads to a divorce in certain cases like that of my cousin, Elderson, of course, in his case he was clever enough to avoid a divorce! He married a Malayalee nurse working in America only for the sake of getting an immediate visa to the United States. Both of them went to America and, until he got a job, he lived with her salary. Of course, he had been a dutiful husband that within a year she became pregnant and delivered a child. For a few weeks, she looked after the child during the daytime when he went to work; and during nighttime, when she went to work, he looked after the child. As days passed, babysitting became a headache for them; they hardly got time to take a rest. Then she suggested bringing her sister from India and he agreed to it.

Within a few weeks, she could bring her sister as a babysitter. Things went very smoothly until she noticed some changes in her sister; her sister was pregnant. At first, there were some quarrels between the husband and the wife; she was in a dilemma, neither could she leave her sister nor leave her child's father. Elderson suggested an easy solution, "After all, what happened has happened! Why not all of us stay together without any quarrel? Both of you are sisters and both the children are mine! I promise you all a real happy life."

And they still live very happily! He could fetch a job for his sister-in-law too. If one goes for night duty, the other will be at home; the next day the second one will go for night duty and the first one will be at home. What an excellent arrangement! And for the night duty, double is the payment in the United States! I smiled heartily at such odd adjustments in family life!

I remembered the words of St. Paul and his advice to the Corinthians:

"It is good for a man not to marry. But since there is so much immorality, each man should have his own wife, and each woman her own husband. The husband should fulfill his marital duty to his wife, and likewise the wife to her husband. The wife's body does not belong to her alone but also to her husband. In the same way, the husband's body does not belong to him alone but also to his wife."

And again, he, in the name of the Lord, says very strictly:

"A wife must not separate from her husband. But if she does, she must remain unmarried or else be reconciled to her husband. And a husband must not divorce his wife."

Unfortunately, even those Christians who respect the Bible more than Jesus Christ, conveniently ignore these words of St. Paul!

Who is going to bother about such verses, I thought. Of course, we live in a world where immorality and inhuman practices are legalized in the name of religion! 'Living together' of man and woman without legal, social or spiritual permission became the order of the day! The system of 'living together' is common in Europe as well as in Africa, especially in Ethiopia, and it has been recently legalized in India too! It has become a ritual like the primitive initiation ceremonies! The Muslims, the Ethiopian Christians and the Americans irrespective of religions circumcise their children without knowing the fact that there is a more than fifty percent chance for them to grow up into sodomites! Among many African tribes, the female genital mutilation or the circumcision of girl-children, using blades and broken glass-pieces is common, making deliveries in future difficult and painful! Those who form Society for the

Prevention of Cruelty to Animals conveniently forget to raise their voice against this cruelty towards children!

Religions were supposed to civilize human beings, to convert them from their brutish tendencies to human tendencies but what happened was that they made laws to legalize their brutish behaviors! While Islam allowed polygamy of keeping four wives at a time, the Ethiopian Muslims are allowed to keep five to ten wives and the Ethiopian Christians are allowed to keep up to seven wives! In Egypt, the parliament was going to legalize necrophilia, a sort of 'farewell intercourse,' that would allow husbands to have sex with their deceased wives up to six hours after death! Even animals would not do such a horrible thing; it would be better if they could legalize cannibalism and carcass eating! They were also likely to lower the marriageable age of girls to fourteen or even less! In Iraq, somebody issued a 'fatwa' implementing Female Genital Mutilation to all women below the age of 49! In Kerala, they would further lower the marriageable age so that some of the politicians and film-actors could escape from the crime of having intercourse with immature children!

In the past, human sacrifice was a religious practice in India and, therefore, it might be considered a legal system! Similarly head hunting and keeping the heads of the people belonging to other tribes like a string was a religious practice in Africa, and it might be considered a legal right! Likewise, child marriage, or a wedding between a girl of three years and a boy of five or six years, was very common in India; and if the boy died after one or two years, the girl had to live like a widow throughout her life!

Of course, in the passage of time, we all left such rotten sloughs and renewed ourselves into rational animals! But in this twenty first century, when man was trying to make his nest in other planets, how could we go back to such obnoxious religious practices of the past? Was it not a shame on all religions? It was high-time for UNESCO to have special auxiliary to control the religious practice of all religions, if they were crossing certain reasonable limits!

Many Indians, especially Keralites, in the United States were maintaining their family by the salary of their wives! Of course, they had jobs for name's sake but the lion's share of the income came from their wives who worked as nurses and only nurses got a higher salary there. Young Keralites who were born and brought up in the States came to Kerala with all the modesty of gentlemen, found beautiful nursing graduates, married them with all pomp and show and took them to America. Once these girls got jobs, and money came to the husbands, they would show their real color! They would start drinking and gambling in attractive casinos and eating in highly expensive restaurants! If their wives objected, they would torture them and the poor women suffered these atrocities just to prolong their married life! They knew that the life of divorcees and widows were similar in India, so horrible that they would decide to suffer their husbands' torture!

As the world becomes more civilized, the people become less cultured; that's the problem we face today! Marriages have become a sort of business festival! It is interesting to note that even in the past marriages were like that! A 12th century book titled the *Art of Courtly Love* laid down 31 rules for the British upper class to love and it says, "True love can have no place between husband and wife," and that marriage should be thought of as a business! If it was like that in the 12th century, the 21st century would be far better!

I remembered what my friend, Lexan told about his daughter's fate! I had attended that wedding; the reception was in a five-star hotel with all the pomp and show of an American wedding! We were all very happy and we appreciated him in arranging his daughter's marriage with a boy born and brought up in the United States. His daughter, Sandra, after her graduation from a very reputed institution, was working as a nursing tutor in a local hospital. The boy's parents came and very cleverly made the proposal, praising the qualities of their son such as though he was born and brought up in America, they were very particular in giving him training in Indian culture and ways of living and he loved Indian food and talked Indian languages better than other Indian boys of his age, etc. and etc.!

My friend brought up his daughter for about a quarter of a century, giving love, affection and care, she was the apple of his eye, and one fine morning, he had to hand over the child to a boy who was born and brought up in another culture, settled on the other side of the globe! Of course, Tom was physically handsome but who could find the mental perversions of a young man just by seeing his profile? In the case of a jackfruit, one can make a small hole in it and check whether it is ripe or not! But in the case of human beings, there's no means to know his or her real nature!

On reaching the States, Sandra understood more about her husband's financial position; he was bankrupt with a huge amount of debt following failure in some business, a drunkard with a few petty cases in the court and a spendthrift on exotic cuisines! He was working in a private company and the salary would be finished within a week! He used to spend the weekends in pubs; once he started drinking, there was no break for it, he continued to drink till the small hours of the day and quite often slept in the pub itself, leaving his poor wife alone in that strange place!

Over and above he was addicted to gambling! Perhaps his failure in business tempted him to gamble and he expected to make money all of a sudden to pay off his debts, and later it became a habit! It would take a longer time for him to realize that gambling would never make a man rich, and a few who became rich saw misfortunes happening to their future generations, as it was devil's wealth! There were a few in India, especially in Kerala, who became rich through gambling or by minting fake currency notes but their progeny faced terrible consequences like mental perversions, impotency, barrenness and other unknown maladies!

Moreover, Tom's parents also began to ignore the couple! They had thought that he would become alright after the marriage, but as his habits did not change, they began to blame Sandra for his waywardness! In such a situation, how could one believe that marriages were arranged in heaven? How long could Sandra patiently wait for the confession and penitence of her husband? If she had a child to look after, she could have forgotten his insolence. But he deliberately avoided her for fear of conception! Perhaps a divorce would be the only solution in such cases! I could only feel sympathy for my friend's miserable fate!

I was thinking about various kinds of family relationships when my friend Mat came to my house. He has been living in the United States for quite a few years and his children were born and brought up there. He always wished his children to marry from his native community in India. When his eldest son Jimmy found a girl of his own community, but employed in the States, he readily agreed to the proposal without enquiring much about the girl. The wedding ceremony was at their church and a grand reception was given to all the friends and relatives. Within one year, a child was born to them and both of them were very happy.

One day, she met one of her earlier husbands and they renewed their relationship. Jimmy who loved her to the core was heartbroken at this sad turn of events. Only then, they came to know that it was her third marriage but that could not change his love towards her. Now she and her ex-husband joined together and filed a divorce case, demanding the share of his father's property. Mat discussed the matter with me and tried to seek my advice in the matter, for he knew that I was an advocate before joining the field of education.

I did not know how to console him and I tried to generalize the matter. I said, "It's a common problem among you, American guys! You want to enjoy the money given by America but not the American culture! Well! You went to America with an inborn Indian culture, perhaps, four thousand-year-old culture, and you failed to adjust with the two hundred-year-old metropolitan culture of the United States. Your children who are born and brought up there tried to adapt with their surroundings and they developed a culture which is neither American nor Indian. Now, the only solution to the issue is that either you leave them to their fate in America or bring them back to India which is quite impossible for you. Of course, the Indian ways of life may be a matter of laughingstock for them too!"

Mat looked quite disappointed. There was clear indignation in his tone, when he said, "See, George! I brought up my kids in Indian culture and that's why my son feels so much at the betrayal of his wife! These Europeans claim that they are Christians! But in personal life what they do is exactly the opposite of what Christ said! Jesus said, 'Whosoever shall put away his wife, except it be for fornication and shall marry another, commits adultery; and whoso marries her which is put away doth commit adultery.' My son committed adultery by marrying a 'put away' woman. He was innocent; he didn't know that she was such a one. But once he loved her, whether she's a nun or whore, he couldn't forget her. My poor child!"

There were tears in his eyes. I really felt embarrassed at such a situation. How could I console his ailing heart? I said, "Dear Mat, be practical! There's no meaning in being emotional in such matters! You see, Mat, now-a-days, the number of men and women with psychiatric problems is increasing considerably. Neither are men satisfied with a single woman nor women are satisfied with a single man! That's the curse of our age! Unfortunately, your son chose a nymphomaniac as his partner! Unless she is treated by alienists, many boys like him will fall into her trap. Better if she could consult a 'shrink' at least!"

"But do you think all Americans are like her?" Mat said with a sneer. He continued, "Of course, divorces and remarriages are more there when compared to India, but people from traditional families always stick to a single marriage. Perhaps, those Hollywood stars may divorce and remarry twice a week, but that's merely a publicity stunt, a means of propaganda! The only difference is that while Indians engage in secret adultery, the Americans have no such hypocrisy!"

I agreed with his opinion and said, "Of course, in America, you can't take anything for granted! It is because in America nothing belongs to you; your house, your car, your furniture, your dress and what not! All those things you acquired are under the hire-purchase system and, once you make a default in the payment of your monthly installment, you will be left with nothing! Of course, if there is no beggary in America, the only reason is that no American has the culture of giving alms, except in terms of formal charity which could be deducted from taxes! In America, no one will give you anything for free; in fact, there is no such thing as 'free' in America; and if they give you something, it will be because they expect to get something in return!"

Mat looked up at the ceiling and said, as if he were in a dream, "Of course, I'm leaving America for good! My only plan for the future is to construct a house at my native place and live with my aged mother for at least a year, God willing! But my children, they are lost for me forever! They won't return to India; they are doomed to be in America and the Indian culture of family discipline, perhaps, it is a sort of hypocritical culture, will always remain a mirage for them!"

I said with a sort of indignation, "America has only a

cultural background of two hundred years and most of the Americans forgot their British culture with which they began! It is a make-believe culture created by certain American philosophers, politicians, economists and film-script writers! It is said that comedy represents life worse than what it is, and those comedies produced in Hollywood by great directors, from Charlie Chaplin to Woody Allen, were so entertaining that they created a sort of myth in the American society; and, instead of working like a correcting force, which was supposed to be the purpose of comedies, they worked as a corrupting force!"

Mat was silent and, looking into his eyes, I said, "Moreover, owing to the flow of immigrants, especially from the African Continent, currently their culture has become more or less an Afro-American culture, what they proudly call Cosmopolitan Culture! When Indians settled in America, they forgot their Indian culture and adopted the Afro-American culture and not the British culture; and that has made all the difference! In the Afro-American culture, they say: Love is a verb and what we need is action or love in its erotic form! And in Indian culture, they say: Love is a noun and what we need is love in its ideal or platonic form! In this difference, comes up the question of divorce, alas!"

I pointed out, "Even Europeans respect Indian culture and heritage but the Indians abroad think of it only as an ornament made of imitation-gold! Think about what the great writer Will Durant said, 'India was the motherland of our race, and Sanskrit, the mother of Europe's languages; she was the mother of our philosophy, through the Arabs....of self-government and democracy; mother India is in many ways our mother.' And the Indians in Europe ignore these facts! Of course, culture depends on circumstances and surroundings; one cannot learn culture through the milk of one's mother nor it is transferable through blood!"

I continued, "Most of the Europeans say that sex is a

biological need and take it as an excuse for every sexual immorality! They share their beds with one or more men or women and lead a corrupted life like that of birds and animals, of cocks and bitches! If sex is a biological need for human beings, how can they practice an ascetic way of life? Ascetic life also is biological in the case of human beings because man is a rational animal, a creature that thinks and dreams and imagines! If sex is a biological need, human beings can have sex irrespective of their blood-relationship, with parents and siblings even! Culture sometimes forces people to become uncivilized but civilization must not make people cultureless!"

Mat agreed with me and said with a sigh, "You see, America is a spoiled culture! The serials presented by the television channels have influenced the young and old generations! Most of these serials, which continued their telecasts for the whole four seasons, brought many changes in American morality! Of course, the Asians, the Africans and the Mexicans were more influenced by them than the whites! These serials displayed scenes and situations of various sexual relationships that the viewers began to believe that one could have sex with every woman except with his mother and sister, and with every man except with her father and brother! Of course, this may be an exaggeration, as there are exceptions in certain personal cases. Just imagine a situation in which you cannot allow even your cousins to stay in your house! You turn your eyes, and they will be in your bedroom! They don't care about the old restrictions of age even! Youngsters and oldies are equally tempted by these serials that one cannot trust any person! Moreover, these momentary entertainers installed deeply the notion among the young men that women who are more aged than themselves and having more experience in sex would be a better choice in marriage!"

I nodded my head desperately thinking that the situation in India too is not promising! I said, "India also is progressing to such a level, of course at present, the relationships have rather more sanctity! Here, generally we think that our brother's wife is our own sister, and our sister's husband is our own brother! Most of the communities also follow the social restrictions related to age. However, one can't ignore the influence of films and serials on Indian social life too!"

"But the most intolerable thing is the exchange of wives and husbands!" Matt said in a tone of indignation. He continued, "Usually on New Year's Day, the men would put their wrist watches or key-bunches in a box; somebody would shuffle them; their wives would come and pick them one-by-one! The real owner of the wrist watch or the key-bunch, whoever he was, would celebrate the New Year's Day with her! And the funniest thing is that once a man has sex with another's wife, he would demand her again, not to please her, but simply for the sadistic pleasure of beating down her husband and snatching away the prize!"

"Of course, they consider it as an act of equality among men and women!" I said. "But does it mean equality of sex? Never! It's just like the retort of a woman 'Fuck you back,' when a man shouts at her 'fuck you!' Both the phrases give the man the same kind of thrill! The more the victim opposes and struggles, the more pleasure a rapist gets! This sense of equality is as foolish as the verdict of a judge on a rape case, who announced, 'A tooth for a tooth and an eye for an eye; it is proved that the man raped the woman and, therefore, as a punishment, the victim is asked to rape the culprit!'"

I continued my words in order to reduce his agony, "Generally, it is said that the Americans change their spouses as they change their dress or food items! While I was studying in North India, I remember a love letter given by a Hindi-speaking girl to one of my neighbors, Kishen! As Kishen did not know how to read Hindi, he showed it to me and I read it for him: Mene aapko hamara dil dey diya; aap usse khana samajkar

271

bhojan kiya! I gave you my heart but you ate it thinking of it as your food! A few Americans, at least, think of married life as some sort of a burger or sandwich, that can be eaten fully or in part and the rest can be thrown into the waste basket! And as Raymond Chandler in his novel *The Long Goodbye* says: 'Americans will eat anything if it is toasted and held together with a couple of toothpicks and has lettuce sticking out of the sides, preferably a little wilted.'"

I found that my joke had no effect on Mat and, so, I continued, "My dear, Mat! The words of St. Paul to the Corinthians might be irrelevant to the modern generation! Yet, let me say them to you: And unto the married I command, yet not I, but the Lord, Let not the wife depart from her husband: But and if she departs, let her remain unmarried, or reconciled to her husband: and let not the husband put away his wife."

A wry smile appeared on Mat's face! Unfortunately, I could not find a faithful solution to my friend's problem. We drank tea and, after some time, he bade farewell to me. One should be very cautious before making an opinion on the family problems of another. I remembered the Lithuanian saying, Neshok virsh bambos; don't jump over your belly button!

When Mat left, I quickly mixed a drink, a peg of vodka with some lemon juice and cold water, and sipped it, relaxing on my rocking chair! I could hear the light sound of some western music coming from the laptop of Xanthu! In many Hollywood films, I had heard similar music while presenting hotel scenes where some of the characters were engaged in dancing! For hours and hours they might dance with slow swinging movements and light steps in the slow rhythm of the music! The dancers usually changed their partners one-by-one! And while dancing, their eyes might be wandering here and there in search of some right partners!

Soon the husband finds his colleague or comrade standing at the bar-counter and he leaves his wife and goes to join his friend for a drink and a hearty talk! The wife stands for a moment without knowing what to do. Suddenly, a stranger comes towards her, as he has been waiting for a long time for the opportunity, and requests her in the most polite manner to dance with him! She agrees and the dancing continues incessantly!

Her delicate palms are in the grip of his hands; he looks into her eyes with excessive desire; his knees touch her thighs while dancing! He brings his mouth closer to her ears so that she can hear his breathing and feel his warm breath! Now it's time for him to talk to her in a very low but passionate voice!

"Do you like my dancing?" He whispers and she cannot but say in a low voice, "Of course!"

"I like to go on dancing with you for hours and hours!" he says with a deep sigh which only she could hear! "Really?" she replies casually.

"Not for hours and hours but for my whole life, dancing and dancing and dancing!" He makes a laughing sound and she giggles, enjoying his joke!

He looked into her eyes and said with a serious look on his face, "There's something in your eyes!" She feels embarrassed, thinking that there may be a bit of sleep in her eyes, and asks timidly, "What's it?" With a hushed laugh, he says, "Oh, it's nothing but a slice of a sweet dream!" She bursts out into a laugh, but suddenly controls herself!

He looks at her beautiful teeth and watches the curves of her lips! He murmurs Hardy's description of Eustatia Wye's lips, "Her lips formed less to speak than to queer, less to queer than to kiss!"

"What!" She looks at his face with confidence! She slowly opens her mouth as if to say something more but realizing that his eyes are locked in her mouth, she keeps it slightly opened!

He brings his nose very close to her mouth as if to inhale her breath! Still the dancing is going on, and in an innocent manner, he is rubbing his groin against her body! She dances forgetting everything, the place, the time and the people! She feels his groin brush her pelvic depression harder and harder but she ignores it in the movement of dancing!

"This is called heavenly pleasure!" he murmurs into her ears and she replies, "Yah!"

"I wish even to die while dancing and holding your soft hands!" he says, feeling the hardness of her teats on his chest. She is no longer speaking but simply cooing like a dove at his words!

He presses his cheek on her cheek and says, "How soft are your cheeks!" She giggles! He continues, "I love the smell of your hair!" She closes her eyes and giggles! He continues, "I love the warmth of your breath!"

Of course, never in his life did he utter such words to his wife, and never in her life did she hear such words from her husband! In her heart, she was comparing the warmth and allure of the moment with the aridity of her married life! In such moments of ecstasy, most of the women whose husbands worked in far-off places used to believe such meretricious words of love uttered by clever lechers!

During such transitory moments of pleasure, who would bother to rack their brains on future consequences! If she had utilized the opportunity of her husband's absence for half an hour in this manner, what would have been her attitude in her husband's absence for a year! Gone are the days of the old saying: Absence makes the heart grow fonder!

Her husband comes back and waits impatiently for a few minutes; he looks into his adversary's face and recognizes that peculiar expression on his face which only a male could realize! He gets hold of her hand and drags her out, and she leaves her dancing partner with an expression of satisfaction!

The reverie was coming to an end! It might have come out from my subconscious mind, perhaps a scene from some films which I had seen sometime in the past! Everywhere husbands had to leave their wives and children and go to far-off places for the well-being of the family! If there was no money, every wife would ask her husband, "What's your idea! Do you expect me to go to the street and make money?" And the husband had to leave her reluctantly!

Once the wife got regular income from her husband, she would think about sex! She would write to him, "Forget your craze for money; come back, it's better to starve here!" He would come back but after a few days, she would begin her nagging for money! And he would be in a situation, as Somerset Maugham said, "…a woman you're desperately in love with as long as you don't see her, but when you're with her she maddens you so that you can't bear her!"

Once this happened only in the western countries, but as the number of antisocial lechers and shameless adulterers increased, poor women were trapped everywhere! For men, there was no risk, as the delicacy, decorum and chastity of Indian women prevented them from disclosing such advances of the scoundrels to their husbands!

Besides, the language itself has a negative influence on the society! Unfortunately, our language is ideological, as Jacques Derrida pointed out. For example, the word 'slut' for a woman who sleeps with many men and the word 'stud' for a man who sleeps with many women perpetuate the cultural belief that sexual relations with multiple partners is a source of shame for women and of pride for men! Such privileged words in the language have contaminated our culture!

I remembered the words of Settu Mammo, an Ethiopian writer, who in one of his short stories says: "A woman feels proud to be loved by a man who is not her husband and, she also desires to be loved by many more, but really regrets when she loses her husband!" How long religious morality can control the instincts of human beings, I wondered.

That afternoon, without any previous information, Mr. Tomcat came to my house! I was seeing him after a break of a decade, though we used to keep contact once a month or so over the telephone. He was my colleague in the Sultanate of Oman and, though I resigned the job on the third year, he continued there for quite a long period! He was from a rich and reputed family but he wanted to make some extra money for the wedding of his daughter and tempted him to come to the desert land of Oman!

In fact, we were not on good terms, or we were not in contact, for the previous few months! Of course, the reason was quite silly, as anybody would say, but in India, if a friend was not invited for the wedding of one's daughter, it was considered a serious breach of friendship! Of course, I came to know about his daughter's wedding through a friend of mine who tried to console me saying that there was some sort of mystery behind it!

I guided him to my study and requested him to relax! I took two glasses and a bottle of cold water from the kitchen! Of course, broken friendship could be retied over a few pegs of whisky!

Taking a sip from the glass, Tomcat made a lengthy apology and told me that his daughter's wedding was conducted under certain strenuous circumstances that he could not invite even many of his intimate friends! He said that his daughter had fallen in love with her teacher in spoken English, a good-for-nothing fellow who was socially and financially inferior to his family status! "That bastard had nothing to lose, just spending a few days to trap the poor girl with his oily art and sweet words, and then, he got everything, the social status, the wealth, the beautiful girl and what not! My heart is burning when I think about that pathetic situation." He was very furious and I could see fire in his eyes!

In order to console him, I said, "Friend! After all, what's

happened is happened! Nobody can reverse the events of the past!"

Still in an angry tone, he continued, "If one's mother suffers from madness, it is fun for others to watch the scene! Inter-racial or inter-caste or inter-religious weddings are good ideas for the politicians to boast! When it happens in one's own life, only then, one could feel the real misery behind it! You can't understand the agony I suffered then! In fact, I planned even to arrange a 'quotation gang' to finish the life of that scoundrel, but my daughter threatened me that she would commit suicide if any such thing happened! How could I see her dead body, after all these years of my love and affection for her! Let her face her fate, I thought. He was not ready to become a Christian and, so, our parish priest was not ready to conduct the marriage in the church! Just imagine, the two thousand-year-old Christian tradition of our family was broken by that silly girl! I had to take them to a far-off place and register their marriage officially."

"And all's well that ends well! Have you settled yourself after such an ordeal?" I asked him.

"Settled myself? How could I? Being a teacher, how could I forgive her sin of marrying her teacher? See, my dear friend, we have been working as teachers for many years and we have seen many abnormal students try to attract our attention by gestures of their eyes and hands, and tempting us by showing their breasts and thighs! I could not look at her face, when I imagine how she had tried to attract the attention of her teacher by using similar gimmicks! I'm ashamed to think that my daughter had looked at her teacher with lustful eyes and sexual intentions! Ugh!" He made a noise of utter disgust and nausea!

"Perhaps, she was innocent! It was he who might have trapped the poor girl!" I said with sympathy.

"He too was a shame to the teaching community! Just imagine a teacher looking at his student with sexual desire! As language teachers, we used to say puns and jokes with double meanings; but we have never stared at our students with lustful eyes, have we? Well! He'll suffer like Othello, the curse on him from his father-in-law, is my curse too!"

"Oh, no! Don't curse your daughter, my friend! What's written on her head cannot be wiped away!" I said, mumbling for words!

"I can't tolerate it, my friend! Think of those years I suffered in the land of the deserts! There was no shortage of anything for my children or for my wife! Food for food; dress for dress! They enjoyed luxuries while I suffered the heat of the burning sun in the Sultanate of Oman! Once my daughter started eating delicious food, itching began at her groin! She forgot her father, her family, her society and her tradition! Then, what she needed was just someone to scratch her groin! And that's what they really call love! Shit!" He gulped the rest of the drink and stood up to bid farewell to me!

He was a bit over-drunk, I realized! I took him in my car to the railway station; of course, on the way we entered a restaurant to take our lunch! Later, we went to the railway station and I saw him off. As the train moved away, I sat for a while on the stone-bench!

I tried to compare human life to a train journey; people come and go; some enter into the train at certain stations, some others get down at some other stations; and the train continues its journey forever! My heart was very heavy at the sad fate of my friend, Tomcat! If everything goes perfectly with his daughter, it is well and good, but if it will be unfortunate if some misunderstanding sprouts up in their life; such things were quite common among people who enter into inter-caste alliances!

I remembered the realistic novel, *Scarlet Song*, written by the Senegalese writer Mariama Ba in which she presented the problems of inter-race marriage. Mireille de La Vallee, the beautiful daughter of a French diplomat, falls in love with a Black Muslim, Ousmane Gueye and secretly marries him. She had to sacrifice her culture, nationality, religion and family for the sake her infatuation! Even after the birth of a child, she had to face social and personal problems! She always lived under the surveillance of her husband's community! She had to face the effrontery of her mother-in-law and the surreptitious love affair of her husband! When she comes to know about his second marriage, which is legally allowed by her husband's community, she becomes mad, kills her child and stabs her husband!

Perhaps, true love between man and woman, like wine and pork, is anathemised by the Koran, I thought. Of course, it is natural that young girls may be trapped by boys and they will not listen to the advice of their parents. They ignore the fact that love is only an obsession, a sort of hysteria, especially among girls, which forces them to forget all the qualities of respectability, decency, sobriety and propriety! Culture is in one's blood; love cannot change it! I returned home, praying for the best in the life of Tomcat's daughter.

Many of my relatives used to come to me for counseling; they might be expecting from me some sort of solution for their personal problems! I wondered how a priest who was hearing the confessions of all the parishioners could sleep peacefully! The faces of many of my relatives and friends stared at me! I wished to have a deep slumber but in vain!

Once I asked Dr. Ahmad Ansari, "What should we do against those anti-social elements who are ready to face any consequence for trapping such helpless women whose husbands are working in far-off places? And the women, due to their so-called Indian modesty, keep the advances of such criminals as secret!"

"If the women keep on with their so-called modesty, there will be no other escape but to suffer the consequences! If they are ready to complain, the only solution is the strict implementation of the Islamic Law! Just cut off the concerned organ! Of course, the Law is applicable only to the ordinary citizens and not to the rulers!" he said with a smile, and winked at me.

I replied in a very serious tone, "When compared to the vast number of citizens, the number of rulers is quite negligible and, so, we can ignore them! But in countries like India, where they believe that a thousand criminals shall be acquitted just for the fear that one innocent may be punished, what can the law-abiding citizens do? Such lechers and adulterers have sufficient money to appoint clever and influential lawyers to plead for them that the Indian courts ignore the seriousness of their crime and may consider them as mentally abnormal persons who need not imprisonment but treatment in mental hospitals, from where they could escape easily!"

Dr. Ahmad said, "I still insist the implementation of Islamic Law in certain criminal cases! Let the court say that such anti-social elements are mentally abnormal and they need mercy killing! If a dog is mad, it deserves a death sentence; in the case of man, he may not be suffering from rabies, but mental abnormalities need electric shocks and strict confinement!"

I said in a helpless tone, "In India, sex-crimes are treated in a very light manner! Even police officers take such cases with a hearty smile! What we need is a system in which immediate punishment should be awarded to such anti-social elements! If a death sentence is given to a criminal who committed cold-blooded murder of the five members in a single family, the sentiments of the people in India are aroused not for the murdered but for the murderer! If a handicapped person, who raped and killed a poor girl in a most inhuman manner, is awarded the death sentence, the so-called cultured people of India conduct rallies in support of the criminal!"

"In such cases, we should appreciate the American system!"

Ahmad said with a cunning smile on his lips. "They preach democracy in each and every situation except in the case of criminals! Nobody knows the exact number of criminals shot down by the police, inside or outside the prison! Some jail doctors even secretly serve exclusive medicines that can curb down the excessive physical, especially sexual, energy of the criminals! Of course, mercy killing is quite common in American prison hospitals! In India, going to jail is literally like going to one's father-in-law's house, as Tagore's Cabuliwallah said! No criminal anywhere in the world could enjoy such freedom as that in the Indian prisons!"

On the next morning, my cousin Pepin and his wife, Merlin, suddenly came to our house! They were working in the Gulf and all of a sudden how could they come, I wondered. Later, I came to know that they came to meet a private doctor who could confidentially do an abortion. How could they think of such a heinous act? In fact, abortion is also a kind of murder and how could parents think of it!

In fact, they had only two girl-children and, a third child was not at all a burden. We live in an age of family planning and we think that an extra child would spoil all our calculations about the future! We left our dependence on God and think like the people who had constructed the Tower of Babel, "Come, let us build ourselves a city; let us make a name for ourselves!" This venture in human autonomy was their sin and human beings were continuing it for generations!

Merlin's argument was that her youngest child was fifteen years old, and it was shameful to have a child after such a gap of time! In Islamic countries, women who could deliver more children would be honored and if an aged woman got pregnant, it was considered a great blessing of God! Among Kerala girls, pregnancy has become a shameful thing, and once they get pregnant, they are not ready even to come out of their houses!

Of course, there must be a limit on the number of children

and the couples must take precautions to prevent unnecessary births of children. But once a woman got pregnant, despite such precautions, she must deliver the child! Abortion should not be suggested or promoted. Abortion is a crime against nature, I thought. I remembered the words of Muammar al-Gaddafi in his *The Green Book*, "The mother who abandons her maternity contradicts her natural role in life."

Despite all compulsions and temptations from different corners, the Catholic Church was adamant in her decision not to allow abortion and it must be appreciated. In a civilization in which to give birth to a child is only the discretion of the woman concerned, God would say, "Come, let us go down and there confuse their language!" The Lord would scatter such civilizations "abroad from there over the face of earth!"

Modern education taught woman that pregnancy and delivery would destroy her beauty, that the child was a burden and an unnecessary obligation and that breastfeeding was a shameful activity to be avoided! When a man or woman bargained over their fertility, the Tower of Babel would fall down! The world would come to an end when the woman dared to say, "Fortunate are the barren wombs and the unfed breasts!"

Pepin and Merlin argued with me on the sanctity of abortion! He pointed out that I was a slave to religious fanaticism and that was the reason why I opposed abortion. He argued that a fetus had no soul; even a human being acquired his soul only when he got the realization that he was a human being! How could you say that Rudyard Kipling's Maugli had a soul? Of course, he would have a soul if only all wolves in the jungle had souls!

But I was adamant with my point of view, and I quoted the words of Tom Harvey's father, "Everything goes by nature!" I continued, "It has nothing to do with religion or God! It's related to the society, to the very existence of our human society! As I am concerned, my last wish is to die, like Tom

Harvey's father in *Roots*, with a loud laugh! To be exact, my last wish is to die laughing at all those irrational religious beliefs and the so-called ideologies which have made human beings mere slaves without being aware of their negative influence on them. And I believe in fate, only in fate, the inevitable fate; the acts of it need not to be explained!"

How could we think about such matters in a light vein! I wondered. In these days, as we run helter-skelter in our craze to establish our legal rights, we ignore our moral rights. Or we failed to claim our moral rights as we ignore our moral obligations. When moral obligations are ignored, we lost our moral right to insist or claim our moral rights. And thus we began to think that we have no moral rights even on our parents, over our children, over our brothers and sisters, but only a kind of name's sake duty which is adjustable on terms of monetary benefits!

Even among siblings, who have been born from the same father and mother, there exists a gap that cannot be filled up by mere blood relationships! We used to say in the past, "Blood is thicker than water," but today we have to say, "Wine is thicker than blood," because wine gives at least a kick or booze!

Pepin was angry at my decision. He said in a humorous tone, "In our utter helplessness, we expect some help in the form of advice or encouragement or consolation from our blood-relatives. But they take the opportunity to make fun of you by giving publicity to those maters which we conveyed to them in full confidence. Pretending sympathy towards us, they spread the news to others and gain a sort of sadistic pleasure out of it!"

He continued, "You say, 'Brother, will you please help me?' And he replies, 'Yes! I am here to help you provided that you should pay for it! You see, brother! Every minute in my life is valuable so that you should pay for those minutes which I have to spend for you.' Of course, the value of a life cannot be compensated in terms of money, but even the court decides a fixed amount for the life we lost in accidents! Even if you are ready to pay for the services offered by your siblings, a chain of obligations will remain with you unpaid! Then you say, 'Well! How much you want for your service? Once your service finishes, everything must be over! I don't like any encumbrance left for me to fulfill.' Once your secrets are with him, he replies, 'Sorry, brother! Find somebody else to handle your problem. I can't guarantee that no encumbrance will be there even after you pay my service charge!' He goes away with a mocking look on his face!"

I kept quiet looking at his face. He might have thought that I needed some bribe for changing my opinion! His face turned dark like that of a criminal! I noticed the glee of a murderer on his face! Let him do whatever he likes! Of course, he and Merlin left my house and went to some doctor, for a 'legal murder!'

That evening I tried to contact Blisso'life who was supposed to be in Ethiopia; the bell rang but nobody replied. I had given my SIM card to him as it had no use in India and as his wife urgently needed one. I knew that it was dangerous to give my SIM card to others without any proper transfer record but I had to believe Blisso'life.

On the next day I again tried and this time, a North Indian took the phone. I introduced myself to him and he cut off the phone saying Blisso'life was not there! I felt some foul play in it; perhaps, somebody had stolen the mobile phone of Ms. Holybook! I immediately called Mr. Glory and enquired about Blisso'life. He told me that he and his family had already left for India!

Mr. Glory briefly told me what happened to Blisso'life. Early morning one day, as he was getting ready to go to the Department, he felt some restlessness, a sort of excessive palpitation, and he and his wife immediately went to see a doctor. The doctor checked his blood pressure and told him that he had high BP that could be easily controlled by medicine.

But it was a shock to him; I am sure, he could not believe that he had any illness! A person who was leading a very pious, normal vegetarian life, strictly a teetotaler, very rarely once in a week or so took two or three puffs of a cigarette when he came to me for a talk, very strict in food habits, who followed the saying "early to bed and early to rise," and such a man got blood pressure and also probably cholesterol! All his principles and philosophies crumbled down like a palace of cards!

Mr. Glory cut the phone, saying, "On the very next day he resigned his job, booked the flight tickets for him and his wife, flew to India on the very next opportunity and almost settled at his home!"

I hurried to the Telecommunication Department and cancelled my old sim-card that I had given Ms. Holybook as a gift. Blisso'life might have given it as a gift to some North Indian, I tried to believe.

I remembered him once talking with great confidence about his health! It was when I told him that I had forgotten to take my tablet for BP. He asked me with a laugh, "Doctor, why do all the people who suffer from ailments and diseases come to Ethiopia? You with blood pressure, Dr. Elderking with diabetics and Mr. Handsome with cholesterol and so on! Do you think that Ethiopia is an asylum for all the invalids?"

He laughed aloud as if he had cut a joke! I felt quite irritated at his words, but calmly asked him whether he had checked his BP, cholesterol and blood sugar, any time in his life!

Suddenly he became serious in his tone and said, "Why should I check them! Food is the main cause for the illness of all you people! You Keralites eat too much fish! Mr. Elderking eats too much chicken and Mr. Handsome eats mutton, at least every month he and his wife consume a whole sheep! And look at me, I'm a pure vegetarian! Three idlis and a bit of chutney for my breakfast, a cup of rice and some sambar for my lunch and two dosas with chutney or sambar for my dinner! Why should a man so strict in diet be afraid of any ailments?"

I smiled remembering the saying: "Man thinks in one way while God thinks in the other way!" Was it true that those who strictly followed disciplined vegetarian lives fear death more than those non-vegetarian Bohemians? But the funniest thing was that those who could not eat, drink or smoke due to personal or social or religious reasons looked with jealousy at those who could eat, drink and smoke! I wished a peaceful retired life for him! As the couple was pretty rich and had no direct heir to their property, many of their near relatives might show them excessive love and respect, but with greedy eyes on their wealth!

Of course, it is foolishness to think that children bind a marriage, I thought. There are husbands and wives who leave their children and elope with their maid-servants or chauffeurs! In certain communities, in which to have more children is culturally a matter of prestige, husbands go for other women! In Baktawang, a village in the Indian State of Mizoram, there is a 66-year-old man named Ziona Chana who has 39 wives, 94 children and 33 grandchildren – all living together under one roof in a four-storeyed house of one hundred rooms! Of course, as a believer in Kum Sang Rorel or the Reign of Christ on Earth for 1000 years, a kind of religion formed on June 12, 1942, he expects to produce more children to help Jesus! Could the number of his children bind him to a single wife?

Whether the couples have children or not, it doesn't make any difference! While in occidental culture the children fail to recognize the love of their parents as the parents are apparently selfish, in the oriental culture the parents fail to recognize the love of their children as the children are a bit selfish. Prof. Blisso'life and family remain in my heart as a model of conjugal bliss!

However, the decision taken by Blisso'life to leave Ethiopia so suddenly was a shock to me! I was sure that they would live together in complete conjugal harmony, anywhere in this world, as couples made for each other. Of course, I could not read their minds; the wife might be blaming the inability of her husband to bless her with children or the husband might be blaming the barrenness of his wife! In the life of every couple, there were always these possibilities and, so to make reasonable adjustments was the only solution. And they did so well in their fight against destiny!

Many a time I used to think pessimistically about human life, especially about married life! Of course, anyone could think optimistically too! But in such cases you were not only betraying your spouse but also yourself! How long could we play blind just to save the face of God! You should come to the practical life and think only in a practical way even if it costs the damnation of your soul!

Well! Let's think in another way! Every husband shatters the dreams of a woman and every wife shatters the dreams of a man! At the same time, one could also argue that every woman realizes the dreams of a man and every man realizes the dreams of a woman! But faith and absolute faith, or complete trust in the spouse would be the only litmus-paper to test the truth! What would have made the life of the latter group a model to the rest of the world? Perhaps, they knew the saying that no one could go back and change a bad beginning but anyone could start now and make a successful ending.

Mrs. and Mr. Blisso'life lived a life quite different from that of others and that would be the reason behind their success! Their maxim was not to compare themselves with anyone else in this world because, as Ralph Waldo Emerson said: "Talents differ; all is well and wisely put!" But to complaint is part of human nature and nobody is ready to change himself or herself rather than complaining about others! And it is easy to judge the mistakes of others but difficult to recognize one's own mistake, as our sages said.

Regular complaints from the spouse would irritate the partner and even leads to temptations! For certain persons, to complain about their partner even on silly issues seems to be a way of lovemaking but once it becomes a habit it will make them suspicious of each other! Naturally, such a situation will lead to divorce!

I remembered the message given by the priest during the wedding ceremony of my friend Prof. Corin's son. A few Indian expatriates in America were also attending the wedding and, so keeping it in his mind, the priest said: "Of course, from the Garden of Eden onwards, it is the breach of the covenant that makes man a sinner, and among married couples it is the breach of faith." All sorts of extra marital sexual affairs are non-Christian and therefore sinful. It might be curiosity that leads youngsters to premarital sex but that too is sin-precedent! The argument that sex is a biological need is true only in the case of animals and it is merely nonsense and a convenient excuse in the case of human beings, as man is a rational creation; sex for man is not merely a means of reproduction but a rational blessing to enhance the sweetness of conjugal life.

Most of the priests in the Indian Orthodox Church were so conservative that they used to insist compulsory annual confessions on the parishioners, I remembered. It seemed the Church kept clear gender discrimination for ages that only male members were allowed for their official meetings, and the annual confession was mandatory for their participation! Well! Did it mean that male members were liable to commit sins more than the female members?

How could you say that all male members in the parish were sinners? Are they all drunkards or are they all womanizers? The only sins they commit are eating non-vegetarian food during the Lent or sleeping with his wife on the previous night of a holyday! And the priests felt a sort of vicarious pleasure hearing the sins of his parishioners!

And people like Dr. Elderking kept one or two concubines and went abroad to make money for their expense! I rang Mr. Glory and asked the whereabouts of Elderking! He said in an indifferent tone: "He was terminated from service; you know he had a brawl with the HOD! And I don't know his current whereabouts and I don't care! Somebody said he managed a post in another Ethiopian university! Bye!" And he cut off the call! Of course, I know the character of Dr. Elderking; he used to quarrel with anybody and everybody after a few pegs of alcoholic drinks! He must have had a quarrel with Mr. Glory too!

On the same evening I got an e-mail from Mr. Jerry; it was from Canada! He wrote: "Hi, old friend! Last week I married an Ethiopian girl; we signed the register at the Registrar's Office in the presence of a few intimate friends! Following it, we served tea for all the guests! It all happened quite unexpectedly and suddenly! Now, I'm back in Canada! Take care!"

Well! Mr. Jerry! Was this the surprise you promised? This was the sweet revenge you planned against those who insulted you! And I don't believe that it was unexpected! Carry on, my dear friend! But this was also a revenge against your first wife who deserted you mercilessly, wasn't it? But you are in your seventies and the bride may be in her twenties! Does it make any difference? No, never! If there is true love between you and your wife, all difficult problems will be turned into daring adventures and all thorns in life will be turned into fragrant blossoms! You are too old to be advised, yet let me remind you the old saying that married life is not a bed of roses! I wish you a very long and happy married life, my old friend! My heart whispered.

My holidays were almost coming to an end and I had to make a lot of arrangements for my return journey. Once you are in a foreign country, you spend your days preparing to go home; and when you are at home, you start packing things to go abroad!

CHAPTER NINE

That Monday morning, I sat in my study, wondering how I should spend the day. I had completed almost all my urgent works and wanted to spend a few days at home without running here and there like a mad dog, as my wife used to say about my busy schedule. On such busy days when I came home very late, naturally it was an entry into a doghouse until I managed the taming of the shrew!

My wife had gone for her yoga class, to be exact, a sort of training given on the art of living. Now-a-days, everybody got proper education in every subject, important or not, except in the most important subject of family life. The life of a housewife in the city was so monotonous that if they did not attend such 'art of living' classes, they might end up in some mental asylums! And my wife selected the former and I could not blame her for that except whether it was necessary when I was with her for a short period on leave. But one dangerous consequence was that some people would become addicted to yoga, like to any other drug, and might become yogis or yoginis!

Once, our religious beliefs and ritual practices were sufficient to lead a happy family life. But in this modern age, our common sense and reasoning compelled us to reduce the severity of such religious beliefs, though we continued to pretend as ardent believers just for the sake of our social security, family prestige and positions offered by the community concerned; and this mental change loosened the supposed Gordian-knot of the husband-wife relationship. Thus, divorces and re-marriages became common events, and people began to change their husbands and wives as if they used to change their dress!

The lessons given in the art of living classes were quite useful, as they discussed all the usual problems that occurred in conjugal life, and this helped the participants to think twice over every issue and to face every problem with courage, patience and equanimity. I appreciated the decision taken by my wife, of course, I also should have attended the course, as for that every husband and wife should attend, provided that my short-term leave did not allow me to do so.

Suddenly I noticed Geetha's notebook lying on my table and I took it in my hands. I moved towards my easy-chair and opened the notebook with great curiosity. She had given even a title for her story! *The Autobiography of a Housewife*! I wondered how Geetha could suddenly become a writer. "There will be some fragrance even for the stone that lay under the jasmine plant, receiving the shower of her pollen grains!" I remembered the local saying.

I was anxious to know what the real problem between Geetha and Rajesh was. Of course, we all show unnecessary enthusiasm and interest in prying into the affairs of others! There's a sort of sadistic pleasure in it, isn't there? I began to read the so-called autobiography of Geetha.

"I was born in a very reputed family in central Kerala. Once, my forefathers were the controllers of that part of the country, during the time of the Maharajas, but those days were gone as the so-called government of the people, by the people and for the people took away our rights and property and made us mere beggars. This position continued even during the British Raj, but everything turned upside down! At first, it was all a shock for us, but soon we began to adjust with the changed situation.

"Of course, we had some land property with an ancestral

house in the middle of it. My father was one among the very few graduates of that area, as the family could send him to a faraway city for his higher studies. My father owned a motor car, the only one in that part of the country. He also maintained a pretty large amount as bank balance, if compared with the money value of those bygone days. Of course, he had a lot of friends and they stuck to him always like leeches, like flies swarm on a sugar candy!

"My paternal grandfather had died a few years before my father's marriage with my mother. He had been an engineer and architect, very close to the then Maharaja. In those days of imperialism, the power and influence of a royal architect was so great that my grandfather received a lot of presents in cash and kind from the Maharaja. His sudden death compelled my father to wind up his carefree life and take up the responsibility of the family. Thus, he married my mother, and the main reason might be that a daughter-in-law was necessary in the house to look after my widowed and aged grandmother!

"My mother too was from a reputed family, but not as rich as my father's family, and the wedding was conducted with the pomp and show of a royal family, as I heard later from my mother. Within one year of their marriage, I was born, perhaps my aged grandmother insisted to see a grandchild before her death. My birth was a festival in the family and, as the first-born, I received all the affection of my father. He brought new clothes for me at least twice a month. He spent his whole time with me, watching every movement of mine, as if he knew he could not see me for a long time.

"He always kept me in his hands and never allowed any others to carry me or take me away from his sight. He did not allow my mother even to visit her parents, as he could not sleep without hearing my noise. He avoided the company of his intimate friends as it would keep him a few hours away from me. Could anyone imagine the protection and security a girl-child felt while she was in the hands of her father? I was only an infant then, but I heard the stories of his love and affection towards me, later from my own mother. And there was no reason to disbelieve what you heard from the horse's mouth.

"One year after my birth, my grandmother fell ill. A paralytic stroke made her bedridden forever. My mother looked after her like a professional nurse, washing her body, changing her clothes and, even, disposing of her urine and stool which the patient usually did on the bed itself. Days, weeks and months went on like that, but my mother never uttered a word of complaint to my father. In fact, he did not know the depth of mother's hardships and suffering in looking after a paralytic patient! In those days there was no system of appointing home-nurses, and my mother did all the work single-handedly. Of course, there was no scarcity for anything in the house, as my father had sufficient money in his bank account. Every weekend, he used to go to the city with his friends in his car, and my mother never objected to it as she knew that 'an outing' was necessary for men, especially for the head of the family.

"One day, my grandmother asked my mother to come near her and she caressed the stomach of my mother. My mother was at the early stage of her second pregnancy! My grandmother whispered a few words of blessings and asked her to open a wooden box which she always kept under her bed, as it contained her special clothes including her own old wedding sari and other dress items she used on ceremonial occasions. My mother opened the box, and my grandmother asked her to take out the clothes and open a secret cellar at the bottom of the box. My mother opened the cellar; it was full of gold ornaments, the ancestral property of my grandmother! She gave them all to my mother and told her, 'This is for your daughter and use them only for her; at the time of her marriage, it'll help you.' She gave her a warm kiss of gratitude, perhaps, for looking after her during those days of paralysis; and that night she breathed her last.

"A death in the early morning was considered ominous in those days, and it was proved true later, the glory of our family came to an end with my grandmother's death. According to the tradition of our family, the land property was always under the custody of the senior member of the family and my grandfather was the custodian. After his death, a few family members demanded the division of the property but due to the commanding power of my grandmother, no one dared to raise their voice. When my grandmother died, again the issue was raised but due to the popularity of my father, the scheme of the family members was aborted. Moreover, they were reluctant to make further claims seriously as my mother was pregnant, for the family tradition had taught them the propriety of controlling such outbursts in front of a pregnant lady.

"When my brother was born, I was only two years old. My father was very careful in giving more love and affection to me lest I might feel a sense of desertion. He spent money lavishly in celebrating the boy-child's birth. Of course, a boy-child was supposed to own all the land property of the family.

"My father continued to buy me new clothes, and I moved in the house like a butterfly. He rarely went out with his friends, as he had to look after all the family affairs. Moreover, the death of my grandmother and the delivery of my mother imposed much financial constraints on him.

"We had no other income except a small share of the total income that we got by selling the products from the land property. Selling of the land property was considered a disgrace for the family in those days. However, my father tried to sell a part of his property but he could not do it due to the opposition from other family members. My father appeared to be gloomy in those days and it was evident from his face that something disturbed him. One day, a few of his friends came to our house as usual and he talked to them in the courtyard. They were arguing on some issue and it was the first time I heard him shouting. Later, when my mother asked him about it, he casually replied that he wanted to get back some money borrowed by a friend. My mother did not ask much about it as it might annoy him more.

"My father arranged everything to celebrate my third birthday. Though there was financial constraint, he managed to buy me new clothes and even a big cake specially prepared for the occasion. All the family members and neighbors were invited and it was like a festival. He carried me in his hands and we went to the nearby shop. He bought me the most beautiful doll from the shop, a Barbie girl with her blue eyes winking at me every time I turned her sideways. But who knew at that time that it was the last presentation from my loving father?

"A few weeks later, on a Friday afternoon, my father took us all for a ride in his car. I was sitting in the front seat, between my father and mother, and my brother sat on my mother's lap. It was a wonderful journey. Throughout the ride, my father and mother were talking about so many family matters, exchanging meaningful looks at each other as well as smiling and laughing at silly jokes. I was watching how fast the trees and plants went backward as our car moved forward! I saw a few hens, frightened by our car, ran and flew away from the road making loud cackling noises! I saw a dog following our car, barking and running fast, as if it was trying to overcome our car or chasing us away!

"In the city, we entered a textile shop, as my mother wanted to buy some clothes for her personal use. My father selected a beautiful frock for me and a pair of shirts for my little brother. I heard my mother requesting my father to buy a shirt for him but he sidelined it pointing out that he had more shirts than needed for a lifetime. Then we went to a hotel and took certain special dishes, the favorites of my mother. I was not hungry and I enjoyed only a chocolate ice cream, so cold and so sweet!

"We returned home by evening. Before we went to sleep, my father told my mother that he had sold the car. He said that he had been suffering from severe back pain and the doctor had advised him not to drive. I knew it was a lie, for he wanted to get some money to maintain the family. He said that he was going to hand over the car to the new owner the very next day. I felt very sad at that decision but what could a little girl do on such situations!

"On the next morning, he kissed me and my little brother, and also made a joking comment at my mother and went out in his car. On the way some of his friends also joined him, as I came to know later, and they all went to the city as usual. He did not come home by lunchtime; he used to come for lunch at any cost. Evening passed and darkness crawled into our house but there was no sign of my father. My mother began to cry as she had the intuition of some sad news.

"Late in the evening, a relative of ours came to the house and told us that there was a car accident and my father was admitted in the city's famous hospital. He told us that there was nothing to worry about as my father had only minor injuries. Even though my mother wanted to go to the hospital immediately, the relatives prevented it as travel by midnight was not safe in those days.

"Early morning, my mother dressed up, and hurriedly dressed us too, so that we could go to the hospital by the first bus to the city. Then, another neighbor came there and told us that it was not necessary to go to the hospital since they had already started from there to the house. We were surprised to see many of our relatives and neighbors coming to our house and standing in small groups, talking in a hushed voice. I saw my mother requesting them to tell the truth about what really happened. After a few minutes, a van came to our house and out of it; they brought my father home in a coffin!

"In fact, I did not understand the seriousness of the

situation. I was only watching the groups of people coming to our house as if to celebrate some birthday party or something like that. But my mother was crying or rather shrieking hysterically, and watching her crying I also began to cry without knowing the reason. I was in my best dress given by my father on my second birthday, I had my Barbie girl in my hand and I wished to show off. Somebody took my brother and made him kiss our father and he did so with a hearty smile. I was also asked to kiss him and I did so in a stupor. I noticed only one thing; all these days, my father's face was never so cold and frozen like that!

"After one or two hours, a Hindu priest accompanied by his assistants came to the house and started their prayers. Once again we were asked to kiss our father and that was the last kiss. They took him away to the burial place and we followed the ambulance in another car. His body could not be cremated as there were some relatives older than him who were still alive, they said. In fact, my brother and I enjoyed the ride as we were in the hands of my mother's sister. How could a three-year-old girl or a one-year-old boy feel the horror of death?

"By evening we returned home and some of our close relatives stayed with us for a week to look after us. My mother was completely exhausted from crying and shedding tears, and she did not care even to look at us as if we the children were responsible for her widowhood! My little brother cried sometimes and wished to be with his mother. I never made any complaints; I was always in a sort of stupefied mood as I could not free myself from that terrible shock. Sometimes, I came to the front of the house and looked at the main road, expecting my father to come to the house at any moment.

"My mother's younger sister stayed with us for a few weeks and looked after us. We called her 'little-mother'! She was very kind and we loved her very much. We slept with her at night and she was just like our own mother. When we asked our little-mother about our father, she consoled us saying that he had gone for a job abroad and would return only after a few months! But my mother cried silently at those words and heaved hot sighs. Gradually, my mother became gloomier, sad and silent, or rather indifferent to daily household duties. Of course, every now and then, my mother's brothers came to the house to enquire about our well-being.

"After a few weeks, my mother took me and my brother to the family temple where we conducted certain special rites and ceremonies for getting peace to the soul of my father! Later, as my mother insisted, we went to the graveyard where my father's body was buried and prayed there. Then, suddenly, I realized that my father would never again come back to us, or give us new clothes or dolls or toys.

"That evening, the relatives of my mother and my father had a serious discussion about our future. My mother's brothers insisted that we should be taken back to my mother's house as my mother was too young to be left alone and her sister was there to look after the children, at least, until her marriage. In fact, my father's relatives secretly enjoyed the decision as my father's land property would be at their free disposal. Thus, we came back to our mother's house and stayed in the ancestral house. Of course, there we also had some property in my parents' name, the share of my mother given by her father as her dowry.

"As days passed, my mother became more active in household activities and it seemed that she was slowly forgetting the death of my father. But our case was quite different and we felt more and more the absence of our father. Sometimes we felt as if our mother was ignoring us, perhaps, our sight evoked in her the sad memory of her husband! My mother worked in the kitchen day in and day out, preparing food for every member of the family in accordance with each one's choice and receiving guests and neighbors in the most hospitable manner, as if she were taking some sort of revenge against her fate. Gradually, she began to take more care of us and tried to forget her grief by looking after us properly.

"By that time, my father's relatives utilized the opportunity in the best way and decided to divide the property. They were kind enough to offer my mother whatever property she liked but she did not care to take her husband's share. She thought of it as a 'cursed land' that took away the life of her husband and made her a widow at an early age. Of course, my father's relatives were very happy to hear such a decision from my mother. Her emotional state was such that nobody thought about her children's future! However, one of the brothers of my maternal grandfather, whom we called Court-Uncle, was a practical-minded clerk in the court, and he interfered cleverly at the right time so that we could get, at least, a small share in our father's property.

"Everybody in the family cared for us. They deliberately avoided all references of my father in front of my mother as such matters would hurt her feelings. Even they never used harsh words while talking to my mother. Gradually, it seemed that my mother was forgetting everything about my father. But I always felt the warmth of his loving kisses on my cheeks.

"On my fourth birthday, my maternal grandfather bought for me a new frock, but I did not even touch it. I insisted on wearing the frock that my father bought for me on the previous day of his death. On that evening, I uselessly waited at the verandah of our house, looking at the road, expecting, per chance, that my father would come before the birthday cake was cut! I even saw a person in a white shirt, just like my father, walking along the road, and my heart throbbed with excitement and joy for a moment. But that was not my father; I was simply hoping against hope!

"Days were passing one-by-one. We received maximum love and care from everybody. Our neighbors and relatives, who came to the house every now and then, never forgot to express their love and concern for us. I knew that they were showing us sympathy, the sympathy towards two little children who lost their father, the sympathy towards a young woman who became a widow just after three years of married life! Perhaps they anticipated the horrible fate of an Indian widow! I hated their sympathy! It was the sympathy people showed towards orphans, derelicts and the destitute! It was the sympathy people showed towards beggars, refugees and the physically handicapped!

"My brother was the pet of my maternal grandfather. He always moved with him wherever he went. As a girl, I had to always live inside the house! If I were a boy, I could also go out with our grandfather! I began to hate being born as a girl!

"With the arrival of my mother in the house, my maternal grandmother completely withdrew from the kitchen. Perhaps, she was clever enough to utilize the opportunity of my mother's widowhood! My mother had to do all the cooking, washing and cleaning. Gradually, my grandmother became a tough supervisor. She found mistakes and errors in everything that my mother did. 'No taste in the food, the rice was overcooked, too much salt in the curry,' the complaints went on like that. She began to scold her, even us her grandchildren, for silly and frivolous matters!

"My mother became almost a maid-servant in the house. She silently accepted her fate, and did all the work without any complaints. My mother had four brothers, one elder to her and the other three younger, and a sister. Her sister was a school-going student and, as she had many things to study, never cared for the household chores.

"My mother's elder brother, who was studying in a technical school in a nearby town, stayed in the house of Court-Uncle whose house was also in the same town. Once every month, this eldest uncle of mine came to our house to enjoy his holidays, and those days were hell for my mother. He never liked my mother and he believed that we were an extra burden for the family.

"In those days, there was no kindergarten system and, so, my grandfather decided to send me to a nearby primary school. To get admission in the school and to buy the new schoolbag, new umbrella and new books, we needed some money. My grandfather was getting only a small amount as pension and that was needed for the maintenance of the family. Then my mother remembered, for the first time, the bank account of my father. From the wooden box in which she kept all her valuables, she took the old passbook, and together with my grandfather, went to the bank. The bank manager told them the shocking news that there was no money in the account except the minimum amount needed for maintaining the account! My mother tore the passbook into pieces and threw it away, then and there! That was, perhaps, the first time that my mother hated my father!

"We knew that my father had given the money to his friends as a loan, but he never cared to keep any records. And none of his so-called intimate friends admitted that they had borrowed money from him! My mother opened the wooden box and, from its secret draw, took a gold chain. Her hands shivered, remembering the words of her mother-in-law. But then, her daughter's education was more important than her marriage at a later time! She sold the chain and, thus, I became a student of the first standard in a primary school.

"The petty quarrels between my grandmother and her daughter were a secret at first, or my grandfather ignored them as silly issues. At times, he scolded my grandmother for her rash behavior towards my mother. But that added fuel to the fire, and she also began to consider us as trespassers. My grandfather, whenever he got an opportunity, consoled my mother and asked her to bear all the sufferings for God's sake!

"One day, he called her to his side and said, 'My dear child,

I am getting old, I don't know when God calls me back. I say this for your better future; don't think I am trying to avoid you! Now your children are grown this much and we can easily look after them even in your absence. But what will happen to you after my death? You must agree for a remarriage. Your Court-Uncle has brought a good proposal. The boy is a widower; his wife died in an accident, just two years after their marriage, without giving a child. He is educated; he is rich enough to look after you. He is from a reputed family and he is ready even to take both your children as his own children, if you insist so. Don't worry about children, we'll look after them. I think only about your future. You're too young and a family life is necessary for you. How long can you live in this house, working like a donkey, suffering all the abuses of your mother and brothers? I have decided and you must obey me.'

"My mother did not reply, perhaps, she had a dream of another married life! On that night, my grandfather took away from the wall the black and white photograph of my father and hid it somewhere in his personal trunk. I noticed my brother, who was only three years old then, realizing some foul play, went out of the house and sat under the huge bread-fruit tree in the front courtyard of our house. I went after him, without being noticed by my grandfather. I saw tears flowing down his cheeks; I also was on the verge of tears!

"After a few minutes of silence, my little brother looked into my eyes and lisped, 'I hate our papa! Our papa is very cruel! Why did he leave us alone? Why didn't he take us with him? I hate him; I hate him!'

"I kissed him again and again, embraced him and tried to console him. I felt my tears blinding my eyes. After a while, I led him towards the house. How sentimental these boys are, I wondered. Girls appear to be more sentimental towards the parents but only until their marriage, but boys, though they will not show it outwardly, are really more sentimental, I thought.

Of course, after their marriage, girls have more things to worry about!

"On a Sunday afternoon, certain guests came to our house in a car. When the guests entered the drawing room and were greeted by my grandfather, I stealthily went towards their car and caressed it. It was as smooth as my father's car. For a moment, I felt as if that car belonged to us! I would also buy a car like that when I grew up, I decided.

"My grandmother beckoned me to come to the kitchen, as children were not allowed to move around on auspicious occasions. I went to the kitchen; she was busy preparing tea for the guests. Usually it was my mother who did all such work. I moved towards my mother's room. She was wearing her best sari. There was a shy-smile on her face. She took the tea, in a tray, to the guests. Usually it was my grandmother who carried tea for the guests, as my mother did not like to greet strangers. I noticed my mother talking to a strange man! Suddenly, a flame of fire came up from my abdomen; this was the man about whom my grandfather was talking! I casually watched the scene; the only emotion in me was simple curiosity!

"After a few minutes, we saw the face of my brother at the front door of the drawing room. Everybody was busy in receiving the guests and nobody had thought about the child! He was dragging a huge pick-axe, as his weak limbs could not lift it up! He tried his best to bring the pick-axe into the drawing room, saying to himself, 'I'll kill him; I'll bury him!'

"My mother burst out into tears and, with a loud shriek, she ran towards my brother, took him in her hands and kissed him again and again. She cried, 'No! My child! My little darling! I'll never leave you! You're my life, my future and my everything!'

"I saw the guests leave the house silently; and as their car moved away, I heaved a hot sigh of relief. And that was the first and last remarriage proposal for my mother! After that incident, nobody talked or thought about her remarriage. And that evening itself, my grandfather took my father's photograph from his trunk and fixed it again on the wall!

"After a few days, my mother became quite normal and adjusted to the household duties. My grandmother became a bit sober there onwards in her dealings with my mother. My mother also became quite assiduous; she helped us in taking baths, gave us the best dress and, even, took us regularly to the temple. She began to participate in certain social activities related to our community. She wished to be engaged always in some or other work, perhaps, to forget the sad memory of my father.

"Much of our land was lying in waste or uncultivated and nobody was daring to cultivate it for fear of financial loss. But my mother talked about it with my grandfather and he allowed her to cultivate the land with sugar-cane or pulses and take the profit. Once again my mother opened the secret drawer of her wooden box, took out another gold chain and sold it to meet the initial expenses of the cultivation. She might have thought of making some income for the educational purposes of her children, without depending on others for anything and everything. Of course, the laborers, who knew the sad story of my mother, worked sincerely and that helped us to get a very good harvest every year that followed.

"One day my eldest Uncle, who was studying in the technical school, returned home quite unexpectedly from Court-Uncle's house where he was staying. In fact, Court-Uncle had kicked him out of his house because, one day when he had returned from the court at an unexpected time, he found the boy on the bed together with his wife! Court-Uncle had loved him as his own son since he had two other sons of the same age, but the boy betrayed him in the most brutish manner. Or his wife might have compelled the boy to sleep with her! He cursed the boy and ousted him away from his sight! How could he divorce his wife, the mother of his four children? The poor man decided to suffer the shame and live with that bitch of a woman, for the sake of his as well as of his children's honor.

"In fact, Court-Uncle never suspected anything wrong when his wife showed extraordinary affection towards my eldest uncle, especially because her own sons of the same age were residential students in a different city. She addressed him always as 'my son, my dear son,' and looked after him like her own son and how could Court-Uncle suspect such a woman? It was said that she started the game in a mild manner, standing very close to him, brushing her breasts against his face quite innocently, helping him to dress with funny comments, asking him to massage her aching legs or hands and, even, using soap on his body in the bathroom! Finally, the poor boy became the prey for her desire! Such relationships might be common or rather ignored in the European societies but in India, they were more than sins against one's soul!

"My grandfather came to know about the incident and he cursed his brother's wife for tempting an innocent young boy. According to our tradition, father's brothers were considered 'young-fathers' and their wives were 'young-mothers'. Then, to have sex with a young-mother was equal to having sex with one's own mother! My grandfather, until his death, never looked at the face of his eldest son! Fortunately, he got a job in a private company at a faraway city, and escaped from the wrath and fury of my grandfather. And for me, I learned lessons from that incident: it is easy for a woman to enchant and seduce any man if she desires so; and there are such promiscuous women in this world who do not care for propriety or morality for satisfying their sexual desires!

"My mother's second brother was a kind-hearted man. In fact, it was he who insisted that we should be taken back to the ancestral house after the death of my father. He got a job in a faraway city and left the house, leaving us to the mercy of my mother's third brother. In those days salary was very meager but he used to send a fixed amount regularly to my grandfather.

And, thus, the financial crisis faced by the family was almost over, to a certain extent. And soon, my brother joined me in going to the primary school.

"By that time, a marriage proposal came for my mother's sister. My grandfather did not know what to do about the wedding expenses! Of course, he had saved some money to be given as dowry for his daughter. But the cost of the ornaments, one could not imagine! Then, my mother came forward, offering a part of her gold, from the cellar of the wooden box. Perhaps, she might have thought that God would provide gold ornaments for her daughter's marriage! Perhaps, my mother had given her the ornaments as remuneration for looking after the children, for a long time after the death of my father!

"The wedding was conducted in the most appropriate manner and my mother's only sister or our young-mother left us for her husband's home! And throughout her life, never did she think about the sacrifice of my mother behind those gold ornaments which she took to her husband's house, but merely kept them as her own rightful property given by her father as part of her dowry or share in the family property!

"My third uncle was the black-sheep in the family. He was neither interested in continuing his studies nor in managing the agriculture. He spent his time with his friends, either angling fish from the nearby river or losing money in gambling. When he lost money on a particular day, he would come home in an angry and irritated mood and quarreled with everyone in the family. His most frequent target was my mother and he quarreled with her either for not giving his favorite food at the proper time or for the tastelessness of the given food. In either case, he would throw away all the food together with the ceramic plate in which it was served. Of course, on those days when he got money from gambling, he would become a good uncle to us and brought sweets and cakes.

"One day my mother noticed a slight shift in the position of her wooden box and immediately checked it. She found that some of her gold ornaments, like rings and bangles, were missing. She knew that the thief was in the ship itself! Another day, she caught her third brother red-handed, while he was trying to take another piece from the box. We tried to get back those ornaments but they had all gone forever, during those 'unlucky' days of his gambling!

"My grandfather wished to send his youngest son, my fourth uncle, for higher studies. My mother came to know about it and she gave the income she had received from that season's harvest for that purpose. Of course, my youngest uncle was always kind towards us and he never forgot my mother's sacrifice for the family.

"A father was supposed to tolerate the foolishness or wickedness of his son. Prodigal sons were undoubtedly a curse for the father, but how could a father deny his parentage? My grandfather knew that once a person tasted the forbidden cup, he would continue to do so. Therefore, my grandfather was clever enough to arrange the marriage of his eldest son at the earliest opportunity. The marriage was conducted and my eldest uncle took his wife to the city where he worked. Of course, he did not send any money to his father even before his marriage, and after his marriage nobody expected any sort of financial help from him. Just like our saying: earlier frail and feeble; now pregnant too!

"The cat that fell in hot water would be afraid of even cold water! My grandfather arranged the marriage of his second son within a few months, lest he should also follow the way of the flesh as his elder son did, he feared. The girl was a nurse in the USA, and after marriage, she would take her husband with her, said the mediator. My second uncle came and saw the girl, but he understood that she was of his equal age if not a bit more! According to our tradition, the bride should be at least five years younger to the bridegroom. Of course, it was not a problem in certain communities which practiced polygamy. My uncle was a man of magnanimity and he thought that if he married that woman, he could take his young brother also to the States and help the whole family at large. He agreed to the marriage; and after the marriage, she took him to America, as promised.

"As a widow, my mother never cared for new dresses and always used her old clothes. Naturally, she did not care what type of dress her children wore! As an ancestral house, there was a rally of guests and never could she save some money to buy new dress for her children! The guests, including relatives and neighbors, ate and drank to their heart's satisfaction, belched aloud and left showering a lot of blessings on us. Of course, kissing and blessing cost them nothing!

"We went to the school and to the temple wearing our old dress. I watched my friends with jealousy when they came to the temple in their new dress, every now and then, even though most of them were the children of ordinary laborers. I always loved new and beautiful dress; I always thought about a future day in my life when I could buy as much dress as I wished. And I learned to keep every piece of my old dresses so neatly and carefully that they never lost their freshness and novelty.

"My second uncle began to send money from the States but my grandfather had to use it for the education of my youngest uncle. In those days, American Indians were thought to be drawing the highest salary in the world, but how could my mother's sister know that they were also the stingiest people in the world, or their circumstances made them misers! She used to come to our house with her child, at least twice a month that my mother had to arrange additional food and milk for them. Our little-mother and her husband believed that she was only taking her rightful share of what her brother had been sending from America! Of course, we enjoyed those weekends as we got a younger brother to play with.

"As I entered high school, which was about ten kilometers away from our house, expenses increased, and my mother struggled much to find the money for my daily bus-travel. High school life for me was a wonderful experience except that I was always watched by my Teacher-Uncle, another brother of my grandfather. He was such a strict disciplinarian that all the students were afraid of him. He did not allow girls even to laugh aloud, for hens, as he used to say, should not crow 'cock-a-doodle-doo!'

"Sometimes I felt jealousy towards those girls and boys who mingled together, talked freely and even spent money in accordance with their whims and fancies. But I knew that I should not do anything that would hurt my mother's feelings or cause disgrace to our family. I would also get a time and then I could enjoy life, fearlessly mixing with people and buying things in accordance with my heart's desires, I thought.

"We were in a mood of festivities when we heard that our second uncle, with his wife and girl-child was coming on leave from the USA. My mother was busy preparing a lot of food items which could be preserved for a long period. They were packed in air-tight plastic containers in order to be taken to the States! We greeted them and they stayed with us for a month. Their child was so cute; the climate of America was so evident on her skin that she looked exactly like my old Barbie girl! I began to hate even my school-going, for I did not like to leave her even for a few hours!

"I noticed that my second uncle had changed a lot in his character and behavior. He appeared to be too docile and obedient to his wife! I came to know that she was drawing a huge salary in the United States, about five times more than that of my uncle. My uncle was working in a textile mill and the cotton-dust created breathing problems for him. Owing to wheezing, he could not go to work regularly and that reduced further his limited salary. Naturally, he depended more on his wife, or rather lived at her mercy and expense!

"My second uncle had always shown much concern for the family. He knew about the careless life of his young brother and asked him to marry a nurse, for it was easy to get a visa for nurses to America, so that both of them could go to the States. My third uncle who had been desperately in need of an escape from his hopeless surroundings readily agreed to the suggestion. Fortunately, a mediator brought a proposal and, within a few days, the marriage was conducted.

"A week before their return to the States, my second uncle and aunt told my mother, of course with some hesitation, about their difficulty in taking the child with them. As both of them had to go to work, nobody was there to look after the child. To get a person for babysitting was highly expensive and the so-called 'daddy care' was impossible for a person like my uncle. Therefore, it was decided that the child should be left with us until she attained school-going age. My mother readily agreed to it and we were all very happy. My uncle and aunt left for the States, leaving their little daughter with us.

"My mother was very careful in looking after the child; the child should never feel the absence of her parents, she thought. Sometimes, we felt jealousy in seeing our mother playing with the child, a situation which was denied to us! My brother one day told me in a hushed voice, 'I thought that our mother did not know how to love children! She really knows how to love the children but of others and not her own!'

"I scolded him and said, 'It was because, in those days, our mother was in her grief of losing our papa! Don't say such abusive words about our mother!'

"He went away with a sardonic smile and never again made such comments. From the school, I always rushed to the house just to play with the child. My grandfather used to scold me for spending more time with the child, as I had much to study as a high school student.

"Months passed and my second uncle could manage to get a visa for my third aunt. She went to the States, registered for her so-called green card and, within a few months, sent the ticket and visa for her husband too. Later, as a green card holder, my third aunt could get American visas only for her own brothers and not for her husband's sister or her children! Of course, my third uncle had to study some technical work in America and for its expense he had to depend on his wife. Even before his marriage, his voice was not rough as that of a man, and after his marriage it became more feminine! Just like our saying: the spotted dog's teeth were powerful, but not very effective as they earlier were!

"The child grew under our excessive love and protection. But even a sweet porridge prepared of gold would not equal the love and affection given directly by the parents! It might be because of our too much love and care that the child, day by day, became naughtier and more difficult to manage. Perhaps she might have felt the absence of her parents! Her hatred towards those parents who had left her was growing day-by-day! She became self-assertive and cried aloud until her wish was granted. The more my mother served her, the more a spoilt child she became! In the temple, she quarreled and even pulled at the hair or attacked every other child she met. It reached to such a stage that we even stopped our regular visits to the temple.

"Pediatricians and veterinarians should be considered the greatest of all medical practitioners because they treated their patients who could not speak about their ailments! My second uncle's daughter began to cry and shriek for everything and nothing! My mother applied all her feline techniques, purring, licking, rubbing and caressing, to console the child, but of no use. My mother was afraid to inform such changes in the child to her parents as it would give tension for my second uncle. Fortunately we came to know that our third uncle and his wife were coming on leave and they would take the girl with them to the States, to be handed over to her parents.

"As usual my mother began to prepare all sorts of snacks, pickles and sweetmeats that could be preserved for a long time, and to pack them in air-tight plastic containers! Then, my third uncle and aunt came home and we were surprised to see our aunt full pregnant! After a few days' rest, she went to the hospital and delivered a girl-child. My third uncle came to my mother and said, 'You're not a sister but a mother to me. You know, it's very difficult to manage a child in the States. My wife is doing even overtime work in her hospital and I go for my studies. We are taking with us my elder brother's daughter and someone should be here instead of her. Sister, please look after my child for at least one year!'

"How could my mother refuse such a humble request? She readily agreed and we also were happy in getting another child in the absence of the first one. My third uncle kissed me and said, 'My dear girl, you must look after the child, agree? For that I will bear all the expenses of your marriage, okay? I blushed and smiled with shyness, and he laughed aloud at his own joke! Before the child could taste the milk of its mother, my third aunt left her child with us and flew to America with her husband!

"My grandfather was the happiest person in the house as he got a little grandchild to look after, in the place of the other one. Perhaps, senility began its cruel pranks on him that he behaved just like an infant in front of the new arrival. He might have been fed up with all the so-called matured people, and found the face of innocent joy in that little piece of his blood! Of course, my brother, then grown up and followed me to the high school studies, was his pet forever. Every evening, my grandfather used to come up to the bus-stop, depending on his walking stick, and waited until our bus arrived! Even though our bus was right on time he would exclaim, 'Oh, my children! At last you came! Thank God! I was worrying why you are so late!'

"Modern Europeans should learn many things from India, I thought. How much our parents loved their children! How much our grandparents protected their grandchildren! I never answered his exclamation but caught his hand and we walked to our house. Of course, I never felt the demise of my father in the presence of my maternal grandfather.

"The little child of my third uncle made our life really worth living, we believed. My mother was so happy and never thought about her widowhood. She felt as she had four children, one left for America! We also found life really meaningful as if we had many other brothers and sisters. Every weekend we had to entertain either of the two boys of my mother's sister, by that time she had one more boy-child, and every vacation we had to protect many more including my eldest uncle's eldest son, in addition to the infant we had!

"My third uncle was very punctual to send some amount in dollars every month. My mother was very particular and sincere enough to spend the whole amount sent by him on the child alone, in the form of baby food of different varieties. Moreover, infants used to suffer from unexpected illnesses like sudden rise in temperature or fever or stomach problems, and our third uncle's daughter was no exception. Every now and then, my mother had to take the child to the pediatrician and it seemed that the child was very particular to develop such illnesses at odd hours or when we had no money at hand! My mother even learnt some homoeopathy just for the sake of the child.

"My mother was an honest maid-servant for her brothers. The tasty food items she bought with my third uncle's money were given only to the child, and we, her own children, were not allowed to see them! She bought milk and other nutritious food items with that money and gave only to the child. She bought biscuits and kept it in secret places, hiding it from her own children, and gave it time to time to her brother's child!

My brother and I watched her doing so with our hungry stomachs and running mouths!

"Years later when I questioned her about such cruel behavior on the part of our mother, she said, without any regrets, in a casual manner, 'How could I give you the biscuits which were bought with the money sent by my brother for his child's sake?' While she looked after her brothers' children, what we lost was the love and care of our own mother! She could never find time to care for our usual needs! She never cared whether we had sufficient dress, whether we ate properly or whether we studied our lessons and did our homework on time! And who would believe the truth that she had loved her brothers' children more than her own children?

"Years later when these kids grew up, married and settled with their rich husbands, they never thought about the sacrifice made by our mother or by us! Perhaps they thought of it as part of our obligation and duty for keeping us in their house! They would be saying: When the widow and her orphans came, it was our parents who gave them shelter; there was nothing wrong if they had to do some domestic work!

"The most interesting thing was that our relatives and neighbors thought that my mother was getting a huge amount from America! The old man's pension was more than sufficient to manage the family and she might be saving a pretty large amount for the wedding of her daughter, some of them whispered. I realized that my mother's sister used to send her children to our house only to get a share of that so-called huge amount!

"We heard that the husband of my mother's sister used to tell his wife, 'Look at your elder sister! She and her children eat and enjoy not only the pension of your father but also the American dollars sent by your brothers. Aren't you the daughter of your father? Or are you the daughter of your father in his second marriage? Let your children also enjoy a part of that money!' And my mother's sister always said 'yes' to her husband, whatever he said or did!

"Were we living at the expense of others? Were we mere beggars trying to live at the mercy of our relatives? My mother's share of land property was lying just in front of our ancestral house and if we could make a small hut there, we would be free from all these hateful allegations! Nobody had taken into consideration the money my mother made from cultivation as it was done on the undivided ancestral land. Each year, the number of gold ornaments she had brought from her husband's house, reduced considerably! In the glare of the American money, her income and her hardships were blurred to nothing!

"I hated the life of a housewife, there onwards! The hard and continuous work of a woman in the house was never taken to account on money terms. For her work, there was neither time-limit nor salary. No rights for her but only obligations like the predicament of a slave! After completing my education, I should go for a job, I would never become a slavish housewife, I decided. I hated to live on the money of others, even if it was from the salary of my future husband!

"One of our neighbors, an old woman and a friend of my grandmother, used to visit our house at least twice a week. She talked with my grandmother for hours and hours and conveyed to her all the news in the neighborhood! She returned home only after taking a sumptuous meal from the hands of my mother, as her 'hands were graceful,' she flattered my mother.

"One day she said to my mother in a hushed voice, 'My daughter! You work hard in this house, but do you think that someone will consider your sufferings? Don't forget to give some care for your own children too. Look at them; they are becoming very lean and unhealthy day-by-day. And you always think about the children of your brothers and sister! Remember, if you pluck out the feathers of somebody's hawk, you will neither have the hawk nor the feathers!' She left the house after taking her remuneration for her sympathetic words, either in cash or in kind, and if it was in food, it would be from our share kept by my mother to give to us when we returned from school!

"I entered college for my graduation studies and it was a thrilling experience for me. The teeming city life, the heavy rush in the buses, the meeting of new faces, friends from different parts of our district, new environment of freedom – all added to my excitement. Of course, it was an escape from the disciplined atmosphere of my house. Moreover, I was away from the stern eyes of my Teacher-Uncle! However, my brother seemed to be more grown up than his years, for he always, with the eyes of a police officer, watched me and my dealings with other male-students! Of course, boys were always more shrewd than girls, and they knew better the techniques of boys applied to trap innocent girls!

"Unlike in the school, young and smart looking college teachers were an additional attraction. They were not like the boring, grave-looking, old school-teachers who neither smiled nor allowed their students to smile. But in the college, the young teachers made their lectures in an amusing manner that we really enjoyed their classes. Their odd jokes, stale-funs, ironical comments and puns made us laugh aloud.

"I did not like the crazy behavior of some of my classmates who, now and then, went to the table of certain young teachers and bent before them, showing most of their breasts, pretending to get some more clarifications on the subject they taught. They spread rumors that they had even shared the beds of certain young teachers! I hated these girls who even created imaginative stories concerning how certain teachers performed in their bedrooms! These insolent girls had no respect for teachers! In our tradition, teachers were given a high respect, placing them in between parents and God, and these girls sat in the class, imagining how the teacher would be if he were nude!

"There was a particular young teacher in the Department of Economics, whom we called Mr. Smartguy. He used to ask questions to me in the classroom and, sometimes, laughed at me calling me Ms. Smiling-pot. If I were absent on a day, he would ask other students where our Ms. Smiling-pot was! Of course, I had beautiful pearl-like teeth and was proud of them. Many of my friends were jealous of my teeth and mocked at me by asking which toothpaste I was using! They were the happiest days of my life.

"Many of my classmates have boyfriends from the senior classes. They walked with them, talked continuously for hours on silly things and got their share of coffee and ice-creams! Of course, I appreciated certain pairs and wondered how matching they were! Most of them were of equal age or an age difference of one or two years. A difference of one or two years between a husband and wife seemed to me ideal. Of course, their calf-love, in most cases, lasted only till the boy completed his graduation. I don't know the fate of those pairs who might have married, but it was cruel to think about them negatively. At least one pair among my classmates married, and divorced after a few years, as I came to know later.

"There was a lot for me to study at home but my third uncle's daughter was really a disturbance or rather was a nuisance! My mother always asked me to look after her, as she would be busy in preparing our dinner. I could open my books only after the child had slept. Though her parents promised to take her back after a year, they conveniently ignored their word, and thought, 'Why can't they look after my child as long as we send American dollars?'

"The child had grown to three or four years old and she could easily climb up on my table and tear or throw away my books. My third uncle and his wife were so busy with their work that it seemed they had forgotten their child! By that time they got a second child, this time a boy, and naturally in their busy schedule, did not care to bring their first born! It seemed that he also knew nothing about the growth of the child and that was evident from the money every month he sent to us; it was always the same amount! On certain months it appeared as if he had even forgotten to send the money!

"He and his wife might have thought, 'What is there to make life so expensive, especially in Kerala? How much can a little child eat? The balance of food thrown to the birds in the morning will be sufficient for our child! Who knows whether they give nutritious food for our child or not! With our money, they all lead a royal life, a life of luxury there! A mother is a mother and her primary concern will be for her own children! God knows whether our child is starving there or not! Moreover, where do our father's pension and the income from his agriculture go? Our brother also used to send money, didn't he?'

"My third uncle always agreed with his wife in such talks. 'Of course! I break my balls to make money here, and they enjoy a luxurious life there with my money! Let me see what happens if I won't send my money!'

"Whatsoever, we did not receive money regularly from him. Once my mother rang him and told him about the urgency of sending some money, and he shouted over the phone, 'Do you think I have a tree here on which money grows? Do you think I'm minting dollar bills here! I break my balls here to make both ends meet! And you spent the money carelessly!' My mother put down the receiver on its cradle without giving him a proper reply!

"During that vacation, my eldest uncle sent his eldest son to our house, asking him to continue his higher education by staying at our house. He also might have heard about the so-called huge amount sent by my American uncles and thought of getting a share of it through his son! How could a grandfather say no to his grandson who wanted to pursue his higher studies staying in the ancestral house? He allowed the boy to stay in the house, and he joined the college for his higher education.

"My third uncle's daughter reached the school-going age and her parents wished to take her back to the States. She was so attached to my mother and even identified her as her own mother that she hated to leave her protection. We also could not imagine a house without the child and my mother felt severe mental agony in parting with her. My third aunt secured a visa for her brother and he was asked to take the child with him to the States. At the airport, she made a heartbreaking scene as she did not like to be separated from us. In short, she was plucked away from us, creating a deep vacuum in our house that would never be filled up.

"It was my mother who felt the greatest sorrow. She felt as if she could not live in the house without the child. She spent her days silently, suppressing her feelings. The house appeared as if somebody had died there! In order to pass time, she began to read newspapers and magazines for which she had no time earlier. One day she noticed an advertisement in the paper, a vacancy of a warden in a women's hostel situated about a hundred kilometers away from our town. She applied for the job. As the post was especially reserved for widows, she was selected and she joined duty within a week.

"Since my mother left the house, my grandmother, to her utter distress, had to return to the kitchen. I too began to help her and, within a few weeks, I learnt to manage the kitchen single handedly. By then, I became a graduate and I wished to continue my study in some professional courses. I tried to get admission for B. Ed., but in the merit list my name did not come, and we had not that much money to get a chance in the management quota, as they demanded a huge capitation fee for those limited seats.

"I wished to study nursing, as it was easy to get a job in that field. Even my friend and neighbor, who was very poor in her studies and who passed her secondary school examination after a number of attempts, had studied general nursing and got a job in a hospital in the city. All my arguments were squashed by the firm decision of my grandfather that I should not become a nurse! Of course, he forgot the fact that two of his daughters-in-law were nurses! If I had studied nursing, my uncles would have even taken me to the States, and my life would have been entirely different! I felt as if all the doors for a job were closed against my face. At least, an improvement in my qualification would help me, I thought, and I joined for my post-graduation course in a private institution.

"It was like a thunder out of the clear blue that my grandfather was bedridden, following an unexpected massive stroke; he was totally paralyzed and the doctors said that his condition was very serious and there was no chance for recovery. We informed the matter to all his sons and, within a week, all his sons reached the place, even from the United States. They spent money lavishly, and as days passed, they became quite restless. They could go back only after knowing 'the one out of the two,' whether my grandfather would recover or pass away!

"For the first time in their life, the brothers felt the absence of their eldest sister. No timely food in the house, not even tea or coffee; and they were afraid to demand such things from their own mother! My grandmother was already fed up with the kitchen work and she began to complain of her body pain and old age. I ignored her malingering and concentrated more in the kitchen work. Of course, a neighbor woman used to come and help us in the kitchen for a few hours, but she had to look after her own family affairs, and she could not be available at the beck and call of the Americans!

"My uncles were very clever! They discussed the problem and found an easy solution, to compel my mother to resign her job and return to the house! There was no possibility of recovery for their father, and if the worst thing happened, their old mother would be left alone! They pleaded with my mother and promised her to pay every month more than what she received as salary from her work as a warden. In fact, they needed a faithful servant in the house and my foolish mother fell into their trap! My uncles were very happy as they began to get their timely food, coffee and tea. There was, at last, a responsible person in the house on whom they could blindly depend, they whispered to each other and laughed aloud in playing a trick on our mother!

"In a way my uncles were lucky because, before their leave period expired, my grandfather expired; otherwise they would have to spend another huge amount to come back once again from the States for his funeral. It seemed that my grandfather knew the difficulty of his sons in prolonging their stay with him! Of course, my uncles could arrange a grand funeral with luxurious ceremonies. After a few days, they performed the last rite of giving a feast to the neighbors and relatives. Then, asking my mother to look after their mother carefully, they left for the States, only to forget their promises to my mother, as we expected.

"My grandfather's death was really a shock for us! We felt as if no one was there to think about our future. For many weeks, we even felt his presence in the house. On certain nights, my brother cried in his sleep, seeing him in his dreams. During late evenings, while I was dozing over my textbooks, I heard his footsteps near me. I clearly heard him saying, as he used to say, 'It's too late, my child; go to bed and sleep!'

"There was a younger brother of my father, and, all these years, he never showed his face to us! He was afraid that we would demand the share of our father which he was enjoying all these years! Of course, immediately after my father's death, he was ready to give my father's share to my mother but she thought of it as a cursed property that had made her a widow, and refused to own it! She did not think even about the future of her children in the heat of anger against her fate! And my father's brother sold the property part-by-part and enjoyed his life lavishly. He forgot the tradition that when ancestral property was sold to someone outside the family, a part of the money thus received should be given to those who had some right over it!

"The only persons in the family, who showed some sympathy for and concern about us, were my grandfather's brothers, Court-Uncle and Teacher-Uncle. They came to my mother and said, 'See, daughter! We are getting old. We wish to see the wedding of your daughter before our eyes are closed. As far as we live on this earth, there's no problem for you. But who knows when God is calling us back!'

"My mother began to think about it seriously. I did not like the idea of my wedding at such an age. I wanted a career first so that after marriage I could be an equal contributor to the family. I knew that marriage is a circle, those who are outside wish to be inside and those who are inside wish to go outside! In fact, marriage constituted a trap for girls from which they could never escape! I knew that a girl's life would be doomed, once she got married to a man. If I got a job, I could help my mother and brother to a certain extent. I did not want them to live on charity. If I had an income of my own, I could spend it as I liked, without the permission of anyone else!

"One day, Court-Uncle came to my house and said that I should not go to college on the next day, for a boy was coming to see me. The boy was a relative of his wife, well-settled in a foreign country, he said. My mother made preparations to receive the boy. I also liked the case because, if I could marry an expatriate, I would also get a job there, and could earn sufficient money to help my family.

"The next day, the guests came and saw me. I was disheartened; I was only twenty-one then and the 'boy' was above thirty-five, perhaps, an age difference of more than fifteen years! Though Court-Uncle insisted the case, pointing out that expatriates usually married only at that age, my mother objected to such an alliance.

"By then, all our neighbors came to know that a boy had come to see me, and they also engaged in finding suitable proposals for me. One day, a neighbor-woman came to my mother and told about a boy, perhaps, expecting some money as the mediator's commission. The boy belonged to a reputed family with much land property; he was highly educated and was waiting for his appointment as college teacher, she said.

"'Veni, vidi, vici,' it was just like that for him; he came, he saw and he married! It was like a festival for our neighbors and relatives. My eldest uncle supervised everything according to the directions of Court-Uncle and Teacher-Uncle. My youngest uncle was always there to help; like a father, he managed to solve every difficulty in the arrangements for the marriage. With a convoy of cars and buses, carrying our neighbors and relatives, I was taken to the temple in his village. On our way, at one time, I missed the sight of all the vehicles that went ahead of us, as if they had all fell down into a ditch! I felt as if my life also was falling into a ditch with this marriage! In fact, the other vehicles were climbing down a hill and I saw them again when our car reached the top of the hill.

"After the wedding, all my relatives and neighbors left me at his house and went back to their houses, as if their headache was over! I sat alone in his study cum bedroom, as my husband was busy dismantling the pandal, erected in the courtyard for the reception of guests, and disbursing money among the laborers and contractors. It was a country house in the middle of the land-property, with no neighboring houses. And I was stranded and I had to spend the rest of my life in this remote house, far away from the city-life of my dreams!

"On the first night, in fact, we slept like wooden logs! Both of us were so tired after the day's restless schedule of a wedding. My husband's mother prepared a glass of hot milk with a few seeds of cardamom and asked me to take it to our bedroom, in accordance with our tradition. I gave the glass to him and he drank only a sip out of it, as he did not like to drink milk as such but only with tea or coffee. He offered me the rest of the milk to drink; he might have learned it from some fiction, and I drank the rest. Then I went to bed, as I was so tired and a heavy sleep was sitting on my eyelids! He also came to the bed and lied down by my side and asked me to give him a kiss and I 'breathed' a kiss on his cheek.

"'Is it a kiss?' he asked in a surprise and requested that I give another one. I 'inhaled' another kiss on his cheek. Again, there was surprise in his eyes; he again told me, 'One more, please!'

"That time, I pressed my lips very hard on his cheek and kept them there for a longer time, in fact, I was in a state between wakefulness and sleep, a sort of 'ardha-sukshupti' or half-asleep! 'It seems you're so tired; of course, the day was so tiresome!' He whispered in my ear and gave me a very formal kiss on my forehead, and we slept like two innocent infants!

"Sometime during the small hours of the dawn, he placed his right hand over me, as if in deep sleep, and drew me towards him; I felt his warm breathing caress my ears. I was in sleep, but I felt a sort of security in his presence.

"I was always crazy about my sleep and my best sleep was early in the morning. My husband pressed his cheek against mine and whispered to me to rise up and go to the kitchen; perhaps he was watching me in my sleep for quite a long time! I woke up and went to the kitchen; his mother had already been ready with two glasses of black coffee. She handed over the coffee and I took it to our bedroom.

"After two hours or so, my husband was ready to go to the tutorial college where he was teaching at that time, and as his payment depended on the days he taught there. I noticed him asking his mother for some money as bus-fare, and it was a surprise for me. Here's a husband who had no money in his hand, and always depending on his mother even for his daily bus-fare, I was really shocked! I have heard that obligations to demanding parents or still-depended-upon parents created strain in our life! Of course, his mother gave him immediately the money and he went to his work without saying even a word of farewell to me, perhaps, he did not like such formalities or showing-off in the presence of his parents. Of course, he looked at me as if silently saying 'goodbye', and smiled at me with an expression of shame or guilt on his face!

"The way of life and manners at my husband's house were entirely different from that of mine. I felt as if I were a stranger there, rather like a fish out of water. Though every member in the family loved and respected me, I could not adjust with the surroundings and I felt lonely among the members of that big house. I knew that I was uprooted from my house and was replanted in my husband's house. Of course, according to our tradition, this displacement was inherent in marriage and I had to undergo that inevitable situation and I should compromise with the new surroundings like an emigrant. By marriage, my family exiled me and I had to tolerate and suffer every adverse or alien situation at my husband's house!

"I used to help my mother-in-law in the kitchen. There was also a servant girl who came early morning to clean the utensils and to fetch grass for the cows. I loved to clean the house and its surroundings; for that was a time in which I could think freely. After breakfast, my husband would go to college where he got an appointment a month after our wedding. He would return only after six pm, often by seven pm. To spend the day alone in the house was quite monotonous, as I could not develop an intimacy with others within a short time.

"In the afternoon, I used to go out to collect grass for the cows. Of course, it was not necessary as the servant girl used to bring it, but I loved to pluck grass from some peaceful part of the land-property. While collecting grass, I used to talk to myself or hum a film song. Sometimes, I used to curse my fate that made me live in a remote village far away from the city. I am doomed forever, I thought.

"The mediator woman who brought the proposal for our wedding was a relative of my mother-in-law. She was a poor woman who used to come to my house to do some odd work and to get some money from my mother for her emergency requirements. Owing to her relationship with my mother-in-law, she had become a sort of aunt for me, and I hated to imagine that rumor-monger as my husband's relative. Whenever I saw my mother-in-law, I thought of her only as the relative of that mediator woman of my neighborhood.

"In fact, even before my wedding, I had asked him about the relationship between him and that mediator woman. But he casually replied that years ago, when he was a child, she stayed in his house for a year or two and helped his mother with household chores. That was also true, and to help a poor relative was not a bad thing, after all! But he did not tell me that she was the daughter of his mother's uncle!

"Later, when I asked him why he did not tell me earlier about this close blood-relationship, he took it as a trivial issue. He laughed aloud and said, 'Who knows about all those relatives of one's maternal grandmother? In our patriarchal system, we care only about the father's relatives. You are more attached to your mother's relatives because your father's relatives isolated or deserted you after your father's death! You are compelled to be attached more to your mother's relatives and you don't know much about your father's relatives! And you never got any affection from the relatives of your father!'

"Of course, there is some truth in what he said. But I did not like a relative of that mediator woman to supervise or advise me as if she were my mother-in-law! I knew that my mother-in-law used to contact that woman secretly, in order to know the detailed history of my mother's family. Of course, there must be a few skeletons in the closet of every great family! When my husband came to know that the mediator woman had complained to my mother for not getting any commission regarding the marriage, of course as a relative she had no right to it, he confidentially gave, even without telling me, a sufficient amount to shut her mouth. Perhaps, he might have borrowed that money from some of his friends because, for newly appointed persons, the salary would be given only after a few months due to the usual clerical delay common in the movement of official papers.

"Within three months of our wedding, we could go for our honeymoon trip, to the city where my fourth uncle was working! My husband might have begged his mother to get some money for it! And our travel in a public transport was tedious and boring, and it lasted for hours and hours! Neither could we relax on the way nor could we eat or drink anything tasty! Perhaps my husband did not know that the way to the heart of a woman is through the mouth!

"Of course, my husband was always with me and we enjoyed a week visiting many tourist spots and viewing wonderful sights. We sat under the shade of trees and inhaled the fragrant flowers! We moved like children talking and laughing at silly things! We ran around the trees, foolishly imitating the hero and heroine of some romantic film! Of course, one of my cousins was with us like a 'black ant in the heaven' but he took a number of photographs which I keep with me still.

"Our plan was to return by train which would be more convenient but, unfortunately, a lightning flood washed away certain parts of the railway track and we had to postpone our journey. Throughout my life it was like that; whenever I wished something good, there would be something like a lightning flood! My husband could not stay there for many days as it was impossible during that probation period of his job to avail more leave. He returned alone by bus, leaving me with my youngest uncle's family, until the railway track was repaired and trains started running.

"After two weeks, I returned with my uncle and my husband was at the railway station to receive me. I reached home only to suffer a month of pain, medicine and hospitalization due to a urinary infection! Though my illness was called 'honeymoon disease,' common among newly married couples, the pain was so severe that I suspected whether it was some sort of venereal disease, perhaps, infected from my husband who had spent a number of years in North India! And North Indian cities were notorious for red-streets and such sexually transmitted diseases!

"I had to take rest for a month and by that time almost all my teeth began to turn black and show symptoms of untimely decay. Doctors said that it was the side effect of certain powerful medicine like 'Mandelamin' which they served me at the hospital. And I lost my smile forever! In the college everybody, including the young lecturer Mr. Smartguy, appreciated my smile due to the beauty of my teeth! I looked into the mirror and shed tears! In the mirror, I saw the reflection of Mr. Smartguy, ogling at me and winking at me and calling me 'Ms. Smiling-pot' in a mocking tone! Gone are those days of my smiles and what was left with me was a married life without smiles, and with severe tooth-pain and headaches!

"I wished to resume my studies and everybody in the family agreed to it, perhaps, observing my melancholic mood. I thought that it would help me to develop a better enjoyable relationship with my husband if I could go with him to the same city where both of us were engaged. I joined a private college and both of us could travel in the same bus. I felt as if I were returning to my old college days. I saw many of my classmates were in love with somebody and those young men employed or not, used to wait patiently to have a chance to talk to them. And my husband, though he had the legal right to visit me, never turned towards that side of our college to see, at least to know, what I was doing there!

"Of course, I never asked him to come to my college to talk to me or meet my friends. He might be busy with his classes in his college, I thought. Of course, if he were of lesser age, he would have showed more enthusiasm or spirit in visiting me even during class hours! As a matured man and a teacher, he could not do so degrading himself to that level, I knew. But love is something which cannot be taught; it must come spontaneously, it must spring from the heart and my husband either did not know that emotion or he felt ashamed to declare it in public or that he could not do so because his wife was only a student!

"One day I was in the bus returning home from the college. The bus stopped near the junction where he used to enter the bus. I saw him standing with other passengers and I smiled at him. But he ignored my smile and entered the bus through the back door. Other passengers were watching me and I felt ashamed or rather insulted. Am I a woman smiling at every passerby? Why did he ignore even my presence in the bus? My honor was wounded and I felt as if I were falling down into a deep pit from where there was no escape!

"Why did my husband behave like that, I used to think. Perhaps he did not notice me standing in the bus. Perhaps, the culture of our society might have prevented him from expressing his love in public places. Or as there was a crowd of women standing by the front door, he had to enter through the back door! But I had seen many couples move freely hand-in-hand and they never cared about what others thought or made ridiculing comments. He would say that love was not a thing to be exhibited and those exhibitionists were cultureless people who belonged to the lower class. Of course, all over the world, lower class people enjoyed more social freedom in married life than the so-called high caste hypocrites! Perhaps, the so-called teacher-image in his subconscious mind might have tempered his heart to live in a make-believe world!

"I always felt that my husband was ignoring my simple desires. He never understood the hopes and aspirations of a young woman! I wished to ride with him holding him with my right hand around his waist and proudly sitting at the back of a motorcycle, but he never bought a motor-bike. I wished to travel with him sitting on the side seat of a car which he was driving, but never had he done so! We were not so poor as not to afford a bike or even a car! If he had wished, he could have bought either of them, and we could have enjoyed our life. Almost all his colleagues had either of such vehicles and I felt ashamed to travel in public transport buses especially to attend a wedding or funeral. Of course, we had not that much money to buy a vehicle, but if we had bought one, we could have managed to maintain it. Now, we have enough money to buy one or two cars but can I get back the thrill of travelling with my husband in a car during my youth days?

"Of course, if I had asked him in a loving manner to do something, he would have done it. But in his presence, I was either too tamed like a sheep or too ferocious like a tigress; for I could not be one in between! And why should I stoop to a disgraceful level and request him for anything and everything? I am his wife and I have the right to demand certain things in life. Am I a beggar to fall at his feet and extend my hands for alms? Of course, if a wife has no job or regular income of her own, she will be treated just like a 'foot-mat', not only by her husband but also by his relatives and even by neighbors!

"By that time, a child was born to us and, thereby, my hopes about improving my educational qualification also shattered. I knew that he wished to have a boy-child but it was a girl-child.

Every Indian parent, to be particular, wished to have a boy-child first as there was no risk in continuing the lineage. I looked at his face; to my surprise, there was real thrill, joy and curiosity of a father on his face. Perhaps, he did not care whether the child was a boy or a girl except that there should be a child to prove his fertility!

"But, in fact, I was sad; why did I give birth to another poor girl to suffer in this world like me? She would also become a slave to her husband and lead a miserable life as a housewife. To be born as a woman, especially in India, is a curse. In addition to all the restrictions imposed upon her by the family, community and society, she also has to face the atrocities leveled against her by sexually restless and jealous members of the public.

"How could a girl grow and survive as a free citizen in a closed society in which almost all male members looked at her only as an object of sex? India will always remain a poor country with her poverty of sex! How could a woman live freely in the midst of a male community that suffocated under suppressed sex? How could she exist under the suspicious eyes of a sexually perverted society which had been misguided by sheer hypocrisy and false notions of a closed culture? Really, I was unhappy in giving birth to a girl!

"Then, we moved to a house that belonged to one of our close relatives, in the city where my husband worked. My in-laws gave me the hope that in the near future we could buy that house! It was really a change for me as I had, at least, a house of my own, with much freedom, and responsibility as well. Of course, my husband could also save the traveling expense as well as time so that he could spend more time with me and my child. Moreover, as the owner of the house had a plan to sell the house, we thought of buying it in the near future. I felt a new enthusiasm and I brought an ideal homely arrangement and discipline in our nucleus family. I maintained the house and its premises as if it were our own property. Of course, I was often disturbed by the thought whether we could make money within a short period to buy and really make it our own.

"As the child began to go to school, I began to feel again some sort of loneliness despite all the domestic work. But it did not trouble me much as I was busy with household duties. Moreover, in the afternoon, I used to go to my daughter's school to bring her home, and that was good entertainment for me. Of course, I could mingle with many homemakers like me but, when I saw some other ladies of my age going for office work, I really felt jealousy towards them. Of course, I had some friends, one should have somebody to talk to, and most of them were jobless and lesser educated than me.

"How happy we were then! Every household thing we bought was a thrill for us. It might be some dress material or costly things like a refrigerator or a television set, but each piece gave us a sort of heavenly satisfaction. Each piece of furniture we bought was a treasure for us. A papaya fruit or a jackfruit from our compound was tastier than any other fruit we bought from the bazaar. A small rose flower or a little lily flower in our garden gave us more delight than any other exotic cut-flowers we saw in the flower shops! And we were blessed with the smiles and lisping of our child!

"We were too busy with our day-to-day life and we enjoyed every moment of it! But, one fine morning, everything turned quite upside down as the owner of our house decided to sell the house, and we did not have sufficient money to buy it. Suddenly, I felt as if we were mere refugees living at the mercy of others! As we had been staying there for a few years, our blood-relative might have thought that we would claim some right over it! It was like a thunder out of the clear blue! Perhaps, he was nagged by his wife or advised by his mother-in-law to behave in an inhuman manner! Of course, I always believed that God gave us problems only with solutions!

"One day, he came to the house with his laborers, without any prior notice, and began repairing the house and beautifying it. Re-plastering the walls, fixing the ceiling, rewiring and painting continued and we had to bear the dust, noise and other disturbances for many days. It seemed as if they were trying to smoke out the rats! Had he informed us a month ago, we would have found a rented house! And it was shameful for us to return to the house of his parents from where we had been sent out once! Nobody was there to help us; my husband ran here and there, like a dog that caught fire on its tail, to find a nearby rented house, and I could do nothing but only shed tears!

"I hated everybody; I hated my relatives and his relatives as well. I hated my father who left me at the mercy of fate! I hated all my neighbors and friends, though they had nothing to do with our fate. I hated even my womanhood that made me a slave to my husband and children! I hated even God who gave uneven justice and unjustifiable fate!

"Fortunately we got a house, of course, with an exorbitant rent, and we moved to it. Though my husband assured me that everything would be changed within three months, perhaps, the house was rented only for three months or he had money only for three months' rent, I was too desperate to believe his words.

"Of course, many a time, I even lost my temper and forgot myself at his very sight, and even reacted so violently like a mad woman! I hated everybody; I hated my husband; I hated his mother, I hated his relative who sent us out of his house; I hated his mother's relative who brought the proposal for my marriage! One day, I became so crazy that I lost my senses; I took the scissors from the drawer of my sewing machine and struck him with it behind his neck!

"Luckily, on the last week of the third month, we managed to buy a small house just opposite to our previous house! I heaved a long sigh of relief and began to walk and talk among my relatives and neighbors with pride and honor. Once again we started a new life, of course, bearing all the limitations of that old and small house. My husband started to take tuition classes for some students by putting a few wooden benches on the outer verandah of our house. But he never asked them the fees, and if someone by chance gave the fees, he did not care who gave it or who did not!

"My husband used to write stories and most of his fiction was obscure or rather philosophical. When he was in the mood of writing, he became quite restless, careless or absent-minded. Even during the early days of our marriage, he used to send me to my mother's house; it is no longer mine after my marriage, for a few days, pretending a sort of extra affection for me and my mother, only to write a story or a poem in my absence. When he wanted to write something, he did not like to be disturbed by me and avoided me or rather ignored even my presence in the house!

"In my opinion, no one should marry a poet or story writer whether man or woman! I wonder why these writers marry! They are living in an imaginative world and a peaceful married life is not for them! I have heard that Shakespeare grouped 'poets, lovers and madmen' into one category and that was absolutely true! Writers and lovers are as mad as madmen, rather worse, and they should not marry and spoil the life of their spouses!

"Do you mean lovers also should not marry? Someone may ask because there are people who think that love is essential in married life. But, here, 'lovers' meant premarital lovers and once they married, their love came to the cipher-point, because their earlier world of fancy was no longer applicable in a practical married life. As lovers, they had to wear a kind of mask, a sort of mere showing-off, which they automatically torn off as and when they began their conjugal life and, then, they would feel dejected and disheartened.

"Of course, I used to read his stories, at least, a few of them, especially when he was away at the college and, I must confess, I loved some of them. I always wondered how a person could write real, life-like stories just by imagination alone! Without practical experience, I don't think that one could write realistic stories. If one meticulously describes a night with a prostitute in a slice-of-life story, there must be some practical experience, I strongly believed so. There is at least a fifty percent chance that the writer must have spent his days with such wayward women. And I felt utter disgust towards such people who engaged in similar obnoxious and abominable situations! I hated such men, who were unscrupulous enough to write about their amorous adventures with such women! I would hate such a man, even if he was my husband!

"Of course, writing stories is a good job if you get money for it, if you can manage your daily bread out of it, and there are many writers who became rich through their writings alone. But as far as I know, my husband did not earn a single coin through his writing! Then, why should he write, wasting his time and energy, and spoiling my simple joys of life? Even when I was sick or suffering from some fever, situations in which one felt lonely and helpless, he neither spent his time with me nor even took a casual leave from his college to nurse me!

"Recently he went to an African country, I believe, only to avoid me; it might be an escape from my presence. Perhaps, he could write more silly stories and useless poems there! Perhaps, he was fed up with me and was seeking new pastures!

"I have lost my talents, my beauty, my health and my life by living as a housewife! And my husband's leaving for Africa was the last straw that broke the camel's back! Of course, I was at the airport to see him off! On my way back home, I sat at the back of the car and thought about the years that passed! I became mad when all the situations of disappointments and rejections, all the issues of dejections and frustrations accumulated in my mind. I reached home as a changed woman.

"During that night itself I wrote a letter to my husband, expressing all my hatred towards him and describing all the anxieties that tormented me all through the past, which I could not tell him face to face. The next day, I posted the letter and felt quite relaxed and relieved of all the bile in me. All the suppressed bitter feelings of my heart were emptied; the tempest was over, the tides and waves were subsided, and I felt the peace of a deep ocean.

"I wanted to see the effect of my letter on him. I waited for his call and, at last, when it came, I talked to him curtly and cut the line. If I had expressed my regret about the letter, there would have been no existence for me as a woman! I knew that it was very difficult to bend a steel rod with your bare hands and there was no possibility that his adamant mind would change! I was always a faithful wife to him and I will continue like that forever!

"Once, while I was a student, a sage came to my house. He read my horoscope and studied the lines on my palms and said that I would be a 'dheerkha sumangali,' a woman with a long married life. Another meaning of that phrase was that until my death I would be with my husband; and that meant, I would die before my husband's death! I am not at all afraid of my death, but I want to die in the presence of my husband.

"A number of illnesses are troubling me and I feel the countdown! And my husband is in a faraway country, unaware of my physical and mental condition. Whenever I complained to him of some illness, he used to laugh at me and said, 'It's all your imagination!' Now, I really desire his presence with me; I need him desperately! Of course, he never suffered any sort of serious illnesses in his life and, therefore, he could not understand my present real agony!

"I met Doctor Phalims, a family friend of ours, and discussed the matter with him. He recommended a psychiatric who had much foreign experience! He told me that some people

337

displayed their 'extra energy' in certain peculiar ways and my husband must be one among them who had such excessive energy! He pointed out that such people used to write literature, draw paintings, make fiery speeches and even risk their life in adventurous activities! They were a sort of idealist and enthusiast, he pointed out, some of them joined terrorist activities others climbed Everest! How true they were all with my husband's nature, I was surprised. I believed that doctor; he appeared to me as an angel! He realized my real situation and promised me all kinds of help, if I could bring back my husband from that African country where he worked. He said that he had some mild and harmless medicines with him by which he could tame my husband.

"I also rang my brother and told him about my sad situation. He promised me to come from the Gulf country where he was working and to help me in taking my husband to the doctor, as and when he arrived at the airport. Throughout my married life, I tried all the four means of samam, dhanam, bhedam and dhandam or advice, allowance, indifference and punishment to bring my husband to a normal life; and I failed miserably. This is my last chance and let me try the last means once again! Pretending my defeat, I will telephone him and make sure of his arrival. Let my husband be with me forever, let me love and protect him, let him love and protect me. I wish nothing more in my life, but only what the sage predicted, to be a dheerkha sumangali!"

Her scribbling ended there; then, a number of blank pages! First, I felt like smiling in a sinister way. It was only a maiden's autobiography and not that of a housewife, as Geetha claimed. I expected more from it about her life as a married woman, only then I could probe into their problems and find a solution, if necessary. Of course, neither was I a psychiatrist nor was I a counselor in family issues. Then, why should I bother about the minute details of their family life?

But what is happening in this world? I wondered. If youngsters divorce, one can understand! How could middle-aged people make such serious allegations and complaints, throwing slime at each other's face like naughty children? And that too, after a married life of twenty-five years! Perhaps, the mind could not become 'aged'?

The husband speaks one thing and the wife understands it differently; the wife speaks another thing and the husband fails to understand her feelings! My God! Many marriages fall apart because either partner cannot imagine what the other wants or cannot communicate what the other needs or feels! Their family life turns into a Babel Tower!

The Tower of Babel is, perhaps, one of the most evocative images in the entire Bible, a spectacle of creaturely aspiration toward deity that finds its counterpart in the mythological story of the Titans who tried to supplant Zeus and were punished by being hurled into Tartarus, as the Dictionary of Biblical Imagery pointed out! Of course, one could not think about the Tower of Babel as a physical or architectural phenomenon reaching massively into the sky, or even as a structure like the Qutab Minar in Delhi or the tower of Madhurai Meenakshi Temple, but something like the Egyptian pyramid or the ancient Babylonian ziggurat or step-temple, a sort of astronomical observatory for use in divination and occult mastery of the universe.

But this image, undoubtedly, denotes confusion and discord and, perhaps, encompasses much more than this like the disharmony in family life! Like family life, the Babel Tower was an attempt made by human beings to reach heaven. In a way, both are ventures in human autonomy, as we see, 'come, let us build ourselves a city' or 'let us make a name for ourselves!' Of course, both represent the timeless human urge for fame and permanent achievement, as well as for independence and self-sufficiency. But in their efforts to solidify their dreams and aspirations, they might have felt pride in their physical strength and the spirit of boasting in human achievement might have dominated them.

There comes the intervening of God, as the top of their towering hopes was 'in the heavens' which God interpreted as 'an attempt to storm God's dwelling place!' Though there was the triumph of both reason and imagination in establishing the unity of man, it was also an attempt on the part of human beings to control and master the world! And then, even God became jealous of them because He knew that 'nothing will be restrained from them, which they have imagined to do.'

Their dream of perfect unity was enhanced by the unilingual situation, as 'the whole earth had one language and few words!' Of course, when the heart is full, words are few! Moreover, as the Malayalam poet Kumaran Asan warned: Oh! Language is so incomplete today that error occurs due to confusion in meaning! However, in perfect conjugal unity, the barrier of language disappears forever! Gradually, I realized the significance of getting this particular passage from the Old Testament, when I opened the Bible with prayer, up above the Arabian Sea, while I was coming to India from Ethiopia!

Married life is really a Babel Tower, an attempt made by man and woman to reach the heaven of conjugal bliss, provided they should understand each other's language! Of course, there's a natural force that destroys the unity of individuals, a force that prevents the building up of a Babel Tower! It is the silent language of the heart, and not the language of the brain or brawn, that helps them to pave the way to the heaven of a peaceful and happily married life. I sighed like a philosopher who was groping in the darkness for a black cat that was not there!

Lucky are those whose marriages could survive the hurricanes and tornados of family problems! Fortunate are those who could keep on with their nuptial bliss when the heavy storms and cyclones of marital despair and other plagues of life blast against them! However, we live in a world in which the so-called romantic myths about married life are broken up, and the nuptial oath '…and both of us shall live happily ever after till death do us part' has become quite obsolete!

Of course, there is no doubt that in certain cases, divorce provides salvation; despite its initial devastation, it may provide a healthy life for both parties. For removing an ulcerous growth, a surgeon has to use his knife, and though his knife at first gives severe pain but it would be a step towards those healthy and happy days in the future!

Well! I knew the stories of both Rajesh and Geetha. With whom should I take sides? I wished to shout like Sir Roger de Coverly that 'much might be said on both sides!' How strange were their notions! No doubt, they loved each other but they did not know how to express their love towards each other! Somebody must launch a school for teaching love and conjugality! One should not be allowed to marry just because he or she has genital organs! Here, both Rajesh and Geetha wanted to be possessive of each other and their love worked on them as an obsession and blinded them. How could they compromise each other and come to an amicable consensus?

It is always dangerous to form a quick opinion or make a comment on the misunderstanding among married couples. Conjugal life is a thin glass vase that, unless you handle it very carefully, it may break into tiny pieces, never to be glued together. It is a fine silk thread and, once broken, you can tie the ends together but with a bulging knot in it! I was in a dilemma; I did not know whether to cry or laugh! Of course, there was a kind of vicarious pleasure when you peep into the life of others!

I remembered the story of a tribal group living on an island somewhere in the east. If a husband and wife quarrel and decide to separate, the Elder will call them, ask them to strip off their clothes and take them in a canoe to a rock in the sea. He will leave them there, without food, water or clothing, and return to the island. Of course, there is no shelter and the couples have to suffer the extreme cold of the night. Every morning, the Elder will come and ask whether the couple have come to reconciliation or not. If they say no, he will leave them there and return until they forgive and forget; and if they say yes, he will take them back in his canoe. It is said that the maximum days they spend on the rock are three! What an easy remedy! It would have been better if the family courts in India or America had attempted a similar experiment!

Of course, every problem that comes in the life of a married couple will be solved if they think that they are human beings, and not animals with options. Human beings are rational creatures and, if so, they should not change their mates just like changing their clothes! It is because man marries a woman not merely for procreation. In an age when semen banks flourish like mushrooms, procreation is not at all a problem, if women are willing, and the presence of men on earth will turn a mere extravaganza!

I wondered how more divorces and remarriages could occur among Christians and Muslims who believe that God created only one Eve for Adam! I could not understand why a Semitic religion like Islam in their Shari-at Law allows more than one marriage even up to four! In this matter Hindus are better models. Of course, in Europe, divorces are sanctioned hurriedly by the court so that the couples would not get even time for a second thinking. They think of marriage as a mere contract between two individuals and not as a cultural institution established for the safety of the society. That is sheer cultureless-ness, and a black mark on their so-called civilization!

Thank God! Everything might have become normal by now with Rajesh and Geetha! They might have sorted out their misunderstandings and come to an amicable settlement. And the saying is 'to err is human but to forgive is divine!' They might have their own errors in their life and they might have forgiven each other. All's well that ends well!

I immediately telephoned to the house of Rajesh. I thought that he might have returned from the hospital. Fortunately, Geetha took the phone and said that her husband was better and he would return home within one or two days. I must visit the house of Rajesh and Geetha and congratulate them, I decided. But before that, I had to visit my aged relatives; I had to make arrangements for my return to Ethiopia. As the days of my return approached, I was really in tension. How fast the days are passing, especially when you are on a month's leave from a foreign country, I thought.

CHAPTER TEN

There was hardly a week more to leave for Ethiopia! I was busy with shopping and I always kept a list in my pocket, a list I prepared even before I started from Africa. Kerala spices were first in the list; pepper powder, cumin-seed powder, coriander powder, turmeric powder, fenugreek powder, mustard powder and chili powder; and then the spice-mixtures like meat masala, fish masala, chicken masala, sambar mix, pickle powder, rasam powder and chat masala.

The coconut powder was not available at the shop; though the word Kerala means the Land of Coconut Trees, we used to get our coconuts from Tamil Nadu and the coconut powder from Sri Lanka because of the windfall and the Communist Party in our State, and the shop-keeper promised me to supply it on the very next day but, in my hurriedness, I forgot to collect it. I also bought certain toilet items like soaps, blades, shaving lotion and creams, which should be kept in the main luggage; otherwise the customs people would pilfer them in the name of security!

Then, from the textile shop, I bought a pair of pants and shirts, a few pairs of underwear, towels and, of course, a few special shirts and gifts for my friends in Ethiopia. And then, the most inevitable item, my medicines for a year which included tablets for blood pressure, cholesterol and stomach illnesses! My doctor also had advised me to start certain mild medicines for diabetics as there was a slight variation in my blood sugar. All these were allopathic, but I also had to take a few ayurvedic powders, oils and ointments!

There was a lot of work to be completed before I left my

home. I should contact my travel agent to confirm and reconfirm my air-tickets and, then, take their computer printouts to be shown at the airport. My newly printed books should be collected from the printers; all banking tasks including bank cheques to be signed and given to my wife; demand drafts, with covering letters, should be sent to the publishers of my favorite periodicals. I also had to make quick visits to my aged parents who lived in the village, and certain other very old, ailing relatives and friends, lest I might regret later throughout my life.

Suddenly it struck my mind that I had not made a visit to my friend's house. Of course Rajesh might have returned from the hospital after a proper recovery of his mental ailment, if I could depend on the words of his wife. If so, he might be taking rest at his house, enjoying all the loving care of his wife. I felt a sort of jealousy, thinking about his luck, especially as I had to leave for Ethiopia without taking my wife with me.

His wife, Geetha, as far as I know, was an excellent wife, always very careful about maintaining the well-being of the family as well as the cleanliness of the house and surroundings. She was an expert in cooking and I knew that Rajesh, after a break of about a year, should be enjoying her culinary gifts and acquiring overweight! Be cautious, my dear Rajesh, or, in future years, you will be taking bundles of medicines, like me! I mused.

Of course, I also must enquire about the date of their coming over to Ethiopia, so that I could give them some sort of help like arranging a convenient house or getting the cooking-gas connection.

While returning home, after making a short visit to my aged parents, I took the roundabout route so that I could call at the house of Rajesh. Of course, I had to change three buses and as the next day being a Saturday, all the busses were unusually overloaded with passengers; I had to stand all through the journey clinging to the iron bars fixed to the ceiling of the buses. I got down at the bus-stop near his house and walked about a hundred meters along a pebbled road to his house.

I opened the gate, passed the courtyard and pressed the calling bell. The courtyard and the small compound in general were so impressive for its neatness and cleanliness. It was just the opposite of what I had witnessed a few days before! The small garden with various plants and multi-colored flowers created a pleasant atmosphere. Of course, the clever hands of an assiduous wife could work miracles in changing a house into a home! And Geetha was really a talented and hard-working woman.

The door opened, Geetha came out with a warm smile and welcomed me to the house. She seemed quite happy to see me, for she thought that I would have left for Africa. I was really happy to see her in that pleasant mood; there was a grace of satisfaction on her face. Perhaps, petty quarrels between husband and wife would enhance the charm and strength of conjugal relationships, I thought.

"You seem too tired from traveling! Would you like to have a cold drink?" she asked me with the true concern of a hostess.

"Alright," I said, "but where's Rajesh? Hasn't he been around?"

"Of course, he's in his room," she replied and hurriedly went to the kitchen to bring me a cold drink. It seemed she had no maid-servants at home.

I heard her opening the fridge, washing the glass and taking a spoon from some steel rack. I looked around; the drawing room was well arranged and there were two or three flower vases with fresh cut-flowers. The showcase was fully packed with toys, perhaps, once used by their daughter, medals and trophies won by her in school sports-meets; and also the old wedding photo of Rajesh and Geetha, with youthful smiles on their faces and holding garlands and bouquets. I smiled to myself, thinking about the uncertainty of human life; a wedding with all pomp and show and, later, a practical life compromising with all shattered dreams!

Geetha came with a glass of orange juice. Taking the glass from her, I thanked and asked, "Where's your daughter? Didn't she come to see her father?"

"Oh, Radha! She has a lot of work in the company where she is currently practicing. She has work even on holidays! She's coming here next week. By the way, George Sir, we're planning for her marriage!" she said proudly.

"That's great! Now, we must find a good boy for her. But, you see, Geetha, it's very difficult now-a-days to find a suitable boy!" I said, sipping the juice.

"Don't worry, George Sir! I think she herself found a boy who's an engineer in the firm where she practices now!" she said with a laugh.

"Of course! Our children are clever; they know our difficulty in finding matches for them!" I joined her in sharing the joke.

I drank the juice and looked at her anxiously. "But where's this Rajesh? Is he still sleeping, at this odd time of the day?" I asked her in a joking manner.

"Come! Let's see him!" she said and guided me to his room. She opened the door and we entered into the room. There was the fragrance of some air-freshener hanging in the room. He was lying on the bed and I said in an embarrassing tone, "Oh, I'm sorry! He's sleeping and it's not fair to disturb him."

Ignoring my comments, she went to his bed and said, "Look, Rajesh! Do you know who's here to visit you? It's your George Sir!" she said in a cheerful voice.

I looked at Rajesh. "Oh, no!" A gasp escaped from my throat; I stood there for a moment thunderstruck! A tremor passed through my veins and my heart was heavily palpitating. Rajesh did not turn his face to look at me! His eyes were open but there was no sign of recognition in them! He was lying on the bed like a vegetable!

There was no change on the face of Geetha, in fact, she looked very pleased. I looked at her with anger, or, rather, with a sort of disgust. However, I could control my emotions, and I asked her, "Geetha, will you please leave us alone for a moment?"

She silently walked out of the room and closed the door behind her. I sat on the bed, very close to his face.

"Rajesh! Rajesh!" I called him softly. My lips were trembling and I murmured, "Oh, Rajesh, my dear friend! What a horrible fate is yours!"

I felt tears in my eyes. There was not even a slight movement on his face! I knew that he was in the coma stage. There was no hope of his recovery. He was doomed for a lifeless life!

Then I noticed tears flowing down from the corners of his eyes. He sensed someway my presence, I was sure. His lips trembled for a while; I felt as if he were murmuring the lines from Shakespeare's sonnet:

'In me thou seest the twilight of such day
As after sunset fadeth in the west;
Which by and by black night doth take away,
Death's second self, that seals up all in rest.'

I took my handkerchief and slowly wiped away his tears. I gave a kiss on his forehead, as if giving the last kiss to the dead body of a dear relative, and whispered in his ears, "You'll be alright soon. Don't worry, my dear friend! I'll pray for you. May God redeem you from this pathetic condition!"

I came out of the room with a drooped head and sat on the chair. Geetha had already taken the glass to the kitchen and returned to the drawing room. Sitting on a chair opposite to mine, she was carelessly turning the pages of a women's magazine. There was still that cheerfulness on her face! After a moment's silence, I said, "Geetha, I'm so sorry! I don't know what really happened to him. It's really a pity! You see, day after tomorrow, I'm leaving for Ethiopia."

"Don't worry, George Sir!" she said calmly. "I'll manage everything here. The doctor promised that Rajesh would recover soon. You see, it was the mistake of the doctor, a sort of overdose of medication! You know, some medicines are too allergic! That's all!" she said quite optimistically.

I wondered whether she was in her normal senses! Or was she hoping against hope that her husband would be recovered? Of course, there was a glow of confidence on her face. I asked her, "Why didn't you file a petition against the doctor? It's too barbaric!"

"Oh, no! Why should I? It creates a lot of problems; going to the police station and long hours of waiting on the verandahs of the court! You know, any doctor can make mistakes! And this doctor is our family friend." She talked in a very casual manner.

I interrupted her and said, "But Geetha, it's too cruel and intolerable! You know, Rajesh was quite a normal person, and how did this fate come up on him? I can't believe even my own eyes!"

She replied in a pleasing manner, "It's okay, George Sir! I love him to be here with me always. He is, at least, quite accessible for me now. No busy schedules, no public meetings, no cultural seminars and conferences on literature, arts or inter-faith harmony; and, of course, no teaching or paper valuation business! We have enough money to manage the family. I'll look after him till my death. I want to see him always and I can understand the meaning of every slight movement of his eyes! I loved him so much and I'll continue to do so. He'll recover soon, George Sir! I know it by my intuition!"

What should I say to this woman? How could I say that she was hoping against hope? Was she crazy or even abnormal? She looked alright and there was no trace of sorrow on her face;

instead I noticed full confidence in her eyes! Anybody who heard her words would blindly believe her! Then, why should I interfere in their happy married life?

I looked at her and said, "Well, Geetha! I'm leaving for Ethiopia day after tomorrow. If you need any kind of help from my side, please don't hesitate to ask me, okay? Goodbye!"

I stood up and moved towards the door. She followed me to the door and said, "Thank you, George Sir! Bye-bye!"

I closed the gate after me and walked towards the bus-stop. I tried to forget the rigid, placid face of my friend. I remembered the bright and cheerful face of Geetha. Is it really love? Of course, true love is an obsession and once you change that obsession into possession, everything changes! She might be too possessive, and possessiveness is there, to a certain extent, in conjugal life. But possessiveness leads to selfishness and selfishness leads to jealousy and greed! Yet, this sort of love is beyond all human behaviors!

I was surprised at the confidence of Geetha! Was she normal in her love towards her husband! Was he quite happy when served or looked after by his wife every moment? I knew that Geetha would definitely look after him with all her sincerity. But what about the unnatural behavior of Geetha! Did she really love him or was it pretense or even revenge? Gosh! Who would give me an answer? I recollected the verse of Prophet Jeremiah: "The heart is deceitful over all things, and desperately wicked, who can know it?"

I remembered Rajesh telling me about a Guruji whom he planned to visit; perhaps, he would give me a solution to this problem. Guruji was famous all over the world and attracted thousands of devotees from different parts of the world! And there was no shortage for such demi-gods or babas in India! Of course, in a world where human beings ran helter-skelter in search of peace of mind, these counselors would be highly useful. Every human being needed the help of a piece of advice from some unselfish Guru or Master! They might be the shovels of some political parties or religious organizations; they might be part of a mafia! Their institutions might have made much money but they really were doing a great job!

That night I got a telephone call and, to my surprise, it was from Dr. Worqu Singh. He said over the phone, "Hullo, Dr. George! I'm sorry to convey to you some sad news! Our old friend Doctor Honey Rao passed away last evening! A few minutes ago, a friend of mine rang me from Hyderabad and told me this news! It was an unexpected cardiac arrest! He had prepared everything to go for a pilgrimage to Kashi and today he was supposed to set out from his house! Man proposes; God disposes!"

"Perhaps, God offered him a better pilgrimage!" I said in a sad voice! The smiling face of Dr. Rao reflected in my mind. Could his soul reconcile with his daughter and daughter-in-law? I wondered. I tried to remember the face of Mrs. Rao, who was very talkative and always careful in looking after her husband! Here Lord Ram's 'vanavasa' had come to an end; but what about the fate of Sita? Mrs. Rao had to undergo a second 'life in the forest,' perhaps!

The next day itself I went to Guruji's ashram and sat with others, without disclosing my identity to any other person. Of course, I was only a spec in the crowd and who bothered about me unless I had an exhibitionist mind! When Rajesh suggested to go to a Guruji, I thought that he was a Hindu 'baba' or spiritual man whom you can see everywhere in India! I was surprised to see the Guruji in the cassock of a Christian priest but he talked like a Hindu philosopher, as I realized later!

In fact, like the culture of India, he was an amalgamation of a number of philosophies, both oriental and occidental! Guruji, might be in his fifties, was a man of good health and well-built body! Perhaps the yoga he did every day could do such miracles! He was always smiling and a sort of grace spread

351

from him! His personality was so attractive that I too fell flat at his charismatic influence! I saw a sort of halo around his head!

He was sitting on a chair placed at the centre of the dais. He was wearing a long cassock with coffee-brown color which reminded me of the mantle of His Holiness the Dalai Lama except for his bright orange-colored khameez. He had long hair and a thick beard but it seemed he had neither combed his hair nor trimmed his beard for a long time! His eyes were very bright and he looked ahead of us, as if looking into eternity! A microphone was placed about a foot away from his face so that the listeners had to strain their ears to hear his words properly!

There was an old woman in a white sari, sitting on the floor behind Guruji! She had a veena in her lap and she caressed its strings, creating a solemn atmosphere. There was pin-drop silence in the hall as if the silence itself had a soothing and consoling effect on the audience!

Fortunately, on that day he talked on human relationships and this was called coincidence or miracle, because the purpose of my visit was to listen to that subject! He began his talk by asking a question: "What was the sin of Adam and Eve?" He himself answered that they profaned the divine and, thereby, an integrated life became fragmented! An integrated good world became a fragmented bad world!

"Today we live in an absolutely chaotic world wondering 'How' and 'Why' human life was fragmented! Usually when somebody asks you 'Who are you?' your answer might be what you have been doing and not what you really are because you do not know your own identity! See! How life is identified by a wrong definition!

"Every human being today faces some sort of an existential problem, and this is the intellectual aspect of that fragmentation! Many of us complain that 'time is not enough' but this is not a qualitative but quantitative problem and, of course, an existential problem!

"Therefore, unity is the practical solution or the only possible reality; what you see around is diversity but it is mere illusion!"

I was shocked to the core because he said a religious dogma which I could not digest! I could understand his stance that everything originated from the Great One or Brahma or God or Allah, will return to him! But as a practical man, I believed, "Diversity is the only reality; unity is mere illusion!" And I knew that while discussing the existential problem both the dictums are one and the same!

Guruji continued, "Of course, some of our great sages could not say what exactly 'reality' was! Our great saint Ramanujan said that 'Reality' must be 'Something'! But Madhavacharya said that Divinity is the only reality! Whom we should depend on or believe for a correct answer? There were great masters who tried to specialize in such universal subjects! At last, they laughed aloud and said to laugh your way through life! For, a specialist is a person who studies more and more about lesser and lesser and finally learns everything about nothing!"

He said, "Most of us underestimate the significance of human life; some of us find its significance in a world outside human existence, some others fail to find any reasonable significance at all! Why can't you recognize the significance of our human life in our present existence itself?"

He was silent for a while and said, "Human life is a search to realize the spiritual and material truth. When we realize that the outside world is incomplete, we begin our search to the inside world. It was the realization that through imagination man can realize many things which are beyond the power of his senses which urged him to think about soul or atma! Man tries to establish that soul or atma is the only truth as it cannot be altered by the three times of past, present and future! When he reached that stage of truth or 'brahma', he begins to think whether even that 'brahma' is true or untrue! *Na sat na asat mukadchade!* Of course, no one can say that everything is discovered; at least a few more digits will be left to fill up, as Morley said!"

Guruji stopped for a while and then continued his talk, "It is said that time and tide wait for none; that also is true! Just think of life in its micro level and think of time in its macro level! Then who could make his or her life meaningful or worthy of living within such a short period? How long could one make experiments with life as Mahatma Gandhi did? Don't you want to gain immortality? Our life will wither away like the lilies in the field! Then how could we achieve eternity; if the soul or atma is immortal where it would make its permanent abode?"

Guruji gave a few minutes for thinking but the listeners did not bother to waste their time thinking; they always wanted quick and easy solutions and they waited impatiently for answers from the horse's mouth!

Guruji said, "The word 'atma' in Sanskrit, what we call soul or spirit in English, has a variety of meanings, each having different nuances! In its noun form, 'atma' means the eternal thing, the immortal existence, the permanent state, the unchangeable entity, the imperishable existence, the unquenchable spark, something that continued forever, a power that is conveyed from one to another, the everlasting stage and so on. In its verb form, 'atma' means to make something eternal, to achieve immortality, to create something permanently new, to change from the old to the new, to preserve from destruction, to prolong one's existence, to perpetuate, to immortalize, to make something continue for a very long time, to disseminate, to keep alive, to make somebody remembered forever, to procreate, to remake something from the old one, to multiply the existing thing, to propagate what's available, to produce offspring by reproduction and so on. Of course, some of these meanings are not direct but nuances of the original meaning."

He continued, "According to Dr. Damodar Thakur, a famous linguist, etymologically the word 'atma' in Sanskrit means to perpetuate! Of course, we developed a culture in which we are compelled to believe that certain words have only specific meanings, and no other meanings to them are acceptable to our psyche! Let me make the idea clear to you without beating the bushes! Our 'atma' or soul achieves eternity or immortality through our next generation. Generation after generation, our 'gene' conveyed from one to another, either directly or indirectly, for it need not be important whether a person has offspring or not, and human life will go on forever! Don't misunderstand that gene is soul; soul is the 'life force' or the spirit that's transferred from one to another!"

He said, "It is like achieving 'moksha' or salvation or nirvana, or even heaven; human beings have no right to achieve it, as Jesus Christ pointed out, but it's a blessing or a gift or a grace of what we call God! Of course, fate supervises the proceedings, and the reasoning of human beings helps or mars the means of achieving that grace! In this fragmented world, human beings face temptations and their reasoning may go wayward! Then what's the final solution to this inevitable problem? First you establish your identity in this world, and then, you achieve your eternity in the other world!"

After a moment's waiting, he asked again, "Then, in such a fragmented world, how could you establish your identity? For, it is the primary matter, more urgent than achieving your eternity in an ideal world, which is secondary! Without finding a solution to the immediate problem related to your very existence, how can you face the second one which is more complex and philosophic than the former? If you do not love your brother whom you can see, how can you love God whom you cannot see?"

The Guruji asked and waited for a moment as if expecting some answer from the audience. Then he continued, "Identity comes only through relationships! It is a question of synonym and not of dichotomy! Rediscover and recognize our relationships, and only then, we could solve our existential problems!"

I smiled remembering a clause in 'Feng Shui", the Chinese pseudo-science related to architecture, like the Indian Vasthu, in which it was advised to change the position of the furniture in the bedroom if the husband and wife quarreled regularly! No doubt, the couples would try a different relationship if they really wanted it!"

The Guruji continued, "There are people who are addicted to abstract ideas like God, freedom, truth, love and beauty as well as to practical things like sex, dress, food, work, literature, cooking, domestic works, prayer, charity, social service and politics! Here we find a good world gradually becomes a bad world! You think that your efforts could make this world better and, thereby, your life better too! You think that a bad world is becoming better and better but what actually happens is that a good world is becoming worse and worse!"

"The main problem with modern man is the lack of wisdom! We collected information and tried to acquire knowledge but no wisdom. As T.S. Eliot says:
'Where is the wisdom we have lost in knowledge?
Where is the knowledge we have lost in information?'

We ignored the wisdom of living; we tried to apply our limited knowledge in analyzing our family life! Remember what King Solomon said: 'Blessed the man who finds wisdom, the man who gains understanding, for she is more profitable than silver and yields returns than gold.'"

"Of course, we try to acquire wisdom in easy ways; we always depend on shortcuts! As Orhan Pamuk says in his novel, *My Name is Red*: 'Wisdom is acquired in an irrational way, a way which cannot be understood with rationality.' And another main problem with man is that only through the passage of time he can gain wisdom, and when he gains it, there is no more time for him to use it; he'll be too late!"

I remembered an incident during a meeting with Guru Nitya Chaitanya Yeti. My friend Suresh, who was running a catering school, one evening rang me and said that the Guru would be in town for an hour at Darsana auditorium! I rushed to the spot; about twenty people were sitting around him; he looked so tired and his voice was so inaudible! Of course, there was a microphone but it was a bit away from his mouth that nothing came out through the speakers! He was talking and talking but not a single word reached our ears, even of those who sat very near to him!

One listener became so impatient that he dared to ask the person who sat near the Guru to place the microphone nearer to him! Guru Nitya heard it, he asked the person near him to keep the microphone away so that people would concentrate on him and not on the microphone! First I considered it a joke and heartily enjoyed it! Soon Guru Nitya said, "You all look here and concentrate your attention on what I am talking. Whether you heard it or not is immaterial! You just think that you are hearing me, that's enough!" Yes, I listened! And I also understood how difficult it was to acquire wisdom, especially through rationality!

Guruji said, "Generally we believe that God chased out Adam and Eve from the Eden Garden but, in fact, it was the opposite; Adam and Eve chased out God from their hearts and that caused all the difference! We wish to have a God who works according to our whims and fancies! We are not ready to humble ourselves before God! In our efforts to become more religious, we used to ignore the real God! When we drive out God from our hearts, sorrow occupies the vacant place!"

After a moment's meaningful pause, he said, "There are many people who consider God a physical entity. Perhaps they love a tangible God and not a transcendental one! The greatest discovery of man is God on whom he can depend during the days of his utter helplessness and loneliness, and throw away all his heavy burden of miseries and failures and, thereby, acquire invincible willpower and indomitable confidence with which he can hopefully survive in this world of momentary victories, equivocal coincidences and unexpected smites of inevitable fate."

He stopped for a while and continued, "Of course, even without God human beings can successfully manage their life. God is not necessary for those people who have properly realized God. However, most of the human beings are mentally weak and they need a sort of omnipotent support to attain and retain their willpower. Here, the question whether God exists or not is immaterial. It is faith that gives confidence; it's the belief that strengthens the willpower! Faith is a potent weapon and many of us need a little bit of faith when faced with difficult situations! God is an experience; the presence of God and the absence of God are two experiences, like the two sides of the same coin! And nobody can question the experience of another person."

His words were thought provoking. The main defect with religions is that the believers want to create a God of their own! They volunteer themselves and take weapons to save God rather than to be saved by God! I remembered the words of E.K. Nayanar, a Communist Chief Minister of Kerala State in India, who asked, "Should God need protector or guard?" He might be an atheist but his words should open the eyes of the religious fanatics who tighten their loin-clothe to protect God! In fact, the biggest fun or 'tamasha' of human society is that the religious believers blindly think that it is their duty to protect God, the Omnipotent, the Omnipresent and the Omniscient One!

Guruji's words echoed in the atmosphere, "We all think that what we believe is the only truth! And explains that the truth in which we believe is directly given by God! We assassinate each

358

other due to our ignorance. Of course, truth is a product of disputes and is the outcome of discourse, as Miguel Foucault suggests. And there is no absolute truth at all! We offer ourselves to become slaves to certain beliefs though freedom itself is divine. Are we ready to maintain healthy relationships among our relatives, among our neighbors irrespective of their religious beliefs?"

He said, "Who can explain what is truth? If truth is only a belief, no one can prove it! In fact, there is nothing like absolute truth! Truth is created and not discovered; truth is established and maintained by those who are in power! The ideologies of the society in which we live force us to blindly believe certain ideas as truth! Our life and experiences are governed by these ideologies which are built into our language and, thus, language is not a reliable mode of communication, as the French philosopher Jacques Derrida points out."

Guruji continued, "We live in a world confused by the instability of language and un-decidability of meaning. This leads to rifts among members in the family, especially between married couples! We use language with puns and puzzles that it becomes ambiguous! The listener always tries to find the other meaning of our words! We look into each other's eyes with suspicion! As the Nigerian poet Gabriel Okara sings, 'Once upon a time, son, they used to laugh with their hearts and laugh with their eyes; but now they only laugh with their teeth, while their ice-block-cold eyes search behind my shadow!'"

Guruji continued his talk on family relationships, "There was a time when woman was considered the pillar of the family! Then, more than beauty, family tradition, wealth and employment, people cared whether the woman was wise and intelligent! Today, we all have pawned our intelligence for material benefits which cannot yield returns for a long period! Let me tell you an old story of a prince and a village girl!"

Thank God! He also knows stories! I was wondering whether the listeners could understand his philosophical talk on existentialism and identity crisis! A story would help them to relax for a while! I thought.

Guruji continued, "Before the arrival of the British, there were more than six hundred city states in India, some of them were very small, some others very big but each city state had a king! There was a small Christendom in Kerala named 'Villarvattom', of course, later it became a part of Cochin, following a marriage alliance. The title of the king of Villarvottom was 'Thoma', following the tradition of St. Thomas who came to Kerala in A.D. 52. He was a kind-hearted man and he loved the farmers in the villages more than the rich lords who stood around him! During the harvest festival, the villagers used to bring their best agricultural products and placed them before the king, and the king watched each one of them very proudly and gave them suitable gifts in return!

"There was an orphan girl in the village; she was very beautiful and intelligent but was working in a lord's house as a maid-servant! When everybody gave gifts to the king, she also decided to give something to the king on her behalf. There was a lemon-tree with a lot of ripe lemons in her courtyard and she planned to give a few of them to the king. But how did she carry them to the king? The farmers took their agricultural products in baskets, bags, pots and other utensils. From the lord's house, where she was working as a maid, she borrowed a big golden cup; she plucked the best three lemons and carefully placed them in the golden cup and gave it to the king. The king was very pleased seeing the golden cup and gave her very costly gifts!

"After some time, she stood with other farmers who were taking back the baskets, bags, pots and other utensils in which they brought their agricultural products and milk products. When her turn came, she took her golden cup, leaving the lemons for the king! The king appreciated her intelligence and asked his son to marry her. He said to his son the words of King Lemuel in the Bible: 'Who can find a virtuous woman? For her price is far above rubies!'

"Are we ready to use our intelligence and wisdom, which were the virtues mentioned by King Lemuel, in maintaining our family relationships? Or are we carried away by sentiments, by anger and by disappointment, by formality and selfishness? 'There are more things in life than disappointment!' These are the words of Gebremichael, the guardian of the Ark of the Covenant kept in the Mariam Zion Church of Axum in Ethiopia, as reported by Graham Hancock in his book *The Sign and the Seal*.

"Human life has only one edition, always remember it! Even the Bible has many editions! Each year in our life is a chapter and each day is a page in the book of life! There may be a few memorable days in our life, like the wedding day or graduation day; they are memorable pages with special notes on them! Generally, we say that in family life, the husband and wife are one and the same! Of course, they must be together but remember to keep 'healthy spaces' in your togetherness! Then, heaven will come down and dance with you!

"Let your life be straight; there should not be bends and curves, there should not be slants and angles; at the same time, we must accept that life is full of bends, curves, slants and angles! Are you ready to ignore a few traits of your partner? See everything but pretend that you haven't seen a few things; and don't try to correct everything but only very few things!

"Are you sure about your decisions? We try to declare that we can decide what is right and what is wrong! And that creates the existential problem in our family life! It is neither an all-good world nor an all-bad world! In such a world only strong human relationships could bring eternal happiness; the strength of our personal relationships will make our relationship with

God and Nature stronger and healthier! Try and try again to reconnect that broken string and maintain that fundamental relationship!"

The message came to an end; it was like a heavy cascade, a strong shower that could purge all the impurities in family life! Most of the listeners returned home with smiling faces! It is easier said than done; I thought and smiled in disbelief!

A heavy hand fell on my shoulder and I turned back to see one of the disciples of the Guruji standing just behind me! He smiled as if we were friends for a long time, and said in a hushed voice: "My name is Savy and I have been serving Guruji for many years! I see a sort of confusion on your face! Let's discuss and find a solution!"

I told him that my first confusion was related to our Guruji! I said, "How could an ascetic like our Guruji find solutions to family problems? What did he know about husband-wife relationships and those unique problems that rise up between them?"

"That's a good question!" Guru Savy said with a laugh. He continued, "You see, an ascetic is the best person to find solutions for family problems! Let me explain. An ascetic has an ideal vision about family life and husband-wife relationships. When people come with their family problems, our Guruji uses his ideal vision as a touchstone or whetstone and finds practical solutions for them! It's so simple!"

"Well!" I said, "Secondly, in married life, nobody is a hundred percent happy couple and most of the couples push on with their life, without knowing why we undergo such a life!"

"I understand what confuses you! We live in the modern world and our minds are modern and rational and we used to ask ourselves what is the purpose of life? The only answer is what our Guruji said, 'Keep up your relationships!'"

"But how could we maintain relationships if our counterparts are unwilling; clapping sound will come only when we use both our hands!" I murmured in a philosophical tone.

He said, "Of course, all human beings are abnormal to a certain extent, and men and women have their own abnormalities. Therefore, husbands and wives should adjust themselves for a normal and healthy married life. Perhaps, 'minus into minus is equal to plus' as the mathematicians say! It's always better to think in a positive way, like what James Stuart says in *Spring Victory*: 'Violets are budding under the dead leaves beneath the snow right now!'"

"Well! I agree that every individual is different in his behavior and attitudes. But could they come to a sort of consensus for the success of a social institution like the family?" I asked him earnestly. Of course, I knew certain husbands and wives who were not a bit ready for any sort of compromise!

The disciple said in a low voice, "See! The abnormality of an individual appears in the form of certain addictions. Whether good or bad, an addiction is an addiction! You know some people who are addicted to drugs, liquor, coffee, tea and various kinds of narcotics. Some are addicted to food, like Bakan in the epics; one group to vegetarian food and the other to non-vegetarian food! We should eat in order to live but not live in order to eat! Some are addicted to excessive sex, literature, science, politics, dress, reading or writing and research. For a few the addiction is sleep, sleeping like the legendary Kumbhakarna! One's blind belief in certain personal principles like discipline, punctuality, cleanliness, maintenance of body beauty, fear of losing respect from others and fear of breaking one's own image are also addictions! Not only certain bad habits but also certain habits which we think great, like craze for power and position, discipline and punctuality or self-assertiveness to certain dogmas, theories and principles whether political social or religious, are also harmful addictions. They are all impediments to a perfect conjugal relationship."

"Well! When you say relationship in married life, we Indians used to think only about sexual relationship!" I said with hesitation. A cloud flashed on his face, but he immediately turned towards a young man and beckoned him towards us. He asked the young man to talk to me and suddenly disappeared among the crowd. The young man was quite polite and matured in his words. He said that his name was Ayeros and asked me to explain my problem so that both of us could try to find a solution!

I repeated what I said to the other disciple and said to the young man, "We live in a world of stress and tension and we could not find proper time or peace of mind to have our free relationship with our wives! Do you think that sex is a great stress-buster?

Ayeros said in a serious tone: "That's true because lovemaking has been found to relieve the pressure of life's burdens; it will definitely ease stress, soothe chronic aches and pains, spur creativity and rev up the energy levels."

I said dubiously, "Of course, anything that makes you feel good, alive and physically excited will make you feel as if you have shed years! But are they related to sex? Does it mean that those who are physically weak, whether man or woman, could not survive stress?"

He replied like an experienced counselor, "Listen, my dear friend! There are two branches in sex; one is active sex and the other pseudo sex. Of course, the latter is better but needs much practice. So let's discuss the former. As you are an active member of family life, I shall suggest a few aphrodisiacs which can add zing to your sex life."

He misunderstood my problem! I thought that he was going to prescribe certain medicines like Penegra or Viagra, or certain hormone tablets, or some weird Ayurvedic potions prepared by the so-called sexologists!

Ayeros continued with the placid look of a dietician: "Fig fruits can do miracles to spice up your sex life as they have Vitamin E, magnesium, manganese and zinc. If you take red water melons, citrulline, a substance in it, will send the signals to release arginine which relaxes blood vessels, and this is exactly what Viagra does!"

I interrupted his prescription and said, "Some people use the fruits of a certain cactus, especially in Arabian countries, as sex stimulants, and there is a heavy rush in certain halwa shops in Delhi where they sell sweet-meat prepared with the juice of aloes! My Ethiopian friend Hadera Halefom said that even passion fruit is such a stimulant! Of course, I had to explain to him that the word 'passion' in the term is not 'sexual passion' but 'Christ's passion' which you can observe in a passion fruit flower!"

The young man ignored my comments and continued, "If you have no inhibitions or taboos, do try some champagne; it enters the bloodstream faster than red wine and works as an antioxidant! The red-hot chili-peppers can recreate the symptoms of arousal by raising the level of heat in your body. Take good quality cheese which releases ten times more endorphins than the great ol'aphrodisiac, chocolate! And chocolate contains two chemicals, phenyethylamine, a stimulant, and tryptophan which creates serotonin, a brain chemical involved in sexual arousal. Remember, my dear friend, it is the right foods that can make you positively sexual!"

"But what about the timing?" I asked. I wanted to get the maximum benefit out of him. I continued, "I read in Sun that a sex therapist named Suzie Hayman proved that making love at 7.30 am is apparently one of the best ways which can make your day healthy because, at that time, the body produces a surge in sex hormones and a rush of adrenalin to get a person going in the morning!"

"Even the great sage Vatsyayana who wrote the Kamasutra recommended morning as the best time to orgasm and conceive! And remember, a few days fasting with prayer, I mean completely abstaining from sex for a few days unlike the fasting of certain people for whom fasting is only for twelve hours and everything is allowed during the night, and the mental preparation of the couples would do miracles!"

He was bidding farewell to me and I hurriedly asked, "Is that all….?"

He laughed aloud and said, "Yes, if only both partners have the desire; it is the will that is important, a mind that is free from 'the voice of education,' and no medicine on earth could provide you the extraordinary patience, invincible enthusiasm and unrestricted practical freedom to achieve the goal! It is left for the individuals concerned! And lucky are those who are able to realize the real significance of human life on this earth!"

"Hell with luck! I will bring luck with me!" I cried at him like Hemingway's Santiago.

"That's cool! But remember the words of the Old Man that luck is a thing that comes in many forms, who can recognize it!" He waved his hands, bidding farewell to me, and disappeared somewhere in the crowd!

Of course, miracles can happen, I mused, perhaps hoping against hope, "for more things are wrought by prayer than this world dream of," as Lord Tennyson says in his *Idylls of the King*. Of course, true love among couples could do magic! If only the husband and wife understand that love is the only anti-dose against the quotidian problems of life. Forget everything and fully immerse in love; for love should not have any limitations or boundaries; it must be free and spontaneous! Be innocent in your love and you will get heavenly joy! As Jesus said, "You cannot enter the Kingdom of Heaven unless you turn into infants!"

We see the lambs play with extraordinary vigor and vitality on the pastures; we watch the puppies playfully bite and climb on each other; we observe little sparrows repeat their efforts a thousand times! They all have a simple purpose in their life, to make their limited period of life worthy of living! But human beings think too much and make their lives worthless!

Most of these divorcing couples were true believers in God and they knew: 'God is Love!' Did it mean that one could not physically or intellectually prove His or Its existence but only experience it mentally and emotionally or, perhaps, spiritually? It would be useful if they read the words of St John: "Beloved, let us love one another, for love is God; and everyone who loves is born of God and knows God! He who does not love does not know God, for God is love!"

But I always considered love as an abstract idea like beauty and truth! I would prefer sympathy to love as the former is pretty solid and practical! Of course, the world prefers the latter because the world is too clever not to face any material loss! It is out of sympathy that one commits sacrifice! Love is only an ideal situation, like God, because God is Love!

For a moment I suppressed my laugh thinking about the disputes among those so-called theists! If those labeled God-fearing theologians could fight about silly issues, what about the couples who face domestic problems in their everyday life! I tried to believe that Rajesh would survive the trauma and would enjoy the rest of his life with his wife and child! I consoled myself while leaving the ashram.

CHAPTER ELEVEN

By evening I reached my home and began to pack my luggage. My wife had prepared some fish pickles and my mother-in-law some garlic pickles as garlic was supposed to reduce cholesterol. My son was there, spending almost an entire month's salary for the flight-ticket which I did not like but secretly appreciated in my heart his manners; he had come from the capital city where he had been working, just to see me off, of course, taking a week's leave, pretending to get some treatment for his throat infection.

My wife was quite silent all through the day, as she used to be during such situations, though busy in preparing the most delicious food for me. She knew that I was leaving her for a year if she could not come to Ethiopia after a few months.

A few of my relatives and neighbors came to my house to say 'bon voyage,' as it was a Saturday, perhaps, a holiday-outing for many of them. We took our dinner in the most warm and affectionate manner though such European dinner manners were uncommon in our part of the country.

After dinner, I went to my bedroom, as my son put on the television to watch some useless Hollywood film. After a few minutes, to my surprise, my wife too joined me; it was for the first time in our married life that she came so early into the bedroom! Usually she made her entrance into my bedroom after finishing all the kitchen work, cleaning all the plates and utensils, sweeping, scrubbing and mopping; then, the washing of clothes, as we got sufficient power supply only during the night, and refreshing herself with a quick bath; and by that time

I would have started snoring! She reminded me the habit of Lyshie Vinod who used to spend her time in prayers, chants and pujas! And on that evening my wife came early, of course, she knew that I was leaving the next morning!

In fact, I was criticizing myself for not properly appreciating, all these years, the beauty of my wife! Then she appeared to me as the most beautiful woman in this world! She came towards me with an elegant smile, like Marlow's Helen whose face "launched a thousand ships and burnt the topless towers of Ileum!" We talked and talked, and consoled each other; we ignored the passage of time; and did not know at what time we slipped into our deep slumber!

Next morning, the taxi car came, of course, Sanjay was our permanent taxi driver, and we put the luggage in it. My wife and son accompanied me to the airport, of course, to see me off. I kissed them farewell and went into the main launch for 'check-in' and the security 'check-up'.

First I had to go from Cochin to Mumbai on a domestic flight. At Mumbai I had to spend the whole night, as the Ethiopian Airlines flight was at 5.30 am the next day. Of course, one would not feel hunger or thirst at Mumbai Airport as the price of snacks and even of drinking water was so exorbitant; they charged them in rupees but at the exchange rate of dollars! The heat of the day and sleepless night made me so tiresome that I wished to sleep the whole five-hour journey from Mumbai to Addis Ababa.

Of course, I always loved the flight on Ethiopian Airlines. I felt the crew was the epitome of Ethiopian hospitality. Despite the poor maintenance of the planes, the pilots were experts in taking the passengers safely to the destination! And after the breakfast, I fell into a deep slumber, hearing nothing but the humming of the plane.

I had to stay in Addis Ababa for at least two days, in order to renew my Resident Permit, before resuming my journey in a domestic flight to Sea Side City. From the Bole Airport, I took a taxi to Tourist Hotel at Arat Kilo, which once had been the haunt of the khat-chewing Arab tourists on their sex and booze safari, where I used to stay due to its reasonable rent! But the receptionist there told me that there was no vacant room and suggested that I try Hotel Tayitu at Piazza, one of the oldest lodges in Addis Ababa; that I went there and took a room.

I loved the antiquity of the lodge as well as the atmosphere and surroundings. Of course, the old wooden planks of the floor and the decayed wooden steps creaked and cracked every time when people walked, creating an eerie atmosphere, especially during the night! I always wished to stay at least a night in that hotel where history sleeps, for it was the first hotel in Addis Ababa or perhaps in the whole of Ethiopia, established during the time of Emperor Menelik II by his queen Tayitu, naming it Itegue or the Empress Hotel. After the Revolution the name changed into Awararis Hotel, and the present government named it as Tayitu Hotel, after the name of Emperor Menelik Second's wife, though the name-board displayed throughout these decades was Itegue Hotel! Despite the nuisance of young girls who offered 'company' for a lunch or dinner, the area was very good, mainly for getting tasty food from mediocre hotels and taxis to different parts of the city.

After keeping my luggage in the room, I went straight to the Ethiopian Immigration Office, submitted my application for the renewal of Resident Permit and they promised to give it by the next morning. After an hour, I came out from the office and walked aimlessly here and there along the streets only to pass my time. Of course, I rang my family and told them that I had reached Addis Ababa safely.

I also rang Mr. Glory and informed him that I was reaching Sea Side City by the next evening. I requested him to find my maid-servant and tell her to clean my house. Mr. Glory was with his family and he did not go to India for the vacation. He was in the middle of his contract and the Ethiopian universities gave air-tickets only once in two years!

I remembered him once saying, "My family is here with me! Why should I go to India, spending my own money? Who's there to greet me? I don't want to see a country that doesn't want me!"

I enquired about my colleagues and he told me that Professor Fluteplayer had already arrived, winding up his vacation a week earlier! There was nothing surprising about it as he wanted to be in the good books of the university authorities! He was in the latter half of his sixties and he wished to continue in Ethiopia until they sent him back to India!

"And what's the news about Elderking? Is he still there?" I asked with curiosity.

Mr. Glory said in a placid tone, "Oh, that man with a big black mole on the face! He disappeared suddenly from Sea Side City and nobody knows where he is! Perhaps, that agent Mr. Smallerao found him a job in some other Ethiopian university!"

"Well, Mr. Glory! Don't misunderstand me!" I said with some hesitation, "If you don't mind, please tell me what really happened to Mr. Elderking."

"Sir, I don't know the details exactly!" Glory said reluctantly, "It seems he was involved in some dirty woman-subject! You know that in Ethiopia you can have relationships with women as far as they are willing! If they turn against you, you're doomed! The university will take immediate action without much enquiry! It seems something like that happened with him too!"

"I'm sorry to hear such bad news about him! Once he was my friend, you know, and many a time I warned him but of no use! Always a pig goes only to the pigsty!" I said with some disappointment at his fate. He was a Hindu fanatic who knew nothing about the great philosophy imbued in that great universal religion! Of course, every believer is happy with his religion because he is satisfied with its practical flexibility and freedom, and is least bothered about its philosophical rigidness and discipline!

"Dear Mr. Glory! You have only bad news for me! Can't you say some good news?" I asked over the phone.

"Well! Then, take this news! I don't know whether you'll be happy with it or not! You have a new Dean! You know that anti-Indian from the Department of Psychology! Dr. Double Zed! I'm sure your life is going to be a hell here with him as your superior!" glory laughed aloud.

I remembered the skeleton-loke figure of that Tigrayan. I heard that he used to enjoy 'chat-eating sessions' with his friends and that he was not in speaking terms with his wife for a quite a long time. As a teacher of psychology, he was self-assertive and incorrigible! I said in an optimistic tone, "Well, Mr. Glory! Everything happens for good!"

"And, by the way, Doctor George!" Mr. Glory said, as if he suddenly remembered something. "There's some interesting news about our colleague Mr. Joken! The university has packed him back to Sri Lanka!" He made a chuckling laugh!

"Why? What happened to him? How could one be terminated during the vacation?" I asked him anxiously.

Mr. Glory laughed aloud and said, "Sir! The case was different! You see, he was sick and the blood-test proved that he was HIV positive! You know about his carefree way of life! Of course, it's very sad! But he who eats salt will drink water! I heard, he has been admitted in a sanatorium in Colombo!"

He switched off his mobile and his chuckling laugh echoed in my ears! It was really a piece of sad news! A moment's recklessness leads one to inevitable fate! Something that began as a pastime, ended up in a predicament from where there was no return! I heaved a long sigh!

By evening I got a telephone call from the Indian Embassy, the Under Secretary to the Ambassador, Dr. Rajranji, wanted to talk to me about an Indian cultural program to be arranged at Sea Side City. I promised to meet him the next afternoon.

Next morning I walked down to the Immigration Office and collected my Resident Permit. Then, I went to the Indian Embassy and met Dr. Rajranji. He told me that the Indian Embassy was planning to celebrate the sixtieth year of its continuous and successful diplomatic relationship between India and Ethiopia. They had selected two Ethiopian cities, Dire Dawa and Sea Side City, to conduct the program. He requested that I coordinate the Indian Community at Sea Side City and, if possible, arrange a lunch for the Goan Cultural Troupe which would follow the official team. For about an hour we discussed the program and then I returned to my hotel.

At night, I slept hearing the wooden planks of the floor contract in creaks and the wooden stairs shrink slightly away from the worn nails cracking, or as Monica Dickens wrote, "crack, crack, crack, like the ghosts of old lovers going up to bed," except that here they were not ghosts of old lovers but real young men and women of Ethiopia, who rented the rooms for 'shorts'!

Next morning, I did some quick shopping, buying those things which were not available in Sea Side City. I took my brunch from a nearby hotel and returned to the lodge. I checked out from Tayitu, took a taxi to the airport, of course, a bit early to catch the 1.30 pm flight to Sea Side City. I entered the launch and found that the flight was two hours late! I pushed the trolley with my luggage to a deserted corner of the launch, sat on a chair, far from the madding crowd, and relaxed.

A few minutes passed; I was thinking of an hour's sleep and, then, an Ethiopian came to my side-seat. He introduced himself as Mekonnen and requested whether I could help him by taking a small spare-part of a coffee machine to Sea Side City. He said that it was urgently needed for his friend's coffee bar named the Blue Bird where I used to take tea or coffee. It was my bad habit not to say 'no' to a person who made similar inexpensive requests and, of course, at times they led me into unnecessary troubles, but most often helped me a lot. When I agreed to his request, he rang the owner of Blue Bird Café and talked to him in Amharic. Then he told me that Mr. Property, the owner of the cafeteria, would come to the airport and pick me up. That's really great, I thought, for I was worried whether I would get Daniel's auto-rickshaw to take me to my rented house, as the flight was two hours late. Moreover, Daniel would be too busy with supplying Mr. Assefa Gion's cooking gas to his customers!

When Mekonnen said "Goodbye," I placed my legs on the luggage for the sake of safety and prepared to sleep. I loved dog-sleeping, especially the afternoon siesta! When I woke up after half an hour, I found another person sitting near my seat. He was reading a newspaper and I looked over his shoulders to see what he was reading, of course, a sort of 'national habit' with us, the Keralites. One could not blame us for this indecent habit, for our mornings began with a cup of black coffee in one hand and a newspaper in the other! And I missed them both in Ethiopia!

He turned to me and asked, "Are you an Indian?"

"Yes! From Kerala," I replied.

"I am also a Malayalee, my name is Govindan," he said; an expression of relief was on his face.

I smiled; it was evident from the Malayalam newspaper in his hand which I was reading over his shoulders! He might be a new fellow to this country and that copy of the Malayalam newspaper would be the only one he could read for the next two years! Or else, why should you bother about a place or its language which did not want you?

"I am a newcomer to Ethiopia," Govindan continued. "I got an appointment as Associate Professor in Gondar University. I am really worried because my flight is two hours late!"

"Don't worry, my friend, it's usual," I consoled him. "You inform the authority concerned and ask them to arrange the transport; of course, they would be there at the airport. But in case of emergency, please call some Malayalees there."

I gave him a few phone numbers of persons whom I knew there in Gondar. I also told him that I was going to Sea Side City and, from there, the flight would take him to Gondar, the city of Fasilidas' palaces. He felt quite tension-free and, as a courtesy, offered me the newspaper he was reading. I ignored the pages on political news and views, for an expatriate should not bother about the dirty politics there, and glanced at the obituary page, mainly for which I had subscribed to that newspaper even in Kerala.

Suddenly, a familiar photograph caught my attention and I looked at it.

"Oh, my God! So soon!" I cried, forgetting all my surroundings. A lightning rod passed through my heart; it was an earlier photograph of Rajesh!

"What's it, sir! Any bad news?" my new friend asked me, as if he were shocked by the change of expression on my face.

"Look at this photograph! Rajesh was my friend and he worked here in Ethiopia for about two years! What a tragedy!" I showed him the photograph with a note below it.

"Oh, this man!" he said in a casual tone. "Is he your friend? Well! It was not an accident, as far as I know, it was a deliberate murder, I must say! Or a culpable homicide not amounting to murder, as the lawyers say!"

"What do you mean by that? Did you say 'murder'? Who did it? You mean his wife?" I asked anxiously. It was clear to me; in fact, I had some suspicion about Geetha's behavior when I saw her last!

"Well! I don't know the details," he said. "But wasn't this Rajesh a patient in the Madrock Mental Hospital a few weeks back?"

"Yes! I think so! Yes, perhaps, that's true!" I said with some hesitation. Of course Geetha never told me the name of the hospital. My heart was throbbing with grief.

"Then, what my cousin, Gopalan, told me is correct. You see, he serves as a male-nurse in the same hospital," he said in a placid tone.

"What did your cousin say?" I asked him anxiously. Of course, I did not tell him how close Rajesh and I were, lest he would not tell me the whole truth!

"Perhaps, what he said to me might not be true!' he said in a hesitating manner, cleverly trying to dilute the seriousness of the subject! "But he said that he had witnessed almost everything!"

I became restless at his circumlocutory way of speaking. Hiding my excessive curiosity, I said, "Well! Rajesh went from here when he received an emergency call from his wife. Of course, there was some misunderstanding in their married life and they wished to come to an amicable compromise."

"Sir, is it true that he had a wife in Ethiopia and also a child in that affair?" he asked me quite innocently. It seemed he was beating the bushes to avoid telling me the truth!

"What nonsense are you talking?" I said bitterly. I was shocked at this new phase of the situation. "If anything like that happened, every Indian would know about it. And I know this Rajesh for quite a long time and he was a disciplinarian, pretty strict in moral issues!"

"Of course, you may be right, but it seemed that his wife believed in a different way! I think, somebody from Ethiopia might have informed her something like that!" he said with an expression of suspicion on his face. Govindan continued, "At least, it was so according to what my cousin overheard! He told me that it was his wife who paid a handsome amount to the doctor and asked him to prevent her husband from going back to Ethiopia, as he had an illegitimate wife and a child there! In fact, the doctor fully believed her and promised to help her, of course, with the good intention of saving her married life!"

What a crazy woman! I thought. Frailty thy name is woman! I insisted my friend tell me the whole story.

"Alright!" he said after a moment's thought. "Sir, this is what I heard about the incident. When Rajesh reached the airport on his way from Ethiopia, he was received by his wife's brother, who was on a short leave from his job in a Gulf Country; perhaps, she had deliberately brought him for the purpose, and by a distant cousin of hers, who had a criminal record, acquitted from a murder case just by luck! Both of them took Rajesh in their car and the poor man did not suspect any foul play! On the way, they gave him some sedative drink, and took him directly to the Madrock Mental Hospital. The doctor, with whom his wife had discussed the issue, admitted him into the hospital. Perhaps, the doctor's plan was to give the patient some sedatives for a few weeks, but when Rajesh came to know about the situation, he became very angry and wild. Of course, any normal person in such a condition would have become violent! The doctor, in good faith, prescribed a mild shock treatment but, unfortunately, it was too much for the weak body of Rajesh. He was brought back from the theatre almost in a coma stage! Of course, the doctor and others hushed up the matter and, you know, what strange things are happening at the Madrock!"

"My goodness! How could a doctor do such cruel things? After all, a doctor is supposed to be a semi-god, a life giver and not a butcher!" I said as if talking to myself.

He heard my words and, as if to convince me, said, "But it was an accident, Sir. Any doctor may make a hand-slip! And Dr. Charlie is supposed to be number one psychiatrist in the country!"

"You mean Dr. Charlie Cheng? My good Lord! He's a madman! I know him from my university days onwards. He's simply a crack! A quack of inhuman experiments! He must be hanged to death for his nasty experiments on helpless human beings!" I was so emotional that my friend seemed a little scared. If I file a case against that brutish criminal of a doctor, my new friend and his cousin will also be hooked by police as witnesses!

"I understand your sentiments, Sir!" he said in a consoling tone. "But, you know, that electroshocks are commonly used to calm down hysterical patients. Of course, it has the side effects like amnesia, profound disorientation, closely related memory loss or regression. All over the world psychiatric patients are treated with LSD, PCD and other hallucinogens, and we can't blame the doctor for a particular treatment he prescribed to his patient, in good faith!"

The announcement came for the check-in of Sea Side City – Gondar passengers and we hurried to the counter. We sent our luggage and moved to the waiting room. We sat there, deliberately keeping silent. My thoughts went back to those couple of weeks in which I had no other option but to stay in the hostel room of Charlie. I did not get any room for myself and I had to wait for a few days. On the first day itself, I understood that he was afraid of darkness and he never turned off the light. Of course, it helped me to get a unique experience that even today I could soundly sleep with all the lights on!

When I went for my classes, Charlie stayed in the room and checked all my baggage and reported everything about me to the student leader, Jayaprakash and, thereby, prepared the ground for my ragging! He never allowed me to sleep; and in the middle of deep sleep, he would wake me up to ask some foolish questions. He was a sadist of the first order and found pleasure in torturing me mentally. The last thing I heard about him was that he had climbed up to the top of the highest water tank in the university campus and threatened to jump down! Of course, he was pacified by his friends and brought down, only to be handed over to his relatives. He completed his studies somehow and with the help of his relatives got a job in some Gulf countries. I did not know how or when he joined the Madrock Mental Hospital. And that student leader Jayaprakash, later became a hermit and was living in an ashram, as I came to know later.

No doubt, Charlie must have got this job through unfair means! When he was kicked out from the Gulf, he could have managed to influence the Health Minister of Kerala to get the job in Madrock hospital! Naturally, he must have studied about the experiments conducted by Ewen Cameron, the Scottish-born American citizen who became the President of the World Psychiatry Association! Charlie could dare any experiment on his patients, as part of his electroshock, drug and sensory deprivation research! Alas, poor Rajesh, how cruel was the play of fate on you! I heaved a long sigh.

I took the newspaper once again and went through the note below the photo of Rajesh. It was on the previous day that he passed away, perhaps, at the time of my departure from Cochin! The cremation time was mentioned there, 10 am the next day!

I looked at my watch; it was 3 pm; his cremation was over! Rajesh might have become a handful of ashes; his pyre might still be fuming, sending a few spirals of smoke into the sky! Tears began to flow from my eyes!

I took my handkerchief and wiped away my tears. It was time to move towards the plane. We boarded the plane and sat on our seats; my friend's seat was somewhere in the back and I bid him farewell in advance. I refused the refreshments offered by the hostess. I leaned on my chair and closed my eyes.

The faces of Rajesh and Geetha, as they were in their wedding photo, came into my mind. Soon the face of Rajesh changed, instead of the smile, an expression of grief appeared there and, then, the whole face disappeared! Changes also came to the face of Geetha, first an expression of wild joy that changed into a sort of ferocious look! Her hair turned disheveled and fell forward covering almost half of her face; and then, a pair of bloody fangs began to protrude from her mouth!

"La belle dame sans merci!" I cried angrily, to the great surprise of the passenger who sat next to me! I felt ashamed and tried to forget everything. The cheerful face of Geetha returned to my mind and I felt genuine sympathy for her. Perhaps, she did everything in good faith, but fate was very cruel to her! Let time console her and give her peace of mind, I prayed silently.

Oh, God! Why did you turn the dream of a Tower of Babel into a nightmare? Why did you shatter and destroy the basic aspirations for a heavenly bliss? But wasn't it a primal act of divine judgment? Aren't we supposed to justify the ways of God? Well! When they began the construction of the Tower of Babel, they had only one language, the language of love, the language of unity, a strange language understood by every human being irrespective of their race, color and appearance. Then God confused that language because people began to mix their natural ways of life with artificial means in the name of civilization!

They lost the spirit of love and sacrifice in the unity of family life; they considered the Tower of Babel a substitute of God, a substitute deity for their selfish motifs! Then, what began as a stunning example of unity ends in dispersal! This was proved by God on the day of the Pentecost when people who spoke different languages gathered in Jerusalem understood the language in which the disciples talked! It was the pre-Babel Tower language, the strange language of love, sacrifice, sympathy and patience...the only language which could bring unity in human relationships, in conjugal life. And I felt the waves of the Chinese song in Im Kwon Taek's film *Painted Fire* humming in my ears: Life was born in dream, live in dream and die in dream!

The plane landed at Sea Side City Airport and, taking my handbag, I rushed outside, without even looking back to say 'Goodbye' to my friend who had to continue his journey to Gondar on the same flight.

There was no need for me to wait at the immigration counter, as I had sealed my passport at the Immigration Counter in Addis Ababa Airport. I collected my luggage and put it on a trolley. The owner of the Blue Bird recognized me and waved his hand. As he did not know much English, he had brought his friend Zalalam with him. Both of them helped me to take my luggage to their car and we rode to the city. I handed over the spare-part to Mr. Property, so that the Blue Bird could resume its flying! They took me to my house, which I did not expect, and even helped me to carry the luggage into my house. Of course, Zalalam asked me for a favor from the university and I promised to do it for him.

Once again, I was in the university campus. Why did I decide to come again to Sea Side City University? How long could I continue here? I brooded over the matter! I loved Ethiopia and Ethiopians and I saw a bright future for the country and her hospitable people. A people who were good at heart cannot remain downtrodden forever! Despite natural calamities, poverty and health hazards; despite internal conflicts and external wars, the Ethiopians are people who survived the test of time! Because they are proud of themselves, they survived all their ordeals in life; and a proud people cannot go unnoticed!

However, it might take a longer period for Ethiopia to come abreast with the rest of the world. A people trapped in an age-old culture, chained to a rotten tradition and shackled to outdated customs and practices might be slow in achieving greater goals. But a change in their ways of life is waiting at the threshold, I hoped.

I had a glimpse of the golden sun setting beyond the Tana

Lake. I could enjoy the 'sunshine', as the advertisement of the Ethiopian Airlines promised, the sunshine of the fifth and last day of the thirteenth month according to the Ethiopian calendar. And the next day would be 'Inku-ta-tash', the Ethiopian New Year's Day!

Well! I shouldn't be too optimistic! There must be an anti-climax for every story! When everything seems good, unexpected events may shatter all our plans for the future! In the midst of all jubilations, unfortunate and sad situations may be lurking behind for their sudden appearance! I felt as if I heard the hushed voice of Julius Caesar, "Beware of that lean and hungry-looking fellow!" Perhaps my mind was disturbed by some unknown fear about that Dean Dr. Double Zed 'Cassius'!

Why should I worry too much about my career? I was always a scholar gypsy, moving from one place to another, delivering my talents, knowledge and experience. My mind said, "Dr. Scholar Gypsy! Every grain bears the name of its consumer!" from India to Oman, from Oman to Libya, from Libya to Ethiopia, it's all the same for me! Who knows the name of the next country waiting for me, of the students who deserve my service? Always be optimistic! "They don't want your service" simply means "They don't deserve your service!"

Moreover, I was pretty proud of my service to this great country. I appeared three times on Ethiopian Television and one time over Tigrayan Radio and that showed how much Ethiopians loved and respected me. At least, those hundreds of my students who could keep at least a faint memory of my name would be sufficient for my immortality!

My friend Misganaw who had recently joined Stay-Beside-Me-Tonight University rang me and said that the Academic Vice President of his University, Dr. Mepleased, wanted to see me regarding the launching of new master and doctoral courses there. I remembered that the first Ethiopian whom I met officially was also one Mr. Mepleased who later ended up in prison! And this Dr. Mepleased might be the last Ethiopian whom I had to meet officially in Ethiopia!

Before I left for India, my student-friends, Solomon Seilu and Nigussie Michael had given me a farewell party in which they pleaded, "Professor! Don't hate Ethiopia or Ethiopians just because there are some arrogant people among us!" "Oh! Never!" I told them. "Before coming to this country, I had promised my friend Dr. Rajuji that I would never say anything bad about Ethiopia or Ethiopians! And I will keep my word! Moreover, I don't believe that one dead swallow can bring a winter!"

I remembered Solomon's query what the problem with the Tigrayans was! I said with a smile, "Tigrayans were great warriors who defeated the mighty Italian army! But then, they had capable leaders and the majority risked their life at their provocative words! Now all the leaders are rich and they don't care for the problems of the people! Of course, they have the culture of suffering and starving; they never complain! They know to live without food, water, clothing, sanitation and all primary facilities! But don't underestimate them; they're explosives waiting for a spark to burst!"

I looked up at the bright blue sky. Where did all those dark clouds, which I had seen before leaving for India, go? Perhaps, they were afraid of the dawn of Meskerem, the first month of the Ethiopian year! Or they might have rained down, adding to the fertility of the soil! The long rains with the lightning and heavy thunders had come to an end, at last!

The gray eucalyptus forests were rejuvenated with fresh shoots. The mountains were covered with thick carpets of green grass. The hills and valleys were full of small yellow 'Ade Ababa', the new Meskel flowers or the bright yellow daisies of Ethiopia! They could grow even on hard rocks! One could see them 'ten thousand at a glance' as Wordsworth, the high priest of nature said.

The Golden Ethiopia, my mind whispered. Nature, like a bride, wore the new yellow shawl over her shoulders! In Kerala too, we had our bright yellow 'kanikonna' flowers to celebrate 'Vishu', our local New Year's Day, I remembered. Those bunches of golden flowers were symbols of grace, fertility, wealth and happiness! Ethiopia was like a newly wedded bride waiting at the bridal suite for her bridegroom!

The Meskel festival was fast approaching. It was not merely the commemoration of the rediscovery of Christ's Cross but also was the celebration of life renewed. People moved in their new traditional white dress, carrying bunches of yellow daisies. Could those golden daisies bind family relationships? Could those Meskel bonfires burn our petty quarrels that led to divorce, our hatred and jealousy that stirred the fragmentation of the family, our dejection and disappointments that made our conjugal life worthless – and turned them into ashes? Could those bonfires spread the light and warmth of peace and happiness, of tolerance, sympathy and love, into our self-centered hearts? Yes! Meskel was the festival of sacrifice and hope! And tomorrow, tomorrow to fresh woods and pastures new, I said, remembering Matthew Arnold's *The Scholar Gypsy*, and entered into my room.

The author's note as tailpiece: *It would be infidelity on my part, my dear readers, if I did not give you this flash news. My dearest character Geetha 'died of grief' a few days after her husband's death and, thereby, I believe, she proved her true love towards him, for it is believed that if the husband and wife die in nearby days, that itself is proof of their mutual love and fidelity. Of course, she could not become a 'dheerka sumangali' as she had always wished! When the heavenly springs of Helicon which gave me materials for writing seemed dry, it was she who directed me to the fresh spring of family life, and I thank her for the same. In fact, it was she who wrote for me 'the autobiography of a housewife' in* *this novel, and if you have any doubt, please do request a linguist to differentiate between her style of writing and that of mine.*

THE END

AUTHOR'S ACKNOWLEDGEMENTS

I have always been fascinated by the beauty of natural human relationships, especially among members of the family. But I think that we misunderstood the term 'individual freedom' and this misperception led us to the desecration of family life. We live in a world in which the voice of modern education taught us to ignore the sanctity of social life in general and of conjugal life in particular, and compelled us to follow the animal instincts of mere survival. We failed to realize the significance of abstinence, self-control and sacrifice, misunderstood the blessings of rationality, considered sex as a mere biological need and sought the means of selfish opportunism to gain pleasure. We accepted our mental perversions as natural guidelines for a satisfied individual life; and forgot the value of disciplined freedom in the attainment of conjugal bliss and happiness. In fact, the concept of the so-called generation gap is rather insignificant as man and woman, with all their perversions, are one and the same from the days of Adam and Eve onwards. At this juncture, we stand confused at the meeting point of male and female chauvinism, or at the encounter between masculine-ism and feminism.

In this novel, the conjugal life of Rajesh and his paranoid wife, Geetha, is the pivot around which more than three hundred real or fictitious persons create a social milieu by which I tried to portray the agony and misery faced by modern families. If Tower of Babel was an attempt made by man to reach heaven, the builders had to face physical, emotional and intellectual impediments. Here, Tower of Babel stands as a symbol of human efforts to attain the heavenly conjugal bliss, and Language as the divine gift given to prudent couples, at times, leading individuals to equivocation, to reciprocal understanding or misunderstanding. Here is a world where every individual is aware of the limitations of language. We are confused and we misunderstand each other due to 'the instability of language and undecidability of meaning.' We ignore the fact that our life and experiences are governed by certain ideologies which are built into our language and, thereby, language is no more a reliable mode of communication, as Jacques Derrida points out. From the heart of every man and woman comes out the deep sigh: "Oh, God! I'm helpless; I can't communicate with my spouse!" When the partners in family life fail to understand each other's language, this Babel Tower falls down! Through the nostalgic experiences of the narrator in between two flights from Ethiopia to India and back, the novel brings out certain tragic realities to remind the readers about the very delicate issues akin to successful family life.

This work of fiction needs some acknowledgements, first of all to its main characters, who were picked up from real life situations but their names are changed or distorted for the fictional purpose, like the narrator of the story, George, then, Rajesh, Geetha, Worqu Singh and Guruji as well as subordinate characters including those borrowed from other literary works (a total of 188), like the following in their alphabetical order, Abala, Aby, Adeodatus, Ahmad Ansari, Alexander Selkirk, Anil, Anish, Anwar, Artqueen, Arun Thapa, Asharaf, Assefa Gion, Awabech, Aweface, Ayeros, Babu, Babuji, Bakan, Balzac, Bency, Bhimasena, Binu, Blisso'life, Bobby, Brahanu, Champion Cheney, Charlie Cheng, Charlotte Alfred, Clearsight, Compensation, Corin, Court-Uncle, Dallas, Dambay, Dametew, Daniel, Danny, Deepu, Dinov, Double Zed Cassius, Doumbledoor, Elderking, Elderson, Elvsted, Eveline Hill, Eyepot, Fanny Browne, Father Flower, Filomena, Frank, Fullgate, Fluteplayer, Gebremichael, Geevarghese, George Banks, Glory, Godwin, Goity, Gopalan, Govindan, Guru Savy, Hadera Halefom, Hamlet, Handsome, Heavenlyfood, Hedda

Gabbler, Helen, Holybook, Honey Rao, Jayaprakash, Jeet Raika, Jerry, Jerusalem, Jimmy, John Papa, Joji, Joken, Jona, Jose, Joyce, Julius Caesar, Junkuson, Kadir, Kalkidan, Kapildev, Kishari, Kishen, Kumbhakarna, Kuroosa, Lady Kitty, Lashie Dinov, Lexan, Maindoor, Malvi, Mamona, Maria, Matt, Maud Gonne, Mebit, Mekonnen, Mengistu, Mepleased (Mr.), Mepleased (Dr.), Merlin, Mintesenot, Mireille de La Vallee, Misganaw, Mobarak, Mohammed, Monica, Mozad, Mrs. Mallard, Mrs. Tolstoy, Muse, Nandu, Nepal Rana, Odds, Omini, Othello, Ousmane Gueye, Pepin, Phalims, Prabha, Prabhakar, President, Prestige Mussalman, Pom, Prepositions, Priest, Property, Pull-ready, Radha, Rajeev Gupta, Rajendra Bhandari, Rajuji, Rajranji, Rama Rao, Ramesh, Reeba, Roger de Coverley, Ryan, Safia, Salama, Salim Mohammed, Sam, Sanders, Sandra, Sajeev, Sanjay, Santiago, Scholar Gypsy, Shylock, Sinja, Smartguy, Spreadinglight, Spread-n-grow, Sreeni, Suresh, Tamarind, Teacher-Uncle, Terry Lennox, Thai, The Poet, Thomas Ramban, Tom, Tomcat, Tomsin Jose, Truzinski, Tsahay, Valina, Veerbhadra, Victoria Rao, Weldearegay, Wellspoke, Wondwosen, Xanthu, Zafu, Zalalam, Zalem, Zarathustra, Zeenath, Ziona Chana and Zoom. I am very much obliged to all of them.

Also I acknowledge my indebtedness to the following one hundred and thirty-nine great personalities of the past to the present in their alphabetic order, who make, if I use the language of the film, a sort of guest appearance in this novel, whose names, sometimes quoting even their words or ideas, as mentioned by my characters during the course of the story: Abdus Salem, Acharya Rajaneesh, Adolf Hitler, Adrian Rich, Ajitha, Alan Loy MaGinnis, Albert Camus, Albert Einstein, Alfred Lord Tennyson, Alvin Toffler, Amish Tripathy, Amitav Ghosh, Anatole France, Annie Frank, Anton Chekhov, Aristotle, Arundhathi Roy, Balarama Gupta, Bertrand Russell, Brunetto Lattini, Carl A. Whitaker, Chandrababu Naidu, Charlie Chaplin,

Charvakan, Chatrapati Shivaji, Christopher Marlow, Clarence Darrow, Dalai Lama, Dante, Dave Meurer, D.C. Kizhakkemuri, D.H. Lawrence, Edmond Hillary, Epictetus, Ernest Hemingway, Ewen Cameron, Fidel Castro, Fikremarkos Desta, Gail Tredwell, Gebriel Okara, George Lamming, Giovanni Boccaccio, Graham Hancock, Gunther Grass, G. von Rad, Hailemariam Mengistu, Haile Selassie, Henrik Ibsen, Henry David Thoreau, Im Kwon Taek, Jack London, Jacques Derrida, James Joyce, James Stuart, Jesus Christ, Jhansi Rani, J.K. Rowling, John B. Watson, John Donne, John Dryden, John Gray, John Keats, John Milton, Joseph Addison, Kabir Das, Kamala Surayya, Kate Chopin, King David, King Lemuel, Kiran Bedi, Kumaran Asan, Lao Tzu, Leo Tolstoy, Lord Buddha, Madhavacharya, Mahatma Gandhi, Malthus, Mariama Ba, Mark Twain, Mark Victor Hansen, Martin Luther King Jr., Matthew Arnold, Meera Nair, Medha Patekar, Menelik Second, Mervin Kitman, Mignon McLaughlin, Miguel Foucault, Milton Friedman, Monica Dickens, Morarji Desai, Morley, Muammer al-Qathafi, Nayanar E.K, Neer Bersilai, Neitzsche, Nelson Mandela, Nitya Chaitanya Yeti, Noam Chomsky, Orhan Pamuk, Oscar Wilde, Pablo Picasso, Pero da Couvliah, Phoolan Devi, Plato, Prophet Jeremiah, Rabindranath Tagore, Ralph Waldo Emerson, Ramanujan, Raymond Chandler, Reidulf Molvaer, Robert Frost, Rousseau, Sam Keen, Sarojini Naidu, Sigmund Freud, Sir Walter Raliegh, Solomon the Wise, Somerset Maugham, Sri Sri Ravi Shankar, St. Augustine, St. Matthew, St. Paul, St. Thomas, Suzie Hayman, Swami Vivekananda, Tayitu, Tenzing Norgay, Thomas Hardy, T.S. Eliot, Valmiki, Vasco da Gama, Vatsyayana, W.B.Yeats, Will Durant, William Cowper, William Shakespeare, William Wordsworth, and Woody Allen. I acknowledge my respect to each and every one of these masterminds.

However, it should be noted that none of the characters portrayed in this work of fiction are meant to represent any real persons, living or dead, except for the names and locales. Let me take this opportunity to thank some of my reviewers and critics like Professors Dr. Ronald E. Asher, Dr. O.P. Mathur, Dr. Vinod Kumar Sinha, Dr. Kanchan Singh, Dr. S. Subhash Chandran, Dr. John E. Abraham and Dr. B. Keralavarma whose words encouraged me a lot.

– Author.

ABOUT THE AUTHOR

Born on April 1st, 1952, Alexander Raju began his career as a freelance journalist as early as 1974, after completing his higher studies in the Universities of Kerala and Saugar, Madhya Pradesh. Touring almost every nook and corner of India, he acquired a firsthand knowledge of the Indian ways of life among various ethnic groups who differed totally in their culture, religion and language. When Sikkim became the twenty-second State of India, he joined the staff of *Sikkim Express* as one of its sub-editors and later became the editor of *Bullet*, a newsweekly published from Gangtok.

"A decade of my wanderings through the length and breadth of India and my not too brief sojourn in the Himalayan Valley gave me an everlasting mine of ideas and a continuous source of inspiration that would last a whole lifespan of a creative writer," says the author.

Returning to his native state of Kerala, he worked as a lawyer for a short while. In 1981, he joined the faculty of English at Baselius College, Kottayam, his own alma mater, and served as Reader in English. For three years, he was Inspector of English under the Ministry of Education, Sultanate of Oman; and for another three years, he served as Professor of English in Bahir Dar University, Ethiopia. For two years he served as Professor of English in Al Fateh University, Tripoli but following NATO's war on Libya, he returned to Ethiopia and served in Mekelle University for three years. Currently he is professor in University of Gondar, Ethiopia. He also serves as Research Guide under Mahatma Gandhi University, Kottayam, Kerala, India.

Alexander Raju, an Indian English poet, novelist and short story writer has many books to his credit. *Ripples and Pebbles*

(1989), *Sprouts of Indignation* (2003) and *Magic Chasm* (2007) are collections of his poems. His first novel *The Haunted Man* came out in 1996; its second edition in 2009. His second novel *Upon This Bank and Shoal* (2008) is published by CCB Publishing, British Columbia, Canada. *Poles Apart on the Same Bed* (2011) is a collection of his twenty-nine short stories. *And Still Plays the Abyssinian Damsel on Her Dulcimer,* a novel based on the history and legends of Ethiopia, is his latest work. *The Voice of Ethiopia* (2008) is an edited work and *The Psycho-Social Interface in British Fiction* (2000) is a critical work.

E-mail:

dr.alexanderraju@yahoo.co.in

or

dr.alexanderraju@gmail.com